The Finer Things

BRENDA JOYCE

St. Martin's Paperbacks

THE FINER THINGS

Copyright © 1997 by Brenda Joyce.

Photograph of the author by Sigrid Estrada.

ISBN 0-312-96155-3

Printed in the United States of America

St. Martin's Paperbacks edition/April 1997

St. Martin's Paperbacks are published by St. Martin's Press, 175 Fifth Avenue, New York, NY 10010.

10 9 8 7 6 5 4 3 2 1

For Michael
because in love and dreams there are no
impossibilities

⚜ *Prologue* ⚜

LONDON, 1850

"PAPA?"

There was no answer. The small, thin child stood just inside the dark, airless cubbyhole of a room. It was very hard to see because of the blackness and the heavy pall of smoke. It was also difficult to breathe. There was but a single candle burning on the small table set against one rotting wall. But here and there small red lights glowed, not in tandem, at first brightly, then disappearing, like miniature red stars. And with every fierce, brief burning, gaunt shadows became visible, weird and grotesque, almost disembodied; hands and fingers, reaching, curling; mouths and eyeballs, the teeth and the whites oddly, starkly light.

Violet hated this place. She stood on the basement landing of the stairs, her narrow back pressed hard into the oily wood banister. She was a creature of instincts. She wanted to turn, run up the steps, and burst forth into the foggy afternoon outside. Into the fresh, clean air. But she could not.

"Papa!" she cried desperately.

All around her, the ends of opium pipes glowed. A pale hand seemed to emerge in the midst of the bitter, foul-smelling smoke. It waved listlessly. Violet, her heart skipping a beat, ran forward.

She peered at the man who sat in an impossibly awkward position. His legs seemed to be broken in places—either that, or he had become boneless in his euphoria. "Papa! Is that yew?" But even as she spoke, dread gave way to relief, and she reached out, clutching her father's bony hand. Every day that hand became a little bit thinner.

He blinked at her not once but many times, and, finally, groggily, muttered, "Violet? Wot's 'appened, gel? Is it yew?"

Violet nodded eagerly as she looked into a pair of watery blue eyes, bloodshot and vacant. But had the light inside the den been better, there would have been no mistaking the familial connection between the pair. Violet's father was as fair as she would be if she were clean, which she was not, although he was sallow now. Father and daughter were raven-haired, and she had gotten her small nose, jutting chin, and high cheekbones from him. But the precise nature of their relationship might very well have been mistaken. Peter could have been taken for her older brother in spite of the weary, death-ridden look in his eyes. Although more dead than alive, he was not yet twenty-four.

"Yes, Papa, it's me, Violet, an' I've come to take yew 'ome." Violet forced a brave, tremulous smile. She was growing nauseated and lightheaded from the acrid-sweet aroma surrounding her. But she did not release Peter's hand.

"Can't," he muttered, putting the pipe into his mouth.

"Papa, please," Violet begged.

"Tell Emilou I'll be 'ome t'morrow," Peter muttered, suddenly pulling his hand away from his daughter's with surprising strength. For a split instant, anger filled his eyes.

Violet panted. "Mama's dead. She's been dead for three years."

Peter blinked at his daughter as if she were a foreigner spewing gibberish he could not understand.

"I need yew, Papa," she whispered brokenly.

"T'morrow," he murmured, his voice growing faint. And suddenly he slumped against the person he sat next to, his head lolling. His neighbor, another skeleton in rags, was too involved in his own affairs to notice. Violet knew her father had fallen asleep.

Tears filled her eyes. "That's wot yew said yesterday," she whispered to herself. Yesterday and every day before that for too many days and weeks and months for Violet to count.

"Violet!" A young, urgent voice sounded above her.

Violet brushed her tears away with one torn, stained sleeve. She turned and started up the stairs toward her friend, Ralph. When she reached the ground-floor landing, he gripped her arm, hard and unkindly. "Why do yew keep comin' back 'ere!" he shouted at her.

Violet's temper snapped. She jerked her arm free as they

slipped outside into the alleyway. Decrepit tenements lined the alley, patched walls falling apart, slate and thatched roofs missing pieces. Men and women congregated aimlessly on broken stoops. Skinny children played in the mud and dirt, hungry babies cried. A pair of drunken coal porters lurched out of one of the alley's five gin mills. "It's none a' yer business," she spat into the ground at Ralph's feet.

He was a pale, sandy-haired boy covered with freckles, perhaps eleven or twelve years old. Like Violet, he was thin to the point of boniness and clad in tattered clothes; like Violet, his eyes were old beyond a child's years, old and wise and shrewd. "'E ain't never comin' out."

"Don't say that!" Violet shouted, hitting Ralph with one balled-up fist.

He scowled and pushed her hard enough that she fell into the street, which was a combination of mud and sewage. Violet stood, furious.

Ralph's expression changed. "I'm sorry," he said. "I'm afraid when yew go down there."

Violet's mouth trembled and she nodded. "But I 'ave to. Wot if 'e dies?"

Two drunk cross-sweepers staggered past them. "'Course 'e's gonna die," Ralph said brusquely. "Everyone dies, yew an' me included, luv."

Violet did not respond. Then she realized that a phaeton had turned into the alley, a very fancy phaeton, one pulled by two gray mares. Violet froze, recognizing the carriage, which did not belong in the East End, much less St. Giles. Ralph exhaled loudly. The phaeton slowly approached. The driver wore livery. And when it was abreast of the two agog children, it stopped. The alley had became unbelievably still and silent. One and all stared.

One black lacquer door opened and a gentleman in a black suit and top hat stepped out. He used a cane to keep his balance, a silver eagle's head on top, and was very careful about where he put each highly polished black patent shoe.

"Not 'im again," Ralph whispered with some fear.

The man had muttonchop sideburns and he smiled slowly at Violet. "G'day, little Violet. That is your name, is it not?"

"Don't answer 'im," Ralph said, taking Violet's elbow. His long face had turned starkly white, causing his freckles to stand out dramatically. Neither child moved.

"'Ow d' yew know my name?" Violet asked, trembling.

She did not know who this fancy man was. But he was very rich, she could see that, and not just from his phaeton and horses, his driver and clothes. A gold fob watch sparkled from one vest pocket, and, like the silver-topped cane, it was clearly real. Ralph was eyeing it, and she knew he wanted to steal it. The gentleman wasn't wearing gloves, either, which was odd, because most nobs wore gloves, and a heavy onyx ring glinted from one of his manicured hands. Diamonds were set in the gold around the black stone.

The gentleman smiled again. "I make it a point to learn the names of pretty little ladies like yourself."

Violet's mouth dropped open and remained that way. She wasn't stupid and she knew she was not a lady and would never be one.

Ralph's stance grew defensive and belligerent at once. "Wot do yew want?"

The gentleman's gaze moved to Ralph, turning ice cold. "Why don't you disappear?"

"I ain't goin' nowhere," Ralph cried.

The man turned to Violet. "My name is Farminger. Harold Farminger. I heard you had a birthday last week, Violet. How old does that make you now?" His smile was far friendlier than before.

Violet's insides curdled. Who was this man? She knew everyone of any repute in St. Giles. This man did not live in, or belong in, St. Giles. This man looked like he belonged somewhere in the West End, Belgravia perhaps. Why was he talking to her? She had noticed him twice before. Watching her from his fancy black coach. But he had never spoken directly to her. What did he want?

Whatever he wanted, it was no good. Violet knew enough to know that. His smile was false, enough to scare the dead, and his eyes were cold and mean.

"How old are you, little lady?" he prompted.

Violet found it hard to breathe, harder than it had been downstairs in the small basement where Peter remained. "Ten. I'm ten. Just."

"Ten. Why that's a wonderful age. I had a daughter who was ten. Course, she's grown up now, a lady in her silks and jewels. I imagine a little lady like yourself hankers for silks and jewels. Wouldn't you like to live in a beautiful house off Regent Street?" His smile widened. "Wouldn't you like to wear silk dresses and pearl necklaces?"

Violet's eyes popped. "Live off Regent Street?! Why, that's where them nobs lives! An' me—wear silk 'n pearls?!"

"I have a large house, Violet, one with two dozen bedrooms, each with its own marble fireplace. Every bed's got velvet and furs, and the floors have rugs from Turkey. You'd even have your very own ladies' maid."

Violet could hardly believe her ears. "Velvet and furs! Me own ladies' maid? Gawd!"

Ralph threw his arm around Violet's shoulders. He sneered. "Wot's she got to do to live in yer house, Mister Farminger—if y' don't mind me askin'?"

Farminger ignored him. "What's your hair like, sweetheart?"

"Me 'air?" Violet echoed.

"Your hair." Another smile.

"Why, it's black," Violet began. Before she could even finish, he took her cap off her head. A pile of dirty black hair fell down to Violet's waist.

"I know wot he wants," Ralph cried.

A look of exasperation crossed Farminger's features. He slipped his hand into the pocket of his morning coat and produced a small, pearl-handled pistol. "Go away, boy."

Ralph's eyes widened. He started to back up. Violet looked from the gun to her best friend, fear making her pulse race. Then Ralph whirled, shouting, "Run, Violet! Run now!"

Violet didn't hesitate. As Ralph ran away, she also turned and fled.

"I never been inside a house with velvet an' furs," Violet said. It was growing dark. Nights in London were usually yellow and foggy, and this one was no exception. She and Ralph sat on empty casks outside of a warehouse that was closed for the night. Ahead of them, they could both see the Charing Cross Bridge. A train, outwardbound, was chugging across the Thames. The last third-class coach was visible, passengers packed in like cattle in the roofless car.

"An' yew niver will be," Ralph said roughly, taking a small knife out of his boot. One hole exposed his big toe, evidence that he wore no socks.

"I'm not sure I understood 'im," Violet said, "but I didn't like 'im. 'E was up to no good."

"I asked 'round," Ralph replied, slipping to his feet. "' 'E keeps whores. 'E wanted yew to whore for 'im."

Violet stared, stunned. "Me?" she squeaked.

"Yeah, yew." Ralph's mouth was tight, his pale gray eyes gleaming. "Turn around," he said.

Violet looked at Ralph, who was holding up his knife. "Wot now?"

"Just turn," he snapped.

Violet obeyed, shifting on the barrel, giving Ralph her back. She watched a rowboat navigate past a barge on the Thames, a lantern casting light from its bow, then felt Ralph lift up a huge piece of her hair. He pulled on it. "Ow! Wot yew doin'?"

He did not answer. An instant later he had sawed off a foot-long chunk of her hair.

Violet jerked, whipping around. She stared down at the dirty, knotted tangle of her hair which was at least twelve inches long. "Gawd!" she finally shouted. With one hand she felt for her hair and was relieved to find half of it still in place. Then she realized she was only left with hair on the left side of her head. "Yew lost yer mind!"

"Shut up," Ralph cried, gripping the other half of her hair. "Or yew want to work flat on yer back with yer legs spread wide servin' the likes of Farminger an' his hoighty-toity friends?"

Violet froze, still craning her neck to look at her hair. Ralph sawed on the rest of her mane. It fell to the ground at their feet.

"No," Violet said slowly. "No. I don't want to be no whore." And she reached behind to feel the nape of her neck. Ralph had shorn her shorter than most boys. It was surprisingly cool and it felt surprisingly good.

"We need t' find us some supper," Violet whispered, shivering in a crouch. It was growing late and she was not just cold but exhausted. But more than that, she was starving. All she'd eaten that day was a small loaf of bread which she'd bought from a vendor outside Covent Gardens with the two pennies she'd earned holding a gentleman's horse for him.

Ralph smiled at her. They were both hanging onto the sides of a brougham. The carriage was empty, and the coachman had not yet noticed the two children riding the brougham's side runners. Both Violet and Ralph were used to jumping onto just about any vehicle that moved. "It's a lovely evenin', now, ain't it, luv? Good way to travel."

Violet smiled. "We're in Mayfair, Ralph. Lot's a places to find us some supper."

"My thinkin' eggsactly." Ralph grinned.

Stately town houses lined this particular thoroughfare. Violet felt as if she had entered a different land—a land of princes and fairy tales. The street was paved and surprisingly clean. Stately oaks shaded it. Unlike St. Giles and the more congested city neighborhoods, the air smelled clean and good. There were no pedestrians at this hour, but a lamplighter was extending his pole and flicking on the black gas lamps lining the broad street. It ended just ahead, where another street crossed it horizontally, forming a capital T. The brougham was approaching a huge mansion, its wide front stairs guarded by a pair of snarling limestone lions. The street in front of the mansion was lined with coaches and carriages of every possible description. The vehicles were double- and triple-parked, narrowing the very wide thoroughfare. Liveried coachmen, grooms, and footmen stood in pairs and groups on the sidewalk, chatting. The house itself was lit up brightly from every window—of which there seemed to be a hundred. "Gawd," Violet suddenly said. "I wonder who lives there."

"Sssh," Ralph began, but too late.

The coachman cried out, "What's this?" Craning to look down from his perch far above them, his eyes widened when he saw the two dirty urchins hanging onto his immaculate, gleaming coach. "Get down!" he shouted, raising his horsewhip and shaking it. "Get down from my lord's coach!"

Violet and Ralph let go, jumping to the street simultaneously. The coachman flicked his reins, urging his team into a faster pace. Violet picked herself up from where she had fallen, watching the beautiful rig disappear as it turned the corner. Her buttocks burned. Closer inspection revealed another hole in the seat of her pants. She sighed.

"Yew awright?" Ralph asked, walking over to her.

"Just hurt me bum." Violet gazed past Ralph. "I can 'ear the music," she said. "I niver 'eard music like that before."

They fell silent. The strains of an orchestra drifted through the night, soft but audible, lively yet serene, peaceful yet gay. Violet sighed again. "Looks like a castle, don't it?"

"Ain't no castle. It's 'Arding 'Ouse. An earl lives there." Ralph scowled and spat into the street.

"Betcha 'e's never 'ungry," Violet said, staring. The mansion looked like it had been comprised of several different buildings, all of different heights. It was made of pale, shimmering stone, and it boasted three high square towers, one at each end and one in the middle. There were turrets and spires everywhere. Gargoyles clung to the roof. Violet wondered why anyone would want monsters on their house, especially when it would have been so very lovely without them.

"Betcha they've got lots of food fer two 'uns like us." Ralph grinned.

Violet's eyes widened. "Yer mad!"

He shrugged. "I didn't eat nuthin' today." He took her hand.

"Wait," Violet said, pulling Ralph into the shadows cast by one of the street's huge elm trees. A gleaming black lacquer carriage was rolling past them. A silver crest graced each door. It slowed and stopped directly in front of the steps leading up to the mansion. As the coachman, liveried in silver and blue, stepped to the ground, the carriage door opened without his help. Violet watched a dark-haired young man step out, clad in black evening clothes. His shirt was snowy white, and somehow the effect was spectacular.

Ralph spat. "Another nob thinks 'e's better than the rest o' us."

"Yeah," Violet agreed. She watched the man say something to his driver and step onto the sidewalk. He bounded up the wide stone steps of Harding House. He moved as if he owned the world, or at least the mansion in this part of it.

"C'mon," Ralph said. They ran from the shelter of the tree across the sidewalk and pressed their bodies against the iron gate that separated the mansion from another luxurious residence. When they were certain that no one was watching, they quickly shimmied up the tree. From an upper branch, they took turns jumping down onto the emerald green lawns surrounding the house.

Ralph smiled at Violet, took her hand, and, avoiding the pools of yellow-white light spilling from the house, they ran toward the back, where experience had long taught them the kitchens would be.

But gardens and terraces were in their way. They stumbled to a halt. The tiled terrace in front of them led not to the kitchens but to a huge ballroom. They stood in the shadows of one huge hedge sculpted like a trio of oversized deer, and from there they could just make out the glittering swirl of dancers inside and the brilliant shimmer of gold and crystal chandeliers.

"Gawd," Violet said in awe.

Ralph, for once, did not reply.

"Let's go take a peek," Violet suddenly begged.

"Yew lost *yer* mind?" Ralph gasped.

Violet pulled her hand abruptly free, and with a defiant glance she was off like a shot. Sighing, Ralph followed her.

A moment later they were crouched beneath one window, the terrace and the open doors to the ballroom directly on their right. More hedges, potted plants, and the blooms of a dozen different varieties of flowers separated the two children from the terrace. Just above their heads was a small stone casement.

Violet could not wait. Slowly she straightened her body and lifted her head, to peer inside the glass window at the ballroom.

Ralph did the same.

This time, Violet was at a loss for words. She blinked, but the fairy world in front of her did not disappear, and it did not change. She did not realize that her nose was pressed flat against the glass windowpane.

She had never seen so much beauty before. Or so many rich people in one place.

Violet had eyes only for the ladies. The ladies wore fantastic jewel-colored gowns in velvets and silks, taffetas and satins. Their skirts, sleeves, and bodices dripped decorations the likes of which Violet had never before seen: white lace, black lace, fur trim, colorful embroidery, seed pearls, even creeping vines and budding flowers that were so skillfully made they appeared to be real. Every now and then Violet would see tiny colored satin shoes with a small heels appearing from beneath the swirling, bell-like skirts and underskirts as the ladies danced. Every single lady wore white gloves. Jewels glittered from their necks and ears. Rubies, emeralds, sapphires, pearls. And diamonds, glittering with hot, shimmering light.

But perhaps the most shocking thing was that everyone was so white.

Violet knew that the ladies used powder, but powder would never make Violet's own skin that white. And not only were their faces pale, like ivory, so were their necks and chests and their exposed upper arms. Violet wondered how a body could be so pale. She had not looked at her face in years, but her hands were usually black, except when it rained. Then they turned gray, with odd little streaks and stripes.

Violet's heart was pounding. She wondered what it must be like to wear such fine clothes, such beautiful jewels, to dance the night away in such a castle-like place.

She stiffened. A dark-haired man was emerging from the

crowd, walking toward her. Although she hadn't seen him up close, she recognized the way he moved, as if he owned the world, as if he were a prince. It was the same dark-haired young man she had seen alighting from the coach a few moments ago. She stared. He was probably a prince, she decided. He was rich and handsome and smiling as if he didn't have a single care in the entire world.

Violet couldn't imagine being so happy, much less having nothing to worry about. An image of her father, followed by that Farminger, flitted through her head, while a gnawing hunger made her stomach hurt.

A woman appeared. She seemed to float, not walk—her pink gown belling out about her—to his side. She was a dark blonde with slightly golden skin, and she was so very beautiful. Violet saw the two exchange smiles. The woman was older than he was—Violet could see that—quite a bit older, but they were gazing at each other as if they were in love. Violet scowled through the thick glass at them.

"Duck," Ralph ordered.

Violet glanced through the window one last time to see the dark-haired man and the golden lady exit the ballroom—and emerge onto the terrace just to her right. She dropped to her knees, alarmed. If she and Ralph were caught now, trespassing, they would be in trouble for sure.

And Violet heard the man murmur. His tone was different, low, yet warm, somehow strange. She had never heard a man's voice sound quite like that before, and when the woman laughed quietly, gazing up at him with shining eyes, Violet realized that she had never heard two people talk and laugh like this. But why should she? In St. Giles, the men shouted and the women cried. Laughter belonged to the drunk.

The man murmured, "Shall we dance, Gabriella? Here in the moonlight?"

But the woman was already in his arms. "How I have missed you, Blake. And it has only been a few days."

He held her tightly, gazing down at her, his smile fading. "How I have missed you," he whispered.

The couple seemed to fuse together as naturally as ice melting into water, and suddenly they were swirling across the terrace, which was cast in beams of mellow light from the ballroom inside and the stars and moon overhead. They danced and danced, a man and woman who seemed to belong together, until they were at the opposite end of the terrace, where they suddenly halted.

Violet stared, her stomach in knots. She watched the man kiss the woman. Deeply. Hungrily. So this was love. She scowled and looked at Ralph. "Let's do wot we came fer. I'm starved now, too." And oddly enough, she was jealous and she was angry. She hated the dark-haired man and his lady love, and she hated everyone inside the ballroom, too. She hated this other world, a world she could never belong to, no matter how she might wish differently.

They ran around the house, widely skirting the terrace where the couple was locked in a passionate embrace. She and Ralph turned the corner and were assaulted by the smell of roasting meats and baking pies.

Her stomach groaned loudly. Gawd. Violet licked her lips, salivating, thinking about roast beef and chicken, apple pies, and hot, sweet bread.

Ralph gripped her arm. From where they stood pressed against the cold stone wall they could see through the tall windows into the kitchens. And the back doors were wide ajar—it would be easy to slip inside. But the kitchens were full of servants scurrying about. A white-coated chef stood in their midst, red-faced and shouting. Apparently preparations to serve a ballroom full of guests were underway.

"Let's do it," Ralph said. "Wot's yer choice?"

Violet looked inside and espied a plum pudding big enough for eight on the counter besides a platter of roasted lamb. It was so very hard to decide. She licked her lips again while her stomach growled. "Puddin'," she said.

"I'll take the meat," Ralph said, his eyes gleaming.

They ran.

Skidding into the midst of servants, all of whom, for a long moment, did not notice the invasion of their domain. Violet grabbed the bowl of plum pudding. Ralph clutched the platter of lamb.

"*Mon Dieu!*" the chef screamed. "Thieves! Thieves! They are stealing my lamb! My pudding!"

But Ralph and Violet were already racing out of the door, clutching the stolen food to their chests. They skidded across the lawns. Behind them, they heard the chef screaming, his cries following them as he pursued them himself.

Violet glanced back and saw the white-coated figure chasing them, a huge knife in hand. He was furious. And on his heels

were three manservants, and two maids, all looking determined
to catch them. "Gawd,'e's gonna kill us," she panted.

"Faster," Ralph shouted, but suddenly they realized their
dilemma. Ahead of them was the high iron fence that enclosed
Harding House from the outside world.

Violet stopped behind Ralph so abruptly she almost collided
into him. She looked worriedly behind her. Their pursuers also
realized their predicament and had slowed, now walking delib-
erately toward them.

"Call the constable," a black-suited servant said.

One of the liveried servants turned and ran back to the house.

"Put down the food," the chef said carefully.

Violet and Ralph hesitated. Then Ralph said, "Toss it,"
throwing the platter of roasted lamb into the grass. "An'
jump!"

Violet held onto the plum pudding hard as Ralph leaped up
and began a mad scramble to climb up the slippery iron fence.
The chef cried out. She stared at the cook, knowing she could
not part with the pudding. Nothing had ever tempted her more.
How could she throw it aside? And into the dirt, at that? Tears
filled her eyes.

"Violet!" Ralph shouted at her.

Violet looked up and saw he was lying on a low branch of
the tree, one arm extended down to her. Violet clutched the
pudding more tightly. The chef and the servants had formed a
semicircle behind her. Someone was asking her for the pudding.
Ralph shouted at her again, with urgency. With a sob, Violet
flung the pudding on the ground and leapt upwards. Ralph
caught her hand and dragged her into the tree. There they collapsed in one another's arms.

"Let's get out of 'ere," Ralph said. Together he and Violet
shimmied down the other side of the tree. But just a few feet
from the ground they both stopped. Violet's heart lurched hard.

Two uniformed bobbies carrying big wodden bats were rushing toward them. "Gawd," Violet whispered. Tears still
streaked her face.

"Run, Violet, fer yer life!" Ralph screamed.

They dropped to the ground, running, Violet on Ralph's
heels. She did not have to look back to know that the police
were right behind them. The constables shouted at them to halt.
Violet ran harder, terrified. But Ralph began to outdistance her.

"Wait!" she panted.

He did not hear her. They cut across the wide street. A coach was coming toward them. Violet screamed when she realized that she and Ralph were about to be run down. She skidded to a halt. Ralph, however, did not stop. With a sudden burst of speed, he managed to dive in front of the coach, missing being run over just by a hair. He rolled and rolled, and, like a cat, was on his feet and running again.

But Violet could not follow him. A huge, hard hand was clamped on her shoulder, so hard that she cried out. She fought, twisting like a maddened creature, trying to sink her teeth into the bobbie's hand, struggling to jerk free, but to no avail. And the policeman, cursing, struck her with his big stick.

Violet could not sleep. Images of the beautiful plum pudding danced in her mind. Images of the pudding, and her best friend, Ralph.

Tears filled her eyes, but she refused to cry. Crying was for babies. Not for her. She was grown up.

She lay in one of dozens of narrow bunks that lined both walls of the room, beneath one thin sheet, shivering. The bobbies had taken her against her will to the closest workhouse.

Violet had fought them like a rabid dog. She'd been hit again, and tossed into a jail-bound conveyance like a mongrel dog. Upon arriving at the poorhouse, she was forced to endure the humiliation of being stripped naked before the cold-eyed warden and two of his assistants. They'd stolen her clothes. Been shocked to realize she wasn't a boy. A plain gray shift had been thrown at her, along with stockings and her old, shoddy shoes. For her supper she'd been given a bowl of watery soup and a small loaf of bread.

Violet choked on a sob. How had this happened? The "union" was a fate worse than death. She'd always heard that once they got you in they never let you out, not even on Sundays to hear the Lord's Prayer. Violet was cold—not because the workhouse was not heated, not because she was still hungry—cold because she was afraid and alone and she wanted to go home, to Ralph and St. Giles.

She stared up at the ceiling, which had been painted white a long time ago and was now a distinct shade of yellow. Tears kept filling her eyes. Where was Ralph now? He'd escaped being run over by the coach. He'd escaped capture by the bobbies. Undoubtedly he was sleeping on the stoop he shared with Violet in St. Giles just across from the Hogshead, a gin mill. Would she ever see him again?

Violet turned on her stomach and cradled her head on her arms. And what about her father? He was going to die. She'd known that for a long time. Ralph hadn't had to tell her. Would she ever see him again?

She hugged herself, trying hard not to cry. She thought about the ladies in their brilliant ball gowns, about the man who'd looked and acted like a prince, about the plum pudding and roast lamb spilled on the lawn outside Harding House.

Violet began to weep.

She cried for a long time, unable to fight her fear. And then finally the tears were gone. She was too exhausted to cry anymore.

But she had come to a realization: One day she was going to be rich and fancy, too.

It was a vow—a vow she made not to God, whom she believed in but knew that would not help the likes of her, but to herself. One day she would wear satin and pearls, furs and diamonds, just like those fancy ladies at the ball, just like that beautiful golden lady. One day she would live in a big, fine house, filled with grand things, with servants attending her, waiting her every beck and call. She'd have a big, fat chef, too, and he'd spend all day, every day, just cooking for her—anything she wanted, from chicken pies and roasted beef to plum puddings, lemon cakes, chocolates, and sweets. Oh, yes, lots of sweets. She would have so much to eat that she would forget what it was like to be so hungry that her stomach caved in, hurting and aching and moaning; she would have so much to eat that she would be big and fat like the chef at Harding House.

And maybe one day a fine, fancy gentleman who looked and acted like a prince would dance with her across a moonlit terrace, love shining in his eyes.

And Violet, comforted by her new hopes and dreams, finally slept, images of plum puddings and princes dancing inside her head.

PART ONE

The Pretender

⸎ *One* ⸎

THE victoria seated two. Its once plush red leather seats were cracking, and the once shiny brass rails refused to gleam no matter how frequently polished, but Sir Thomas Goodwin would not consider purchasing a new conveyance. Violette did not care. When Sir Thomas had brought his young bride to his home in York six months ago, just outside of the village of Tamrah, she hadn't noticed the torn leather or the tarnished brass of the victoria. She hadn't noticed the excessively faded upholstery in his home, the smoke-darkened, torn wallpaper on the walls. Sir Thomas was gentry, and it had been a miracle that he would call on a mere shop girl, much less take her to wife. In many ways, Sir Thomas had saved her life. In any event, he certainly had changed it drastically.

Of course, Sir Thomas was old enough to be Violette's grandfather, perhaps even her great-grandfather, and this was his second marriage. His first wife had died a decade ago. But her life had changed from the moment he walked into her shop and smiled at her. He courted her, gently and respectfully. But best of all, Sir Thomas had agreed that Ralph could leave London, too, and join them as a servant of sorts.

Sir Thomas drove the victoria down Tamrah's single main street, keeping their gray gelding at a walk. Violette kept her chin high as several shopkeepers and pedestrians turned to look at them from the stone sidewalk. Her heart sank a little when she noticed Sir Thomas's daughter, Joanna Feldstone, staring at her from outside the cabinet maker's. Violette looked away from the older woman's icy stare.

At first, she hadn't cared about the difference in their ages.

Not really. Marriage was a matter of convenience, a business arrangement. Everyone knew it, and she and Ralph had discussed it at length. Violette had been thrilled to accept the proposal of a gentleman who would take her away from London and the grim life she had always known. She had been thrilled to marry a knight and become Lady Violette Goodwin. Sir Thomas had suggested that she spell her name in the French fashion. Violette couldn't spell or read, so she did not care. She had agreed.

They had been married for six months. Violette had just turned eighteen.

How she loved York. She loved the countryside, and she loved Goodwin Manor, but she hated this small village. It wasn't the village itself, which was quaint, with its stone buildings and timbered roofs, flowers in the windowsill pots. It was that no one here liked her—no one, that is, except for her husband.

And Violette knew what everyone thought. They all thought she was dirt, not good enough for Sir Thomas, and that she had married him for his money. But everyone was wrong. She had married him to better herself. She had married him to escape her grim existence.

Now Sir Thomas stopped the victoria in front of the druggist's, a small shop with stained-glass windows, and Violette felt her cheeks begin to burn—not that she cared what these hoighty-toity villagers thought. However, she did smooth down her magenta-colored silk dress, one overlaid with a darker red lace tissue, red roses decorating the flounced hem and the high neckline. She fingered the pearls at her neck. She tucked an escaping wisp of hair back into her dark blue velvet bonnet, which was decorated with a small bird and fruit. Then she picked up her reticule. She could not help being nervous.

"Do what you have to do, Violette," Sir Thomas said mildly.

Violette smiled at him. He was very tall and very thin. Cook was always scolding him for not eating, and his face was pale except for two brilliant red spots on his cheeks. Violette, of course, ate enough for the two of them. He was close to seventy, or so Violette had heard, so of course he was very wrinkled, but his eyes were as mild as his tone had been, and they were kind. Violette had liked his eyes from the moment they had first met. "I promise to 'urry." She stepped down from the carriage carelessly, landing on the dirt street with a small, restrained jump.

Her pulse accelerating now, Violette turned to glance back the way they had come. The moors stretched out into what appeared to be infinity, on the one hand bleak and inhospitable, nearly treeless; yet it was late summer now, and they were abloom with purple gorse. Sometimes it seemed to Violette that she lived on top of the world, that she could see out forever, to China if need be.

But even Violette knew that was an impossibility. However, from where she stood, she could see a good ten kilometers. A few miles in the distance the ground was more elevated, and atop that hill there appeared to be a pile of stone; but it wasn't stone or rocks—it was Harding Hall, the country seat of the earldom.

And the Hardings were in residence. Sir Thomas was calling on them that noon—to introduce his bride.

Swallowing, Violette entered the druggist's, trying to tamp down her nervousness. She was terrified of facing the earl and the countess. She might look like a lady, but Violette was always aware of the truth, and thus far it did not seem that she had fooled anyone. She was no longer hungry, not ever, but often, like now, she had a sickness deep in the pit of her belly. If these villagers disliked her so, she could imagine the reaction of Lord and Lady Harding.

Yet she was also curious. She and Ralph had driven the victoria past Harding Hall many times, when Sir Thomas was abed, as he so often was; they had gazed at the sprawling palace, wondering what it might be like to live in such a place, or even to visit within those beige stone walls.

Violette shoved her thoughts aside, aware that she was perspiring, a part of her hoping that something would happen to postpone the visit. It was dim within the druggist's. Standing at the counter was Harold Keepson, clad in his white jacket and horn-rimmed spectacles; next to him was the rector's wife. Both Harold Keepson and Lillith Stayne ceased conversation the moment she entered the shop. They turned simultaneously to look at Violette. Her cheeks burned more violently now, especially as Missus Stayne made no effort to disguise the fact that she was looking Violette up and down with sheer dislike and utter condescension.

Her chin lifted another fraction. Violette had the feeling that she had committed some monstrous mistake, but for the life of her, she did not know what that mistake could possibly be—other than entering the ranks of a society which wished so fervently to exclude her. "G'day, Mister Keepson. G'day, Missus Stayne."

Lillith winced. "Good day, *Lady* Goodwin." Most of the villagers had trouble pronouncing the word "lady" whenever it preceded Goodwin. "My, what an *interesting* dress."

Violette glanced down at the big, beautiful roses she dearly loved on the flounced hem of her favorite dress, then fingered the roses on her bodice. "Thank yew. Mister Keepson, do yew got rat poison fer me?"

Keepson nodded, staring at her through his thick lenses. "Do you have a problem with rats, Lady Goodwin?" His tone was kinder than Lillith Stayne's had been. But Violette had already figured out that the men in the village were much nicer than the women—some of them, in fact, wanted to be *too* nice. She wasn't a fool.

She shook her head and gave a small smile. "Infortunately, we do. Cook asked me to bring the poison 'ome."

Missus Stayne wore a frozen smile. "I'll be right back," Keepson said, as the shop door opened, its bell tinkling. "Just how much rat poison do you need?"

"I ain't really sure. Mebbe enough to kill off four or five?" Violette's hands were trembling. Joanna Feldstone had just entered the store.

Keepson disappeared into the storeroom. Violette was never sure whether Joanna would acknowledge her presence or treat her like a piece of furniture, so she nodded quickly, glancing at the older woman out of the corner of her eye. Lady Feldstone was old enough to be Violette's mother. She was a big, buxom woman with an ever-present glare.

She turned her back on Violette. "I didn't know there were rats at Goodwin Manor. My father never had rats before, not once in his entire life, I should know. I say, I cannot understand what is happening over there these days!"

Violette clenched her fists. She didn't even think of holding her tongue. "The cat died. That's why we've got rats."

Joanna Feldstone turned, raised both heavy brows in a look at once incredulous and dismissive, then gave Violette her broad back again.

Keepson returned, assuring Violette that he had given her enough arsenic to do away with a good dozen rats, and Violette proudly paid with a fiver she took out of her purse. She loved paying for everything with cash. The fiver actually was a part of Violette's pin money. Goodwin gave her a five-pound note once a month to do with as she pleased. Violette had been overwhelmed by his generosity.

Violette thanked the druggist, but did not bother to say good-bye to either woman, giving them *her* back. Outside, she found Sir Thomas still sitting in the victoria, but he was talking to the rector, George Stayne. Both men paused as she appeared. Violette handed her husband the bag containing the poison, then clambered up into the victoria. As she settled down on the seat besides Sir Thomas, she saw where the rector was looking. Several inches of stocking and one black high-low had been revealed by her movements. Violette tugged down her bright skirts to cover her ankle and shoe.

"Did you make your purchases?" Sir Thomas asked.

Violette nodded. "G'day, Parson."

"Good day, Violette," George returned. "I hear you're calling on the earl today." He smiled.

Violette's heart lurched. "Yeah." Although the Hardings had been in residence briefly when she and Sir Thomas were first wed, he had not been feeling well then and they had never gone calling. Instead, Sir Thomas had sent Ralph with his card and an apology.

Now Sir Thomas was rubbing his abdomen, wincing.

Violette was concerned. "Yew got stomach pains?" Sir Thomas' stomach had been bothering him for the past two months. It seemed to be a condition that was growing worse, not better. "Mebbe we should go t' the 'All another day?"

"It will pass." Sir Thomas lifted the reins. "Good day, George."

"Is this an experiment?" the earl of Harding demanded of his younger son.

"No." The one word was said flatly. Blake crossed his trouser-clad legs, leaning back comfortably in the plush leather chair. He faced his father, a tall, striking, silver-haired man who stood behind his massive rosewood, leather-inlaid desk. Blake's older brother Jonathon also stood, but over by the one large window that overlooked the sheep-dotted moors. Outside, the sky was a brilliant shade of blue.

The two brothers and their father were in the earl's private study, a huge room with gleaming oak floors, Aubusson rugs, a green marble–manteled fireplace, a frescoed ceiling, and two walls of floor-to-ceiling books. The third wall was comprised of four double-sized windows, and it was papered in mint green silk. Damask sofas, Louis Quatorze chairs, striped ottomans, and several small and medium-sized tables completed the room. Sunlight streamed inside.

"This has to be an experiment! Either that, or you are as mad as the prince." The earl was furious.

Blake stood, stretching. He yawned. "At least I am in good company." He smiled lazily, a flash of white teeth in skin slightly, unfashionably, tanned. His hair was short and dark. He ressembled the earl almost uncannily, except for the difference in their years.

"You know, Theodore," the earl said coolly, "I could disown you for this."

Jon stepped forward, his blue eyes mild. Unlike his brother and father, he was blond. "Excuse me, but may I referee? You cannot disown Blake, Father, it would be a far graver scandal than Blake building these 'row houses,' as he calls them. Besides, he has weathered the scandal about the bank. Really, wasn't that far worse than building?" Jon smiled, then shot his brother a dark, warning glare that belied his mild, placating tone. It was a command to be silent and behave.

Blake sighed. Two against one, as always. Why was it that he could never do anything right? The earl was never pleased.

"No," Richard Blake, the earl, said. "Being a banker, by God, is only as bad, not worse, than being a builder! The Hardings do not trade, by damn! The Hardings are not plebeians. Theodore, you are doing this merely to annoy me."

Blake no longer smiled. "I wish it were as simple as that," he snapped. "I am a grown man, Father. And the younger son. How would you like me to live?"

"I give you an allowance. And when I am dead, your brother will do the same," the earl said firmly. "Peers do not trade. Peers do not earn money. It is not done."

"This peer not only trades, he buys, he sells, he builds, and dammit, he earns money," Blake said tersely. "And I refuse to be dependent upon you and Jon. Nor do I care how the rest of society lives."

"You made that clear twenty years ago, when you tried to run away to the Indies at the mere age of eight." The earl shook his head.

"I was not running away," Blake returned with a smile. "I told you my plans."

"Fortunately," the earl glowered.

"Even at eight, Blake was seeking an independent fortune," Jon interjected lightly, smiling.

Blake also smiled. "I know you will not believe this, but I was more interested in seeing the world. I still regret being dragged home by Tulley."

"Thank God for Tulley," Jon said. He faced the earl. "Father, you will not get Blake to change his mind, much less his ways. He never does what you wish for him to do. He is the rogue in the family, the self-proclaimed black sheep, remember?"

"How can I forget," the earl said. He threw his hands up into the air. "It has been one misadventure after another, and I had truly hoped things would change when you came of age. Yet what has changed? First I had to explain to the world that my son trades in China. This was the major topic of discussion in the club when the Lords was in recess seven years ago. But three years past I had to explain that he bought a bank. And everyone was appalled, Blake, let me tell you this! Do you know that the prime minister actually asked me if he had heard correctly, that you were a moneylender?"

Blake couldn't help it. He said, mildly, "I am a money-lender."

Jon groaned.

The earl flushed. "Don't use that word in connection with yourself in this household! And now I have to explain that you are building row houses in the East End?"

"Have you ever been to the East End, Father?" Blake asked grimly. "Have you ever been to St. Giles? Seven Dials? Southwark?"

Harding froze. Then he stalked out from behind his desk. "I want you to know something, Theodore. I was one of the first peers in the Lords to support the Reform Act of '32, and then the poor laws and the factory laws after that. I've been on thirty commissions in the past twenty years, half of them dealing with investigations into the abominable conditions that exist in this country, commissions involving factory workers, miners, tradesmen, even children, women, you name it! Do not ask me if I have visited London's slums."

Blake's jaw flexed. "Have you?" he challenged.

Jon's eyes widened. The earl did not move. A thick silence cloaked the room, broken only by the periodic ticking of the library's single-pendulum clock. Blake regretted his lapse of temper and judgment.

Suddenly one of the library's two teak doors was pushed open, and the countess appeared. Suzannah looked at the tableau in front of her, from her husband to her two sons. Like Jon, she was blond and fair, and about ten years younger than the earl. She was wearing a pale blue moirée morning gown, her wedding rings, and small sapphire ear studs. "I thought I heard shouting, but when I approached, there was this very unnatural silence." Her voice was soft and melodic, in accordance with her appearance.

"Hello, Mother." Blake moved first. He crossed the room with long strides and took his mother's hands, kissing her cheek. "Forgive my appearance, but it was a long, dusty trip. You are beautiful, as always."

"And you are, as always, immaculate and impossibly dashing," Suzannah Blake, the countess of Harding, replied with a smile. "You do not appear to have suffered an interminable railway journey. I imagine you have broken a few hearts along the way."

Blake smiled. "I owe it all to my tailor. But if I have broken any hearts, I am quite unaware of it."

"I doubt that," Jon interjected. "At least, that's not the latest word to float around Londontown."

Blake eyed his brother in annoyance.

Suzannah smiled at her younger son. "I am so glad you could come, Blake. It's been too long since we had the entire family here at the Hall. Am I interrupting?"

The earl turned and slammed closed a ledger on his desk. The noise was loud and emphatic. "Actually, darling, you are, and in the nick of time. *Your* son is building houses. What will he think of next?"

The countess sighed. "Oh dear. I suppose the sky will fall as a consequence?"

Blake and Jon laughed in unison. The earl glowered. Suzannah moved to him and patted his arm. Finally, grudgingly, he gave up his pout. "What is afoot, madam?" Harding asked, shrugging on his tweed riding coat. Like Jon, he was clad casually, in breeches and boots.

"We have callers. Sir Thomas Goodwin is here with his

bride. I have left them in the keeping of Catherine. Please, come and bid the knight and his wife good day.''

The earl sighed, crossing the room. ''God, I didn't know Goodwin was still alive. We didn't see him, did we, last year?''

''He was ill. But he is very much alive today, although I must say, he doesn't look all that well.''

''Mother, Sir Thomas is seventy if he's a day,'' Jon said.

Suzannah paused at the door. ''I think I should warn you, though,'' she said to her husband and sons. ''His bride is not what you are expecting.''

''And what are we expecting?'' Blake asked with some amusement.

''I do not think Lady Goodwin is even eighteen,'' the countess said hesitantly.

Blake and Jon looked at each other and started to laugh. ''Good for Goodwin.'' Blake chuckled.

''I didn't know he had it in him,'' Jon agreed, grinning.

''And she is . . . different,'' Suzannah added. And she appeared quite worried.

❖ *Two* ❖

VIOLETTE was in awe. She had never been inside a house like this before.

She sat stiffly on a yellow velvet sofa in the drawing room, not hearing a word of the polite conversation being exchanged between Lady Catherine Dearfield, a friend of the family's, and Sir Thomas. Her eyes were wide, taking in every detail of the drawing room, which was almost as large as the entire ground floor of Goodwin Manor itself. A huge yellow, white, and gold carpet covered the entire floor. A dozen distinct seating arrangements were evident, consisting of sofas and loveseats, bergères and ottomans, and tête-à-têtes. Four huge crystal chandeliers hung from the high, molded ceilings, which were painted mauve, with beige and gold accents. Innumerable paintings graced the walls, as did various busts and statuettes on their pedestals. This home, Violette thought, should not belong to a mere earl and his countess, it should belong to a king and his queen.

And the outside of the country house was as palatial as the

inside. For from afar, Harding Hall truly resembled a royal residence, with the house's numerous wings, its high roofs and towers, its terraces, balconies, and Gothic spires.

"So how do you find the country, Lady Goodwin?"

It took Violette a moment to realize that she had been addressed. She flushed, shifting carefully; it was at times like these that she desperately wished she had been born a lady and was used to crinoline cages. "I . . . er . . . I love me new 'ome," Violette said, just as the Harding family entered the room.

Sir Thomas stood, as did Lady Catherine. But Violette was frozen. She had just met the countess, who had been amazingly pleasant, not at all like the villagers, not that Violette had dared utter a word in response to her. Being in such esteemed company was intimidating enough. And now the countess had returned with the earl and their two sons. Harding did look like a king, even in his country clothes, but he appeared to be a somewhat annoyed king. Violette could not help but stare. His sons were as dashing as princes, one fair like the countess, the other as dark and as handsome as sin. Her heart fluttered a little.

"Violette," Sir Thomas said with a slight cough.

Violette realized that everyone was looking at her. She jumped to her feet. Her heavy skirts, adorned with heavier roses, caught the small clawed foot of the sidetable besides the yellow velvet sofa. It tilted precariously, a small china lamp sliding towards its edge.

Violette watched it, horrified. But the dark handsome man in the black suit and silver brocade waistcoat rushed forward and caught the lamp before it crashed to the floor. "Gawd, I'm sorry," she whispered.

He set the lamp on the table and looked at her. His eyes were a brilliant shade of blue. He stared directly at her, making her feel uneasy, making her want to run away—or come impossibly closer. And then he smiled. "No harm done, Lady Goodwin. May I perform the introductions? Theodore Blake, at your service. But you may call me Blake, everyone does." Before Violette could digest the impact of his devastating smile, much less his words, he had lifted her gloved hand, almost but not quite to his mouth. He kissed it without touching the skin of her glove.

She gaped at him, her heart seeming to turn over. Suddenly, eight years slipped away and she recognized him as the man who had danced on the terrace all those years ago. He gave her another smile, this one different, somehow intimate, then he pushed her hand down to her side, where it belonged. "Sir Thomas, so good to see you again. May we wish you somewhat belated felicitations?"

Sir Thomas came forward and the two shook hands. Violette wet her lips, backing up a step, trying to mind her skirts, watching now as her husband was greeted by the earl and the eldest son, whom she gathered was Lord Farleigh. Her pulse was racing, but she decided that was because she had almost broken what had to be a priceless Oriental lamp. She didn't realize that she continued to stare at Lord Theodore Blake until he looked her way, catching her in the act. He smiled at her again. He had a dimple in his left cheek and a slightly cleft chin.

Violette ducked, blushing. Good gawd! She had never had such a handsome man look at her before, and certainly not the way this Blake had looked at her. And he had kissed her hand.

The greetings over, it was time for the ladies to sit back down. The countess took a seat on the yellow sofa and smiled at Violette. "Lady Goodwin, do come and sit by me."

Violette stole a glance at the assembly. Lady Catherine was taking a wide chair to accommodate her crinolines, Sir Thomas was standing besides the earl, discussing some issue currently being debated in Commons, and both of the sons were regarding her openly. Violette felt that her cheeks remained red. Forcing a smile, she maneuvered carefully past Lady Catherine and the sidetable, not wanting to knock anything over. She sat.

"Do our moors agree with you?" the countess asked, her gaze steady upon Violette's face.

"Yes, ma'am. I mean, yes, me lady. I am very 'appy 'ere." She stole another glance at Blake. She hadn't been mistaken. He continued to watch her, but she could not fathom his expression. It was just slightly amused, she decided.

And Violette did not like being the butt of jokes, even ones she did not understand. She lifted her chin. "I grew up in London, I did. I niver in me life saw such beauty afore."

The countess smiled. "I love York as well. I think, even when I am in town for the Season, my heart remains here."

"The season?" Violette frowned. "Which season?"

A choked coughing sound made Violette turn her head. She watched Lady Catherine hand Jon her handkerchief, which he pressed to his mouth as he continued to cough.

"There is a season in London . . . ," a male voice said gently. Violette looked into Blake's blue eyes. ". . . during which

all of society throws itself into an endless round of fêtes and
soirées, of dinners, dances, and balls." He smiled. "It is really
overdone and quite boring."

Violette's pulse pounded. She could not imagine balls and
dances being boring. "I would not be bored," she said carefully.

Blake's smile flashed but his eyes held hers. "Yes, I can
understand that."

Sir Thomas came forward, flushed. "Come, Violette, we
have outstayed our welcome. My lord, my lady, we are so
pleased to have you back again."

The countess was standing. "Thank you so much for calling,
Sir Thomas. I am truly delighted for you and your bride. Lady
Goodwin? Thank you."

Violette had stood, and was feeling relieved that she hadn't
caught the clawed foot of the sidetable again, but now her
mouth dropped open. The countess was thanking her? For
what? "Why . . . er . . . yer most welcome," she said haltingly.

Jon started coughing again.

"Are yew ill?" Violette couldn't help asking with concern.
He was a strapping man, all golden-like, with broad shoulders
and long legs—he did not seem sickly.

Lady Catherine was at his side, once again allowing him the
use of her lacy linen. She smiled at Violette. "Jon has come
to the country to recover from a winter flu that would not go
away. I do believe it has lodged in his brain as well as his
lungs." Catherine turned and leveled a cool green stare at Jon.
"As he has forgotten how to comport himself," she said in a
very low, censuring tone.

Violette did not understand. She wasn't certain what "comport" meant, but she thought it had something to do with behavior, and the Harding heir certainly behaved as well or better
than anyone Violette had ever seen.

"Sir Thomas, again, felicitations," Blake said, distracting
Violette. His voice was as rich as honey. It was a voice that
could never be ignored.

Suddenly he turned and bowed slightly at her. "A real pleasure, Lady Goodwin." As he straightened one hand touched
the left side of his chest slightly, as if he were covering his
heart. "I am so pleased that we are neighbors."

Violette thought wildly for something to say. "Me, too,"
she finally said. And then, "I always wondered wot it was like
inside yer 'ouse."

Blake laughed. "And now you know." His eyes twinkled. "And hopefully you will have many more opportunities to enjoy my home. One day I shall give you a tour."

"Blake," Jon said, his tone warning.

"May I escort you to the door?" Blake asked, holding out his arm.

Violette blinked at it, but it did not go away. She knew she was supposed to place her arm in his, but she couldn't imagine being escorted outside by such a man. So she said, "I can manage, thank yew." And she followed Sir Thomas out.

"What do you think you're doing?" Jon demanded.

"I'm not doing anything," Blake said, staring out of the drawing room window as the Goodwins rolled away in their decrepit victoria. He and Jon were alone with Catherine. The moors were covered with heather in full bloom. Finally the purple landscape swallowed up the knight and his bride.

"I think the two of you behaved reprehensibly," Catherine said. She tucked two strands of platinum blond hair behind her ears. She faced Jon. "How dare you laugh at that poor girl."

"Me?" Jon's tawny brows lifted. "I was hardly laughing at her; she is sweet enough. Although you must admit Mother was right, Lady Goodwin was hardly what one would expect." He smiled again.

Catherine jabbed him with her elbow, a quite unladylike gesture.

"Ow," Jon said.

Blake continued to gaze out of the window.

"At least I wasn't flirting with her." Jon eyed Blake.

Blake finally tore his gaze away from the rolling moors. He shrugged helplessly. "I confess. I was flirting. It is my second nature. You have to admit, in spite of the accent and the garish dress, she is stunning." But it wasn't Violette's looks Blake was thinking about. There was something about her that wouldn't leave him alone—and was almost disturbing him.

"Quite," Jon agreed. "Blake, why in God's name didn't you tell Father the truth?"

Blake grimaced. "It did not seem like the time."

"I think you choose to annoy him," Jon accused.

Catherine's hands found her hips. "Blake! You did not tell your father about the honor Prince Albert bestowed upon you?"

Blake smiled ruefully. "No, I did not."

Jon glanced at Catherine. "But he told Father all about his latest project, practically giving Father an apoplexy."

"You exaggerate," Blake said mildly, glancing back out of the window. He turned his back on Catherine and Jon.

Catherine and Jon exchanged looks. "Blake," Catherine said softly, "the fact that the prince has titled you in reward for your good works will soon be all over town. Your father will find out. He is going to be so pleased, but he will be furious if he learns of this from an acquaintance. Why don't you tell him tonight?"

Blake did not answer. His gaze was on the rippling, purple-hued moors. His thoughts remained on Lady Violette Goodwin. Oddly enough, he found her fascinating.

"He refuses to say or do anything to promote a calm moment between himself and our father," Jon remarked, somewhat sarcastically. "And I do not think Blake is very concerned with Father right now." Jon smiled. His chin had the same cleft as Blake's. "Are you smitten, little brother? Finally, after all these years?"

Blake turned with a laugh. "Smitten? Hardly. But you have to admit, she is charming." Yet his smile was gone. How could she be married to Sir Thomas, even if it were done all the time? Was she even eighteen?

"Charming?" Catherine said. "That is not quite a word I would use to describe Lady Goodwin."

"Sometimes 'charm' has a different meaning for a man—when in reference to a woman," Jon explained. "She is adorable, I agree. Charming, to say the least."

"This topic is not at all seemly. She is married," Catherine said, stepping between the two brothers, "married, as in: she is a wife, she has a husband. And Sir Thomas is our neighbor."

"You don't have to define marriage to me," Jon said, grinning.

Blake remained silent.

Catherine huffed. "Perhaps I should. After all, the one of you has a reputation as a rake a mile long, and the other has a familial duty to perform which is long overdue."

Jon put his arm around his brother, and together they faced Catherine. "Who said I am failing in my familial duties?" Jon asked.

"Your mother. Your father. All of society," Catherine said.

"And you?" Jon asked softly.

Catherine sighed, but a faint pink color marred her lovely

cheeks. "No, Jon. I am your friend. I have known you for too many years to count and I would never judge you."

Jon removed his arm, giving Catherine an enigmatic look. "Blake," he said somberly, "what is wrong?"

Blake's gaze had wandered to the window. "Is she eighteen?" he asked. "It is such a common arrangement, but I am having trouble with the concept."

"Blake, you *are* smitten," Jon said, teasingly.

"She is married," Catherine repeated firmly, "to our neighbor. And, yes, she is eighteen."

Blake and Jon regarded one another. "She is very young, Blake," Jon finally said. "This is not at all like you."

Blake sighed. "Very young. Very young and very lovely and married to a man old enough to be her grandfather." The brothers' gazes held.

"Blake," Catherine protested, "I suspect your thoughts are scandalous. Can you not confine your bachelor ways to the fast lanes of the city?"

Blake did not answer. He had not come to the country for a brief liaison with a young woman of questionable antecedents. Surely he would forget a woman named Violette Goodwin had ever existed by tomorrow morning, wouldn't he? After all, she was hardly the kind of woman he kept company with. And briefly, in spite of so many years, he thought of Gabriella.

Jon spoke, not unkindly, but frankly. "Where in God's name *did* Goodwin find her?"

"They say she was a shopgirl in London," Catherine explained.

"Or worse," Blake said. Now he thought he knew what was bothering him, for he had spent enough time in the East End. "With that accent, a matchgirl is more likely."

"Well, in spite of her past, she certainly held her own today." Jon smiled. "And she has done admirably well for herself in marrying Sir Thomas."

Blake thought about how she had almost knocked over his mother's blue and white lamp and he smiled. Then he thought about her marriage and his smile faded.

"Perhaps she even loves Sir Thomas," Catherine said pointedly.

Blake met Catherine's green gaze. "I am not an ogre, Catherine, even if I am a bachelor. In fact, I am considered to be a very gallant man. I do not seek out women who do not wish to have the pleasure of my company, so cease your fretting.

And as Jon has pointed out, she is too young for me. Too young, obviously naïve, and hardly my type.''

"I am not relieved," Catherine said. "To the contrary, having seen the two of you together this single time, I have an extraordinarily bad feeling, perhaps even a premonition of sorts."

Jon made a scoffing sound and put his arm around her. "How foolish you are being," he said softly, "and that is not like you."

"I have never had this kind of feeling before," Catherine said. "Blake? You will stay away from her?"

Blake hesitated. And finally, more disturbed than ever, he nodded, wondering if he was being truthful.

She kept intruding upon his thoughts. Had he become jaded like some of his bachelor friends? Was that why he found Lady Goodwin so fascinating? Because she was young, fresh, different? He could not shake her from his mind. Yet he had not lied when he had said that she was not his type. The women he had thus far spent time with were all older than she, and far more worldly and sophisticated. They were women whom he could not hurt—and could not love. But, then, Blake did not believe in love. Not anymore.

Goodwin Manor lay ahead. Blake slowed the racy phaeton, until his black gelding was at a walk. He had not been able to concentrate on the papers he had brought with him and had felt compelled to take a drive. He squinted into the distance. Someone was outside in the small garden, which butted up against the square stone house. Blake saw that it was a man, undoubtedly a servant. He halted the phaeton. Catherine's warning returned to his mind, but he dismissed it as overly melodramatic.

The servant turned, pushing back his cap. He was an extremely fair young man of no more than twenty with long, sandy blond hair. He laid down his hoe and strolled toward Blake, his strides awkward because his legs were so thin and long. Blake hadn't been aware of the fact that Goodwin kept a manservant. Most country folk had a do-all maid and a cook and no one else.

"G'day," the young man said. "Wot can I do fer yew, sir?"

Another Cockney accent. Blake stared, thinking about Lady Goodwin. "You are Sir Thomas's gardener?"

"That an' his coachman an' valet an' everything else," the young man said, unsmiling. "Me name is 'Orn, Ralph 'Orn."

"Ralph, you have done a wonderful job with Sir Thomas's garden. Tell me, are those a new species of rose?"

Ralph looked at him as if he had lost his mind. "Don't know," he said. "I plant wot me mistress told me to buy."

Blake had been keeping one eye on the house. He, of course, did not give a damn about this garden or any other one. He was rewarded now when the door opened and Lady Goodwin came outside to stand on the stoop. It was very hard to explain his racing heartbeat and his eagerness, as he could not fathom it himself. But one thing was clear: he was beginning to smile, so was she, and their gazes had connected instantly.

Perhaps he was wrong, he thought. She was young, she appeared naïve, but most ladies in her position would take a lover without thinking twice about it.

She came forward with a small exclamation. Blake winced. She was wearing a lime green dress. The color itself was awful, especially so for a woman with pearl white skin and sky blue eyes. Emerald would have been a much better choice. But to make matters worse, the dress had large orange appliqués sewn all over the skirt. Clearly the appliqués were supposed to represent some object, but he could not begin to fathom what. In between the appliqués were small embroidered green leaves. He then realized that the appliqués were replicas of oranges.

He lifted his eyes and met her gaze again. He tensed. It was impossible for him not to feel the invisible force that pushed and pulled between them, some kind of inexorable bond, invisible, compelling, but almost physical, because he could actually feel it. And Blake was afraid. In his entire lifetime there had only been one woman who had drawn him this way, so inexplicably, so strongly—and she had thoroughly rejected him in the end, ultimately marrying another man.

Blake shook himself free of his past and his thoughts, leaping down from the phaeton at once. "Lady Goodwin," he said, smiling, bowing briefly. "How good to see you. I was on my way into the village and I had to stop and admire your garden."

"Lord Blake," she said, worrying her lime green satin sash. "G'day. I . . . this is a sorprise."

He stood beside his horse. "Yes, I imagine it is. And how is Sir Thomas today?" He glanced briefly, dismissively, at the gardener. Ralph stared rudely back and did not disappear.

"Me 'usband is abed today," Violette said. " 'E ain't feelin' up to stuff."

Blake bit back a smile. Gently, he said, "Up to 'snuff,' Lady Goodwin. The expression is 'up to snuff.' "

She blushed more brightly. "Oh, er, 'scuse me, me lord." She glanced down at the dirt road they stood upon.

And Blake wondered why Goodwin didn't hire her a tutor. She was embarrassed. She didn't want to make mistakes, that was plain to see. "Would you like to show me your garden?" Blake asked.

She jerked in surprise. "Yew want to see me garden?"

"You may give me a small tour," he said, a soft command. "Perhaps you should dismiss the gardener."

She blinked. "Oh, right. Ralph, g'on with yew. Yew got things t' do, don't yew?"

The gardener glowered—at Blake—and jammed his cap down more tightly. "Yeah, Lady Goodwin. I got plenty t' do." He turned, but not before giving Blake a dark, hostile look. Blake watched him stalk off, amazed by the servant's display of emotion and brazen audacity. Horn stirred up a bad feeling inside him.

"Is he a friend of yours?" he asked, gesturing for Violette to precede him.

Her cheeks remained flushed. She glanced up at him and averted her eyes. "Now wot makes yew think that?" She laughed somewhat loudly, nervously.

Blake wondered what she was hiding. As they strolled to the garden, he glanced back over his shoulder one more time, and found Ralph watching them from the shade of the small carriage house, his tall, lanky frame hunched over. Blake automatically took Lady Goodwin's elbow. Horn was close to her in age and he spoke with the same horrid accent—a dialect not common in York. Were she and Horn more than servant and mistress? But why had he thought that? It was a stunning and unpleasant thought—and a distinct possibility.

"Well," she said quickly, " 'ere's the garden."

Blake looked into her eyes and felt a sharp stabbing in his chest—as if kicked there by a miniature mule. "Perhaps some time I can show you the gardens at Harding Hall. They are quite spectacular."

Her eyes widened as he spoke. She was as still as a deer. Then she said, her tone hushed, "Oh, me lord, I would luv that!"

Blake suddenly folded his arms, his smile fading. She was as much a child as a woman. And she seemed every bit as naïve as she appeared. "You like flowers, Lady Goodwin?" he asked seriously.

She nodded, her eyes luminous. "I luv flowers. An' trees. An' the sun an' the sky when it's blue, like t'day. But I 'ate the rain," she said with a flash of passion.

He almost told her that her eyes were the exact shade of the sky on that country day. And that would have also been the truth. "Why? Why do you hate the rain?" He had to know.

She hesitated, their gazes locked. Then she wet her lips and shrugged. "I don't like bein' cold an' wet an' 'ungry."

Blake stared. It took him a moment to fully comprehend her, because she had just opened the door on a world he was aware of, but had never before really entered. "What does being hungry have to do with being cold and wet?" he asked slowly.

She opened her mouth, but did not reply. She turned away from him, staring out at the purple moors. "Stupid thing t' say."

Blake didn't think so. Blake thought it had been brutally honest. He was very disturbed. How vulnerable she was, misplanted in his world the way a jungle fern might be in a cultivated London hothouse. "I will show you the gardens at Harding Hall," he said flatly. "You shall be immersed in flowers and greenery, but not on a day when it is wet and damp."

She turned, openly eager. Her eyes were shining, her smile wide.

When had a woman ever looked at him that way? Or even a child, for that matter? He was merely offering her a tour of the gardens, he was not handing her a ten-carat diamond ring. Compassion welled up inside of him. "Perhaps Sir Thomas will feel better tonight? We are having a small dinner. At seven. Do come."

Her blue eyes were wide. "Gawd," she said. "Thank yew. We'll come. Yew can count on it." Her smile was even broader now. "Supper at 'Arding 'All," she whispered to herself, with no small amount of awe.

Blake finally smiled. But it was forced, because he realized the extent of her naïveté. She was too innocent for him to even consider dallying with her, and, if he dared be honest with himself, that was what had brought him to Goodwin Manor that day. He was vastly disappointed, yet he was also terribly relieved.

He had made a monumental mistake a decade ago of entrusting his heart to a woman, and he had no wish to ever be so foolish again. And he had the most unrealistic, absurd sense that Violette Goodwin could affect him the way no lady ever had, not in recent memory—and that included Gabriella. And that was to be avoided at all cost.

❖ *Three* ❖

VIOLETTE ran into the house, holding her skirts well above her ankles. Ralph had been in the kitchen, and he appeared in the front hallway as Violette hit the first step of the stairs. He reached out and grabbed her wrist, halting her in her tracks.

Violette turned, her face wreathed in smiles. "Did yew 'ear?" she cried. " 'E's invited me an' Sir Thomas over fer dinner, can yew believe that?"

Ralph let her go, crossing his arms. "Oh, I can believe it all right."

Violette continued to beam. "Dinner at 'Arding 'All!" she exclaimed. "With the earl an' the countess! My gawd! I can not believe it meself, I must be dreamin'!"

"I don't think so."

Violette turned eagerly. "An' 'e's gonna show me the gardens. Ralph, they've got at least a 'undred gardens up on the 'ill, don't yew think? It'll be like dyin' an' goin' t' 'eaven!"

" 'E's goin' to show yew more than the gardens," Ralph spat.

"I got to go an' get Sir Thomas up an' tell 'im the news." Violette dashed up the stairs. She ran down the hall and barged into her husband's bedroom. It was a room she never entered except when she was caring for him when he was ill. And he had never entered her bedroom, not even once. Now she did not think to knock. And she skidded to a stop abruptly, her heart sinking.

He lay on his back, very still. His eyes were closed, he was pasty white, and he was breathing shallowly and rapidly. Almost but not quite forgetting the incredible dinner invitation, Violette walked over to the bed and carefully picked up her husband's hand. She did not have to be a doctor herself to know that he was worse. "Sir Thomas? Yew ain't feelin' any better?"

His eyes opened. He smiled slightly at her. "Oh, Violette. Seeing you is enough to make me feel better, for it's like the sun coming out from behind dark storm clouds.''

Violette smiled at the man she had become so fond of in one short half-year. ''Don't be ridiculous. I ain't no ball of sunshine.''

''But you are, my dear,'' he said gently. ''And I knew it from the moment we first met. I understood the joy you would bring me even then.''

Violette harrumphed, blushing with pleasure, and went and opened a window. ''The air is so fine 'ere. It's got to be good fer a body, if not fer a soul.'' She turned and smiled brightly even though she was worried. ''I'm goin' to town to fetch Dr. Crumb.''

''Don't go,'' Sir Thomas said, his watery blue eyes upon her. His tone was thinner than usual, far more weak than normally. ''I'm lonely when you leave me, dear.''

Violette quickly crossed the room and sat down on the bed besides his hip. ''Yew ain't well, are yew?'' she asked worriedly.

''I'm an old man, Violette, but no, I do not think that I am well.''

Violette clenched her fists. ''Not that old!''

Sir Thomas smiled, then suddenly, he gasped.

''Another pain?'' Violette asked.

''It will pass,'' he said, his eyes closed. ''It always does. Having you here with me these last few months has made it all so much easier, Violette.''

Violette strode to the door. ''Ralph!'' she shouted. ''Ralph! 'Urry to town an' get the doctor, d' yew 'ear me?''

''I 'eard,'' Ralph called from downstairs. ''Yew bellow to wake the dead!'' The front door slammed closed.

Violette turned, her back against the wall. She forced a smile. ''Doc Crumb will be 'ere soon.'' She quickly, purposefully, changed the topic. ''Lord Blake was 'ere. 'E invited us to sup tonight at the 'All.''

''That was very kind of Lord Blake.''

''Yeah, it was,'' Violette said miserably. ''But don't yew worry. We ain't goin', not with yew so down the weather, an' that's that.'' But she wanted to cry. She wasn't a fool, she knew she was never going to receive another invitation to dine with an earl and his family and guests.

''Violette, you go. You go and enjoy yourself.''

Violette blinked. ''Yew lost yer mind?''

Sir Thomas chuckled, then groaned. ''No, dear, I want you

to go. I want you to enjoy an evening the likes of which you have never had before. No one deserves it more, especially for putting up so sweetly with an old goat like myself. Don't mind me. I shall sleep.''

"But . . ." Violette's hopes warred with her sense of responsibility and her genuine concern. "But . . ."

"No buts! I truly want you to go and enjoy yourself." His tired eyes held hers.

Tears filled Violette's eyes. She rushed forward, dropped to her knees, and hugged Sir Thomas so hard that his smile faded and he gasped. "Oops, sorry," she said, sniffing and wiping her eyes.

"That's quite all right." He stroked her hair with one gnarled, trembling hand.

Suddenly Violette leapt to her feet. "Gawd!" she gasped. "Wot do I wear?"

"Yew ain't goin' out like that?!" Ralph said.

Violette's hands found her hips. "Wot's wrong with me dress?"

"Everythin'," Ralph shouted.

Violette looked down at herself. She was wearing a pale blue satin gown, the only evening dress in her wardrobe. It was the same dress she had worn to her wedding. The neck was high, the bodice pleated with white satin, and the skirts consisted of five blue and white draped layers. "I know this ain't as pretty as me other dresses, but . . ."

"Yew got skin showin'," Ralph said tersely.

"I do?"

Ralph jabbed his finger at her throat. The collar of the bodice exposed about three inches of Violette's throat and neck. "Yer mad," Violette said. "An' jealous, 'cause yew don't get to sup with the nobs."

"I don't want to sup with the earl," Ralph said. "We got to talk, Violette."

"No, yew got to drive me over to the 'All." Violette donned her white kid gloves and picked up a lightweight ice white cashmere shawl. It was trimmed with white ermine fur. Ralph followed her through the front door. Sir Thomas was sleeping. Dr. Crumb had given him laudanum for his stomach pains.

The victoria was waiting, the gray hitched up. Violette's pulse, already dancing, raced. Ralph walked around the horse and jumped up. Violette lifted her skirts and climbed inside as well.

"Yew stay away from Lord Blake," Ralph said heatedly, picking up the reins with his freckled hands. The victoria jogged forward.

"Why? 'E's a nice man."

"Wot 'e's thinkin' ain't so nice," Ralph said angrily.

"'Ow d' yew know wot 'e's thinkin'?" Violette protested.

"I know 'cause I'm a man, same as 'im." Ralph glanced at her. "'E wants to lift them blue skirts of yers, Violette, an' don't yew go forgettin' it!"

Violette hesitated. She wanted to deny what Ralph had said, but she couldn't. Surely Ralph was wrong? Blake was so nice, so wonderful—she was certain of it.

"I sorta seen the way 'e looks at me," she finally said, downcast. "I ain't stupid." Her heart had stopped dancing. "But 'e looks at me different, not like dockworkers an' such, Ralph."

Ralph spat. "'E ain't no different, luv, an' yew make sure yew don't go forgettin' it."

Violette worried now. She had never forgotten that horrid man in the top hat who had wanted her to whore for him when she was a ten-year-old child. Since then, there had been many men, all with the same lewd thoughts, all with groping hands and leering smiles. Violette was not a fool. She had learned the art of fending off unwanted letches before any advance was made years ago.

"Promise me yew'll be careful," Ralph said.

Violette hugged her wrap closer to her body. The reality of her life warred with her admiration for Blake. "'E's a genny-ine gent, Ralph," she said slowly. "'E don't want t' use me like I'm some fancy whore." A sadness she did not want to feel was ruining the summer evening. "I'm sure, Ralph."

"Sure—an' wrong," Ralph said. "Be on yer toes tonight."

Violette was silent. Above them, the night had turned blue-black.

The countess greeted Violette at the entrance to the grand drawing room. She smiled, taking both of Violette's hands. "So good of you to come, Lady Goodwin," she said, squeezing Violette's palms.

For an instant Violette could not reply. Nine people had al-

ready gathered in the room, chatting in pairs. And the first
person Violette saw was Blake. He had been dashing, of course,
that morning in his tweed country clothes and high boots, as
he had been the first time she had met him, in his black city
suit. But Violette was unprepared for her reaction to him now.
Her heart slammed to a stop and she could not breathe.

And he had seen her, too, for he was smiling at her. Clad in
a black tailcoat and black satin-piped evening trousers, he
strolled slowly toward her and the countess.

"Thank yew fer invitin' me," Violette whispered, beginning
to tremble.

"Is Sir Thomas not with you?" the countess asked as Blake
arrived at their side.

Violette found it hard to reply, for Blake was staring directly
into her eyes, no longer smiling. She felt her cheeks heating as
he reached for her hand. Violette managed, " 'E ain't well. Dr.
Crumb gave 'im some laudanum an' 'e's sleepin' like a baby.
'E told me I should come without 'im."

"I'm so sorry," the countess said, worry flitting through her
blue eyes.

But Violette was frozen. Blake was kissing her hand. And
even through the thin lambskin, she felt the pressure of his
palm, the warmth of it, the strength. The oddest thing happened
to her. A jolt of liquid sensation, fierce and hot, the likes of
which she had never before experienced, pierced through her
entire body, her entire being.

He released her hand, unsmiling, staring back. Their gazes
locked.

The countess looked from the one to the other, frowning
somewhat. Then she took Violette's arm and tucked it in hers.
"Come, dear. I shall introduce you around." She actually
turned her back on her son, forcing Violette to do the same.

And that was when Violette saw Lady Joanna Feldstone,
glaring at her from across the drawing room.

After the most wonderful dinner Violette had ever had, one
including baked pheasant, roasted lamb, and sautéed Scottish
salmon, not to mention lemon meringues, strawberry tarts, and
plum puddings (there had been twelve courses!), Violette joined
the other women in the drawing room while the men wandered
off for a cognac, a cigar, and perhaps a game of billiards or
whist. Violette had not spoken during dinner except when ad-

dressed. She had spent the entire two hours eating and listening, while stealing glances at Blake, who sat directly across the table from her.

Every now and then their eyes had met and he had smiled at her from behind the silver epergne. And she had blushed.

The countess left the two mahogany doors open and she now smiled at her guests. "What a wonderful summer evening," she remarked as the ladies sat themselves down in the closest seating area. A fire crackled in the oversized hearth. Made of pale stone, it was ceiling-high and engraved with angels, pennants, flowers, vines, and other biblical symbols.

"Our summers are very fine," Lady Feldstone said, eyeing Violette. "Of course, only a mad person could remain in London right now."

Silently Violette agreed. London was hot, humid, and airless in the summer, and usually the stench from the river was overwhelming.

"Come, Lady Goodwin," Lady Catherine Dearfield said pleasantly. "Do sit down."

Violette hesitated. Her stepdaughter had taken the middle of the red-striped sofa, Catherine on her right, while the countess was seated across from her on a beige tête-à-tête. Violette felt it would be awfully nervy to go and share the tête-à-tête with the countess, but she had no wish to sit besides Joanna, who had stared coldly at her during most of the supper. Finally Violette chose to sit on a small tufted ottoman, but she felt as if she were on the fringes of the group, and not a part of it.

Which she was. Because she was really Violet Cooper, not Lady Goodwin, and this evening was making her acutely aware of just how fragile—and precious—her world was.

Joanna ignored her. "I dearly look forward to the fox hunt this Saturday, don't you?"

"I'm afraid I stopped riding with the hounds ages ago. Catherine, however, is quite fond of the sport," the countess said.

Violette's eyes popped. Lady Dearfield was not just ivory-skinned, blond, and green-eyed, she was one of the most gentle, ladylike women Violette had ever come across. She could not imagine her dashing across field and stream on some huge steed. But Catherine smiled. "Yes, I adore hunting. In fact, I adore anything to do with horses. My mornings are spent in the riding ring practicing my dressage. My father keeps one of the finest stables in the north of England."

Joanna snickered. "Why don't you invite *Lady* Goodwin to join you this weekend? I'm sure she would make a wonderful hunting companion."

Violette froze. She hated horses, was terrified of them, and Joanna knew it. For one instant, she looked from her malicious stepdaughter to the somewhat confused faces of the countess and Catherine. The countess smiled, breaking the moment quite smoothly. "Do you hunt, Lady Goodwin?"

Violette swallowed, knowing she was beginning to blush. "No, I'm sorry. I niver learned."

Joanna snickered again. "I do love the hunt. I used to hunt with my father when I was but a child. Of course at my age, I'd rather watch from the sidelines."

At her age—and with her bulk—Violette couldn't help it. "That's probably a real good idea," she said smoothly. "'Cause a fall might kill yer horse if he went down beneath yew."

It took Joanna and the other two women a moment to realize what Violette had meant. Joanna gasped, turning red. Catherine quickly smiled, her posture frozen, saying, "It is a dangerous sport. One must be an accomplished rider in order to participate."

The countess was looking at Violette, her serene expression difficult to read. Violette knew she had made a terrible mistake and was ashamed of having lost her temper. But Joanna Feldstone was always sending her daggers with her eyes! But then the countess said, "Lady Goodwin might wish to join me on the sidelines, then. As I also prefer to wait for the men, rather than to ride with them."

Violette was overwhelmed. The countess and Lady Dearfield, and Blake, too, of course, they were all so kind! And to think tha she had been so afraid to call at Harding Hall with Sir Thomas. To think that she had doubted Blake's intentions, even for a moment. "Thank yew, me lady," she whispered somewhat hoarsely. "Mebbe I'll do just that."

Joanna looked from Violette to the countess. She was gripping her hands so tightly in her green taffeta lap that the seams of her gloves appeared ready to pop.

"Excuse me," Blake said warmly, poking his head around the doorway. "Dare I interrupt?"

Violette's heart skipped a half a dozen beats. Little did she know that her feelings were mirrored on her face.

The countess smiled not quite naturally as Blake stepped into the room. "You are never interrupting, Theodore. Don't tell me you have finished your port and cigar?"

Blake's smile was easy, his gaze slipping to Violette. "It was a cognac, actually, and, no, I neither finished that nor my smoking. But I made Lady Goodwin a promise." His eyes held hers. "Do you remember?" he asked softly.

Violette could hardly breathe. Of course she remembered. She was already on her feet. "Yew promised to show me the 'undreds of flowers yew got bloomin' 'ere at the 'All."

He threw back his head and laughed, the sound as warm and rich as the plum pudding had been, and then he strode forward. "I promised to show you the gardens. But I am afraid, Lady Goodwin, that we do not have a hundred flowers here."

Violette's nerves were strained with excitement. "'Course yew do. Yew can almost count 'em from the road."

Blake's smile faded, but his gaze remained trained upon her face. "You must be an eternal optimist," he finally said.

Violette did not know what an "optimist" was and was not about to reveal her ignorance to the present company, so she did not reply. Their gazes remained locked.

The countess was also standing. "Actually, we have one hundred and twelve different species of flowers and flowering plants here at the Hall."

Violette's excitement over the Harding gardens dimmed. Blake was still gazing with unusual intensity at her. A different kind of excitement seemed to come alive inside of her, leaping from nerve ending to nerve ending. She could not seem to move.

But Blake came to life. He took her elbow. "A hundred and twelve. How perceptive, Lady Goodwin." He turned to his mother. "We shall be but a minute or two." He bowed at the three women, ignoring Joanna's narrowed eyes, and led Violette from the drawing room.

⊰ *Four* ⊱

THE moon was bright. Violette was acutely conscious of the man who held her elbow as they strolled onto the slate-floored terrace. Thousands of stars shone down upon them. Violette couldn't help recalling that night, eight years ago, when she had watched this man dancing on another terrace with another woman in the waxen moonlight. She knew that the man had been Blake.

"A penny for your thoughts?" Blake said, stopping, pausing to face her.

Violette looked up at his handsome face. His eyes were gentle, soft, kind. Was Ralph right? Violette hoped not. She wanted Blake to remain a prince in her mind and her heart, an unattainable one, but a prince nevertheless. She smiled at him. "I'm thinkin' yew should be a prince, not an earl's son."

Blake started. Then he smiled slightly. "That is excessively flattering, Lady Goodwin. But I am no prince. Not even close, in fact."

Violette had to look at her toes. His proximity, his appearance, his unrelenting gaze, were doing strange things to her insides. She felt dazed. And, frankly, had she ever been happier? This entire evening had been magical. It was almost like a dream.

"You're not looking at the flowers," he said softly.

She glanced up, into his intense eyes. For an instant she forgot to breathe, was shaken from her head to her toes.

And then he lightly touched her elbow. "Come," he said, breaking the moment.

Violette followed him to a flower bed shaped like a figure-eight. Tulips in rainbow hues blossomed everywhere. "I luv tulips," she said.

Blake continued to regard her.

Violette felt self-conscious. What was he thinking? His eyes were bright. She was so nervous, in spite of her happiness. Surely he did not think badly of her the way the villagers did. But she wished that she were a real lady, like Catherine Dearfield.

She walked away from the bed of tulips to admire a hedge of rioting orange flowers. "Wot are these called? I niver seen such flowers afore."

He followed her. "I do not know, but they are very beautiful."

Violette glanced at him, smiling.

His smile faded. "Almost as beautiful as you."

She froze.

He was stationary—as if surprised by his own words. He hesitated. "I am sorry, but you are beautiful, which you must know." His gaze searched hers. "Surely there is no harm in a compliment that is sincere."

Violette was at a loss for words. She wet her lips, which seemed dry. She knew she was not beautiful. His mother was beautiful. Catherine Dearfield was beautiful. "Yer teasin' me. Yew have to be."

He studied her. "No, I am not teasing you."

She looked up sideways, feeling shy, her heart beating hard, wildly. "Now yer the one eggsessively flatterin' me."

He chuckled. "It's 'excessively,' Lady Goodwin. E-x-c. Excess-ive-ly."

Her smile faded. "Yew makin' fun of the way I talk?"

"I would never do that." He was somber.

She wet her lips. "E-x-c?"

He nodded.

"Ex-cess-ive-ly," she said carefully.

"That's right," he murmured. "In fact, that was perfect."

Violette smiled with real pleasure. "Excessively," she said again. Then she sobered. "Do . . . do yew really think me a looker?" Her pulse raced.

His dimple had appeared. Now it disappeared. He hesitated. A long moment passed. "Yes," he said flatly. He suddenly stepped away from her, shifting so that he gazed out on the moors, away from her.

And that simple affirmation sent chills sweeping through her. Violette felt like crying, but not with sadness. "Yew are the most beautiful man I seen, too, an' I thought so from the first time I ever seen yew," she whispered.

It was his turn to be frozen. His eyes were wide as he turned back to her. "An optimist—and a woman who is genuinely frank, without pretense. How unusual you are."

Violette knew that her cheeks were hot. "Can't I give yew one of them complyments, too?"

He regarded her silently.

She felt her cheeks continuing to burn. "I said something wrong, didn't I?"

He nodded.

She wet her lips. "I don't want to talk wrong the way I do. I don't want to walk funny an' break fine things 'cause my skirts are so big an' wide."

"I know," he said harshly, his jaw flexed. Violette did not even see him lift his hand, but suddenly his palm was touching her cheek, an exquisite molding of his callused skin to her jaw. Her gaze went from his darkened eyes to his mouth. A thought dashed through her head. What would it be like to be held by such a man? To be kissed by him?

"Violette," he said tersely, finally dropping his hand.

She loved the way her name sounded when he said it. It sounded like the name of a real lady. She did not move.

A long, tense moment passed. She sensed that he was warring with himself. Ten years ago he had not hesitated. Almost a decade ago he had kissed that golden lady on a moonlit terrace. Violette was suddenly, acutely, disappointed.

And he knew, for he was staring at her as if he intended to read every thought on her mind, every feeling in her heart, and suddenly he gripped her elbows, leaning toward her. His mouth brushed over hers. Violette was afraid to move. Afraid to even breathe and destroy the precious moment. His mouth feathered hers again.

He pulled back, staring at her, still holding her arms. Violette swallowed with great difficulty, her pulse rioting, unable now to recollect anything other than the man beside her and the night they were immersed in. A huge bubble was swelling inside of her heart. Her thoughts raced, tumbled, wild and incoherent, her mind filling with images and hopes and dreams . . . and being cherished by a prince like this was one of them.

"Gawd," she heard herself whisper. "I ain't niver been kissed like that afore."

His eyes darkened impossibly more and suddenly he pulled her into his embrace. Violette did not protest as her body was crushed against his. His mouth claimed hers, hot and hungry now. Violette had to cling to him in order to remain standing upright. Her legs had lost their ability to hold her up, and she had lost the ability to think.

And he kissed her and kissed her for a small eternity until her body had turned to mush and a small soft sound escaped from her own lips. He dragged his mouth from hers. Violette leaned against him, in his arms, shaking and breathless. When she managed to raise her face and open her eyes, she found him staring at her, his gaze mesmerizing with its brilliance. Violette remained motionless.

"You are shaking," he said abruptly, putting his arm around her. Shadows had crossed his face. He seemed disturbed. He dropped his arm from her waist and gripped her elbow instead. His body no longer touched hers.

And Violette began to comprehend what had just happened. This prince of a man had kissed her, and it had been the most incredible kiss of her life. Her body was alive like never before. She yearned for his embrace, for more of his kisses. But she was married to Sir Thomas.

As that last, final thought intruded, Violette's stomach lurched, and with it her heart.

"I guess we got to go inside," Violette said, her tone choked. The immensity of what she had done—of what they had done—overwhelmed her.

He looked down at her grimly. "I think we must talk."

She stared up at him, slowly pulling her arm free of his grasp. She folded her arms across her bosom. "Talk? Wot about?" she asked fearfully. Trying to stop the stupid, foolish images from racing through her head—images of moonlit terraces, exotic gardens, and this devastating man. But suddenly there were other images too, images she did not want to entertain, not now. Images of Sir Thomas, old and wrinkled and ill, lying in his bed. Images of Ralph, angrily warning her of what the night would bring. Images of herself, many years ago, her hair chopped off, clad in ragged boys' clothes, sweeping streets for fine gentlemen like Theodore Blake.

Oh, gawd. Ralph had been right.

But Blake's kiss had been so beautiful. Just as the evening had been so beautiful. Just as he was so beautiful.

Violette wanted to weep. A desperate yearning rose up from nowhere, an intensity Violette had never before felt, a yearning she did not quite understand. It was far more than physical. Yet hadn't she thought Sir Thomas to be the answer to her dreams? *But he is an old man*, her mind shouted silently, stubbornly at her. *But he is my husband*, another, frantic part of her responded.

Abruptly Blake halted, causing her to do so, too. He released her elbow, his face carved in stone. Violette gazed at him, even though her cheeks burned violently now, with shame and even with some anger.

"I owe you a sincere apology, Lady Goodwin," he said stiffly. "In my own self-defense, I can truthfully say that I was overcome by my passion for you. I am sorry."

Violette stared. She was trying to understand what he was saying, but his words were so hurtful, stabbing through her breast. Everything was so hurtful. "Yew was overcome by yer passion," she repeated thickly, thinking now about their differences, and the fact that he knew she was married, that Sir Thomas was his neighbor.

He shifted his weight. "I pride myself on being a gentleman, but tonight I behaved like a cad. My apology is sincere."

Violette hugged herself. "I don't want yer apol-o-gie."

He flinched. "I beg your pardon?"

"Yew 'eard," she whispered, batting her eyelids frantically. She wasn't going to cry, not in front of him. Ralph had been right.

"Don't cry," he said suddenly, his tone as soft as the velvet night air, "please."

Violette wiped the back of her eyes with her gloved hand. "I ain't cryin'," she said defensively.

"I have hurt you," he said.

"No." She shook her head. And because he was staring so intently, Violette looked anywhere but at him. They faced the sloping, endless moors. It was very hard to tell where the blue-black land ended and where the blue-black sky began, even though the heavens above were star-studded.

She had trusted him. Even though they had only just met, she had trusted him more than she had ever trusted anyone— and he had betrayed that trust. Because she was Violet Cooper and they both knew it. Everyone knew it.

"Why have I hurt you, Violette?" Blake asked abruptly.

Now he was calling her by her first name again. "Yew didn't 'urt me."

He was silent. "I shall be leaving the country in a few days. I don't want to leave with bad feelings between us."

Violette stiffened, eyes wide. All she could think of then was that he would shortly return to London. And it was very likely that she would never see him again.

"Can you not accept my apology?" he asked quietly— gravely.

He was going to leave. The magical evening was over. And all she would have was the memory of him, the gardens, and his kiss. Loneliness overwhelmed her. And with it an inexplicable sorrow. Violette could not reply.

"Lady Goodwin? Violette?" He started to reach for her, but quickly dropped his hand.

Slowly, still unable to speak, she nodded. Her eyes had become moist in spite of her better intentions.

"Thank you," he said.

And they returned to the house.

*   *   *

"What some company?" Jon asked.

Blake turned. He remained on the terrace under the watchful stare of the candle-colored moon. He shrugged. He felt ill. How had he let himself get so carried away, with the evening, with her?

His brother crossed the terrace, carrying two snifters. "I imagine you could use a drink." Jon's gaze was mild yet penetrating.

Blake grimaced, his mind filled with thoughts of Violette Goodwin, whom he had never meant to hurt or insult, feeling as low as a man could feel, feeling like the dirt under his shoe. He accepted the cognac. He sniffed it without any appreciation. "I don't know how this has happened," he finally admitted.

"How what happened?" Jon asked.

Blake did not answer.

Jon sighed. "I can guess. You took a beautiful woman out into the gardens and there is a full moon, in case you have failed to notice. I also happened to notice that both you and Lady Goodwin seemed extremely distressed when you returned to the house. Can I assume that she rejected your overtures?"

Blake took a draught of cognac. "I had intended only to befriend her. I doubt we are friends now." He sipped again. The feeling of illness he was afflicted with did not go away. "Of course, I do not think I am capable of having a friendship with her anyway."

"Why not? You have some very good women friends in town, Blake." From the kennels, one of the dogs began to bark. "Of course, they are older, intellectual, not particularly attractive." Jon smiled.

"You are annoying me," Blake said firmly.

Jon's brows arched. "I do not think that I am a player here."

"What the bloody hell does that mean?"

"It means that Lady Goodwin is fascinating, even from my boringly conventional point of view. She is not like any woman either of us have ever known. In her own way, she is as extraordinary as Gabriella."

Blake stiffened. He failed to speak.

Jon eyed him. "The mere mention of her name still distresses you?"

"Absolutely not." Blake was angry. He clenched his snifter. "She married Cantwell eight years ago. Why would her name upset me now?"

Jon's eyes softened. "Because she is an amazing woman, still, beautiful, kind, intelligent, and you were head over heels in love with her in spite of your age differences, and she refused to marry you, even though she loved you as deeply."

Blake could not believe what he was hearing. Did Jon purposefully wish to open up old wounds? Make him bleed? "She made the decision she thought correct," Blake said with a calm he did not feel. "I did the honorable thing. I retreated. She is, I believe, happy. I have certainly moved on."

"Have you?" Jon asked.

Blake set his glass down on the terrace wall. "That is the most ridiculous question I have ever heard. But if you are asking me if I am carrying a torch for Gabriella, the answer is 'no.' "

"Then you are a rare man, being that half of the men I know do yearn for her, in one fashion or another." Jon sipped his own cognac. "And they were not passionately involved with her for three years."

"I was eighteen," Blake ground out.

"You wanted to marry her."

Blake stared, furious.

"You have refused to even look at a decent woman since then," Jon said. He was angry now, too. "Is that why you are pursuing Lady Goodwin? Because she is unavailable—and therefore inherently safe?"

"I have had enough," Blake ground out. "But let me get the last word in. I am not *pursuing* Lady Goodwin. Just as I do not *yearn* for Lady Cantwell. Good night." Blake whirled.

"Whom are you trying to convince? Me, or yourself?" Jon called.

Blake halted. "What are you trying to accomplish?"

"I am tired of seeing you play so hard at being a randy bachelor," Jon said very seriously.

"You are hardly one to call the kettle black."

Jon only smiled at that. "I also like Lady Goodwin. Yes, she needs a little polish, but any fool can see beneath the garish dress and horrid accent. Sir Thomas will not live forever, Blake."

Blake gaped, stunned with what Jon was implying. "Have you lost your mind?" he finally asked.

Jon laughed. "No, I have not." He sobered. "But even I could see something between the two of you—a tension, I guess one would call it. And I saw it between you and Gabriella, too, Blake. Everyone did.''

Blake had heard enough. ''You are a romantic fool. And to think that we grew up together and I did not ever guess.'' He turned, striding across the terrace.

''Blake, one last thing,'' Jon called after him.

Blake slowed but did not pause.

''Lady Feldstone is Lady Goodwin's stepdaughter.'' Jon hesitated as Blake halted. ''Actually, I was not the only one to see her stumble into the drawing room ten minutes ago. Joanna Feldstone obviously despises Lady Goodwin. To use a very common expression, I believe she has an ax to grind.''

''What is your point, big brother?'' Blake asked seriously.

''Lady Feldstone wants to cause trouble—and you may have given her the ammunition she needs, Blake. If I were you, I would be careful in the future where Lady Goodwin is concerned.''

Blake stared, realizing that Jon was probably right.

''So when are yew goin' t' tell me about 'im?'' Ralph asked as the hitched gray jogged away from Harding Hall. The victoria's springs were not in the best condition, and the victoria's two occupants bounced and jarred along the winding dirt road.

Violette sat with her arms folded across her chest, refusing to cry. Her jaw was grinding down so hard that it hurt her face. She did not answer Ralph.

''I'm sorry,'' Ralph said suddenly, intensely. ''Violette, I'm just tryin' to protect yew.''

Violette wanted to weep. Her lovely evening—the most wondrous of her entire life—had been ruined. Everything had clicked into place since she had left the terrace and Blake. His passion had overwhelmed him, but only because she was not a real lady, would never be one. He would have never been overwhelmed by passion if in the company of a true lady like Catherine Dearfield. He had treated her as if she was some kind of light-skirt tramp. ''Mebbe I'm sick an' tired of yer protectin' me! Mebbe I can take care of meself!'' Violette snapped.

Ralph's mouth tightened. He stole a glance at her as Goodwin Manor appeared ahead of them. Except for the light which was on in the kitchen, testimony to the fact that Cook was waiting for them to return, the house was cast in complete darkness. "Fine. Yew take care o' yourself. See if I care."

Violette turned blindly away, sniffing once, twice, then swallowing her remaining tears. Her shoulders hurt from being held so stiff and so square for so long.

The victoria rolled into the short graveled drive in front of the manor. Violette hadn't realized before how small her home was. She lifted her satin skirts and leapt to the ground. Not waiting for Ralph, who had the horse to put away and who lived behind the two-horse stable anyway, she stormed into the stone house. The front hall was pitch-dark, but Violette knew where the matches were. She lit a kerosene lamp, then shrugged off her mantle, starting up the stairs.

There was no sound coming from Sir Thomas's bedroom, but of course he was sound asleep, dosed with laudanum. Violette entered her own small bedroom. She had her very own bed, one with a carved wooden headboard and a mohair throw. Even on the coldest winter night, she was toasty warm when abed. She also had an oak wardrobe, an intricately carved dresser, a plump upholstered chair, and a full-standing mirror. Violette couldn't help noticing, though, that the fabric on the chair was old and faded, as was her striped and flowered wallpaper, and that her furnishings, once so remarkable, looked somewhat dowdy now. She turned and faced herself in the looking glass as she set the lamp down, which was tin, not even silver or porcelain. She reminded herself that she was lucky to have her own bedroom, much less a home like Goodwin Manor. She paused, regarding her reflection. Was she beautiful?

Had Blake meant it?

She looked at the ivory-skinned woman facing her. Looking at herself this past year was always a surprise. She didn't look like Violet Cooper, the daughter of a man who had once been a welder. It was an illusion, but she looked like a lady, even in the plain blue satin dress. But what did it matter? She might be addressed as Lady Goodwin now, but the truth would never change—and Blake and all of his world knew the truth.

Violette did not have a ladies' maid—she had insisted to Sir Thomas that she did not need one—so it took her some time to struggle out of her dress and cage and petticoat. But when she was clad in her plain flannel nightgown and robe, she picked up the lamp and went to check on Sir Thomas. It was *awfully* quiet. Usually he emitted the occasional snore.

Sir Thomas was sleeping soundly. Violette crossed the room

and looked down at him, worried now because he was so unnaturally pale. But he was wearing the slightest of smiles. She hoped he was having happy dreams. Impulsively Violette bent over and kissed his forehead.

He was terribly cool. Violette froze, suddenly noticing that his chest was hardly moving. And usually his breathing was shallow and fast. Fear pierced her, but she shoved it aside. Of course he was breathing! Dr. Crumb had been there that day.

But she stared and stared at his chest until her vision blurred and she did not see it rise or fall even the slightest bit . . . not even once.

Violette realized that he was dead and she screamed.

⋛ *Five* ⋚

THE Harding coach was drawn by a four-horse team of blacks. It was black lacquer and shiny brass, the silver crest of the earldom embossed on the two carriage doors. As the coach rolled away from Harding Hall, its five occupants were unusually silent.

The countess sat beside the earl on the red velvet seat facing forward, clutching his arm. Across from her were Blake and Jon, Catherine in their midst. It was Catherine who had galloped over that morning from her father's hunting box to tell them the horrific news. Dearfield Way was but a mile south of Goodwin Manor, and one of the grooms was married to Sir Thomas's cook. She had learned of Sir Thomas's death before she had even had breakfast.

"I do hope Lady Goodwin is all right." Catherine broke the silence, twisting her hands, gloved now in black.

"This is terrible," the countess said, her blue eyes soft with sympathy. "But he did not look well when he called the day before yesterday with Lady Goodwin."

The earl regarded them all. "He looked positively ill, but I did not wish to say so. He looked as if he did not have long to live."

"In any case," Jon said, "Lady Goodwin must be very distraught."

Blake remained silent, staring out of the window. He did not see the passing countryside. He kept remembering how upset Lady Goodwin had been last night, in spite of his sincere apology. It was hard to believe. She had left Harding Hall, only to go home to find her husband dead in his bed.

Of course, Sir Thomas had been very old. Everyone had to die sometime, and he had lived a long, full life. Long enough and full enough to have taken a young, beautiful bride to wife.

The coach turned off of the main road. Ahead was the small stone village church, built in Norman times. Behind it lay the windswept cemetery. Blake could see that the entire village had turned out for the funeral. A sea of black suits, black dresses, and black hats crammed the treeless area.

The coach stopped amidst the many horses and vehicles parked around the square church. The earl alighted first in order to help the ladies down. As Blake leapt out behind his brother, he espied the coffin, a wreath of white flowers atop it, on the ground besides the pit where it would be laid. His gaze roamed the crowd. He saw Joanna Feldstone, her husband, Baron Feldstone, beside her. She was weeping copiously, supported by the small, short baron. But where was Lady Goodwin? Surely she was present. Or was she abed, dosed with laudanum?

"Oh dear," Catherine said suddenly.

Blake had seen her at the same time and his stride faltered. The villagers had gathered around Joanna Feldstone, the baron, and the coffin. On the other side of the still-empty grave Lady Goodwin stood with her manservant, spectacularly alone.

Blake was briefly frozen, but his family was not. The countess and the earl were hurrying toward Lady Goodwin, Catherine and Jon behind them. Blake recovered, following. Why in hell was she alone? Why was no one there to comfort her except for a single servant? He was furious.

As his mother hugged her and his father bowed over her hand, Blake regarded her, unable to look away. She was not crying. She stood as still as a statue, stiffly erect, staring out into space. She did not really seem to be cognizant of his family, the crowd, or what was taking place. There were terrible dark rings beneath her eyes, and clearly she had not slept at all last night, nor did he blame her. He saw no sign of tears. Her composure, he decided, was admirable. But had she been a weeping wreck he might have found it odd, for she hadn't married Sir Thomas for love.

Blake awaited his turn. When Jon and Catherine had finished extending their condolences, he bowed. "Lady Goodwin."

She focused on him. Her eyes were, he saw, the exact same shade as the brilliant sky. Impulsively he touched her arm, vaguely aware of the manservant eyeing him. "I am so very sorry."

She stared, nodding very slightly, a small jerk of her head.

Blake looked up into the watchful gaze of her manservant. The two men stared at one another for a moment that seemed to stretch on and on. Blake realized that he did not like this man. This man felt like a rival, although that was too ridiculous to dwell upon.

The rector, George Stayne, had stepped forward. "My lord, my lady," he greeted the earl and the countess. He was somber. "My lord, would you care to say a few words?"

The earl nodded. "I would very much like to," he said, stepping forward and clearing his throat. "Ladies and gentleman, I have known Sir Thomas my entire life," he began.

As his father started speaking, Blake made his decision. He moved closer to Violette, standing hip to hip with her, taking her arm and tucking it in his. "Feel free to lean on me," he whispered, "if you are in fear of fainting."

She blinked at him and he thought he finally saw a tear sparkling on the tip of one spiked, ink-black eyelash. "I niver fainted in me life," she said.

It had been clear to Blake that none of the mourners were adjourning to Goodwin Manor to comfort the widow in her grief. A quick discussion with his family had hardly been necessary, for one and all agreed that a visit to the manor was the order of the day. Still, Blake was appalled when the Harding coach turned into the graveled drive in front of the stone and stucco house. The only other vehicle in sight was Goodwin's tired victoria.

"This is unacceptable," Jon said grimly, voicing Blake's very thoughts. Clearly Lady Goodwin had never been accepted by the villagers.

The brothers exchanged glances. Blake pushed open the carriage door, almost forgetting himself. He waited impatiently for his father, his mother, and Catherine to alight.

"After you," Jon said, understanding him exactly.

Blake stepped out of the coach and strode to the house. The front door had just been opened by the manservant, who seemed surprised to see the Hardings. But he ushered them inside. It was clear that he was not pleased to have visitors, which Blake found as unacceptable as the events of the entire day.

Lady Goodwin was standing at the window in the parlor, apparently having seen them driving up to the house. She turned as they entered the room. The countess took one look around and said, "I shall speak with the cook and see what can be done about refreshments." She exited the room.

Jon walked over to the liquor cabinet. "Lady Goodwin, if you don't mind, might I have the key?"

Violette remained standing, staring. Her gaze had immediately found Blake. Nor had he been able to look away from her since entering the room.

"Lady Goodwin?" Jon prompted.

Blake went forward and took her hands in his. She was not wearing gloves. He managed to smile at her. It was not an easy task, because her hands were very small, and very cold, in his. "Lady Goodwin, I think my brother needs a drink. And I would like to join him. I imagine that we all would. The key?"

"I . . ." Her voice was husky. She glanced at Jon, the earl, and Catherine, bewildered. "I ain't sure where it is. I don't drink."

Blake had to smile. "That is a given. Ladies do not drink. Except for a glass of sherry, perhaps, and wine at suppertime."

She lifted her gaze. Confusion was mirrored in her eyes. "Wot's goin' on? Why are yew 'ere?"

He put his arm around her and guided her to the settee. Something was wrenching at him. "Come. Sit. It is the custom, you know, for friends to gather around the bereaved."

"Why are yew bein' kind again?" she whispered as he sat down, taking her with him.

For a moment he could only gaze into her eyes. He finally smiled, said as lightly as possible, "It is a fatal flaw of mine."

Her small nostrils flared. The tip of her nose was turning red.

As Jon and the earl began searching for the key to the liquor cabinet, Blake produced a handkerchief. His initials, T.E.B., were embroidered in maroon on the ivory square. He handed it to her.

"This is too fine to use."

"Nonsense," he returned.

She lifted it to her nose and blew very noisily. Blake's heart seemed to be trying to pound its way right out of his chest. He could not understand himself or his feelings. He had never felt quite so protective of anyone before.

Catherine had joined in the search. Blake ignored the rummaging going on in and around the sideboard containing the liquor cabinet. His hand moved over her back, which was small and hard. Her gaze lifted, doelike, and held his. "Thank yew," she whispered.

His hand paused. Their gazes remained locked.

"Hallelujah," Jon cried, holding up a key.

"In the nick of time," the earl agreed, watching as the cabinet was opened and a bottle of scotch whisky was produced. "Dewar's, I am happy to say," the earl announced.

"Bring two when you come," Blake instructed. He removed his hand from Violette's back. He was feeling protective, but not brotherly. And she was grieving. Even a fool could see that.

"Blake, you are not giving her a scotch whisky," Catherine admonished.

"I most certainly am," Blake said mildly. Jon handed him two hefty glasses. Thanking him, Blake put one down and turned to Violette. "Lady Goodwin," he said softly, "this will help."

She shook her head. "Yew said ladies don't drink eggscept for a sherry or a wine."

"Except," he murmured. "E-x-c."

She nodded. "Except." She managed a small smile.

He smiled back. "There are exceptions to every rule. Mourning is always an exception—and that is a rule."

Violette's brows furrowed together. Blake became alarmed. She appeared about to cry. "Do drink. Please," he said.

Violette stood abruptly. She did not speak, walking over to the window, her back to the ensemble. Blake found himself standing as well, unsure of what to do. He exchanged a helpless glance with his brother. Jon said, "You may as well drink up. I think you need a drink more than she does, brother."

Blake watched Catherine move to Violette. "My dear," Catherine said, "it is very acceptable to cry. Perhaps not publicly, but privately. Should I send for your maid? Do you wish to go upstairs?"

Violette said huskily, "I don't cry."

Silence greeted her words.

Blake gripped the whisky glass and drank half of it. It definitely made him feel better.

The countess returned, smiling. "We shall have sandwiches and tea in a flash."

''Oh, no,'' Violette whispered.

''Lady Goodwin, you do not wish to serve refreshments?'' the countess asked, perplexed.

Violette shook her head. Blake looked past her and saw Joanna Feldstone and her husband climbing down from the Feldstone carriage.

''I don't want 'er 'ere,'' Violette suddenly cried.

''Lady Goodwin,'' Catherine said calmly, ''Lady Feldstone is Sir Thomas's daughter. It is only proper that she come to share this time of mourning with you.''

Violette turned toward Blake. Her eyes were wide, wild. ''She 'ates me. She's come to make trouble.''

Blake couldn't agree more, but quickly recovered. ''You have nothing to fear,'' he soothed.

''I have everythin' to fear,'' she cried.

Joanna entered the room, a smile pasted on her tear-ravaged face, Baron Feldstone behind her. ''My lord, my lady, how wonderful of you to come,'' she said, rushing over to the earl and countess.

They had already spoken at the funeral, condolences having been exchanged. The countess said now, ''Of course we came. It was a lovely service.''

''Yes, it was. No help from her, though.'' Joanna glared at Violette.

Violette did not move. She did not even appear to breathe. She resembled a fragile yet stunning porcelain doll.

''You did nothing to help with the preparations,'' Joanna accused.

''Joanna,'' her husband said, low. He was sweating.

''But she did NOTHING.'' Joanna shrugged her arm free of his grip.

''Lady Feldstone, have a drink,'' the earl commanded sternly.

Her eyes widened. The earl poured and handed her a huge scotch whisky. ''This will ease your pain.'' He stared.

Blake silently applauded. No one could refuse his father when he spoke in such a tone. Joanna accepted the glass, appearing positively shocked, and took a hesitant sip of whisky. Immediately she began to choke. The baron pounded her on the back. Blake couldn't help hoping she would choke for a very long time, if that would keep her silent. He glanced at Jon, who smiled at him, clearly thinking the very same thing.

But she did not continue to choke. She set the glass down

and faced Violette. "Well," she said, "one thing is clear. My father is dead—God rest his soul. And this last half-year he was insane."

Violette's bosom heaved. "Sir Thomas wasn't mad."

"Don't you dare interrupt me!" Joanna cried. "I have had enough of this . . . this . . . PRETENDER!"

Violette stiffened. "I ain't no—"

"I want you out of my house!" Joanna shouted. "Go back to the streets—where you belong—you tart!"

Almost seeing red, Blake stepped between the two women, but before he could speak, the countess put an arm around Joanna, a smile fixed on her face. "Lady Joanna. Please, calm yourself. There is no cause for incivility. We must respect the dead."

Tears filled Joanna's eyes. "Respect the dead? I loved my father! He was a wonderful man! But my life has been insufferable since he married this trollop, this tramp! I do not know how she managed it, but I want her out of my home!"

The countess was taken aback. Violette was frozen, her expression glazing over. Blake said, very coldly, "Lady Feldstone, I suggest you share this moment of mourning with your husband elsewhere. Good day."

"Blake!" the countess gasped.

The earl, highly annoyed, stepped into the midst of the gathering. "Lady Feldstone, you may or may not like your stepmother, but facts speak for themselves, and she was Sir Thomas's wife. Sir Thomas had no sons. It is impossible to guess what provisions he has made for either yourself or Lady Goodwin, but until his will is read, Lady Goodwin has every right to remain in this house under the common law of this land."

Blake refrained from saying, *Hear, hear.*

Joanna gaped at the earl. "You take her side, my lord?"

"I refuse to take sides in this matter. I am merely stating the facts under the law."

Blake turned to Violette, whom he saw was shaking. He didn't think twice as he put his arm around her. "It will be all right," he said quietly.

Joanna began to weep, loudly, into her handkerchief.

"Father?" Jon interjected. "Given the emotions running rampant today, perhaps we should unearth Sir Thomas's will. What is the point in waiting? He was a fair man. I am sure he has made provisions for both his wife and his daughter."

The earl sighed, glancing at his pocket watch. But he directed himself to Violette. "Lady Goodwin, do you have any idea where your husband's will might be?"

Violette, her face a mask of fear, shook her head. "I ain't got no idea."

Blake was already crossing the room, his brother falling into step beside him. "The library. We shall mount our search there."

"Of course," Jon said.

As the two brothers entered the library, a small, dark, cluttered room, Jon said, his voice low, "You are wearing your heart on your sleeve. It is not appropriate. Did I not tell you to be careful?"

Blake started, looking for matches, which he found on a small table. He lit a lamp. "Are you mad? What are you talking about?" Had his concern for Violette been so obvious?

"You can deny it, even to yourself, but your affection for the widow is glaringly obvious. And Joanna Feldstone is not oblivious, even in her grief."

Blake tensed. "She is more child than woman. I feel nothing but sympathy for her. She is in mourning, for God's sake. I would sympathize with anyone in her position."

"You did not think her a child last night," Jon said, "and she may be young, but she is no child." He gazed at Blake. "And if I can see where your sympathy will lead, so can everyone else."

Blake halted besides the desk. "My *sympathy* is not leading anywhere." He meant it. But he was also confused, because his own feelings were not quite clear, even to him. But Jon was absolutely wrong if he thought that Blake would purposefully or inadvertently comfort the widow.

Jon stared. "I think you are lying to yourself."

Blake hoped that Jon was wrong. "Did we come here to analyze my relationship to Lady Goodwin, or to find the will?"

"I am sorry," Jon said. "Dammit." He raked his hand through his thick, gold hair. "But this is a small village, and we both know how the villagers love a little scandal."

"There is not going to be any scandal," Blake said flatly. "I promise you that."

Jon grunted. Blake frowned as they turned their attention to the desk. The top contained an open book on the taxonomy of insects, several pens, a ledger, and some unused sheets of vellum. Unable to remain annoyed with his brother, he opened the center drawer. And he whistled instantly. "I think someone knew his time was coming, Jon." He held up a large envelope.

It was clearly marked in black ink: The Last Will and Testament of Sir Thomas Goodwin, Knight.

✢ *Six* ✢

VIOLETTE remained riveted by the window, her back to the windowpanes. She was dazed. She had seen death before. Many times. But somehow this time was so very different. Sir Thomas had given her almost everything she had ever wanted, had ever dreamed of—he had been so good, so kind. It did not seem at all fair that he was dead, but Violette was no fool. Life was not about fairness or justice; it was about those who were smart and strong enough to survive.

And shouldn't she have anticipated this? Sir Thomas had never been well, not from the moment they had first met. And he had been an old man.

Violette was afraid. With Sir Thomas gone, what would happen to her now? She had never really felt secure in the role of Sir Thomas's wife. She had no confidence now. She could envision the dark, dirty streets of St. Giles as if she had been there yesterday. She could remember being dirty, cold, and hungry. In these past few months she had almost forgotten what it was like to be homeless and vagrant, and she did not want to go back.

Violette wiped her brow with her sleeve. What if Sir Thomas had failed to mention her in his will? They had been married for six brief months. Joanna Feldstone would toss her out on her ear. Of this Violette had no doubt.

The countess squeezed her hand briefly. "There, there. Everything will end well, my dear."

Violette looked at her blankly. What did the countess of Harding know? She could not understand. She had been swaddled in silk, not shreds, born with a silver spoon in her mouth, not a rag teat soaked with water-diluted milk. The countess had everything. Violette only had Ralph and Goodwin Manor—and perhaps not even that.

The brothers returned to the room, smiling. Violette stopped breathing. Blake was carrying an envelope, and his bright blue eyes went directly to her. "We found it." Still regarding Violette, he handed the sealed envelope to his father.

The earl said to the company at large, "May I?" He did not wait for an answer, promptly breaking the seal. He extracted a single page that appeared to be a legal-looking document and scanned it. "Well, this has been witnessed by the rector and Harold Keepson, and executed by Messrs. Stanhope and Cardiff—a well-known London firm. The will is simple. Sir Thomas left Goodwin Manor, its furnishings and the property it sits upon to his wife, Lady Violette. He has left his monetary estate to his only child, Lady Joanna Feldstone."

Violette sank down into the nearest chair. She began to breathe again. Sweat poured down her body, causing her underclothes to stick to her skin. Relief overwhelmed her.

She was not going to be cast out into the streets.

"He left the house and property to her?" Joanna shrieked. *"To her?!"*

"To me." Violette closed her eyes, trembling violently.

"I am afraid that he did," the earl said, returning the document to the envelope. "This belongs to the estate, and I shall retain possession of it until the solicitors settle any necessary transactions and file with the Justice of the Peace."

Joanna squared her shoulders. "My father was insane. And I shall not take this meekly, oh no." She stared furiously at Violette. "I will get this house—my home—if it is the last thing that I do. You shall be back on the streets—where you belong."

Violette lurched to her feet, flushing. "Get out. Yew 'eard the earl. This is my 'ouse now. Scat, yew fat old toad!"

"Lady Goodwin," the countess protested.

Violette ignored the countess, staring angrily at Joanna, for the first time in six months truly speaking her mind, defending herself—and how good it felt.

"You heard Lady Goodwin," Blake said coolly to Lady Feldstone.

Joanna hesitated, looking from Violette to Blake and finally to the entire assembly, then curtsied abruptly to the earl and the countess. Without another word, she marched from the house, the ashen baron puffing after her. The front door slammed closed so violently that the surrounding walls shook.

Violette remained standing, her hands clasped to her breasts.

"Lady Goodwin," Catherine said gently from her side, "I think you must be exhausted. Let me ring for your maid. You should retire and rest after this extraordinary, tragic day.''

Violette nodded. She was numb. She had one coherent thought. Goodwin Manor was hers. Dear, dear Sir Thomas. He hadn't forgotten her after all. ''I don't got a ladies' maid,'' she managed. ''But I'll be fine.''

The countess looked at Catherine and Catherine said, ''Come. Let me at least help you upstairs.''

Violette allowed the other woman to take her arm. Then, impulsively, she burst out, ''Thank yew, all of yew, so very much.''

''There is nothing to thank us for,'' Blake said softly, his gaze holding hers.

Violette led Catherine into her bedroom. Catherine glanced around at the small, dark room. It was immediately apparent that Violette slept there alone. Her narrow bed could not possibly accommodate more than one person. But Catherine couldn't help wondering why the furnishings were so tired and worn. Why hadn't Sir Thomas refurbished the room for his bride, as was customary? If Violette were not about to nap, Catherine would have opened the yellowing muslin drapes to brighten the interior.

Violette sank into a chair covered with faded magenta brocade. ''I think I'm tired.''

''I would imagine so,'' Catherine said, studying her. She wanted to understand why Blake was so interested in her. She was, Catherine thought, terribly beautiful, yet there was also a waiflike aspect to her. Was that the reason Blake was so intrigued? She was so different from Gabriella.

Catherine had been friends with Blake and Jon since they were children. She knew both brothers as well as they knew one another. Her father was an earl who had acquired both his title and Dearfield Way some dozen years ago. Catherine still remembered as if it were but yesterday the first time she had met the two brothers—they had all been astride, Catherine in pigtails, accompanied by a groom and riding a fine Arabian mare. Blake and Jon had been breaking rules and riding about the countryside unescorted on two handsome hunters. The boys had been twelve and fourteen, respectively, Catherine only seven years of age. Somehow they had raced across the moors, and Catherine had given both boys a run for their money. She hadn't won, but she had crossed the finish line on the brothers' heels. And they had all become instant friends.

She had known of Blake's three-year love affair with Gabriella, who had then been widowed for several years and apparently in no rush to wed in spite of the numerous suits she had garnered. Blake had been eighteen in the beginning of their liaison, Gabriella thirty. Everyone had known of the affair. They had been quite inseparable.

Catherine had debuted five years ago, and since then become somewhat acquainted with Lady Cantwell. She was, of course, quite beautiful, but it was her extreme intelligence and outspokenness which was outstanding, that and her generous, warm nature. No two women could be more different than Gabriella Cantwell and Violette Goodwin. Blake's interest in Violette, which was glaring, almost made no sense.

Yet there was something about Violette Goodwin that even compelled Catherine, and after a moment's reflection she realized that it might be her stubborn pride, which was clearly at odds with her vulnerability, both the result of her being miscast as the elderly knight's young wife. Catherine could not help but admire Violette's courage, both in transforming her life by marrying so upwardly, and in clinging to her new life now with Sir Thomas dead. And Blake, she knew, admired traits like courage, honesty, and pride far more than he did either gentility, decorum, or mere beauty.

Perhaps, Catherine thought suddenly, Gabriella and Violette had more in common than one might assume at a first glance. "Can I help you out of your gown?" Catherine asked kindly.

Violette smiled wanly. "Thank yew. In truth, I ain't in the mood to struggle meself."

As Violette stood, Catherine began undoing the numerous buttons down the back of Violette's black serge dress. She helped the younger woman pull the heavy wool garment over her head, then began to unfasten the tapes holding the crinolines in place. They whooshed to the floor when released.

Violette stepped out of the cage, clad in a plain petticoat and chemise. "I'm fine now, thank yew, Lady Dearfield."

Catherine smiled. "Lady Goodwin, you may call me Catherine if you wish."

Violette blinked. A smile spread over her face. "I would love to call yew Catherine," she said slowly. Then added eagerly, "Yew may call me Violette."

"Can I help you with anything else?" Catherine asked. Violette appeared dazed and lost. "Do you want to talk about it?" she asked gently, referring to the death.

Violette met her gaze. Her eyes were moist. It was a moment before she spoke, as if trying to decide whether to share her thoughts or not. " 'E was old, but I was 'appy." A shadow flitted across her terribly expressive face. "Look at this room." She glanced around. "It's me own, me very own, not even to share. D'yew know that Sir Thomas gave me pin money?"

Most husbands do, Catherine thought, but refrained from saying so. She wondered what Violette was not saying.

" 'E was a good man, and 'e was my friend," Violette said firmly. " 'E changed my life."

"I am very sorry that he passed away," Catherine said sincerely.

"I will miss 'im. A lot." Violette sat down heavily on the bed, her white petticoats belling about her. "Sometimes . . . ," she stopped.

"What, dear?"

Violette stared down at her ruffled knees. " 'E's gone an' I'm scared," she said frankly.

Catherine did not know what to say. So she reached for the other woman's hand.

And at precisely that point, there was a knock on the door. Violette merely cocked her head, but Catherine was alarmed.

"Who is it?" Catherine asked, already suspicious.

"It is I, Blake," came a warm male voice.

Violette leapt to her feet, holding her dress up to her chest, as Catherine cried, "Do not even think of entering this room!"

Too late. Blake had opened the door. His smile faded when he saw Violette. In spite of the dress she held up, her shoulders and arms were entirely bare and he stared far too intently for Catherine's taste.

Violette lifted the dress to her chin. "I ain't fit fer yer eyes."

"Blake, whatever can you be thinking?" Catherine was aghast.

Blake held up a snifter, not removing his gaze away from Violette. "Brandy. For Lady Goodwin. I insist that she drink the entire glass." He met Violette's eyes. "You need some sleep. This will help. Either that, or I shall send for Dr. Crumb. He can dose you with laudanum."

"I don't need laudanum," Violette said flatly.

Blake handed Catherine the glass. "We are preparing to leave." His gaze slipped to Violette. "May I call in the morning? To see how you are getting on?"

Violette was motionless for a moment. "O' course." Pink colored her cheeks.

And Catherine looked from one to the other, well aware that at that moment, they were both completely unaware of her presence. Tension spiraled between them. Had Catherine possessed a match, and had she lit it, she thought the air itself would have burst into flames.

Blake arrived at Goodwin Manor just before noon. He slid off of the fine gray stallion he had been riding. Clad in a tweed riding coat, tan breeches, and Hessian boots, he stared at Goodwin Manor, which appeared almost eerily still. He saw no sign that anyone was present. Clearly, once again, no one from the village had bothered to call that morning to see if the widow was in need of comfort or anything else.

His temper rose—and with it, pity for Violette Goodwin, an outsider and an outcast. As he stared, he watched the front door open and the lanky, sandy-haired manservant appear. Ralph Horn was wearing his usual expression of undisguised hostility, and he eyed Blake coldly from where he stood with his back to the entry hall.

Blake sighed inwardly, unable not to wonder once again about the servant and his relationship to his mistress. Blake led his horse forward and tied it to the small jockey statue which belonged to the pair at the head of the drive. "Is Lady Goodwin at home?"

Ralph did not move aside, rather, his body barred the open doorway. "She is still abed." His thin lips bared his teeth in an almost feral way.

But an image of Violette asleep in the small bed he had glimpsed the day before filled his head, distracting him. He imagined piles of blue-black hair streaming over the white sheets, while her slim arms and shoulder were bare and uncovered. He shook himself free of his very unwelcome thoughts. "At noon?"

"Yeah. At noon." Ralph smiled at him as unpleasantly as before.

Blake stared back at him, more than annoyed. What was this servant to Lady Violette? Only a fool would dismiss the fact that they both spoke with the exact same Cockney accent, were about the same age, and that Horn's behavior was hardly subservient: "Than I shall leave my card and take some dinner in town—and stop by on my way back to Harding Hall," Blake decided.

"Ralph?!" Violette cried loudly, clearly from upstairs. "Whose 'orse is in the yard?"

Ralph scowled, while Blake smiled. The manservant turned, and shouted, "Yer *friend*, Lord Blake."

Silence greeted his words.

"I shall wait in the parlor," Blake said, moving past Ralph. Because the manservant was slow to step aside, Blake actually had to shove past him, their arms brushing very solidly. If Ralph worked for him, he would last two minutes and be out on the street. But the moment Blake entered the dim front foyer, his annoyance vanished, because Violette was coming down the stairs.

His heart flipped. Her hair was loose and streaming over her shoulders almost to her waist. He could not move. Such a sight was rare. Women only let their hair down in the most intimate moments, and every woman of his acquaintance wore the current fashion of shoulder-length curls.

She faltered, her hand on the wood railing, halfway down the stairs. An eager smile faded. "Yer starin'. Wot 'ave I done now?"

He cleared his throat. "I thought that there might be some matters which you wish to discuss with me."

But she had just realized why he continued to stare and her eyes widened; she reached up and grabbed a tress, and she cried out. "Gawd! I fergot . . ." She turned abruptly.

He gripped the banister, hard, because his impulse was to bound up the steps and catch her before she could flee. "Lady Goodwin, please, it hardly matters."

She faced him from above on the steep, narrow stairs. Her cheeks were brightly flushed. "It ain't proper, is it?"

He hesitated. "No, it is not really proper."

"I can braid it real fast." Her liquid blue eyes were worried, but more than that, shining, luminous and direct.

"Very well."

She turned, took a step, stopped abruptly and faced him again. "Yew ain't goin' t' leave?" she cried in alarm.

"Of course not," he assured her.

She smiled, lifted her skirts, revealing both black leather high-lows, and ran up the stairs.

Blake watched her stockinged ankles, aware of what he was

doing but incapable of looking elsewhere. Then he turned, only to find Ralph staring at him, not even attempting to disguise his hostility. It struck Blake then that Horn was in love with his mistress, whether she knew it or not.

When Violette entered the parlor, Blake stood up. She smiled shyly at him. Her hair was braided now into one single, thick blue-black rope.

"Are you feeling better today?" Blake asked.

"Yeah, I am." She sat down in a wide chair, pushing down her skirts. Apparently the cage she wore beneath them annoyed her. Blake bit off a smile. "That brandy did the trick," she continued. "I niver felt so good in me life."

Blake took the seat facing her, chuckling. "It elevated your spirits, did it?"

She glanced at her knees, then into his eyes. "I don't understand. Yew use big words, words I don't know."

"El-e-vate," he said softly. "It means to raise or lift up."

She brightened. "Yeah, it elevated my spirits." She pronounced the word exactly as he had.

He smiled. "That was perfect."

She blushed, clearly with pride.

He studied her. She was so transparent. He had the oddest notion that a man could see right through her to her very soul. He shook off the thought. It was far too romantic for a realist like himself. "So you slept well?"

"Like a newborn baby."

"Then I am pleased."

She fidgeted with the satin-trimmed edge of her bodice. "Now wot?"

"Actually, I came over today to see if there is anything that you need, anything that I can do for you," Blake said.

She tore her gaze away, smiled at her lap. "No. I thanked Gawd last night that Sir Thomas didn't fergit me. I'll be fine." When she looked up, her eyes were sheened.

He studied her. Every single feature, from her slashing eyebrows to her delicate, tipped-up nose. "Lady Goodwin, I am sorry for your loss. But at least Sir Thomas lived a rich, long life."

"I know." Her tone was husky and low. "But whenever I think about me dinin' at 'Ardin' 'All an' 'im abed, dyin', I get all sick inside."

Her expression affected him so strongly that Blake rose and

was at her side, where he knelt. He took her hands in his. They were small, callused, and warm. He would comfort her, but only for a minute or two. "You could not have known. Do not feel guilt, or blame yourself."

" 'E wanted me to go an' 'ave a good time, 'e said so," Violette said miserably.

"He was a good man, apparently," Blake murmured, but he did not rise.

" 'E was a very good man," Violette said fervently. " 'E was my friend." Violette smiled to herself. "He used to tell me I was a ball o' sunshine."

Blake did not smile. He began to understand Sir Thomas better, envisioning now a lonely old man who needed this bright, seemingly uncomplicated, beautiful child-woman in his life. He released her hands and sat back down. "He cared for you. And you truly cared for him." Somehow he was no longer amazed by that latter conclusion.

"O' course. Look at all 'e did fer me. Bought me clothes, fed me like a 'og, an' fer me birthday 'e gave me this." Eagerly, Violette lifted a thin gold chain from beneath the high neckline of her dress. On it was a medium-sized single pearl capped with a diamond.

"It's very nice," Blake lied. The trinket could not have cost more than thirty or forty pounds.

"Ain't it?" Violette enthused. She replaced the pearl and chain inside of her bodice. "He gave me a fiver every month."

"For what?" Blake asked, unsmiling.

"Fer me pin money," she said as if he were foolish for not understanding immediately.

"He gave you an entire five pounds every month?" Blake kept his voice detached.

She nodded, smiling happily.

His heart seemed to be breaking. But he did not want it to break—not ever again. But it flashed through his mind that if he had been married to Violette, he would have adorned her with sapphires and diamonds and given her a nearly limitless allowance. He rose abruptly to his feet. Was he insane? "How did you and Sir Thomas meet, Lady Goodwin? If you do not mind me asking?"

She paled. "Wot does it matter?"

Blake saw fear in her eyes. "I'm sorry. The question was far too intimate."

She stood. "I was . . . I was a shopgirl. In an apothecary's. 'E was shoppin'," she said tersely.

"I see," Blake said. So the story was true. Sir Thomas had found her employed in a shop. "How fortunate for Sir Thomas, then."

She breathed a little. "Why are yew always bein' kind to me?"

"My fatal flaw," he said lightly. He wanted to ask her a dozen more questions. About her parents, about her childhood, where she had been born, and raised. He knew he could not. Not when she was distressed at having to reveal meeting her husband while employed as a shopgirl.

"Are yew kind to everyone?" Violette asked almost shyly.

"I am hardly unkind," Blake said.

"And to women? To ladies like Catherine Dearfield?" Violette's cheeks were crimson.

"I suppose I am kind when kindness is called for," Blake said, truthfully enough. He could not help but being amused. "Tell me about Ralph," he said suddenly, softly.

She became motionless. "We been friends our entire lives," she said after a very long, careful pause.

Blake studied her. "Friends?" His tone was as careful.

Hers became defensive. "Yes, friends."

Blake walked over to the window and stared out of it. He did not really see his horse, nibbling the grass at the feet of the jockey statue. He did not think Violette capable of pretense or deception. Her face mirrored her every feeling. She might think her and Horn to be friends, but Horn felt differently, Blake was certain.

"How did you and Horn meet?" Blake asked carefully.

Violette stiffened. "Wot does that got to do with anythin'?"

She did not want to tell him and Blake retreated as a gentleman should. He changed the subject. "Lady Goodwin, I came here today to advise you if I can. Now that you are a householder, you undoubtedly have many questions for me."

She blinked, but relaxed visibly now. "I don't got any questions. Why would I 'ave questions?"

"You have new responsibilities now, Lady Goodwin," Blake said gently. "Has it escaped your notice that you have a staff to pay? That you must provide for yourself? That there shall be taxes due?"

Violette shook her head, her complexion growing pale.

"Sir Thomas apparently did not leave you a pension."

"A pension," Violette whispered. "Yew mean, money."

"Yes." He was grave. "I mean money."

She hugged herself, her gaze riveted to his. "Sir Thomas left 'is money to Lady Feldstone."

"I am aware of that," Blake said. He saw that she understood what he was arriving at.

"Oh, gawd," she whispered. "Wot will I do?"

"Do not fret," Blake said quickly. "I called today because I have an uncanny knack for budgetary matters. It occurred to me that you might need my help. I own a bank, Lady Goodwin. I dispense financial advice frequently."

She worried her hands now. "Yew 'ave a bank?"

"Yes. Lady Goodwin, the first task before you is to analyze your expenses." Blake was blunt. "The second task before you is to consider your income—or lack thereof. And then we must find a solution to your dilemma."

"Wot are yew sayin'?" she asked fearfully.

"Lady Goodwin, do you have any income?"

"No." She trembled. "I got me savin's. From me pin money. Thirty-five pounds."

He winced. "Lady Goodwin, this house requires an income. You have a staff to pay monthly. And taxes. Taxes are very high in England."

"I don't need a cook," Violette said quickly. "An' Ralph don't need a salary."

"You cannot pay your taxes with thirty-five pounds. And how do you propose to feed yourself on a daily basis?" Blake felt as if he were being cruel, when he was only trying to advise her. He wanted to help her, very much so.

"Gawd!" she cried. "Is this why you came? To frighten me to death? Wot will I do?!"

"No." He was alarmed. Tears had filled her eyes, and he reached for her, but she moved away. She had not shed a tear at the funeral. How jarring it was. "I want to help you find a solution."

"You came to tell me I'll be out on the streets again, didn't you?" she flung. "That's the solution. I'll be 'omeless and 'ungry! Like Lady Feldstone wants!"

What he was witnessing was sheer panic and he could not be immune to it. "That is not going to happen. I promise you, Lady Goodwin." His words were not premeditated. And the moment he uttered them, he saw her relief, and her belief in him, and knew he could not take them back, no matter the weight of responsibility he was assuming. He ignored the warning voice inside of his head which told him that he was getting far too involved in matters that were not his affair.

"But the justice will take this 'ouse away, won't 'e, when it's tax time?" she whispered, ashen.

He wanted to reassure her, but he could not. "I'm afraid so. Therefore I advise you to sell this house immediately."

"Sell it?" she gasped.

"Yes." He had cut off her gasp by brushing his fist over her damp cheek. Immediately he dropped his hand. "You could raise a considerable sum of cash for this property, enough for you to live well for several years in a small flat."

She gazed up at him. "Really?" Her expression softened. Her eyes became hope-filled. "I love the manor, but it's too big and grand fer just meself." She smiled at him. "Fer me an' Ralph," she amended.

For me and Ralph. He shoved her disturbing words away. For surely if there was something illicit between the two of them, she would never be so open about it. "I can help you with the sale, if that is what you wish to do."

She nodded. "I don't have no choice, now do I?"

"No, you do not have a choice." He produced his handkerchief and handed it to her.

She smiled at him and blew her nose. And then she surprised him by saying, "But after a few years the money from the sale of the 'ouse will be gone. I won't be able to pay me rent. Wot will I do then?"

Her acuity pleased him. "You need to plan now for the future."

Her expression was intense. " 'Ow can I do that? Gawd, I'll 'ave to go back to workin'-in a shop." The moment the words were out she flushed.

"Perhaps not." His smile was brief, his gaze direct, holding hers. "There is always a solution," he said, "to every dilemma. You can do what all widows eventually do."

"An wot's that?" Her eyes were glued to his face.

"Remarry." He stared into her eyes. Oddly enough, he found it hard to visualize her remarried to some anonymous, elderly man. Instead, he had an image of her standing in the salon at Harding Hall, in sapphires and diamonds. "Catch yourself a second husband, one with means," he said.

Her eyes were huge. Silence reigned. He could not break her

stare. And she asked, trembling, "Yew mean, catch meself someone just like you?"

⬦ *Seven* ⬦

BLAKE started. "Someone like myself?" he echoed.

Violette's pulse was hammering so hard she was lightheaded. She could not take her eyes off of him; she hardly heard him repeat her words. The images were there again, inside of her head, but stronger than before. But now they were welcome. Blake, dancing in the moonlight, with that golden lady. Herself, and Ralph, hiding in the shrubs just below the terrace, two grubby, hungry orphans hoping to steal some food. And the other night, Blake, on a moonlit terrace, with Violette in her blue satin best. She had been in his arms. He had kissed her passionately. It had been the most wonderful moment of her entire life. But then she had been married to Sir Thomas, and it had been terribly wrong. Today, Sir Thomas was dead.

And God bless him and rest his soul, but he had been old, wonderfully kind but so very old, too old, while Blake, standing before her now, suggesting that she remarry, was young and handsome, gallant and kind. The answer to every woman's dreams. She stared into his brilliant blue eyes, remembering her own childhood dreams, born one anguished night in the union. That night, she had hoped for and dreamed of having all that she now had, with one exception—the love of a prince of a man.

Maybe, just maybe, she had dreamed of being loved by Blake even then, when she was only ten years of age.

She dreamed of being loved by him now.

And Violette felt it, the headlong, spinning, breathless fall, she felt every single inch of it, as she tumbled head over heels in love with this devastating man. She could almost feel his arms around her again, could taste his mouth, hear his warm, rich laughter in her ear. *Oh, my gawd*, she thought, stunned. *I love him, I truly do.*

And maybe he loved her. Violette trembled. She could hardly imagine what it would be like to be his wife, to be loved by him, day after day, night after night. How easily she could see herself at Harding Hall in one of those glorious rooms, clad in silks and chiffons, belonging there because of Blake. Violette was faint with the prospect.

"Lady Goodwin?" Blake prompted. "What I am suggesting, actually—"

She cut him off, blurting, "Do yew mean we should marry? Yew an' me?"

His eyes widened. And his expression changed; he appeared shocked.

But surely she had not misunderstood. Had she? She loved him. She had never felt such love before. Not ever, not even for Ralph, whom she considered a brother. She loved him the way the moon loved the night sky, the sun the day. Her tremulous smile disappeared. "Blake? Didn't yew mean that we should marry?"

"Lady Goodwin." Blake forced a smile. He was oddly pale. "I am sorry I was not clear. I did not mean to suggest that we marry. I meant only that all widows eventually remarry for economic convenience. It is more than common."

In that instant, Violette realized the immensity of her mistake. She had misunderstood. He had not meant that they should marry, not at all. She could not move, could not even breathe, and where as a moment ago she had been exhilarated, now she stared, feeling a crushing weight lowering itself pound by pound upon her shoulders, her chest, her heart. He had meant that she marry someone *else*.

"Lady Goodwin," Blake said, suddenly seizing her arm. "Please, this is a terrible misunderstanding."

Somehow, she lifted her chin, held her head high. She blinked back hot tears, managed a smile, prayed it wasn't lopsided. " 'Ow stupid can a gel be? I must be an idiot. O' course yew wouldn't marry the likes of meself." She swatted at her tears with her hand. "Gawd. Sir Thomas ain't even cold yet."

He continued to hold her arm, and he jerked on it. "Who you are has nothing to do with it. I am not marrying, not ever, or, if I do, it shall be for convenience and nothing more."

" 'Course it's who I am. I can't talk proper an' I can't walk without knocking things over an' I ain't a real lady an' we both know it." Violette backed up again. Her heart hurt her terribly now. Worse, she felt humiliated for having been such a stupid fool.

"No. If I wanted to marry you I would in spite of all that." Violette inhaled.

Blake winced. He threw up his hands. "Blast! That did not

come out the way I intended it to. I am not at all interested in marrying anyone, period. Marriage is not even on my mind.''

"Why?" Violette asked bluntly. She did not believe him.

His tone was ice. "That is not your affair."

She stared. He stared back. "One day yew'll marry," Violette finally said, deadly certain. "Someone like Lady Catherine Dearfield." She felt far more ill than before at that thought.

"Catherine is practically my sister," he said flatly. "I assure you, I have no plans to wed at all in the near, or not so near, future."

Violette did not reply. She had no reply to make, she just wanted him to leave, so she could grieve for Sir Thomas, and for herself. And she still did not believe him.

But he lingered, making no move to depart. "Lady Goodwin, perhaps we should change what has turned out to be a painful topic?"

"Aggtually, I'm real tired," Violette said, hoping he would take the hint. She wanted to be alone. To crawl into her bed, hug her pillow, and berate herself for being a stupid fool. Berate herself and rid herself of the remnants of any lingering wisps of her crazy dreams.

But if he understood, he was refusing to leave. He continued to stare at her. "Do you wish me to proceed with the sale of the house?" he asked. "I can arrange everything. You shall not have to lift a single finger, except to sign the bill of sale."

Violette turned her back on him and stared out of the window at his beautiful gray horse, a huge animal she would be afraid to even walk past, silhouetted against the heather-covered moors. She despised his horse. Suddenly it symbolized everything he was and everything she wasn't. "I can't write." She felt a grim satisfaction in uttering those words, as if in revealing and declaring the final truth about herself to this man who was so kind yet so indifferent to her would kill off any last hopes she might have. She wished she had never met him. But then she didn't wish that at all.

"You can't write?" Blake echoed. Violette glanced at him and saw his complete shock. Instantly she regretted her admission. Then, "Not even your name?"

"Not even my ABC's." She glanced away, humiliated anew. Why did Sir Thomas have to go and die? Leaving her and Ralph alone? Allowing her safe world to come crashing down upon her? Tempting her with the impossibility of loving this prince of a man when he would never love her back? Violette did not want to be alone. She was scared to be alone, but she had never felt more alone in her entire life than she did at that moment. "Just go," she said tiredly.

Except that she really didn't want him to leave.

"Of course you are tired. How thoughtless of me."

Violette did not turn. But she strained to hear, heard not a sound, and knew he continued to stand there.

From behind her, he said, "When you wish for me to start the sale, contact me at Harding Hall. Good day." Still he did not move.

Violette was afraid to speak. So she said nothing. She was afraid to say good-bye, afraid it would be final and she would never see him again.

He turned and, his footsteps loud on the wooden floors, departed the manor.

She wasn't certain how long she remained staring out of the window after he had gone, when she heard a movement behind her and knew it was Ralph. She sighed and turned to face him.

"I 'eard everythin'." His oddly pale gray eyes flashed. "Yew must be an idiot."

"Don't," Violette warned, her own eyes filling with anger.

"Yew want to marry 'im? Are yew crazy? 'E wouldn't marry yew, m'lady, if yew were the last woman on this earth."

"Yer a fine friend," Violette cried, balling up her fists. Her vision was blurring.

"Yer in luv with 'im, ain't yew? An' yer 'usband ain't even cold yet." Ralph spat. His own fists were clenched.

Violette hit him. Hard, in the stomach. But Ralph was reed thin, and he knew her as well as he knew himself, and he sucked in his abdominal muscles as she wielded the blow, so Violette was the one to hurt her fist and wrist. She cried out. Ralph opened up his arms and Violette fell against him. She wept against his chest.

He stroked her hair. "C'mon, luv, this ain't the brave gel I know so well." He smiled above her head. "Can't blame yew fer fallin' fer the likes o' Lord Blake. They say 'e's a real ladies' man. Got lots of skirts back in town, 'e does. I just don't want to see 'im usin' yew. Yew don't want that, do yew, Violette?"

Violette was frozen, her face buried against his clean white shirt. She knew that Ralph didn't mean to rub salt in her wounds, but he was doing just that. " 'Ow do yew know 'e's a ladies' man?'' she whispered.

"It's a fact." Ralph tilted her chin up so their eyes locked. "But 'e's a smart man. We'll sell the manor right away. It's a good idea. But don't yew even think of remarryin'." He frowned down at the top of her head. His gaze was intense. "Sir Thomas turned out all right, we were lucky, we were. But I won't let yew marry again. Yew an' me, together, we'll do just fine—like in them old days."

Violette stiffened against his chest, recalling how Ralph had initially been set against her marrying Sir Thomas—but Violette had been determined to accept his proposal and become his wife, for his gentle nature had been apparent to her from the start and she knew he was the answer to her dreams—or most of them. She would have probably accepted his suit even if it had meant sharing his bed, which it hadn't. But Ralph had been afraid that they would be separated by her marriage. Violette had explained that Ralph was the only family she had, and Sir Thomas had been good enough to hire Ralph to work at the manor without any further questions.

But now Violette didn't quite like what Ralph was saying. What if she did eventually decide to remarry, for "economic convenience"? It would be her decision, not Ralph's. Yet because Blake's image remained seared upon her mind, she decided not to argue pointlessly. She met Ralph's gaze. "An' 'ow are we goin' to do *just fine*? I don't ever want to be 'ungry again, Ralph Horn. I don't ever want to sleep on a stoop. I don't want to go back to St. Giles."

"We won't starve an' we won't go back, I promise yew that," Ralph said grimly.

Violette was sarcastic, but not intentionally so. "Yew think there's some pot of gold out there fer the likes of yew an' me?" She shook her head. "Before I married Sir Thomas, I was a shopgirl, an' I worked 'ard to get me job, but I don't recall yew workin', Ralph."

Ralph stared at her. His eyes narrowed. "I brought us 'ome some coin."

Violette started to push away from him, unable to stop thinking about Blake, wishing that he had said yes, he wanted to marry her, take care of her, love her. How had this happened to her? She had only met him three days ago. "Yew stole purses, Ralph, when we'd agreed to be respectable folks."

The front door opened and closed.

"Now who the bloody 'ell is that?" Ralph said with exasperation. But Violette knew he was relieved and that he would not answer her. He turned slightly, sliding one arm around Violette's waist. She remained pressed against his side, too exhausted now to move away. She was being too hard on Ralph. He was family, all that she had. And he was doing the best that he could, just like she was. It was so easy to be rich, so hard to be poor. Thank Gawd, she thought, for Ralph. If anything ever happened to him, she would really be alone.

And Lady Joanna appeared on the threshold. She saw them together and she gasped.

The brothers walked their mounts alongside a trickling stream. The moors were a blanket of purple all around them. The sky was brilliantly blue, unmarred by even a single cumulus cloud. Below them, the terrain sloped gently away, and the towers and parapets of Harding Hall could be seen in the distance.

"Catherine warned you not to flirt with her," Jon said frankly.

Blake raked a hand through his hair. "It was the most awful moment of my life when I realized what she said. And I truly do not want to hurt her, not ever; she does not deserve it."

"No one does," Jon commented. They paused as Jon's bay stallion began sniffing the water in the stream before drinking.

"How could she think that I would be interested in marriage?"

"How could she think that you would think of marriage to her?" Jon eyed him.

Blake frowned. "She said the same. That is *not* the issue even if we do come from entirely different worlds."

Jon tugged on his mount's reins. "So you would marry her in spite of her antecedents?"

"I did not quite say that."

"Then what is the issue?"

"I am not interested in marrying anyone, and why should I be? I am not the heir to the earldom. Thank God."

"One day you will get your due." Jon mounted, gathering up his reins.

"What does that mean?" Blake asked.

"It means that you shall be struck by a bolt out of the blue and go out of your mind with wanting for a particular woman. You will know that this is the woman for you, the only possible woman for you, and that you wish to spend the rest of your life with her—and that a mere thirty or forty years will not, cannot, be enough."

Blake stared. "Does this amazing statement mean that you have been struck by a bolt out of the blue?"

Jon smiled wryly. "Am I at the altar?"

Blake stared, unable to penetrate his brother's thoughts. "Love is for fools," he finally said.

Jon stared. "I see. So you were a fool when you were in love with Gabriella? Our parents are fools?"

Blake was grim, silent. Finally he said, as he mounted, "Look, you do know me better than anyone. And the whole world knows I offered Gabriella that thirteen-carat marquis. Yes, she crushed me. I loved her in the manner you have described, a manner in which you know that spending an eternity with a particular woman is not enough. And it was far worse because I know she loved me back, and it was fear which made her refuse me, fear of the future because of the difference in our ages. I have behaved the way any man would, given the circumstances. But do you know? To this day, a part of me still loves her. Will always love and admire her."

Jon rode his mount alongside Blake's. "I am sorry about what happened, Blake. I just hope that you change your mind. I recall a time when you wanted nothing more than a wife and children. It is terribly sad that because of a disappointment eight years ago, as vast as it was, you must give up all your hopes and dreams."

"That is life," Blake said. "It is not rosy, and it is not fair." Surprisingly, it was Violette's image that came to mind, chasing away Gabriella's.

"How cynical you have become. Life is also full of surprises." Jon smiled slyly. "Surprises like Violette Goodwin."

Blake spurred his mount forward. It was beginning to seem as if Jon was trying to seriously steer him toward Violette with honorable intentions. But that made little sense. Blake knew his brother and Jon was very conservative. "Violette Goodwin is full of surprises," he said reluctantly. "She appears fragile, but she is quite tough to have survived as well as she has." Tough and courageous, he couldn't help thinking.

Jon laughed, his blue eyes twinkling. "C'mon. Mother will tan both of our hides as if we are nine or ten years old if we are late for supper. She has guests."

They galloped across the heath, their steeds sending clumps

of dirt and gorse flying, enjoying the exhilaration of the fast-paced ride. Two grooms met them in front of the house, taking their mounts as the brothers dismounted. The front door of the hall flew open and Catherine came down the steps. "Have you two enjoyed your afternoon?" She smiled at them both. "Who won?"

"I did," Jon said, putting his arm around her waist briefly and kissing her cheek. "Blake was—is—distracted. How can I not enjoy this day?" He smiled at her. "It is even better now."

Catherine smiled back at him and turned to Blake. "What is wrong?"

"Jon exaggerates." He, too, kissed her cheek.

"We have been discussing Lady Goodwin," Jon said, his tone mild.

Catherine looked from Jon to Blake. "Nothing ill, I hope?"

"Why would we be speaking ill of the widowed bride?" Jon asked. "To the contrary."

Catherine's expression was one of worry. She clasped her hands, wringing them.

"What is it?" Jon asked, studying her.

She hesitated. "I was in the village today. I have heard the most ghastly rumor. It is so ghastly I am loath to even repeat it."

Jon's gaze was riveted upon Catherine. "Now you must tell us," he said.

"It is a rumor that must be stopped, Jon, and either you or your father should do something about it." She gripped his arm. "It is about Lady Violette."

Blake had started to walk past them into the house. He had to turn. "What is the rumor?"

Catherine regarded him soberly. She finally blurted, "Lady Feldstone says Sir Thomas did not die a natural death!"

"That is ridiculous," Jon said flatly as Blake stared. "He was seventy years old and unwell."

"But his health was satisfactory—she says." Catherine began tugging at her sash. Her gaze went from one brother to the other.

Jon took her hand in his. "Catherine, dear, I have never seen you so distraught. There is more, isn't there?" He was gentle.

"Yes, but it is despicable." She glanced again at Blake.

"I am involved?" he asked slowly. "In this rumor?"

She shook her head, wet her lips. "They are saying that Sir Thomas was murdered."

"Murdered!" Jon exclaimed.

"By Lady Goodwin . . . and her manservant, that fellow Horn."

❖ *Eight* ❖

"MY lord," the Harding butler intoned. "A solicitor is here to see you. He says it is quite urgent, begging your pardon, my lord."

The earl was taking breakfast with his sons; it was not yet nine in the morning and the trio had returned from an early morning ride. A fog was just lifting from the countryside. Blake and Jon exchanged glances as the earl accepted the caller's card. "A Messr. Cardiff." He regarded his sons. "That is the name of the solicitor who handled Sir Thomas's will." He nodded to the butler. "Show him in, Neddingham."

Neddingham left. Blake pushed his breakfast plate away, instantly uneasy. "Sir Thomas has been dead but four days. I have a distinctly poor feeling about this." Violette Goodwin's image filled his mind. He had not seen her since he had rejected her so thoroughly the day after the funeral. Every time he thought about their last encounter, he grew grim. But not as grim as he became whenever he thought of Lady Joanna's malicious slander. She had been spreading rumors, as Catherine had said. It was absurd. Blake knew that Violette Goodwin was no murderess.

But just last night he had heard two maids in the hall outside of his door, whispering about Lady Goodwin murdering her husband—poor, poor Sir Thomas.

Cardiff entered the breakfast room, smiling. He was extremely tall and thin, his dark suit hanging loosely on him. The earl stood and they shook hands. "I am so glad to make your acquaintance, my lord, and so sorry for disturbing you at this early hour, but my business cannot wait."

"I imagine not." The earl introduced his sons and invited Cardiff to sit. Somewhat reluctantly, the solicitor did so. He refused to take anything more than a cup of tea.

"What brings you to Harding Hall?" Blake asked, watching

their guest spoon sugar into the Wedgwood porcelain cup.

"Word of Sir Thomas's death has already reached certain parties in London, parties whom, I am afraid, I was not previously aware of. In any case, I understand that you, my lord," he addressed the earl, "are currently in possession of Sir Thomas's will. Lady Goodwin told me so herself."

"You have been at Goodwin Manor?" Blake asked, aware that Jon was eyeing him. He had been unable not to wonder how she was—and why she had yet to call on him for aid in selling her house.

Cardiff nodded.

"I do have the will, but surely it can wait until after we finish our breakfast?" the earl said.

"Of course," Cardiff responded, but he appeared perturbed. He continued to stir his tea.

"Do you mind my asking what has happened?" Blake inquired. "There is usually quite some time involved in the matter of settling estates. And this one is quite small and simple, there should hardly be a rush."

"It is not as simple as you think." Cardiff hesitated. "Well, you shall all find out soon enough." He sighed. "Sir Thomas was heavily in debt. To the tune of thousands of pounds. His creditors in London have learned of his demise and are eager to possess his estate."

Blake froze.

Jon leaned forward. "Surely you do not speak literally, sir?"

"I do speak literally. His debt was unsecured. He has already been named a bankrupt. When I left Goodwin Manor, a bailiff was on his way to secure the property and all possessions. The entire estate shall be liquidated to pay off Sir Thomas's creditors. They are hoping for an October auction of the house's furnishings, in order to proceed with the sale of the house itself immediately after that."

Blake was on his feet. "And Lady Goodwin? Has she learned of this?"

"I am afraid so. After all, she is the one who has the most to lose."

Something twisted inside of Blake, hard. Knifelike. "And how did she take the news?" He could imagine her reaction.

"I am not sure. She stared at me and did not say a single word."

Blake did not hesitate. "I am going to Goodwin Manor," he announced.

Jon rose as Blake started from the room. "I am coming with you."

The earl and the solicitor stared after the two brothers.

Lady Joanna was in the front foyer conversing angrily with her husband when Blake entered the house with Jon. Recovering from his surprise at finding her in Violette Goodwin's home, he bowed. "Good morning, Lady Feldstone," he said stiffly. "Baron."

She curtsied and the baron nodded. "Good morning, my lords." Then her baleful gaze lifted. "This has to be a mistake."

"You have heard?" Blake asked.

"Yes. My own solicitor contacted me late yesterday. The accounts my father left to me and George are also frozen. Apparently they, too, will be liquidated to pay off my father's creditors." Tears filled Joanna's eyes.

Blake did not feel sorry for her; the baron was well off. "Where is Lady Goodwin?" Jon asked.

"I imagine that she is upstairs with a case of the vapors," Joanna said. "She must be frantic at having married my father all for nothing."

Neither brother replied to that inciteful comment.

"I knocked, but no one answered, not even that wretched manservant." Joanna folded her arms across her big bosom.

Blake nodded, but did not move. "Lady Feldstone, are you aware that it is against the common law of this land—and common decency—to spread slander?"

Joanna jerked. "I beg your pardon?"

"Blake?" The baron was flushed. His easy expression had vanished.

"Unless, of course, you wish to bring formal charges of murder?" Blake queried.

Joanna blanched.

The baron looked from Blake and Jon to his trembling, pink-clad wife. "Good God! What are you talking about?"

Blake faced Feldstone. "Your wife has been speaking her mind quite freely in the village. She claims that her father was murdered by his second wife—by Lady Goodwin."

The baron's mouth dropped open. "You don't say!" He regarded his wife. "Madam? Surely young Blake has misheard!"

Joanna tilted her double chin, the bottom one hanging. "My father was not at death's door. I have every reason to believe that he was murdered by that . . ."—she swallowed, seeing Blake's expression—". . . by that woman!"

Blake crossed his arms and stared.

Jon stepped forward. "What reason, Lady Feldstone? What reason could she have? I myself saw her grief over your father's death. And he was an elderly man."

"What reason?" Joanna cried. "She is a fortune hunter and that has been obvious from the start. She enticed my father into marriage, and we all know how! She married him for his money. I am surprised the marriage lasted six months—that she did not do away with him five months ago. I imagine she is distraught to learn that she only got the house and not his bank accounts," Joanna said vehemently.

"Many women are fortune hunters," Blake said coolly. "But that does not equate to murder, Lady Feldstone."

"You defend her!" Joanna cried. "I have no doubt that she murdered him with the help of that insolent manservant—her lover!"

The baron gasped.

Blake was silent, but only for a moment. As Jon gripped his arm warningly, he faced Joanna squarely. His pulse raced. "I am an excellent judge of character. Violette Goodwin is no killer. I suggest you refrain from spreading any further malicious slander. And that includes attacks upon the lady's character and morals."

She said, hoarsely, "I saw them together."

Blake jerked. "Indeed?" His tone remained cool, but his wits escaped him.

"Lady Feldstone," Jon said smoothly, "whatever you saw, you misinterpreted." His voice was a command.

Blake wanted to agree. Whatever Joanna had seen, she was undoubtedly exaggerating—or was she? He had been suspicious of the relationship from the very start.

"Well, we do not need a scandal," the baron said. He gave his wife a warning look while mopping his brow with a handkerchief. "No need for a ruckus, I say. My wife absolutely misunderstood whatever it was she saw. And no need for you to bother yourself anymore with a mere rumor, my lords." He smiled. "I am sure it will die down and be forgotten in no time." He glared at his wife.

Blake remained icy while Jon bowed. "A good show, my lord," he said. "Now, shall we find the widow?"

Before Blake could start for the stairs, Jon grabbed his arm.

"Blake," he warned in a low voice, "this is Lady Goodwin's home."

Impatience filled him. But Blake leaned on the banister, gazing up the stairs. "Lady Goodwin?" he called loudly. "Please, it is I, Blake, and my brother. Do come down."

There was no answer.

"To hell with decorum," Blake said, and before Jon could halt him he bounded up the stairs, taking them two at a time. He strode down the hall, aware that both his brother, Joanna, and the baron were following him. As he already knew where Violette's room was, he proceeded directly to it. It crossed his mind as he heard Joanna's affronted gasp that she was remarking just how familiar he was with the upstairs terrain. To hell with her, he thought savagely. She had caused enough trouble as it was.

Her door was ajar. Blake's unease grew. He rapped on the jamb. "Lady Goodwin?" But he already knew she was not home. There was no response.

Blake thrust the door open and stared.

Jon, Joanna, and the baron crowded behind him, peering past him into the deserted bedroom.

And it was far more than deserted. Blake's pulse pounded with unusual force. The bed had been stripped down to the frame and mattress and nothing else. The blankets and coverlet were gone. The wardrobe door hung open, and the wardrobe itself was scathingly empty. Not a single toiletry remained on the small sideboard, not even the lace doily he had noticed the other day. And the worn, threadbare rug was also gone.

All that was left in the room was the stripped bed and the tired old furniture.

"She is gone!" Joanna gasped. "Good Lord, that hussy has left—taking everything of value with her that she could!"

Blake's heart was dropping rapidly through his body with the force of a boulder-sized rock. Sickness welled inside of him. Jon laid his hand on Blake's arm. Blake could not look at his brother. He could only stare at the abandoned room.

She had run away.

"I wonder what else she has stolen," Joanna cried, turning and rushing down the hall and into her father's room with the red-faced baron on her heels. "I shall inventory this house," she shouted over her shoulder.

"Blake?" Jon asked, low.

Blake finally faced him, his heart hammering, his jaw flexed.

"I am not sure what to think," he returned in as low a tone.

"This does not look good," Jon said. "I know you like the lady in question, but it is quite evident that she has run away."

Blake did not respond.

Joanna reappeared. "She has not taken a single thing from my father's room that I can see." Her fists found her broad hips. "Did I not tell you, Lord Blake?"

He was more than ill. "I beg your pardon, Lady Feldstone." He wanted to get away, to go outside; he needed to think.

"She is nothing more than a fortune hunter, and the moment she learned of my father's debt, she absconded with what she could."

Blake could not reply.

"Lady Feldstone," Jon said calmly, but authority laced his tone, "it is apparent that Lady Goodwin only took her own personal possessions—her clothing and toiletries."

"She took the blankets! She took the rug!"

Blake had the oddest urge to weep. "She doesn't like the cold," he said.

"What?" Jon started.

Blake shook his head, unable to speak. It was bad enough that she had been left with nothing, but it was far worse that she had run away. Far worse.

It was, possibly, damning.

"She is a thief," Joanna said flatly. "A thief from the streets. And worse. Oh, yes. For why do you think she has run away now, upon learning that there is no estate for her to inherit, with such haste? Why flee like this? Like she is some common criminal?" Lady Joanna was triumphant.

Blake looked at her, feeling rather dazed. And rudely so.

"Because she is a common criminal. Because she is a murderess. *Because she killed my father.* That is why she has run away like this."

Blake shoved past Joanna, whom he detested more than he had ever detested anyone before.

And he was thinking the exact same thing.

PART TWO

The Accident

✢ *Nine* ✢

CHELSEA, LONDON

THE flat was in the East End, one of the dozens built "back to back" for the neighborhood's working class. Made of thin, flat bricks, the roof shingled, it had three rooms: a single, windowless bedroom; a front parlor, which also served as a front hall; and a small kitchen. The privy was outside and shared by the row's tenants.

Violette knew that she should be grateful that she had a roof over her head, but she was not grateful, not at all. She was dazed and frightened.

She had not yet recovered from losing Sir Thomas. It had been one blow after another. Violette was well aware of the horrid rumors spread by Lady Joanna, yet how could anyone think her a murderess? Sir Thomas had not just been her husband, he had been a godsend and her friend.

And did the entire village also think her an adulteress?

Had both vicious rumors reached Harding Hall?

Violette despised London; she had so loved the countryside. She had loved Goodwin Manor, and she had loved Tamrah, in spite of the way most of the villagers had treated her. In spite of the rumors, she had not wanted to leave York.

But with the arrival of the solicitor of the estate she had not had any choice. Ralph had insisted they flee, and immediately. There had been no reason to remain in Tamrah, especially because of Lady Feldstone's nasty rumors. Ralph had saved most of his salary, and with the savings from her pin money, they had decided to return to London, where at least they both knew how to survive. They had rented the cheapest but cleanest flat they could find in a respectable but hard-working neighborhood. They told the landlady that they were brother and sister which, in Violette's mind, they were.

Most of the women living in the rows worked in one factory or another, sewing or shoemaking. Most of the men worked in and around the docks of St. Katherine's as coopers, carpenters, and stevedores. Ralph was also working at the docks in an iron foundry, which he despised.

Violette and Ralph had returned to town over a week ago, but she was still in shock. At night she dreamed about the evening Sir Thomas had died. She would be dining at Harding Hall, seated opposite Blake, sated and smiling and content, so very content, and then she would be shaking Sir Thomas, who lay as still as a corpse in his bed. And suddenly Violette was not standing over her dead husband in her pale blue satin evening gown. Suddenly she was nine or ten years old again, clad in holey trousers and a dirty shirt, her hair chopped off to her ears. The sights and sounds of St. Giles surrounded her, the wailing of a hungry baby, the shouts of a drunken man, the sobs of the woman he was beating. A rat stared at her with beady red eyes. And Violette would awaken with a scream.

Her scream awoke Ralph every night, who slept in the other room on the floor.

It was the final blow, finding herself once again in London town, nearly penniless, where only the rich lived well.

But they weren't beggars and they weren't thieves. They weren't homeless and they weren't starving, not yet. They were, just barely, respectable.

Violette had tried to get her old job as a Bloomsbury shopgirl back, but she had been replaced by her employer many months ago. The past two days she had been canvassing Fleet Street, Regent Street, and Oxford Street, hoping to get a job selling custom apparel to the ladies and gentlewomen of London's West End. She had yet to succeed.

But she was determined. She was Lady Goodwin now, a respectable widow, and whereas before no hoighty-toity custom shop would even consider her as an employee, now there was a chance that someone would hire her. Violette couldn't help but imagine working in one of the fancy West End shops, selling beautiful gowns and gloves and hats to ladies like Catherine Dearfield and the countess of Harding. And what if, one day, Blake happened to walk in? Perhaps to buy a gift for his sister or mother? Violette couldn't bear the thought of never seeing him again.

Violette had always prided herself on her common sense. She knew that her thoughts were dangerous. It was far more likely that she would never see Blake again. And that one day she would hear gossip about his marriage to a lady like Catherine Dearfield.

She wondered if he thought about her, even in passing. Had he heard the ugly rumors about her? She desperately hoped not.

Violette was preparing supper, immersed in her thoughts, when Ralph returned. She had boiled up a small piece of beef with some carrots and onions and had purchased a fresh loaf of bread earlier that day. It was such a meager meal. Violette was starving, even though she had bought a meat pie from a vendor that afternoon with their scarce, rapidly dwindling coins. Violette recalled how she had always been full at Goodwin Manor, where Cook had delighted in feeding her. She hated being hungry. Being hungry was the same as being afraid. She was starting to feel ten years old again.

Ralph entered their dark, airless apartment, which, outside of the table and chairs in the kitchen, remained unfurnished except for one small mattress in the bedroom and the pallet he slept on in the parlor. He was blackened with dirt and sweat and grime. He gave her a dark look and threw his cap straight across the kitchen at the far wall. It crashed there and landed on the floor.

"An' wot does that mean?" Violette asked calmly.

"It means we 'ad a good life, an' we ain't goin' to stay like this fer long." He was carrying a mug of ale. There was a gin mill two blocks from the flat. He sat down on one of the kitchen's two rickety chairs and slugged it down. "I 'ate me job."

Violette already knew that. "Supper'll be done soon." She turned to the stove, grim. Working in a foundry was as bad as begging and stealing on the streets—except that it was honest. They had had such a good life with Sir Thomas. How she missed the York countryside. The fresh air, the blue skies, the flowers and trees. How could they ever recapture that kind of life? Even if Violette did land a job in one of the city's finer shops, unless she remarried and well, they would spend the rest of their lives struggling to afford a simple flat like this one, with Ralph working himself to death. Blake had advised her to catch a second husband with means.

Her heart tightened. Her memories of that day were bittersweet.

"Yer late t'day," Violette said, spooning the stew into two chipped bowls.

"I'm late 'cause I stopped at the mill with two new buddies o' mine."

Violette carried the two bowls of stew to the small, square kitchen table. She sat down facing Ralph. "I ain't found a job yet, but I'm sure I will."

"Yew were down t' the guvnor's end again?" Ralph asked, ignoring the food.

Violette nodded and said hesitantly, "Ralph, mebbe Blake was right. Mebbe I got no choice. If I was a fancy shopgirl, mebbe I'd find me some rich chap to marry."

Ralph had been sipping the ale; he choked. He slammed the mug down. "Yew think everythin' 'Is Lordship says is right? 'is Lordship didn't want nuthin' t' do with yew, 'cept to lift yer skirts, an' no fancy gent will think otherwise."

Violette was stricken. "That's not fair. Sir Thomas married me. We 'ad such a good life with 'im."

"Those days are gone. Wake up. Yew ain't gonna remarry." He stared.

Violette stared back. "Why are yew bein' so mean to me?"

"Because I don't want some old lech usin' yew. Yew was lucky with Sir Thomas. Yew want to have some fat old gent in yer bed every night?"

"I wouldn't marry someone old," Violette heard herself say. She couldn't help thinking about Blake, picturing him as clear as day in her mind. And the thought crept unbidden into her mind, *I don't want someone just like him—I still want him.*

And Ralph knew. "Get 'im right out o' yor mind. 'E ain't fer yew. No young lord is gonna marry one of us, Violette. Where's yer smarts gone?"

Violette stabbed her stew with a spoon. She had lost her appetite, filled with anxiety over the future. Ralph was right. Blake didn't want her—and she did not want someone else. And she had little faith in what lay in store for her and Ralph.

"Don't be sad," Ralph said suddenly, surprising her. "That's not yew, Violette."

Violette inhaled. "I don't know wot I'm thinkin'. I'm so confused," she confessed. "Everythin' was fine, until a few days ago."

"Everything was fine until Sir Thomas died an' that fat bitch started those rumors about yew an' me," Ralph agreed. He kicked his chair, then sat back down to eat.

Violette did not quite agree. Things had been turned upside-down even before Sir Thomas died. Everything had changed the moment Blake had so suddenly strolled into her life.

The hansom turned the broad, tree-lined corner in the quiet residential neighborhood. Violette's heart stopped. Harding House loomed ahead, at the end of the street.

Violette almost knocked on the roof to order her driver to stop, turn around, go back. But her muscles failed to obey her panic-filled mind. She could not lift her arm, although her fist was clenched.

She swallowed, her heart trying to wing its way out of her chest. What was she doing? Was she mad? To seek Blake out now, to ask for his help, even though he had offered it to her two weeks ago?

Violette had pride, and her pride warred with a very real fear. She had not been able to gain any kind of respectable employment. Door after door had been slammed in her face. And Ralph had started going to his job late—or not at all. He was running the streets again with his new "buddies," at times not even bothering to come home. Violette was terrified. Their money was dwindling, as was their attempt to cling to respectability. Ralph's behavior was far too reminiscent of a past that Violette only wished to forget.

It had become clear to her that she, at least, must find employment, and immediately. It would not just replenish their coffers, but it would boost her fragile self-esteem and failing hope.

Violette inhaled, reminding herself that she was not a ragged urchin now even if she felt like one. She was Lady Goodwin, and she had a legitimate reason for seeking Blake out. He had offered to advise her in her financial affairs. She needed far more than his advice now, she needed his help in finding her a job.

And, of course, in spite of all common sense, she couldn't help wanting to see him again.

The hansom rolled closer. Violette was perspiring when it finally came to a halt. She alighted without help from the driver, who was slower than she in climbing down to the street. Violette dug into her blue velvet, beaded reticule. It was a dark shade of blue, unlike the violently royal color of her fur-trimmed dress. Violette handed him the required fare, watching as one and a half precious pounds disappeared into his trouser pocket.

"M'lady," he said, his accent almost identical to hers. "Fer another pound 'n a 'alf I'll wait fer yew to do yer busyness." He smiled at her, missing numerous teeth in his round, jowled face.

Violette shook her head, ribbons and cherries dangling in her eyes, incapable of speech at that moment. The hansom moved away. Violette swiped at her bonnet in annoyance, then turned, sucking up her courage. Two liveried footmen, at once resplendent and intimidating in their blue and silver uniforms, stood sentinel outside of the two oversized front doors of the Harding mansion.

Violette lifted her skirts with one gloved hand, clutched her reticule with the other, and started up the wide stone staircase. When she reached the door it was immediately opened by one of the footmen, who ushered her inside with a blank expression. Violette blinked, gaping.

She stood in a rotunda of sorts, one whose ceiling was as high as a cathedral. Far above her head, the ceiling was trimmed in gold sworls, and painted with clouds, blue sky, trumpets and angels. She glanced quickly down. She stood on an amazingly pristine white marble floor. From where she stood she could see past closed doors on her right, where she suspected the ballroom was, and down the marble-floored corridor. A wide, elegant staircase with an iron banister and red runners swept upwards into the house. On her left were a pair of open doors, through which Violette glimpsed a huge, elegant salon. Works of art covered every available wall.

Harding Hall, their country home, was huge. But this mansion was every bit as large, and somehow far more spectacular, far more palatial.

The footman was staring at her, his gloved hand extended, palm up.

Violette looked at his face, than at his palm. How did he keep his gloves so white? Hers were already dusty just from the hansom ride through town.

"Your card, my lady?"

Violette clutched her reticule with both hands. She did not have any cards. There had been no need for cards in the country. In fact, she had never used a calling card in her life, and she was singularly unprepared for this request. *I need cards,* she managed to think, dazed. Her knees were knocking together.

"Is Lord Blake 'ome?" she whispered, hoarse.

He blinked, briefly registering his surprise. "I beg your pardon. Lord Blake does not reside at Harding House."

Violette turned white. " 'E doesn't? I . . . I didn't realize."

At this point another manservant appeared, this one clad from head to toe in black. "Joshua, is there a problem?" he asked with authority.

"No, Mister Tulley. Her Ladyship has failed to leave her card, and has asked if Lord Blake is in residence." The footman spoke without inflection.

The servant faced Violette with censure in his eyes. He was slim, his face long, his pate bald. "If you leave your card, my lady, I shall make certain he receives it."

Violette was unnerved. She was not stupid, and clearly she was doing something terribly wrong, but what? Surely such a fuss wasn't about her failing to leave her card? "Sir. I beg yer pardon." The servant's eyes widened as she spoke. Violette lifted her chin. "I ain't got no card. But Lord Blake told me I could come t' 'im fer advice, an' that's wot I am doin'. It's eggscrucyate-inly important, sir."

Mister Tulley stared at her as if she had grown two heads.

"Please!" Violettte blurted. "Just tell me where I can find 'im! Me 'usband died, they said 'e's bankrupt, an' Blake promised me 'e'd 'elp me!"

Tulley turned to Joshua. "This is extraordinary," he said, low. But Violette heard. Tulley faced her, and some of his veneer had slipped, for he regarded her with pity. "I shall tell Lord Blake that you have called, Lady, er . . . ?"

"Lady Goodwin," Violette said, her chest heaving. She did not want his pity. It had been hard enough for her to come to Blake in the first place. "Is the countess at 'ome? Or Lady Dearfield?"

"They remain in the country," Tully said quietly.

"Blake told me 'e was comin' back to London." Violette turned blindly away. She did not know what to do. Blake had been her last hope, her last resort. She did not see Tulley and Joshua exchange glances.

"Lady Goodwin, I shall send word to Lord Blake that you have called. In the meantime, might I have an address where he may contact you?" Tulley asked.

Violette looked up. The last thing she would ever do was reveal to Blake the location of the small, spare flat where she lived. She shook her head. "I'll come again t'morrow. Mebbe 'e'll be 'ere, then. Thank yew. G'day."

She turned, managing to hold her head high when she wanted to slink out of there. The footman rushed ahead of her and opened the door for her. Violette smiled tremulously at him. Stepping outside with her, he closed the door behind her and went to stand on the door's other side as one part of the pair of statue-like sentinels again.

Violette walked slowly to the top step but then made no move to go down. The grand Mayfair neighborhood was spread out panoramically before her, one palatial home after another surrounded by green trees, groomed lawns, and rioting gardens, but none as wonderful as Harding House. Her pulse raced dangerously—she felt miserable, lightheaded. She reminded herself that they had food at home, a roof over their heads, and enough money to pay the rent for the next three months. But she wasn't certain that she should try to reach Blake again tomorrow. She had seen the butler's condescension, worse, his pity.

She started down the steps.

"My lady."

Violette turned at the sound of Tulley's voice. He stood in front of the house, the door behind him wide open. His expression grave, he hurried to her. "My lady, what I am about to do is wrong, terribly wrong, but Lord Blake is not my employer—his father is. And the earl is a man of compassion, and he is extremely fond of justice."

"I don't understand," Violette said.

Tulley's face softened fractionally. "The earl would agree with what I am about to do, if my suspicion about what Lord Blake has done is correct."

"I still don't understand."

Tulley sighed. "His Lordship has a townhouse in Belgravia. Number One, Sloane."

Violette's face brightened. "Belgravia! That's not too far—I can walk!"

The butler raised his hand. "But he is not at home at this hour. I doubt His Lordship will return home until much later this evening. At this hour, he is at his club—on Pall Mall."

"'Is club," Violette echoed.

"If you truly wish to reach him, I suggest you waylay him as he is leaving, which should be shortly."

"Yes, I wish to reach 'im. 'Ow long will it take t' walk there?" Violette smiled eagerly.

Tulley stared. "Now I understand," he said, gazing at her face.

"Beg yer pardon?"

"God forgive me," Tulley looked heavenwards, then smiled at Violette. "I will have a coachman bring you around in one of our smaller, unmarked vehicles."

"God bless yew, sir!" Violette cried.

⪧ *Ten* ⪦

BLAKE leaned back in his leather chair, one trouser-clad knee crossed, immersed in the *London Times*. He was in his club's reading room, a well-lit library paneled in dark oak. All the other gentlemen present were as studiously involved as he; a few of the gentlemen were sipping port or smoking cigars as they read. No one spoke.

Until the marquis of Waverly entered the carpeted, bookcase-lined room. Heads turned as various gentlemen murmured greetings to the heir to the dukedom of Rutherford. "Hello, Blake," Dom St. Georges said quietly, smiling.

Blake laid down his paper as his best friend—after his brother—took the red leather chair besides his, stretching out his long legs. "Hello, Dom. You are looking well. What are you doing in town?"

Dom grinned, a flash of white teeth in his perpetually tanned face. He was amber-eyed and golden-haired. "Anne and I have stolen away for a few days, and, although currently at Rutherford House, we are spending the weekend in Paris."

"How very romantic," Blake said. "And how is your lovely wife?"

"Lovelier than ever—and as vexing."

Blake laughed. Dom had more than met his match when he had married the very capable, very sincere, and very beautiful Anne Stewart, an American orphan raised with her English cousins. Until Blake had seen the pair together, he would have sworn that in spite of being heir to the dukedom of Rutherford, Dom would never marry. "And how are the twins?"

"They do not sleep," Dom said of the one-year-old children.

He and Anne had been blessed with a boy and a girl. "We do not sleep. Even the nurse doesn't sleep."

Blake chuckled. "Perhaps it is time to adjourn to the salon for a drink."

"My idea exactly," Dom said, both men standing. As they left the library, he said, "You know, Blake, I saw something quite odd outside when I was on my way in. Are you the only Harding in town?"

"I believe so, why?" They trotted down the carpeted staircase.

"I am positive I saw one of your family's unmarked phaetons across the street, and someone, a woman, was sitting inside."

They strolled across the salon and took a table not far from the mahogany bar where a bartender polished glasses. As it was mid-afternoon, only a few of the many other tables were occupied. A waiter instantly materialized to take their orders. That done, Blake shrugged, leaning back on the small moss green sofa. "You must be mistaken, Dom."

"Apparently so." Dom grinned. "After all, what woman related to the Hardings would wear a hat with truly atrocious papier-mâché cherries hanging off the brim?"

Blake froze, quite sure color was draining from his face. "A woman in an atrocious hat? In one of our unmarked carriages?"

"Have I said something wrong?"

Blake was standing. "A beautiful woman? With black hair and blue eyes?"

Dom also stood, regarding Blake with open curiosity. "I merely drove by the carriage and glanced inside. I have no idea whether the woman in question was attractive or not, much less raven-haired and blue-eyed. Blake, where are you going?"

Blake did not hear him. But surely Violette was not outside in a Harding vehicle. And as he entered the foyer he faltered.

"But yew must get this message t' Lord Blake," Violette Goodwin said loudly, shaking off two grim ushers. She stood in the foyer, an usher on each side of her, actually inside of the club. And, yes, she was wearing a ghastly hat.

A half dozen club members were congregating in the foyer as well. Blake felt Dom stop beside him. "Good God," Dom said. "A woman in the club?"

Blake didn't know how to react.

"Madam, you must leave, at once. No . . . females . . . are allowed in this establishment.'' The club manager had appeared. His face was as red as his waistcoat.

"But it's most urgent. O' eggscrucyate-in' importance. I beg yew!'' Violette cried. It seemed that she would soon stamp her foot.

"Violette,'' Blake said, starting forward.

Dom followed. ''*Violette*? Who *is* this, Blake?''

But Blake ignored him. Violette had seen him and she rushed past the ushers—as if she were going to throw herself into his arms. Murmurs of astonishment and disapproval sounded all around them as more members came downstairs and out of the salon to view the historical event of the invasion of their club by a woman.

"Blake!'' she cried, her eyes lighting up.

He gripped her arm before she could actually embrace him—for he had the suspicion that was what she would do—and halted her in her tracks. He was aware that he devoured her face with his eyes. His wildly racing heart did numerous, odd flipflops, as if he were some fresh-faced Eton boy. He hadn't been certain he would ever see her again. "Lady Goodwin, do you wish to have me displaced as a member of this club?'' But a twinkle appeared in his eye. A dimple accompanied it.

"Gawd, no!'' She saw his expression and started to smile, but uncertainly. '' 'Ave I done somethin' wrong?''

"You have. And it's 'have.' With an 'h.' You must stop dropping those h's.'' His gaze held hers, warmly. He was pleased to see her and could not deny it, even to himself.

"H. Have.'' She did not remove her eyes from his face.

"Well done,'' he said softly, still holding her arm as if afraid she might escape—and still looking into her blue, blue eyes.

A smile spread slowly across her features. "Thank yew,'' she whispered.

"You,'' he said. "Your mouth should not open and form an 'o.' It's a small, brief movement of one's lips.''

"You,'' she repeated, perfectly. Their gazes remained locked.

"Well, well,'' Dom murmured. "What an interesting turn of events.''

Blake ignored him. "Ladies are not allowed inside of a gentlemen's club, Lady Goodwin.'' His tone was gentle.

She was startled, then dismayed. "They ain't?! I'm so sorry! I 'ad no idea!''

He smiled again. Was it possible that he had missed her?

"Excuse me, Lord Blake," a man said huffily.

Blake recognized the voice as he turned to face the earl of Hutton, a round, portly man twice his own age. "You do realize that this . . . this . . . creature must go, and immediately," Hutton said, red-faced. "And that there shall be complaints filed against you!"

Before Blake could respond, Dom stepped forward. The heir to the dukedom of Rutherford smiled, but it did not reach his golden eyes. He laid a hand on Hutton's thick shoulder. "Hutton, there is no need for distress. Blake, *Lady Goodwin*, and I were just leaving. And as for complaints, I imagine it would be a sad day for such an estimable club were it to lose a bevy of members at once." Dom's smile widened. He stared.

Hutton was taken aback. "Surely you don't mean . . . ?"

"But I do," Dom said easily. "Neither I nor my grandfather, the duke, would wish to continue on here if Blake were no longer welcome. I imagine the earl of Harding and the viscount of Farleigh would feel precisely the same way."

Hutton paled. "I beg your pardon, my lord."

"Thank you," Dom said.

Blake bowed. "Good day, Hutton," he said, still holding Violette's arm.

She curtsied, not very well. Her foot caught her skirts and she almost tripped, but Blake kept her upright. "G'day, me lord," she said, blushing.

Blake looked at Dom and they winced.

If she had arrived in one of his family's smaller, unmarked phaetons, used for the purpose of traveling to London in some discretion and with privacy, that carriage was now gone. But on the sidewalk outside of the club they said good-bye to Dom, who was staring at them and smiling strangely, and Blake steered Violette across the street to his own waiting coach. His coachman did not blink an eye as Blake handed her up and onto the plush royal blue velvet squabs. She had taken the backwards-facing seat, another faux pas, for a lady always faced forward, but he was prepared to ignore it. He had other more pressing concerns.

He sat across from her. She met his eyes and blushed. He did not signal his driver to go forward, and they remained stationary. "This is a surprise," he said, no longer smiling. He studied her downturned face. She did not reply. "Lady Goodwin?"

She looked up. "I need t' see yew, an' I'm so sorry to have caused yew trouble, m'lord!"

He could not help himself. He reached across the space separating them and took both of her hands in his. "Are you going to cry?" he asked gently, releasing her hands in order to extract a handkerchief.

"Me? Niver! I'm 'ardly in napkins."

He half-winced and half-smiled. "Take this anyway. I have the oddest notion you might wish to use it."

She took the linen square and gripped it tightly.

"Lady Goodwin?"

She inhaled loudly. "I don't know wot t' do. Is it true? Yew—you—said I could come t' yew—you—fer advice. 'Ave I lost everythin' t' some bleedin' city nobs?"

"I'm afraid so. Sir Thomas was heavily in debt. I am frankly astonished that he made no real provision for you."

"Gawd," she whispered, her eyes huge.

"There are always solutions," he reminded her, sympathy flooding over him.

She nodded, looking grim and forlorn and waiflike and beautiful all at once. When she spoke, she startled him. "I was 'opin' t' find me a job in some fancy shop. On Regent Street or Oxford Street where the real ladies an' gents shop."

"A job?" he echoed. "You wish to be a shopgirl again?"

"Wot choice do I got?"

"What choice do you have, with an 'H,' " he corrected automatically. But his mind was racing.

"But I've already tried everywhere. At first everyone's so nice, but then they chase me away like I'm no good fer 'em." Her tone was plaintive, her eyes trained on his face.

Blake could imagine how it had been. Violette, although a distinct victim of bad taste, did appear genteel. Many gentlewomen dressed abominably anyway, thinking that more frippery was better than less. So she would be greeted with some enthusiasm—until she walked and talked. Then her antecedents became obvious, and she would be told in no uncertain terms to leave the premises. He ached for her.

He hated to bring up the subject, but he was a realist and he said, "What about remarriage?"

She quickly avoided his eyes. "I was thinkin' that, in time,

I'd meet some fancy gent in the shop the way I met Sir Thomas." Her gaze lifted. It was almost defiant. "Some *nice* fancy gent. Someone who's young." She hesitated. "Like yew."

Blake stared.

She did not look away.

Her gaze was oddly challenging. He did not know what to say. He did not even know what to think. He had adjusted to her having been married to the elderly Sir Thomas. He couldn't quite see her married to someone closer to her in age. And if she were looking for some young lord to marry, then she was harboring grave illusions. No peer of his would marry a girl from the East End. It just wasn't done. The best she could hope for was another crone, perhaps another knight if she were very lucky. If she wished to marry someone close to her own age, then she would have to set her sights much lower, perhaps on a merchant, perhaps even lower than that.

"Lady Goodwin, most ladies do not seek husbands in retail shops."

She stared at him, her chin tilted up aggressively. " 'Ow do I find me a good husband? Someone with means, someone like you?"

He hesitated, not wanting to tell her the truth, not wanting to hurt her. "Primarily through introductions." He was certainly not going to suggest she put herself on the marriage mart this Season—she would never get in.

"Will yew introduce me?" she asked.

"That is impossible." His reply was instantaneous.

"Why?"

"I have no one to introduce you to."

"Yew don't 'ave friends?" she asked with skepticism. "Or I ain't good enough fer 'em."

He could hardly believe his ears. "My friends are not interested in marriage," he finally said, hesitating. "Violette, this isn't about you're not being good enough. Titles marry titles. Or money. Like marries like, just as water seeks its own level. In my world, the daughter of an earl marries the son of an earl, or even higher if she can. Do you understand?"

"Yer tellin' me I don't got a chance," she said, the tip of her nose pink. "Yer tellin' me like marries like, an' I ain't like yew."

He was silent. Then, "Yes," he said soberly. "You do not have a chance, not amongst my set."

But like a terrier, she would not quit. "An' Sir Thomas? He wasn't in your set?"

Blake sighed. "I am merely telling you the way of the world, Violette. No, Sir Thomas was not really a part of my circle. He was on the fringes only because the seat of the earldom is outside of Tamrah."

"I don't like yer rules," Violette said bluntly.

Blake did not know how to respond. He wasn't so sure that he liked them either.

She stared at her lap for a few minutes, then looked up, directly into his eyes. "I don't want to get married again anyway. I was just checkin' the sityation."

He did not believe her. "Sit-u-a-tion," he said gently. "Situation."

She nodded. "Will you get me a job, then? Is that possible?" She seemed nervous now, playing with the fur trim on her skirt. Blake didn't know anyone who wore fur, even trim, in September.

"I can certainly find you a job," he said slowly. He wasn't exactly thrilled with this prospect either. What was wrong with him? She had been a shopgirl before. And she desperately needed an income now.

"A good one? Where I'm servin' ladies like yer mother and Lady Catherine?"

Something tautened inside of him. "Yes. A good one. Where you shall sell to ladies like my mother and Lady Dearfield." He was grave. He could not quite come to grips with this solution, either. He kept envisioning Violette the way she had been the night Sir Thomas had died, clad in a simply elegant blue satin gown, facing him on the moonlit terrace, with shining eyes. It was a disturbing image, one that had haunted him frequently these past two weeks.

He looked across the small space separating them and saw that Violette was smiling. "Thank you, Lord Blake, thank you very much," she said.

⁑ *Eleven* ⁑

THEY sat in silence, staring at one another. The carriage suddenly seemed uncomfortably small and closed to Blake. He glanced out of the window at the passing coaches and broughams, riders, and pedestrians. "Lady Goodwin, might I take you home?"

She stiffened. "I . . . er . . . I ain't goin' home just yet."

He noted her discomfort. What was she hiding? "Where are you staying?"

She spoke after a pause, her words tumbling in a rush. "I got me a room at a 'otel."

"Hotel," he said. "With an H. Which hotel?"

"Why do yew want t' know?"

"Why are you now belligerent? Let me take you back to your rooms." He smiled.

"I'm stayin' at the St. James."

His brows lifted. "Why, that is a favorite haunt of the Europeans." He rapped on the ceiling. "Godson. To the St. James."

Immediately the carriage rolled forward. Violette sat without expression, staring at him. Blake studied her, causing her to drop her gaze. He knew she was not staying at the St. James; she could not afford even a night or two. But why would she try to deceive him about this matter?

He continued to stare out of the carriage window, thinking now about Sir Thomas's death. He still believed the elderly knight died from natural causes, in spite of Joanna Feldstone's wild accusations. But Violette had fled Goodwin Manor the moment she had learned that her husband's creditors would possess everything—just two days after his death.

"Wot's wrong?" she asked quietly.

He met her gaze. "Lady Goodwin," he said slowly, "was there a reason you left the country in such haste?" His gaze was direct, piercing.

Her stare widened, but did not swerve. "Yew mean, after I learned o' me 'usband's debts?"

Blake nodded.

She folded her hands in her lap. "I don't know why, eggsactly, we ran away."

We, he thought. "Exactly," he murmured. "But you did run away."

She nodded, mouth pursed. "I was scared. Scared o' losin' everythin' I ever dreamed o' 'avin'."

He wanted to reach out and touch her, but he did not. "Is that the only reason you were scared?" he asked softly.

"Yeah." But she hesitated.

"There is more, is there not?"

She shrugged, avoiding his eyes for a moment. "Yeah. There's more. Ralph wanted t' leave. 'E wanted t' leave fast, right away."

Blake's heart was hammering now. *Ralph*. Violette was not capable of murder. But was the manservant? Was *he* a murderer? If there had even been a murder? "And do you always obey your manservant?" The question was caustic, which he had not intended.

She jerked. "I told yew. I've known Ralph since we was little. We growed up together, 'im an' me. 'E's me family."

"I see," Blake said. "Are your parents alive, Lady Goodwin? Do you have any brothers, sisters, cousins?"

"No," she said. "Just Ralph."

He stared.

They did not speak again until the phaeton paused in the circular lamp-lined drive in front of one of London's tonier hotels. Violette smiled at him. "Wot about me job?" she asked, preparing to rise.

"I will make inquiries this afternoon and tomorrow."

"An' 'ow will yew—you," she smiled at him, "leave word fer me?"

"I will leave a message here at the St. James."

She looked everywhere but at him. "Thank you, Lord Blake."

"Blake," he corrected, seizing the door handle before she could grab it herself. "Lady Goodwin."

She froze, crouched in the coach.

"A gentleman always precedes a lady out of a conveyance, in order to aid her in stepping down."

Her eyes widened. "Oh." She sank back down on the seat.

He shoved the door open, climbed out, and reached up to take her hand. "No jumping," he added.

Violette hesitated, then stepped carefully down onto the street.

Blake bowed. "On the morrow, then."

She nodded with an eager smile. "On the morrow . . .
Blake." And she curtsied—perfectly.

He followed her, of course.

She waited for his carriage to drive away and turn the corner,
standing in front of the hotel, watching him leave, waving. How
obvious she was. The moment his phaeton turned the corner,
Blake ordered it to slow and he jumped out, then told his driver
to continue home to his town house. He hurried back toward
the hotel and arrived just in time to see his quarry enter a
hansom cab. Blake followed suit.

The hansom headed west, toward Mayfair and Belgravia,
then turned sharply south. The stately residences of the upper
classes disappeared, double- and triple-story red-brick dwell-
ings on shady streets taking their place. The hansom veered
again. The pleasant, well-kept homes and gardens of the city's
merchants and traders also vanished. In one instant, Blake
found himself transported into a crumbling neighborhood of
back-to-backs, groceries and grog shops, with the smokestacks
of several different factories belching overhead.

Her cab had stopped. Blake rapped on the partition separating him from the driver, far more than grim. There was a knot
in his stomach, one acutely unpleasant and unpalatable.

He observed Violette as she disembarked from her hansom
and paid the driver with a friendly smile. As the cab rolled
away, she paused, staring up at one of the flats. These row
houses had no front yards, no porches, no fencing. When she
finally hurried up the three front steps and unlocked the weathered door, Blake alighted from his own cab. He was barely
aware of paying his fare. He stared at the tenement where she
had disappeared.

He should have guessed. This was what she could afford. He
himself was building row houses like this one for London's
poor, as were several of his peers, so he should not be dismayed
at her choice of residence, but he was.

It was one thing to build homes for those less fortunate than
himself. It was another to actually see such homes up close,
occupied, in an actual working-class, impoverished neighborhood.

And he did not have to walk closer to instantly remark that
these particular row houses had been constructed both rapidly,
cheaply, and poorly. He could see at a glance that the thinnest
bricks had been used, a cost-saving device. But that meant that

the walls would soon crumble in places and leak when it rained, which was, in London, on average one out of every three days. Inferior shingles had been used on the roofs. Undoubtedly they would leak too.

Blake strode slowly up the walk; the pavement was broken in places. The sidewalk was littered with rubbish and even broken glass, although not, thank God, with sewage and other excrement. He hated the fact that Violette lived here. He hated it violently.

He knew he should leave her with her pride intact, but he could not.

He continued up the walk and to her front door. The factories behind the tenements were causing an unpleasant odor, one that could not be healthful, one containing the fumes of gas. He could also, finally, detect the odors coming from the privies, which he knew were behind the row houses. Blake refrained from using his handkerchief to cover his nose. He did not hesitate, but knocked loudly, not once, but several times.

The door opened immediately, revealing Violette, who had removed her hat. She turned starkly white when she saw him, then started to slam the door in his face.

Blake thrust his shoulder against it and shoved past her.

She cried, "Yew can't come in 'ere!"

But he was already inside. He stared at the small, dreary foyer where he stood, a windowless room which he knew doubled as a parlor. He recognized the rug which had adorned Violette's bedroom floor in Goodwin Manor. But there was not another stick of furniture in this room, other than a small pallet on the floor.

"Wot yew think yer doing?" she shouted.

He ignored her, striding to the doorway that let into a small, dark, ugly kitchen. He saw the outdated stove, the wooden counter, the chipped plates and bowls atop it. He saw the single wooden table and the two spindly chairs, one of which was distinctly off balance.

"Yew can't come in 'ere," Violette repeated from behind him. Her tone was laced with tears.

He didn't really hear her. He was too appalled. He turned to look at her, stunned, then walked over to the other doorway to peer into the bedroom. It contained a single mattress and numerous blankets, and all of Violette's clothes, hanging on wall hooks.

"How dare yew," she cried from behind him.

He faced her. "I had to know."

She was close to tears. He saw that now. "Well now yew know! Are yew 'appy?"

"Not at all," he said quietly. "You cannot remain here."

"Oh, right! An' where will I go?" She was bitterly sarcastic. "T' 'Ardin' 'Ouse?"

It was a possibility, athough not a solution. Blake extracted his billfold and opened it.

"Wot are yew doin?" Violette asked fearfully.

"I am writing you a banknote. Surely you have a pen and inkwell?"

She stared wildly, not answering him.

He walked into the kitchen, looked around, and realized that he would not find what he was looking for because Violette could not write. He turned, extracting one of his business cards from his breast pocket.

She took it and stared as if she had never seen a card before. "Wot's this?"

"The address of my bank," he said. "Tomorrow you shall find a draft there, made out to you, for the sum of five thousand pounds. You may cash it then and there, or at any other bank you choose."

She gasped. "Five thousand pounds? Are you daft? I can niver in me life pay yew back."

"I do not want to be paid back. It is a gift. There are some pleasant flats in Knightsbridge. Also in Bloomsbury. Shall I take you there now?"

She continued to stare at him. "I don't understand. Wot do yew mean, a gift?"

"Have you never received a gift before?" he asked.

She blinked at him. "Sir Thomas gave me the necklace. An' me clothes. An' me pin money." Tears suddenly filled her eyes. "A fiver every month."

His jaw flexed. "We now know that Sir Thomas was indebted and could not afford more." But Blake knew he had not been that indebted. He had been miserly with his bride. In spite of loving her, he had been cheap.

"I . . . I . . ." She faltered. " 'Ow can I take this?"

"You can and you shall. There are no ifs, ands, or buts about it. It is a gift." Blake did not take his gaze from her pale face, her trembling lips. "Come to the bank tomorrow. If I am not there, ask for my assistant, Christopher."

"A gift," she whispered, staring at him like a child bewildered on its first Christmas by too many presents to contemplate.

Finally he started to smile. "It is my pleasure, Vi—Lady Goodwin."

Their gazes locked. "Yew can call me Violette," she whispered.

He did not move. He had not been having illicit thoughts until that very moment. But her eyes were shining, her face rapt. She was so beautiful, so vulnerable, and so damnably honest. The silence within her horrid flat was astounding; he could hear his own soft, even breathing, and hers, harsher and more ragged. And somewhere, outside, he could hear the distant sound of machinery grinding and whirring. In one of the neighboring flats a child was crying.

But none of that really registered. Blake looked at her mouth, recalling its taste and texture. It was hard to remember why she was forbidden to him. He ached to hold her, to make love to her, and then teach her the ways of the world. It had been such a long time since he had been so strongly drawn to a woman, not since he had loved and lost Gabriella—eight years ago.

His heart lurched, his body stiffened, dread battling desire. Violette was different, and not just from Gabriella, but from anyone he knew. She was far more than beautiful, and he was in danger of losing control of himself and his emotions. He could not, must not, let that happen.

She remained motionless. Her gaze was glued to his face, her heart—her love for him—shining in her eyes.

Christ, he thought, ready to reach for her.

And the front door suddenly slammed, footsteps sounding. Blake started. So did Violette.

Ralph entered the kitchen, staring at them both. "Wot the bleedin' 'ell?"

Blake's pulse began a distinct roaring in his ears. He suddenly recalled the single mattress in the bedroom. And Violette had fled Tamrah with Horn. "Are you visiting Lady Goodwin?" he asked. It was hard to maintain one's calm, hard not to snarl like a jungle animal. For he already knew the answer to his question, and in that instant, the depth of his anger and jealousy amazed him.

It was inappropriate, beyond the pale, for them to be sharing a flat, even if Violette considered Horn family.

"Visitin' Lady Goodwin?" Ralph laughed. "No, I ain't visitin' Violette! I live here, by gawd."

Blake did not move. Incapacitated, even though he recalled the pallet on the floor of the parlor. And just how long would Horn remain brotherly toward Violette? Without another word, he shoved past Ralph and strode out of the house.

To his credit, he did not slam the door violently behind him. Nor did he wrench it from its hinges. Nor did he glance backwards even once.

⊰ *Twelve* ⊱

VIOLETTE jumped at the sound of the front door slamming shut. She was still stunned over Blake's gift, stunned and bewildered. Her gaze met Ralph's. He was smiling with satisfaction. Suddenly furious, Violette ran past him and into the parlor. She swung the front door open just in time to see Blake climbing into a hansom. Her heart seemed to have stopped beating, her lungs to have filled with air. She clung to the door, wanting to call out to him, but he did not even glance back in her direction. The hansom rolled away, Blake staring stiffly straight ahead as if she did not exist, had never existed.

Violette felt Ralph come up behind her. She whirled. " 'Ow dare yew!''

'' 'Ow dare I wot?'' Ralph asked.

"Yew know wot! Yew chased 'im away,'' she said furiously.

He blinked at her. "I didn't do nuthin', luv. Just told 'im the facts. I do live 'ere with yew.''

"Yew didn't 'ave to tell 'im,'' she cried. Violette slammed the door shut. She realized that she was shaking. What if she never saw Blake again? He was so furious. And why did he dislike Ralph so? Didn't he understand that they were lifelong friends? Hadn't he believed her when she had told him the truth? Surely he hadn't heard the rumors about her and Ralph— the rumors that were completely unfounded?

"Wot's that in yer 'and?'' Ralph asked.

Violette blinked and looked down at the card she clutched in her palm. "It's just Blake's card. 'E's got a bank. 'E's given me a gift.''

"Wot kind of gift?'' Ralph said suspiciously.

"Five thousand pounds!'' Violette cried. "Gawd, can yew believe it?!''

But Ralph stared, wide-eyed. "An' just wot did yew 'ave t' do t' get this?" he cried angrily.

"I didn't do nuthin'," Violette whispered miserably. She shoved past Ralph, walking into the kitchen. She plopped down on one of the rickety chairs, cradling her face on her arms on the table. Her heart felt broken. And what did his gift mean?

No one had ever been so generous to her before. It was inconceivable—a miracle.

Ralph seized her shoulders, shaking her. "Wot'd yew 'av t' do fer this?" he shouted. "Dammit, Violette, I want t' know."

She stood so abruptly that her chair crashed over. She pushed hard on his chest, but he didn't budge. "Go away! Yer ruinin' me life! An' I ain't done nuthin'—it was a gift!"

" 'E lift yer skirts?" Ralph demanded, lowering his face so it was level with hers. His eyes had turned savagely charcoal gray. " 'E feel all guilty-like, huh?"

"Wot?" Violette gasped, recoiling.

Ralph pounded his fist once on the table. "Well, yew just go an' return this to 'im. 'Cause we both know what 'e expects fer yew t' do."

" 'E don't want nuthin' fer this! Nuthin'! Blake's good an' kind and a real gent—yew don't understand."

"Yer a fool," Ralph spat.

"No," Violette protested. "Just stop it, Ralph. Just stop it." She started to leave the kitchen. "An' I ain't returnin' the money, it's a *gift*, a gift from Blake to me."

The message arrived the following morning. Violette was at home when her door knocker sounded. She dried her hands on a towel, her heart skipping. Her immediate thought was that it was Blake, that he had come to apologize, to see her.

She rushed through the house, patting her coiled hair. But when she opened the door she was disappointed. Blake did not stand outside on her stoop. But the footman standing in front of her wore outstanding clothing: tan breeches, white stockings, black buckled shoes, a red frockcoat and felt hat. Violette peered past him and immediately recognized the phaeton she had traveled in the day before—it was Blake's rig. The footman, she realized, beginning to tremble, was holding a sealed envelope out to her.

Violette made no move to take it because she could not read. Her disappointment increased, accompanied now by shame. Violette took a breath. "Could . . . could yew kindly read it t' me, please?" she asked the footman.

He did not blink as he opened the ceal and read. "As promised, I have procured employment for you. Please report to the shop of Lady Allister at 103 Regent Street tomorrow morning at ten A.M. I have also made arrangements at my bank for your draft to be drawn anytime that you wish." The footman cleared his throat. "It is simply signed 'Blake,' my lady."

"Thank yew," Violette whispered. She knew that she should be ecstatic. He had given her an incredible gift and had found employment for her at her request. But she wasn't ecstatic. The tone of the note seemed singularly cold. Or was it her imagination?

She managed to smile at the footman. "Please tell His Lordship that I am much obliged."

The footman bowed. Violette watched him walk to the phaeton, wishing intensely that Blake had delivered the note himself.

Lady Allister was a kind, stout widow who had operated a ladies' specialty shop for more than a dozen years. Her husband had been an inventor of mechanical gadgets, knighted by the Queen for his service to the English people. Lady Allister had no airs. She did not care that ladies were supposed to remain at home, take tea, call on other ladies, and attend fêtes and soirées. "I would be so very bored," she told Violette as she looked her up and down that first day.

Violette liked her immediately. But she wasn't sure that the no-nonsense Lady Allister felt the same way. Violette was immediately assigned to one of the senior clerks—in Lady Allister's shops everyone was a clerk not a shopgirl—for an entire week of intensive training. "You are not to sell a single item until you are intimately familiar with every item in this store," Lady Allister warned her.

Violette nodded meekly. "Yes, me lady," she said.

Lady Allister frowned.

But her nervousness was taking a back seat to her curiosity. Lady Allister's clientele consisted of the most noble, elegant, and wealthy ladies in England, and Violette had never seen so many spectacular fabrics, furs, hats, gloves, veils, reticules, shoes, and other accessories before. In the window two fantastic ball gowns were displayed, one orange, one silver, shown with fur stoles, one mink, one chinchilla, white gloves, and matching satin shoes. Nothing in the store was ready-made, Violette learned, except for what was in the display window. And that was just to whet the appetites of Lady Allister's customers. They required that everything be custom-made, ordered anywhere from a few days to a few weeks in advance.

The first three days went very quickly. There was so much to learn—and so much to see. A parade of elegant ladies entered the store every day. Orders were taken on credit. Lady Allister did a thriving business. It quickly occurred to Violette that one day she could have a business like this one—if she worked very hard, saved her money, and applied herself with the utmost determination.

It suddenly seemed like one of Blake's solutions. Lady Allister was so clearly happy—and very well off. Although she was a widow, she had never remarried, and Violette knew from the gossip amongst the clerks that she had no intention of doing so. Violette could remain an unwed widow, too, if she were in Lady Allister's position. Suddenly the future appeared far less grim. Violette began to think that she might even be happy in such a situation. Not ecstatic, of course. But comfortable and content—living without fear.

So Violette threw herself into her training with near violent intensity. She memorized the names of the very important customers, along with their preferences in clothing and accessories. She was unfailingly polite. She went out of her way to charm. She listened to and watched the other clerks very carefully, trying to learn the styles and fashions these noble ladies preferred. One day, some of these ladies might shop in her store, and she never forgot it.

Lady Allister seemed to approve. Her stern facade became warmer, and occasionally she even smiled at Violette.

But Blake did not come to inquire after her welfare, or to even see how she liked her new job. It was the one blemish in Violette's new life.

But one gentleman, about Blake's age, handsome and auburn-haired, returned to the store a second time. The first time he had been, according to Violette's fellow clerks, with his mistress, an exquisite blonde. Violette had watched the blonde order dress after dress, stunned that anyone could wear so much and make so many purchases in the blink of an eye. The gentleman, Lord Farrow, had seemed bored. He had not objected to his mistress's excessive shopping. But Violette had caught him repeatedly studying her, not the blonde, and each and every time that their gazes had caught she had quickly looked away, ignoring his rather penetrating and speculating regard.

The bell rang. Two ladies were already in the shop, studying swatches of fabric with Theresa, the other clerk. Lady Allister was in the back, where a shipment of merchandise had just been delivered. Violette went to the door as Lord Farrow came in. Her smile faltered; he smiled back at her. As Violette closed the door, she strained to see if his beautiful blonde mistress awaited him in his elegant, open coach. It was empty.

Violette was very nervous. Theresa merely glanced at her once and said, "Please see to whatever His Lordship requires," turning her full attention back to the other two customers. Violette followed Lord Farrow over to a glass case containing beaded reticules in all sizes, shapes, and colors. "Did you forget somethin' yesterday, me Lord?" Violette was trying to enunciate as carefully as she could, not opening her mouth so wide on the word "you" and remembering her H's. It was very trying to do.

"Actually, I did," he said, his gaze on her face. "I think I forgot to introduce myself properly. I am Lord Robert Farrow. And you are Violette?"

Her pulse was racing, with some alarm. She did not have to be told point-blank to know that Lady Allister would be furious if she saw Farrow flirting with her. She stole a glance at Theresa, but the discussion was animated now, the lady who was buying trying to decide on trim for each gown. Violette swallowed. "Actually, me name is Lady Goodwin."

He paused. "Ah, I see."

Coloring, Violette said hastily, "Wot can I do fer you today, me lord?"

He did not answer her. "I am sure that many gentlemen have told you this many times before, but you are very beautiful, Lady Goodwin."

She stared uneasily. His gaze was compelling; she could not be immune to his charm and good looks. "You are gonna get me dismissed, me lord."

"I am sorry, Lady Goodwin. That is the last thing I wish to do. Can you help me select a scarf? It is a gift for a woman of extraordinary beauty." He smiled at her.

Violette nodded, relieved that they were on safe ground again. "An' wot colors might please yer lady friend?"

He smiled and said softly, "I do not know."

She blinked into his unwavering gaze. "Wot do you think she'd like, then?"

"Something bold, beautiful, like the lady in question. Something special. Very special."

Violette had the crazy thought that he was referring to her, but that was impossible. She quickly opened a case and selected several scarves for him to inspect. He smiled at her. "You choose. Which do you prefer?" he asked calmly.

Her hands were trembling. "I . . . I like the red."

"I am hardly surprised. Can you gift wrap it for me, Lady Goodwin?"

Violette nodded, relieved his purchase was finished. As she took a foiled box out from beneath the case, he moved closer. "Would you care to meet me in the park sometime? For a drive, perhaps?" Farrow asked.

Violette almost dropped the gift box. The bell tinkled over the front door. Violette was about to refuse—confusion overcoming her—when she espied the countess of Harding and Catherine Dearfield entering the shop. She beamed, flooded with relief. Lord Farrow followed her gaze.

"Ladies Harding and Dearfield," he murmured, his tone speculative. "Are they good customers of yours?"

"I niver waited on them in me life, but I had dinner at 'Ardin'—Hardin' Hall," Violette said with pride. She waved. It was obvious that they were surprised to see her.

"I see." Farrow regarded her, then said quietly, "Sunday at noon? When the shop is closed?"

Violette hesitated. Farrow did not interest her. Only one man held her heart. And one day, if she worked very hard and was very clever, she would have her own shop, a shop like this one, and her future would be safe and secure. Yet Farrow was not at all like Sir Thomas. He was like Blake, young and handsome and so very noble. She could not help but being slightly tempted. What if he was in love with her? In spite of his elegant, beautiful mistress?

Blake had warned her that she could not find a husband in his world. What if he was wrong? Violette almost wanted to prove him wrong.

"Lady Goodwin?" Farrow prompted.

"I . . . no. No thank you." Once the words were out, Violette was relieved. She could not risk losing her job.

Farrow was crestfallen, but only briefly. He smiled, bowing.

"Our paths shall cross again, Lady Goodwin. I am certain of it." He nodded at the countess and Catherine before crossing the store and leaving with the gift-wrapped box.

Violette stared after him. She felt that she had made the right decision.

"Violette," Catherine exclaimed, smiling with pleasure. She gripped Violette's hands, kissing her cheek. "It's so good to see you! You left Tamrah in such haste—without even saying good-bye or leaving a forwarding address."

"How are you, dear?" the countess asked, her blue eyes alight.

"Fine, thank you," Violette said, hardly able to believe that these ladies were so thrilled to see her. And she was thrilled to see them. They were surely the nicest people in the world. "An' you?"

"We are well," the countess said cheerfully. "Lord Harding had some business in town, so I decided to accompany him, as did Jon."

"And I could not possibly remain in the country," Catherine said as easily. "Father is so busy hunting that if I had stayed at Dearfield Way it is quite like being alone."

"Well, I am real glad to see you both," Violette said firmly.

"Violette, do you work here?" Catherine asked, puzzled.

Violette blushed. She was well aware that real ladies did not work. But she held her head high and said firmly, "I do. An' I like it a lot. Lady Allister has been wonderful to me. I been learnin' all about the business."

"We heard about the poor state of affairs which Sir Thomas left you burdened with," the countess said softly. "Are you all right, dear?"

Violette nodded. "I got no choices, me lady. He didn't leave me with nuthin'. I had to find me a job. Actually, Blake got me hired here." She had to smile.

Catherine and the countess exchanged glances. The countess laid her hand on Violette's shoulder. "I see. Was this, then, his idea?"

"No, it was mine. I do like it here. There's so much to see, so much to do. I been learnin' all that I can."

"That is very commendable, and very brave of you, my dear," the countess said.

"I finish me trainin' tomorrow," Violette said enthusiastically. Lord Farrow had been her first sale.

"Violette," Catherine said, unsmiling. "What did Lord Farrow want? He seemed to be very interested in you.''

Violette cast her eyes down. Had it been so obvious? ''He came here to buy a scarf. But he invited me to drive with him in the park.'' She looked up with a small, uncertain smile. ''I refused.''

''You did the right thing. It is not proper to drive with a gentleman unless one has a chaperone,'' Catherine said firmly.

''Lady Allister wouldn't like me drivin' with a customer,'' Violette said.

''No, I don't think she would,'' Catherine replied.

''Violette, perhaps you should know. Farrow has quite a reputation. He is not very honorable where beautiful women are concerned,'' the countess said frankly. ''It is best that you stay away from him.''

Violette nodded. So Blake had been right. She couldn't help feeling somewhat disappointed. It would have been thrilling to have a man like that fall in love with her and court her. Then, ''Can I help you both? Did you come to shop? Bein' as Theresa is busy, I'm allowed to serve you.''

''Oh, yes,'' the countess began, but at that point Lady Allister entered the shop from the back room, saw Lady Harding, and sailed forward, smiling. The two women began to chat.

Catherine shifted so her back was to the pair, while she herself faced Violette. ''Violette, are you certain that you are all right?''

''Yes, Catherine, I am.'' Violette hesitated. ''Have you seen Blake?''

''Yes, I had dinner with him and the family last night. He did not mention that he had seen you, or that he had helped you procure employment.'' Her brow furrowed.

Violette bit her lip. ''I see.'' She hadn't even been worth a passing reference. Or a small visit. Or anything.

And then she thought about his incredible gift. She had gone to his bank and opened an account there. If Blake had been present, she had been unaware of it, for she hadn't seen him. He was, she thought, incomprehensible.

''Violette,'' Catherine asked, ''when *did* you see Blake?''

Violette was taken by surprise. She fidgeted. ''I went to see him. 'E told me he would help me with me finances before I left Tamrah.''

Catherine nodded, regarding her closely. ''It is odd that he never mentioned it.'' Then she shrugged and put her arm around Violette. ''But in any case, it is so good to see you.

Now we must exchange addresses so we can visit from time to time.''

Violette managed a smile—recalling Blake's reaction to her tiny, horrid flat. Although she had moved to Knightsbridge, with Ralph coming and going as he pleased, she didn't particularly wish to invite Catherine over. "I been stayin' at a hotel," she said. Then, "Do you wish to shop?"

And Catherine, diverted, smiled and agreed.

The shop was closing; it was five in the afternoon. But as Violette began pulling down the shades per Lady Allister's orders, she stilled. There was no mistaking the sleek black phaeton driving toward the store. Her heart skipped too many beats to count. Violette, frozen, watched Blake alight from the carriage.

He had come. He had finally come to see how she was faring in her new job. He had finally come to see her. She felt faint.

"Violette? Are you daydreaming?" Theresa asked.

Violette started as Blake approached from outside. "No, I . . . er . . . Lord Blake is here."

Theresa, plump and blond, gave Violette an odd glance. "Perhaps you had better unlock the door and let him in."

Violette hurried to obey. But her eager smile vanished at the strained expression on Blake's face. He bowed briefly, then entered the shop. "Good afternoon, Lady Goodwin."

"G'd afternoon, Blake," Violette said. "I mean, Lord Blake." She twisted her hands. Was he still angry with her? But what had she done wrong!

He eyed her as Lady Allister hurried out of the back room. "My lord!" she cried, hands extended. "Another pleasant surprise?"

Blake took her hands in his and kissed her on the cheek. He was smiling warmly. "How are you, Lady Allister?"

"I have had a very good week." Allister glanced from Blake to Violette. Her brows lifted questioningly. She said, "Lady Goodwin has been a model employee. She has thrown herself into her duties here with all her heart."

Violette ducked her head, filled with pleasure, for it was Lady Allister's first direct compliment to her. But not before she caught Blake's eye.

Blake said, no longer smiling, "I cannot say that I am surprised."

"Thank you for bringing her to me," Lady Allister said.

"I wish to speak with Lady Goodwin," Blake said flatly. "Privately. Is she finished for the day?"

Violette could not imagine what he wished to speak about, but she did not like his look or his tone. Trouble was coming and she felt her insides curdling. How she wished that he had smiled at her the way he had smiled at Lady Allister. What had she done now?

"Of course. Good night, Lady Goodwin. Until tomorrow."

"Thank you, Lady Allister," Violette said, casting a searching glance at Blake.

He gestured toward the door. "Let us walk outside."

Violette nodded. Blake followed her out onto the overcast street. It had been raining earlier, and the air was damp and pleasantly cool.

Blake took her elbow and they began walking. Violette looked at him nervously. When he still did not speak, she said, "Thank you so much for gettin' me the job. I do like workin' for Lady Allister, an' I been tryin' real hard."

He halted and gave her a long look. "What is this I hear about you and Farrow?"

It took Violette a moment to comprehend him. "Me an' Lord Farrow?" It quickly crossed her mind that either the countess or Catherine had had a recent discussion with Blake.

"Yes, you and Farrow. He was here today? He asked you to drive in the park on Sunday?"

Violette had stiffened. Her chin tilted upwards. "Yes, he was here. But that wasn't my fault. He came to shop."

Blake snorted. "He propositioned you."

"I said no," Violette snapped. "Not that it's yer affair!"

"So you do have common sense?" His tone was like a lash. "Farrow is a rogue. When it comes to women, he has no morals, none. I hope you did not encourage him to return."

Her pulse pounded with anger. "An' if I did? Mebbe I like him. Mebbe 'e likes me!"

Blake laughed harshly. "So that is the lay of the land?"

"I beg yer pardon?"

"Do you like him enough to become his mistress, Violette?" Blake asked cruelly.

Violette's shoulders jerked back with a snap. "'Ow could yew!" she cried.

Blake took a breath. "I know the man," Blake said, his eyes flashing. "He wishes to amuse himself at your expense. He does not intend marriage, not to you, not to any woman. His reputation as a ladies' man is legion, Violette.''

Violette hugged herself. "Like yers?"

Blake stared angrily. His dark brows slashed together. "I suppose that I do have a small reputation in that regard. But my reputation is minor compared to Farrow's."

Violette was hurt by his admission. "Wot do you care if I take up with the likes of Farrow?"

Blake was rigid. "So you will accept his invitation?"

"I don't know," Violette cried. She turned her back on him abruptly and stared unseeingly across the street. She felt like crying. This was not the kind of visit she had anticipated.

He touched her shoulder briefly from behind. "Violette," he said softly.

She had to face him. His soft tone had washed over her like a warm, warm wave.

For a long moment he did not speak. And when he did, the anger had left his tone. "Oddly enough, I do care. That is why I am concerned, that is why I am here."

Violette could hardly believe her ears. "You care? About me?"

"I do not want to see you hurt by anyone," he said harshly.

She wanted to fling herself against him. She smiled. "Blake, I care, too. Fer you. If only you—"

"Stop," he cut her off. "Do not make more out of this than what exists. We are friends. That is all."

"Friends," Violette echoed, "you mean, like me an' Ralph?" She covered her heart with her hand. It was hurting her all over again.

"No." His jaw flexed. "I mean friends, as in I have helped you to gain employment, helped you to get back on your feet. Nothing more."

She backed away from him. "I don't know why yew came 'ere today," she cried.

"Violette," Blake said. "I came to warn you away from Farrow. You are too innocent to understand him and his kind. I am sorry." He reached out his hand toward her, as if to pluck her sleeve, or touch her.

She swatted it away. "Don't yew go feelin' sorry fer me! Because mebbe, just mebbe, yew are wrong. Mebbe Farrow 'as a bigger mind, an' a bigger heart, than yew, me lord! Mebbe one day 'e might like me enough to make me 'is *wife*!"

Blake stared. He did not speak for a long time. While Violette fought the urge to shed hot, bitter tears.

"He will not," Blake said quietly. "He cannot. Your stations in life are far too different. It is not done."

"Go away," Violette managed, meaning it. "Go find someone else to be friends with. *Leave me alone!*"

"Even if he loved you," Blake said as quietly, "he would not marry you. I am sorry, Violette."

Violette backed away. His brutal words were stabbing painfully through her chest. "Go away," she whispered thickly.

"I am sorry, Violette," Blake repeated heavily. "But I am a realist. Let me drive you home."

"A realist," Violette said bitterly. "Yew know wot, me lord? I feel sorry fer yew!" She turned, reaching blindly for the door. But his palm came down flat and hard on the frame, holding it closed.

"What the blazes do you mean by that?" he demanded from behind her.

She half-turned. Violette stood so close to him now that her skirts enveloped his legs, and she thought that he could surely see the glitter of hot tears in her eyes. "I mean yew think the world is all dark, dirt, and smoke, don't yew? An' I'm the one born in St. Giles! But the sun shines, Blake, it does—every single day." She tried desperately not to cry.

"Of course the sun shines," he said, his gaze on hers. "But it shines on dirt and through smoke, and even beautiful roses have thorns."

She wanted to hit him, her fists were clenched into tight, hard, hurtful little balls. "An' wot about rainbows?" she cried. "Wot about pots o' gold?"

He blinked. "Rainbows?" he asked, as if he did not understand her English. And then he shook his head. "Violette, rainbows are not only an illusion, they are fleeting. And there are no pots of gold at the end of any rainbow."

Violette finally wiped her eyes. "Rainbows are real and they are also magic," she said. "I believe in 'em, I do, and I believe that one day I can find me one that will last *forever*." She stared defiantly.

He was silent. Then, "I hope that you do."

She choked, turning away. Reaching for the door, Blake dropped his hand, allowing her to open it. "At least I got hopes an' dreams," she said. "Not like yew." And she went inside.

Blake did not move, and he did not reply.

⋟ *Thirteen* ⋞

BLAKE'S phaeton rolled up to the curb in front of Harding House. Three weeks had passed since he had spoken with Violette outside of Lady Allister's specialty shop. In those three weeks, Blake had thrown himself singlemindedly into his business affairs.

Blake bounded up the wide front stairs and past the two stone lions. The footmen bowed and immediately swung open the immense door. As soon as Blake entered the rotunda, he heard a pair of female voices which he recognized and he smiled. He hurried into the parlor, reserved for the family's use, just a few doors down the hall.

Catherine and the countess were in a lively discussion about the countess's first event of the Season, a ball. It would also be the very first ball of the Season. Blake hardly cared. Last week he had found himself thoroughly bored at the two dinner parties and the single dance which he had attended. He intended to put in a very brief appearance at his mother's ball tomorrow. He had also been working late most evenings. It was preferable to the inane conversation he endured at the parties he did choose to attend.

Hugs, kisses, and greetings were exchanged. "How are you, Mother? Catherine?" Blake asked warmly.

"I am so very worried," the countess said. "The ball is tomorrow and there is still so much to be done!"

Blake smiled fondly. "You are always worried to distraction before any social gathering you sponsor—and it is always, without fail, a great success."

His mother frowned, already lost in thought, and walked over to the secretaire where she sat down and began making notes and lists. Catherine plucked Blake's sleeve, her smile gone, her eyes on his. "Blake, we must talk. About Violette."

He was immediately all ears. "And what is there to discuss?" He tried to sound indifferent when he did not feel indifferent at all. It was almost as if he missed Violette and yearned to hear about her.

"I am afraid I have done something terrible," Catherine said, gnawing on her lower lip.

"I doubt it," Blake replied easily.

Catherine sighed. Taking Blake's arm, they moved farther across the salon. "The other day I stopped by Lady Allister's to visit her. I have repeatedly tried to find out where she lives, so I might call there, but Violette has always changed the subject, making me wonder what she is hiding. Anyway, Violette did not seem well. She seemed tired. And, well, sad." Catherine regarded Blake. "Impulsively, I invited her to your mother's ball."

Blake's eyes widened. And his pulse positively leapt. "Is that the end of the world?" he asked calmly, but his thoughts were far from calm. All he could think was that Violette would be at the ball tomorrow night. He was far more than surprised. Suddenly he was looking forward to the event.

"I am very worried now about this. Blake, the countess's ball is one of the most elegant of the Season. Invitations are coveted and fought over. Violette was thrilled to be invited. I know she will come. But what will happen once she is here? This is not like a dinner at Harding Hall." Catherine wrung her hands. "She is very sensitive and I am afraid she is going to be hurt. You know how cruel people can be."

Blake realized that Catherine was right. He turned away, his hands jammed into the pockets of his trousers. His crowd would be appalled to have Violette Goodwin in their midst. She would be cut dead.

"I haven't told the countess, either." Catherine worried the ivory sash which adorned the waist of her cream yellow gown. "Oh, dear. I sense a huge disaster in the making."

Blake's mind raced. "Do not worry about Mother. I shall explain to her, and she has a heart of gold. Well, I am afraid we have no choice but to close ranks around Violette and protect her, so to speak."

Catherine brightened. "What a wonderful idea! In fact, not only shall I make it clear that she is a dear friend of mine, why do you not give her your attention? If people see you courting her, they will think twice about being rude and uncivil, I daresay."

Blake regarded Catherine. He said slowly, "Catherine, I do hope this isn't some mad scheme on your part to throw me together with Violette Goodwin?"

Catherine gasped. "Blake! How could you even say such a thing!" If she were dissembling, then she belonged on the stage. If he did not know Catherine so well, he would think she was taking on Violette as some sort of project or experiment with which to amuse herself. But Catherine was a genuinely compassionate woman. Her motives were pure.

But Blake continued to stare.

Catherine smiled at him now. "Lord Farrow has stopped by Lady Allister's three or four times in the past few weeks. He has even given her a gift. A very beautiful scarf."

Blake stiffened. "She should not have accepted it."

Catherine's green gaze was level. "I am afraid that she did not know any better." Suddenly she brightened. "Jon!"

Jon was sauntering into the room. The countess did not glance up. "What are the two of you whispering about?"

Catherine flushed. "I was just explaining to Blake that I impulsively invited Violette to your mother's ball."

"That was a capital idea," Jon said, kissing her cheek. "Don't you think so, Blake?"

Blake met his brother's far too benign gaze. He had little doubt that he was being set up by them both. He turned and walked over to a window. It did not matter. He was looking forward to seeing Violette Goodwin again, even if it meant flirting with danger.

When Blake had left, Jon invited Catherine with him outside. Arm in arm, they strolled in the countess's resplendent gardens. "You have been very clever, Catherine," Jon remarked warmly.

She laughed with delight. "I do think so. I am also lending Violette one of my gowns. I do want everything to go so well tomorrow night."

"She will be stunning, I am sure," Jon said as they paused to watch the goldfish in one marble pond, "although not as stunning as you."

Catherine cast her gaze down, smiling, her cheeks pink. "Thank you."

He released her arm. "It's a shame," he said, "that Violette does not have a real mentor amongst our set, because all she needs is a little polish and no one would ever suspect that she is not one of us."

Catherine stared. "A mentor? A little polish? Jon, she needs a tutor. She needs to learn how to speak correctly, without that accent, to walk and move gracefully, even to stand up, sit down, and curtsy! Why, she needs a complete course in fashion, and I dare say, etiquette. In short, she needs far more than a simple polishing!"

Jon smiled at her.

Her eyes widened. And as it was so often the case between them, she understood him perfectly. "How clever *you* are," she said.

Ralph stared as Violette finished dressing. His eyes were cold. Violette knew him well enough to know that he was angry and unhappy. But she couldn't be too sorry. She was filled with a combination of excitement and dread.

She was going to her first ball. At Harding House. Violette was so nervous that she was lightheaded. She was terrified of making a mistake, of talking the wrong way, or saying the wrong thing, or behaving in some manner that was considered rude or unfashionable or déclassé. She had been working at Lady Allister's long enough now to know that there were all kinds of rules which the upper classes relished following. Violette hardly understood any of them.

But Catherine had been kind enough to invite her to a grand event, a real ball, just like the one she had witnessed eight years ago. Nothing would keep Violette away.

And Blake would be there.

Her heart lurched. She stood in front of an oval mirror, but closed her eyes. In the past three weeks, Violette had thrown herself into her work. This week, Lady Allister had told her that she had made more sales than the other clerks. Her employer was so pleased that she had given Violette a raise.

What would happen tonight? What could she do? To gain Blake's attention, to win his heart? Or at least to make him see her differently than as a mere friend?

If only he would kiss her again the way he had at Harding Hall on the summer night in York. It was only a month ago, but it seemed as if it had been another lifetime.

"Yer goin' to get into trouble t'night, I can feel it!" Ralph cried, breaking into her thoughts.

Violette opened her eyes. She faced her very pale reflection in the mirror. Somehow she had managed to arrange her hair into a chignon, although numerous tendrils were escaping around her face. Catherine had lent her an ice-blue taffeta ball gown, one Violette at once loved for its rich and sensuous feel, yet thought terribly plain. It was the first time she had ever worn her shoulders bare, for the bodice of the gown was cut straight across her chest and arms, the small velvet cap sleeves hanging. Violete wished the gown had lace trim, or roses, or even beads. All it was adorned with, other than the velvet cap sleeves, was a darker blue, stunningly wide satin sash. The underskirts, exposed when she moved, were a wonderfully rich shade of iridescent green that at times glinted purple or mauve.

"Did yew 'ear me?" Ralph demanded.

Violette faced him with an anxious smile. "You are daft." She intended to speak with utter precision tonight. "What could possibly 'appen—happen—tonight?" But she thought, *a kiss*. A wild, savage kiss, one that would show her that Blake did not really think of her as a friend but as a woman.

" 'Is Lordship's goin' t' dance yew right out o' the ballroom int' the library or some such place, an' 'e ain't got marriage on 'is mind—yew remember that!"

"How could I forget?" Violette glanced at herself in the mirror. She thought she was lovelier than she had ever been, but she was afraid, not hopeful. Tonight, she prayed with all of her heart, was the beginning of the rest of her life. *Please, God.*

"Yew ain't one of them, Violette. Yew ain't niver gonna be one of them," Ralph said furiously. "An' no fancy job or fancy dress is gonna change the facts."

"I don't care," Violette said. But it was a lie, and she knew Ralph was right, which was why she was so scared. The truth was unavoidable now. Tonight she was entering a world where she did not belong. She was determined not to make a fool of herself. But how could she not? What if she tripped while on the stairs, perhaps even falling down them, or stepped on a gentleman's feet while dancing—if a gentleman even asked her to dance, and Violette had the terrible notion that no one would. Yet she did not know how to dance, so if someone did ask her, she should refuse. But Violette knew she wouldn't refuse; she would somehow fake it, pretend. And wasn't that what Joanna Feldstone had called her? A pretender? Violette had never wanted to do anything more than to go to the Harding ball, but she was a pretender, because she wasn't really Lady Goodwin, she was only Violet Cooper. The ball was proof that she wasn't a real lady, that she was completely unprepared for the evening that loomed ahead.

Ralph cut into her thoughts. "*I don't care*," Ralph mimicked. "Wot airs yew got now, me lady!"

Violette faced him, trembling. "I just want to better meself. You shouldn't make fun of me talking properly."

Ralph stared at her as Violette faced him. "Yew gonna get 'urt tonight, I can feel it, an' I don't gotta be a wizard to know it."

"I ain't going to get hurt," Violette said firmly. "You're jealous, Ralph Horn."

He glared. Abruptly he turned his back on her, making Violette feel terrible—she hated fighting with Ralph, her dearest friend in the world, dearer than any brother could ever be. "I'm sorry," she said.

He whirled. "No, yer right. I'm jealous. I'm damn jealous, luv."

Violette stiffened. "Of me airs?" she whispered incredulously.

He laughed slightly and cupped her bare shoulders with his callused palms. They were damp. "No, not o' yer airs. I'm 'appy fer yew if that's wot makes yew 'appy, talkin' like some nob."

Violette searched his pale eyes, finding a tenderness there she rarely saw. "I don't understand."

"I'm jealous o' 'Is Lordship." Ralph's eyes darkened. "I 'ate the way I seen yew look at 'im, an' I 'ate the way 'e looks at yew!"

Violette stared, stunned.

Ralph's grip tightened and his eyes flared and suddenly he pressed his mouth against hers. Violette was so surprised that she did not move. He immediately stepped away from her, ending the brief kiss before it had even begun. His own eyes were wide and stunned and somehow frightened.

"Ralph?" She could not believe what he had done.

"I . . ." He stared. "Gawd, I'm sorry!" He turned and strode out of the bedroom, as fast as his legs would take him.

When Violette arrived at Harding House, servants were in the foyer, relieving the ladies of their wraps, the gentlemen of their hats, capes, and canes, if they carried the latter. Violette had nothing to give over and she felt her cheeks flaming—she had already committed a mistake, which she prayed no one would notice. But the two couples in front of her were not even glancing at her. And then Violette saw Tulley, the butler.

She beamed in relief, for he felt like a dear old friend. He saw her, starting, then quickly recovered. His expression became benign. He bowed. "The ballroom, Lady Goodwin," he intoned, gesturing.

Swallowing, Violette said, very carefully, "Thank you, Tulley."

He shot her a brief smile, a twinkle in his eyes.

Violette's pulse was rioting. But at least she had one ally in the house. She followed the two couples down the three steps into the massive ballroom. But once inside, she was frozen, incapable of movement.

It was larger than she had remembered, more majestic. White pillars lined each long side of the rectangular room. The mint green ceiling was domed and beautifully wainscoted in white plaster and gold. A half-dozen huge crystal chandeliers were lit with hundreds of flaming candles. The floors were wood parquet and polished so highly that they gleamed. Dozens and dozens of assorted small chairs lined the room's gold-clothed walls, beneath marble busts set upon pedestals and numerous works of art. Violette would have been happy just to wander around the room looking at the sculptures and the landscapes, but she did not dare.

And there were so many people present that Violette could not hazard a guess as to whether the guests numbered two or five hundred. Along the edges of the ballroom the beautifully gowned, bejeweled women and gentlemen in evening dress gathered in groups, chatting and sipping champagne. In the center of the room dozens of couples were performing a quadrillen. The orchestra, Violette realized, was skillfully hidden from view at the far end of the room behind a thick arrangement of flowering shrubbery decorated with papier-mâché figures of men and women waltzing.

And past the dancers and the band, wide doors led into another room, where Violette glimpsed more guests and buffet after buffet of refreshments.

Violette hesitated, unsure of what to do. Three other couples were passing by her as they entered the ballroom. Violette looked around, realizing that she did not see anyone she knew. But the Hardings, of course, had to be present. The Hardings—and Blake.

Then she recognized Catherine Dearfield as one of the ladies on the dance floor performing the quadrillen. She was stunning in a bright pink moirée gown, and she moved so gracefully that Violette was filled with yearning. Her partner was a handsome, swarthy gentleman. They looked wonderful together, Catherine ethereal and fair, her partner dark and attractive.

Violette turned away. She could not remain by the steps like a statue. She would look for the countess, Jon, or Blake.

And as she walked alone through the ballroom, she was aware of men and women turning to regard her somewhat quizzically. One or two gentlemen who appeared to be unescorted studied her and smiled. Then Violette faltered, espying Lord Farrow, who had seen her and was coming purposefully her way.

"Lady Goodwin," he said, his eyes gleaming. He took her hand and kissed it. "I am so delighted to see you."

"G'd evening, me Lord," Violette said nervously, aware that they were being watched by several guests. She did not want his attention. He had been stopping by the shop far too frequently. Lady Allister had actually given Violette the same lecture about his character as the countess. And he had given her the beautiful scarf, insisting that she accept it.

"You look ravishing tonight, as always," he said. He tucked her arm in his. "Shall we go and have a glass of champagne?"

Violette hesitated. She still saw no one else that she knew. "I . . er . . . I guess so." She stole another glance at the party watching her encounter with Lord Farrow. And she heard one gentleman murmur, "Who *is* that?"

A woman said loudly, "I have *no* idea! Did you hear that Cockney accent? Good God—do you think she has crashed the Hardings' ball?"

Violette stiffened. And if Farrow heard, he gave no sign. He began pulling Violette away. But Violette heard another man remark, "What a shame, a woman like that with those looks. So she is Farrow's newest, eh?"

Violette stumbled alongside Farrow, refusing to look at him, barely aware of where they were going. She no longer wished for his company; in fact, she wished to disappear entirely. And she had thought her speech was improving.

As they crossed the ballroom Violette did not look at anyone, but now she felt as if everyone were watching her. She tripped as she and Farrow crossed into the dining room.

"Are you hungry?" he asked.

Violette finally met his dark gaze. It was very hard to keep a rein on all of her emotions, and she did not trust herself to speak. But somewhat miraculously, a voice behind her said in response, "I think Lady Goodwin wishes to decline."

Violette whirled, facing Blake.

His eyes held a dangerous light, a muscle flexed in his jaw. His gaze helds hers only for an instant, and then it skewered

Farrow. Farrow eyed him coldly in return. The two men stared with undisguised hostility at one another. And it took Violette a moment to realize the extent of the tension between them. It was almost as if she had caused it. Had she?

Could Blake be jealous?

"Good evening to you, Blake," Farrow said without any warmth.

Blake nodded, then faced Violette. His eyes softened, and a moment later he bowed, taking her hand. "I am so pleased that you are here, Lady Goodwin."

He sounded as if he meant it. She melted inside, forgetting the humiliation of the past few moments. "Yew are? I mean, you are?"

"Of course." He tucked her arm in his. "I hate to be rude, my friend, but Lady Goodwin and I have several urgent matters to discuss. I am her financial advisor."

Farrow stared, his lips curling. "Right." But he recovered, bowed stiffly at Violette and said, "Will you mark a waltz for me on your card?"

Violette blinked. She had not yet recovered from the amazing fact that Blake had not just sought her out, but that he was pleased to see her. Perhaps her dreams would come true tonight. She crossed her fingers.

"Do you have a card, Lady Goodwin?" Blake asked softly. "A dance card?"

Violette did not dare ask what a dance card was. "No."

"We shall get you one," Blake said, his gaze unwavering on her face.

Farrow bowed again. "A waltz," he reminded her.

Violette smiled. "That's fine, me lord."

Farrow turned and disappeared into the crowd. Violette smiled shyly at Blake.

"You look lovely tonight," he said. Blake led her toward a buffet. "Farrow is up to no good, as I have told you before."

Violette nodded. "I . . . I am beginning to think you are right."

He glanced at her. "Are you hungry?"

"No." How could she think of eating when she was arm in arm with Blake, the most stunning, noble, intelligent, kind man she had ever known in her life?

They paused. "Shall we dance?" he asked.

Violette felt herself blushing. With Blake, she was not afraid to confess the truth. "I don't know how to dance."

"Ahh, I see." He regarded her. "Then perhaps you should stay off of the dance floor tonight, Lady Goodwin." He smiled at her.

"I think you are right," Violette said, smiling back at him.

"Let me introduce you to some of my friends," Blake said.

Violette allowed Blake to lead her over to a group of guests. A mixed group, both in gender and age, they all became quiet when Violette and Blake approached. Violette was pinching herself to make sure that she was not dreaming.

Blake bowed at the oldest gentleman present. "Your Grace, good evening. Might I present a friend of mine? Lady Goodwin of York has recently come to town. Lady Goodwin, the duke of Rutherford."

For one moment, Violette was frozen. She almost gaped. She had never laid eyes on a duke before, much less been oh-so-casually introduced to one. Blake squeezed her elbow and Violette came to life. Aware that her cheeks were burning, Violette curtsied—a curtsy she had been practicing on numerous customers. "Yer Grace, good evening. It's wonderful to meet you." Her pulse was racing.

And if the duke heard her "awful Cockney," or noticed that her manners were far less graceful than those of the class he belonged to, he gave no sign. He bowed over her hand. "A pleasure, Lady Goodwin. Is it not a magnificent ball?" His eyes twinkled, surprising Violette. She immediately sensed that here was another kind, compassionate man.

"Yes, sir . . . I mean, me lord."

Someone coughed behind Rutherford.

"And how are you, young man?" Rutherford asked Blake.

Blake smiled. "On a night like this one, with such a woman at my side, need I even answer the question?" Blake asked.

It took Violette a moment to realize what Blake had meant. She gawked at him. Was this the same man who had been furious with her outside of Lady Allister's—who had told her he wished to be mere friends?

"Lady Goodwin, I do believe that you have met the duke's son, the marquis of Waverly. And this is the marchioness," Blake continued.

Violette was now recognizing the very handsome, golden-haired, amber-eyed gentleman who had been standing beside the duke. She began to flush. He had been present in Blake's club with Blake when she had forced her way inside quite inelegantly and uproariously.

But Dom St. Georges grinned at her, his eyes containing the very same twinkle as the duke's. "It's a pleasure to see you again, Lady Goodwin."

Before Violette could respond, the lovely, petite woman by Waverly's side was smiling at her and introducing herself as the marquis's wife. "You are in town now?" Anne St. Georges queried. Her manner was open and friendly, her accent American.

Violette nodded, at a loss because this exalted family was being so gracious toward her.

"Oh, then you must call upon me at Rutherford House." Anne St. Georges smiled. "And soon. We will take breakfast together and you shall tell me all about how you first met Blake." Her blue eyes sparkled. "I do adore gossip," she added.

"Yes," was all that Violette could manage. She was dazed.

Blake performed introductions amongst the rest of the group, and then everyone began to chat animatedly. Violette remained silent, listening as the opera was discussed, her eyes constantly glued upon Blake's face. After a few moments, Blake excused them and led her away. "There are many more people here that I wish for you to meet," he told her.

Violette met his brilliant blue eyes. "Yes," she managed, as he maneuvered them toward another cluster of conversing guests. Arm in arm with him, she had one coherent thought. God had answered her prayers.

"You seem somewhat tired, Lady Goodwin," Blake said, about an hour later.

He had just handed her a glass of champagne. Violette nodded at him. "Meeting so many people is eggssaucting."

"Exhausting," he said, his gaze on hers. "E-X-H. Ex-hausting."

"Exhausting," Violette whispered, taking a sip of the champagne. She had never tasted champagne before and her eyes widened. "This is delicious," she exclaimed.

He laughed, the sound rich. "Dom Perignon; 1849 was a premier year."

Violette took another sip. She had been so tired, but the bubbly champagne was rapidly restoring her spirits. "I do like this."

"Be careful," he said. "It can go right to your head."

"I niver been drunk in me life," she said flatly. "Eggsept

when you gave me that brandy after Sir Thomas died." She sombered. "Except," she amended. She did not want to recall that day now.

"Well, at the rate you are finishing that glass, I imagine that this shall be the second time." Blake seemed amused.

Violette stared at him, hardly having heard him. Thus far they had been so busy meeting so many people, and now she had time to think—and to yearn. Blake was so handsome. She could look at his face forever, never getting enough. She wondered if he would always make her heart stop, always take her breath away.

Blake tore his gaze from hers. He sipped his own flute of champagne.

Violette couldn't help gazing at his mouth and recalling the kiss they had shared. Her body tightened with the recollection. She thought about the gardens outside of the house. "Will you take some air with me?" she asked impulsively. "It's so hot in here."

He stared at her, unsmiling.

Violette wasn't warm, and she was afraid he could read her thoughts. But she ducked her eyes and fanned herself with one hand. "I was so nervous tonight," she murmured, a kind of explanation.

"It's cool out. You would need a wrap."

"No. I don't want a wrap." Violette kept her gaze downcast.

A brief silence greeted her words. "Very well. For a moment, then." Blake took her elbow and they left the dining salon. They passed several guests as they walked down a hall. He halted before a pair of French doors. Outside was a flagstone terrace and moonlit gardens, a pretty gazebo in its center. "Are you sure you are warm?" he asked, glancing at her.

Violette was actually on fire. "Yes."

He shoved open the doors and they stepped outside. "Pale blue suits you," he said somewhat tersely. "It is a shame you do not have sapphires and diamonds to go with the gown."

Violette laughed hoarsely. "Me? Gawd!"

"God," he said, stepping away from her. "Never *gawd*. And a lady does not use that kind of language in any case." He had moved to a stone bench, his back to her, facing the gardens, the moon, and the gazebo. Violette devoured his back openly. But before she could go to him, he turned slowly around.

His eyes were so intense that Violette, about to follow him, froze. "God," he said, almost to himself.

"God," she whispered breathlessly. "Wot language can a lady use?" Not that she cared. Not in that moment.

"Oh dear," he said, his jaw flexed, no, ground down.

Neither one of them laughed. A few feet separated them. Moonlight drenched them. Blake stared. Violette's pulse raced with alarming speed. It seemed difficult, even unnatural, to breathe. But perhaps that was because of the rioting fragrances they were immersed in. The gardens were almost suffocating. Roses, lilies, amber, freesia, and tuberose mingled together, at once overpowering and erotic, exciting. It was another onslaught on their already overburdened senses.

Violette thought about his kiss on the terrace outside Harding Hall. Every fiber of her being quivered with anticipation, with need. She met his brilliant gaze. "Wot?" she finally managed in another whisper.

His temples were throbbing. "I think that taking air is not a good idea. Let us return to the ball. I shall introduce you around some more."

"I don't want to meet any more guests," she said bluntly. Why didn't he come closer to her? Surely, surely, he would kiss her. Violette knew he could see her trembling. "Blake?" It was only half of a question. It was also an invitation.

But Blake did not step closer, nor did he pull her into his embrace. Instead, he turned his back abruptly on her, and stared up at the moon.

⊰ *Fourteen* ⊱

VIOLETTE had the awful feeling that if she did not do something, Blake would leave her standing there alone in the gardens. She summoned up all her courage, took a deep breath, and walked over to him. He turned slightly but did not move.

She could not smile. She failed to think of a single intelligent thing to say. She could only speak from the heart. "Blake," she said huskily. "I've yet t' thank you fer your gift an' . . . for everything you've done fer me since we met." She wet her lips. "And fer tonight. Fer this lovely night."

His gaze, holding her eyes, dipped to her mouth. "It has been my pleasure," he said slowly.

"Do you know," she continued shakily, "the first time I ever saw you I really thought you were a prince?"

He started. "Come, Violette," he began, mildly amused.

"No, it's the truth." She felt herself drowning in his long-lashed, turquoise-blue eyes. "Eight years ago. There was a ball. Here. At Harding House." Perspiration trickled down between her breasts. "I wanted something to eat. We were going to steal plum puddin' an' lamb from your kitchens. But I couldn't help sneakin' up to the window to look inside the house at the ball an' the dancers. I saw you. I remember it as clear as if it were yesterday."

His gaze roamed over her face, his expression not merely strained, but somber. "You are probably mistaken."

"No." She shook her head. "You were with a woman, older than you, a golden lady. I remember you took her onto the terrace an' danced with her."

Blake's chest seemed to heave under his snowy white shirt-front and black tailcoat. "I do not remember. I was a boy eight years ago."

"Not to me." Her smile was shy, tremulous. "I was eight years old."

They stared. Blake finally lifted his hand and touched her cheek with his fingertips. He did not say a word.

But his eyes spoke volumes. And Violette's heart sang, and she trembled, swaying toward him.

And suddenly he had her shoulders in his palms and she was pressed against the entire length of his body. Before Violette's lids closed she caught a glimpse of the wild brilliance in his eyes, and something explosive crested inside her. Blake slid his powerful arms around her, bent her backwards, his mouth taking hers.

Violette had never even dreamed a kiss could be so powerful and earth-shattering, so overwhelming. His mouth was hard, hungry, yet hardly hurtful, and his strong, large hands roamed her bare shoulders and upper back, only to press down hard on her waist. His grip tightened. His mouth opened hers. His tongue sought out and flicked hers. The pressure of their lips continued, increasing.

A soft, wild sound escaped Violette as she clung to his broad shoulders. He ripped his mouth from hers, only to cover her throat and jaw with hot, hungry kisses. Violette moaned, shivering with pleasure.

His grip tightened yet again and he claimed her mouth an-other time, even more forcefully than before. Violette tried to kiss him back with all of the passion inside her body, inside her soul. He was so beautiful; being with him this way was so beautiful. Her palms slid from his shoulders to his face. She wanted more. So much more.

And then Blake stopped kissing her. His harsh breathing sounded loudly as he slowly straightened. "God," he said, their gazes meeting. "God," he whispered again.

Violette smiled at him. Tears of happiness filled her eyes, tears of happiness, of wonder, of joy. How she loved him. How she loved him with all her heart and all her soul. She had never known she could feel this way for anyone—man, woman, or child—before.

But his expression changed as he stared back at her. He dropped his hands, stepped away from her. His eyes had darkened with dismay.

Violette did not understand. "Blake?"

"I apologize. Once again. That should not have happened." He was harsh. Rigid. Tense.

She gasped. "Why not?!"

He raised a hand, as if to forestall her denial. "I lost my head. Your beauty is uncommon."

"No," Violette whispered. Even she knew that this was about far more than beauty. "Wot can you be saying? Wot can you be thinking? That was wonderful, the best thing I ever—"

"No," he snapped, his tone like a whiplash. "Don't you understand?" he cried.

"No," Violette panted. "I do not understand. But don't tell me we are just friends!"

He stared at her.

"I think you love me," she heard herself say, "just like I love you." And then she wished, desperately, that she had not stepped so far out on such a shaky limb.

He blanched. A huge, monumental silence had settled over the gardens, around them. "No." His voice rang out. "I am sorry you do not understand. But a man does not have to love a woman in order to want her the way that I want you. I am sorry, Violette."

She wanted to clap her hands over her ears. " 'Ow can you say such a thing to me?! 'Ow can you be so cruel?!"

"We had better go back inside," he said heavily. And without waiting for her to reply, he gripped her arm and led her to the house.

*   *   *

He did not look at her as they rapidly traversed the corridor. Violette refused to cry. Her heart was broken, thoroughly, but she would not shed a single tear in front of him.

She was stunned.

His strides faltered as the sounds of the guests became louder, coming from the library where the gentlemen smoked cigars, drank scotch whisky and French brandy, and played billiards and whist. He glanced at her. "Are you going to weep?" he asked.

Violette shook her head, unable to speak. *He could not have meant what he had said, he could not.*

"Violette," he said, his tone harsh, "this is all my fault. We should not have gone outside. I should not have danced attendance upon you. I am sorry."

"But I do not want yew to be sorry," she whispered, forgetting all about her you's.

He froze, his gaze scanning her face. "I cannot," he began, and hesitated. "I can*not* give you what you want."

She felt her face crumble even as she saw his regret and she shoved the back of her hand to her mouth. Something welled inside of her, but she was bloody well damned if she would let it out. *Oh, gawd. A fool. An utter, stupid, idiotic fool—that was what she was.*

"You cannot go back to the ball in the state you are in," he said flatly, taking her arm. Violette did not protest as he turned her around. She ducked her head because a lady in a pale gold dress was coming toward them. Blake was gripping Violette's elbow and she felt his tension increase.

"Hello, Blake," the woman said politely, her voice low and soft.

Violette immediately looked up, staring at the woman who was breathtakingly beautiful, her features strong and arresting, her gaze green and direct. She had honey blond hair pulled back tightly into a simple chignon, and she was older than either Violette or Blake. She wore a spectacular diamond and emerald choker but no other jewelry.

"Hello, Lady Cantwell. How are you?" Blake asked.

His tone was odd. Violette's gaze flew from the lady's gown—one of the most exquisitely beaded lace creations she had ever seen—to Blake's face. She could not decipher the look in his eyes.

"Very well, thank you." Lady Cantwell smiled into Blake's eyes then regarded Violette. "Hello. I am Gabriella Cantwell."

Violette could not smile back. She had glimpsed something wistful in her smile and sorrowful in her eyes when she had been speaking to Blake. Did he mean something to this woman?

"This is Lady Goodwin, from York," Blake interjected. "She has but recently come to town."

"I do hope you are enjoying our wonderful city," Lady Cantwell said. She turned to Blake. "Once again, your mother has outdone herself. The ball is an outstanding success."

"Thank you," Blake said.

"Lady Goodwin, it was a pleasure meeting you, and it was good to see you again, Blake." With one final warm smile that somehow encompassed them both, Gabriella Cantwell moved past them and down the corridor.

Blake regarded her back for an instant and then took Violette's arm. He did not look at her and a few moments later they were in an unlit room. Violette did not move as Blake struck a match and turned up the wick on a gaslamp. They were in a beautifully furnished parlor, one opulent with fabrics and rugs from the Orient. Violette sank down on a tufted beige ottoman, her elbows on her thighs. She refused to meet his eyes.

"I am going to get Catherine," he said.

Violette did not answer. Blake left, closing the door behind him. Violette finally looked at her taffeta-draped knees. She did not understand what had happened. The evening had been perfect, like a fairy tale in which she was Cinderella. She was afraid to understand. Was it as simple as Blake claimed? He lusted for her in a common, sordid way? Or was it that she wasn't good enough for him? *Was that it?*

And who was that woman? Lady Cantwell had somehow seemed familiar. Violette felt more miserable than before. Lady Cantwell might be close to forty, which was what Violette suspected, but she was one of those women who only became more intriguing with time, and Violette knew that she could not compete with her if she wanted Blake, too.

The door opened and closed. Catherine stared, then hurried over. "My dear! Violette, Blake said you are distraught and in need of female company. What has happened?" Catherine pulled up a bergère and managed to sink into it in spite of the fullness of her skirts. "I saw you earlier and thought you were having a wonderful evening!"

"I was. It was perfect. A dream come true." Violette shook

her head. "I wish I could 'ate him, but I can't."

Catherine regarded her with concern. "What has he done. Why are you so close to weeping?"

"I won't cry," Violette said thickly. She raised her eyes, her mouth firmed. "Niver. I ain't cried since they locked me up in the union when I was a little girl."

"The union?" Catherine whispered, her eyes wide.

Violette stood abruptly. "The union. The workhouse. The poorhouse. It's where they put orphans, feeding 'em gruel an' making 'em tread steps that go nowhere." She wasn't in the mood to make the effort to speak like a real lady. After all, she wasn't genuine, she was a fraud, and Blake knew it. She rubbed her gloved fist over her eyes.

Catherine gasped. "You were in the poorhouse? You poor dear!"

"Don't feel sorry fer me." Violette walked away. She stared blindly out of the window at the gardens where Blake had just kissed her. Her heart was filled with pain. *Why didn't he love her back? Why was she born Violet Cooper? Why couldn't she be a real lady?*

Catherine also rose to her feet. "What has Blake done?"

Violette turned. " 'E kissed me. I didn't know a kiss could be so wild an' grand."

Catherine pinkened. "Oh, dear."

"Bloody 'ell," Violette said savagely, almost spitting. " 'E kissed me, then said 'e's sorry, so sorry, but it's just lust."

Catherine gasped. "Blake said *that*?"

Violette stared at Catherine. " 'As 'e ever kissed yew?" Her chin was tilted up.

Catherine started, and shook her head. "No. Not in the manner I believe you are speaking about."

"An' 'e won't. Not unless yer 'is wife. Because yer a lady, an' I'm dirt."

"My dear, you mustn't think that way," Catherine cried, rushing to her. She took Violette's hands and smiled, but it was forced, her eyes filled with worry. "I am sure that he does care for you."

"No." Violette rubbed her eyes again. "One day 'e's gonna marry a lady just like yew. Me 'e'd niver consider."

Catherine hesitated, touching the diamond-and-pearl choker on her throat. "Violette, dear. You mustn't think of Blake that way. He doesn't wish to marry at all, at least not for a very long time."

Her nostrils flared. She felt choked up again. "I'd wait."

Catherine did not respond.

"But I guess I'd 'ave to wait forever, now wouldn't I?" she asked bitterly.

Catherine was frozen, her color fading. "This is all my fault," she whispered.

" 'Ow could this be yer fault?" Violette asked glumly. "Yew ain't t' blame."

Now Catherine blushed.

"Wot? Wot's goin' on?"

"I am sorry," Catherine said with apparent guilt. "I was worried about how you would make do during this evening. I asked Blake to help, perhaps to court you, so that everyone would accept you."

"Yew wot?" Violette gasped. "Yew told 'im to court me? Yew mean, 'e was just playin' a game?"

"No! We were trying to protect you because we are both so fond of you," Catherine said quickly.

"Did yew tell 'im to kiss me, too?" Violette asked harshly.

"Of course not."

Violette turned her back on Catherine abruptly. She placed her palm over her thundering chest. It was hard to breathe. "Why did I come 'ere tonight? 'Ow stupid I am!"

Catherine rose and walked over to Violette. "Dear. I am a new friend, but truly I *am* your friend. I want to help you. I have an idea. I think that I can."

"Yew can't help me." Violette felt her nose turning red. "Not unless yew got magic t' make me the kind o' lady Blake would think o' the way he thinks o' yew.' "

Catherine smiled now. "Unfortunately, I am not a magician. But perhaps I can be a teacher of sorts."

Violette was cautious. "A teacher?"

"Yes." Her eyes bright, Catherine sank down on the crimson sofa. She clapped her hands, more animated than Violette had ever seen her. "Violette, if you spoke correctly, and walked more gently, and understood the propriety which guides us all, the rules and etiquette, and, of course, changed your wardrobe, why I do believe you could have everyone fooled into thinking that you are one of us!"

Violette made a face. "Wot are you blatherin' about?"

"Do you want to be a real lady?" Catherine cried, on her feet.

"A real lady?" Violette blinked. "O' course I do. But that s impossible. It'd take a miracle."

"No. It is not impossible. It would not take a miracle. What it would take is a very determined teacher, and a very dedicated pupil."

Violette stared, suddenly understanding.

"I shall be your teacher," Catherine declared. "And I shall turn you into a lady that we could actually present at Court!"

Violette did not move. "An' Blake? Can we fool 'im?"

Their gazes met. "We can try," Catherine said vehemently—and a conspiracy was formed.

Violette couldn't help feeling a little bit better. She watched Catherine move across the ballroom, pausing repeatedly to converse with those she knew. Catherine was the epitome of grace and gentility. Maybe all was not lost. Violette wasn't sure that Catherine could turn her into a real lady, but she was determined to try Catherine's wild scheme. She had never wanted to try anything more. The stakes were so very high.

She saw Blake standing across the room.

The stakes were the love of an incredible man.

Blake had seen her as well. For one moment their gazes locked, and then he turned away. Violette stiffened, her small smile instantly fading.

She walked closer to a pillar, hiding behind it. Blake didn't think she was good enough for him to love. Was she a fool to think that she could change his mind? What if Catherine were successful in teaching her to act and speak like a lady? Wouldn't he feel differently about her then? And if he did not?

Her final thoughts were too painful to contemplate. Violette moved away from the pillar. Although it was early, and she hadn't eaten or drank anything other than the flute of champagne, she would go home. There was no point in lingering, not tonight. And tomorrow at eleven A.M. she would call on Catherine at her father's town house as Catherine had suggested.

But Violette had not taken more than three steps toward the steps at the other end of the ballroom when she faltered, dismayed. Standing not far from those steps was a very formidable, stout figure—that of Lady Joanna Feldstone.

Inwardly Violette groaned. She wanted to leave, but she did not wish to walk past her stepdaughter. Oh, no. Joanna had always hated her, but at least when Sir Thomas was alive she'd been forced to be civil. Violette couldn't help but recall their last encounter at Goodwin Manor. She paused, undecided as to what to do, certain a disaster would ensue if Joanna saw her now. And this time she had no doubt that Blake would not rescue her.

And then she glimpsed Lord Farrow standing with a group of guests. And although he was immersed in a pleasant conversation, his gaze was turned upon her. Violette immediately smiled at him.

He returned her smile, quickly detaching himself from the ensemble. He strode to her, obviously pleased. "Lady Goodwin. I was hoping we might speak again tonight."

Violette saw, from the corner of her eye, the moment that Joanna noticed her. The other woman froze, staring openly, with hostility. Violette took a breath and smiled again at Farrow. "Actually," she said, her heart hammering, "I was about to leave."

His brows rose. "So early?! The ball has only just begun, and we have yet to share a waltz."

Violette hesitated, because Blake had just walked into her line of vision, behind Farrow. He was regarding them both impassively, making it impossible for Violette to guess what he was thinking. But first Joanna, now Blake. Violette didn't think she could take too much more tonight.

Blake turned abruptly away from her. It was such a simple action, yet it said more than words ever could. Violette stared, stricken, unable to look away.

"You will stay a while longer? No one leaves a ball just as it is just beginning." Farrow took her arm.

"Me brother is ill an' I am worried about 'im," Violette fabricated quickly. "I niver intended to stay the evening. But would you be a good enough gentleman to walk me to the door?"

He studied her, finally acquiescing. "I am sorry about your brother. Will I see you at the Merritts' dance tomorrow evening?"

"I don't know," Violette said. Of course she had not been invited, but she could not tell Farrow that. As they crossed the room she darted one last glance at Blake. If he was aware of them leaving, he did not show it, for his back remained turned to them as he spoke to a group of guests. Violette could not wait to leave.

And while Violette avoided looking at Joanna as she and Farrow approached, Joanna stared very directly at them both. Violette's cheeks started to burn.

And then Joanna said, quite loudly, so all those standing around the steps could hear, "I do not believe it! My father is not even cold in his grave and she has taken up with someone else! She is not even in mourning!"

Violette flushed, meeting Joanna's blazing regard. What had she done to make this woman hate her so?

"But of course, a female like *that* would not understand the concept of mourning," Joanna cried while another matron patted her arm soothingly.

Farrow smiled down at Violette as if he were oblivious to Joanna's words—which was an impossibility. There was no way he could not have heard. Violette shrugged free of his arm. Enough was enough.

Her hands found her hips. "Mebbe you're just jealous, you fat old witch!" she said loudly. "Could it be that you're in love with Lord Farrow?"

Joanna gasped. Beside her, Violette heard Farrow chuckle. "We had better go," he said softly.

But before Violette could agree, Joanna shrugged free of the baron, who had tried to restrain her, and she positively blocked Violette and Farrow's path. "You!" she cried. "You liar— adulteress—murderess!"

Violette gasped, blanching.

Farrow was stunned. "Lady Feldstone, did we actually hear you correctly?"

"You most certainly did," Joanna said, red-faced. "How can *she* be here? *When she killed my father?*"

Gasps sounded from all around them. People were turning to stare. Not even pretending otherwise.

"I didn't kill Sir Thomas," Violette began in a throaty voice. Sweat gathered on her brow.

"Rat poison," Joanna shrieked. And she leapt forward. But before she could attack Violette physically, Blake appeared, grabbing her arms and restraining her.

"Lady Feldstone. If you insist on continuing this very un- seemly conversation, I shall insist that you leave my father's home." Jon had materialized behind him, and so had Catherine. In fact, Blake, his brother, and Catherine had formed a semi- circle around her and Farrow, as if protecting her from Joanna.

Violette had never been more horrified, and at the same time, she wanted to hug Blake for supporting her against Joanna. She could not, though, for Farrow held her arm even more tightly than before. But she was grateful to him as well.

Joanna faced Blake. "Why do you defend her again? Why don't you ask her yourself about the rat poison? I *know* she poisoned my father."

Violette cried out. She clung to Farrow. Her wild eyes found Blake, who started.

Blake's eyes narrowed. He said, "I beg your pardon, Lady Feldstone. I have no wish to continue this discussion."

Violette opened her mouth to deny purchasing the arsenic, but no words came out. She had bought the rat poison, but not to kill Sir Thomas, only to kill one big, annoying rat.

Blake snapped, "Farrow, as long as you are escorting Lady Goodwin to the door, why don't you do so now? I suggest you put her in a Harding carriage. I will loan her mine."

Farrow nodded, but said, "Actually, I will see Lady Goodwin safely home myself." And he propelled Violette past the crowd before she even knew what was happening. All around them people began to talk in animated, speculative whispers. Everyone stared at her.

And as she went up the steps she half-turned, to meet Blake's glinting eyes. She wanted to stop, go back, tell him it wasn't true. But surely he knew that?

He took a step backwards, away from her, his piercing gaze on her face.

And Violette cringed. Panic overwhelmed her, and with it, despair. He thought the worst.

⊰ *Fifteen* ⊱

VIOLETTE stumbled as Farrow guided her past the two footmen standing silently in front of Harding House. His grip was firm enough to hold her upright. Violette was in the throes of despair.

The evening had been a disaster. But surely everyone did not believe that awful Joanna Feldstone? Yet Violette was afraid. If only she hadn't bought rat poison the day before Sir Thomas's death.

They paused on the sidewalk. "I will take you home," Farrow said, signaling his carriage.

Violette glanced up at his handsome face. He did not make her catch her breath the way that Blake did. He was an impressive man, but nothing like Blake. She did not trust him; Blake she trusted implicitly. She had no wish to be accompanied home by Farrow, especially as she had not forgotten Blake's warnings. "I don't mind takin' a hansom," she said thickly.

"It is my pleasure, Lady Goodwin," Farrow said, his penetrating gaze holding hers.

Footsteps suddenly sounded behind them and they both turned. Blake said, "I am sure it is your pleasure, Farrow. But I have already ordered my phaeton around for Lady Goodwin."

Violette was relieved, yet she had not forgotten all that had transpired between them that night. Aware of Farrow's hand on her elbow, she desperately searched Blake's face for some clue as to what he was thinking. But his expression was cool and unreadable. Violette's heart sank.

She did not care, she decided, if the entire world thought her guilty of murder—as long as Blake thought her to be innocent.

"Ah, so you will escort Lady Goodwin home?" Farrow said coolly. "Am I poaching, Blake?"

Blake stiffened. "That is unforgivable, a slur upon Lady Goodwin's character. I would watch my tongue if I were you, Farrow."

Farrow's smile flashed dangerously. He glanced at Violette. "I hold Lady Goodwin in the highest possible regard."

Violette looked from one man to the other, feeling as if they were about to leap at one another like hungry dogs fighting over a single mutton bone.

"That is a relief," Blake said, his smile as brittle and as brief. "And, no, I am not escorting Lady Goodwin home, I am loaning her the use of my vehicle. Ah"—his smile was as cold as his eyes—"here it is. Violette?"

She jerked at the sound of her name. Farrow had finally released her, but she felt him start, too. Violette knew he was waiting to say good-bye to her, but she only had eyes for Blake. "Blake. Thank you."

He didn't quite shrug, gesturing toward his racy black phaeton, avoiding her eyes.

Violette turned toward Farrow, trembling, managing a small smile. Nothing had changed. She was hurt to the quick. "Thank you for yer concern," she said, finally unscrambling her wits.

"I look forward to seeing you again." Farrow bowed. He

did not seem very pleased, either with Violette or the turn of events.

Blake took Violette's arm, his grip uncompromising. Before Violette could take another breath, he was propelling her to his phaeton. Violette shot another glance at his hard face; he did not even glance at her.

The coachman held the door open. Blake began to hand Violette up, but she balked. "Blake. I . . ."

He interrupted. "I do not know where you now live. You will have to give the address to Godson yourself."

Violette finally stepped up into the carriage. The door was almost slammed in her face. Blake returned to the curb. His gaze seemed to focus just above her head on the phaeton's gleaming gold molding.

"Blake," Violette cried, gripping the sill of the open carriage window with both hands. "Surely yew do not believe that 'orrid Lady Feldstone?"

He eyed her as the phaeton dipped under the coachman's weight. The vehicle shifted.

"Blake?"

Their gazes finally met and locked. "No," he said. "I do not believe the accusations."

Violette stared at him as the phaeton began to roll swiftly away. Why was she not reassured? His face was set in stone. There were no traces of warmth there.

She continued to stare out of the window at him as she was driven away. Violette watched him turn and walk back up the wide stone steps of Harding House. She finally collapsed on the cool leather seat, perilously close to tears. And now all that she could think of was that Blake had the entire evening to enjoy—with someone like the so very beautiful Lady Cantwell.

When Blake reentered the house, late guests were arriving, but he ignored them, striding down the hall. Blake let himself into the parlor where he had sent Catherine to comfort Violette. He strode directly to the liquor cabinet and poured himself a double scotch whisky.

He could not shake Violette's stricken expression from his mind. He himself could easily strangle Joanna Feldstone for her outrageous accusations. Violette was not capable of murder, and although she had clearly married Sir Thomas for his wealth and position, he knew her well enough to know that it had been far more complicated than that. She had married him, he knew, to escape from the life she led; to escape the streets of London and her impoverished beginnings. And she had been, amazingly, very fond of Sir Thomas. Her grief over his death had been genuine. As had her gratitude for all that he had done. Violette had not killed her husband, of that Blake did not have a single doubt.

But he was very uneasy. Violette had not denied buying rat poison. But perhaps she had been too shocked with the accusations to respond. And what if Sir Thomas had been murdered?

Ralph's glowering image came immediately to mind.

And there was always guilt by association.

Blake paced, downing half of the scotch. Perhaps only one thing was clear. He had made a vast, nearly irreparable mistake tonight by kissing her. He had found Violette startlingly beautiful from the moment he had first met her, beautiful and enchanting. He had wanted her then, but not half as much as he wanted her now, and that was where the real danger lay. In fact, tonight was the first time that he had spoken with Gabriella without being swept away by too many memories to count.

He had left the door to the library open and Jon suddenly appeared. Blake was glad to have his thoughts interrupted. Jon walked over and laid his hand on Blake's shoulder. "I thought I might find you here."

Blake intended to smile, knew he grimaced instead. "Have a drink?"

"Why not?" Jon's smile was characteristic, revealing his dimple, one identical to Blake's. "This is a party; too bad you are so unhappy."

Blake moved back to the sideboard and poured his brother a hefty scotch, handing it to him. "Lady Feldstone should be strangled."

"Or muzzled at the very least," Jon agreed. "I'm sure our dog master has the appropriate items in the kennels. Shall we call him?"

Blake leaned his hip on the sideboard, unamused. "Violette is not capable of murder. Anyone can see that."

"Really?" Jon studied Blake.

"You think her a murderess?" Blake was shocked.

"Whoa! Slow down. I personally believe her incapable of murder, just as I believe that Sir Thomas died a natural death. However, Lady Goodwin comes from questionable origins, and that is what the world shall consider first."

Blake sighed. "That is what I am afraid of. Did you see her face? She was humiliated, mortified."

"Yes," Jon said, his gaze piercing. "You seem very concerned."

Blake jerked. "What does that mean?"

"It means," Jon said softly, "that you are fighting a losing battle. Why don't you admit it?"

Blake stiffened. "All right. I am fighting a battle. I will admit that I am very fond of Violette Goodwin. But *that* is as far as it goes."

Jon had the audacity to laugh.

"Do you seek to provoke me?"

"No," Jon said, still grinning. "Well, maybe just a bit."

"You know," Blake said calmly, "I am fully aware that you and Catherine set me up tonight, suggesting that I court Violette in front of the guests."

Jon feigned a wide-eyed look of innocence. "Come, Blake! That is farfetched. But tell me this. Who told you to take Violette Goodwin outside? To kiss her?"

Blake stared. Then he had to smile. "Touché."

"Perhaps," Jon said mildly, "you should court Lady Goodwin in earnest, honorably, sparing both you and her much grief."

Blake's smile vanished. "I am *not* looking for a wife," he finally said.

"How adamant you are," Jon returned. He studied Blake. "Let me give you some brotherly advice. Lay Gabriella to rest, Blake. And do it now, before you lose Violette to someone like Robert Farrow."

Violette stood in front of the Dearfield town house, screwing up her courage, as the hansom which had deposited her there drove away. Clad in a navy blue dress with black lace trim and a black sash tied in a bow, she clutched her lime green reticule tightly. She was afraid. What if Catherine believed the ugly accusations and no longer wished to tutor her in the behavior of a lady?

But they did have an appointment for that morning. Unfortunately, though, if Catherine had wished to cancel it she would not have been able to even send Violette a note, because Violette had never disclosed her current address to her.

Taking a deep breath, Violette approached the five-story town house, walking through wrought-iron gates. Petunias lined the elm-shaded walk, azaleas bloomed on the front stoop. Violette used the door knocker. A butler instantly appeared.

"Lady Goodwin?" he intoned.

Violette flinched, waiting for him to deliver a fell blow and tell her that Catherine no longer wished to see her.

"Do come in. Lady Dearfield will be downstairs shortly. She hopes you will take breakfast with her."

Flooded with relief, Violette followed the elderly butler into a sunny, spacious foyer. Oak floors gleamed. Portraits were hanging on the papered walls. She glimpsed her reflection in one tall Venetian mirror. Two pink spots had appeared on her cheeks.

Violette tucked escaping strands of hair into her bonnet, which was bedecked with orange silk flowers, and hurried down the hall after the butler. She peeked into a spacious, graciously appointed salon as she did so. Although the Dearfield town house was in no way as impressive as the Hardings' city mansion, it was very, very pleasant.

The breakfast room was also drenched in sunlight and papered in a tree-of-life print. Yellow silk draperies were pulled back to expose the flowering back gardens. One ornate side-table was cluttered with covered dishes, and Violette sniffed appreciatively. She could smell baked ham and fresh bread.

The butler hesitated. Violette smiled at him and sat down at the table. He turned and left. A moment later Catherine appeared, looking almost angelic in a pale blue morning dress. And although she was beautiful, Violette thought the dress quite plain.

"My dear," she said, smiling. "I am so glad to see you." But her smile faded as she glanced at Violette, who had stood up. Catherine looked her over carefully.

"I'm glad, too," Violette said, her hold tightening on her reticule. "I was afraid you might have changed yer mind after last night." She spoke very carefully. She was going to become a lady, she had no other choice—and if it were at all possible, she would win Blake's heart.

Catherine frowned. "That was horrid, Violette. I was appalled with Lady Feldstone's behavior—and by the by, her behavior was not that of a lady." Catherine did not sit down. "A lady is gracious, genteel, and polite—*always.*"

"She'll get hers," Violette said seriously.

"I beg your pardon, Violette, but what you just said is not ladylike either." Catherine was reproving in spite of her gentle tone. "And a lady would never call another lady names as you did last night."

Violette frowned. "You mean, I'm supposed to be all nice and charming when she shouts to the world that I murdered me husband?"

"Yes. Two wrongs never make a right. And it is *my* husband, my dear. It is *my* lord, *my* dog, *my* cat." Catherine patted her arm. "We are beginning our lessons now. You must be gracious, genteel, forgiving. You might answer me by saying, 'I am sure Lady Feldstone did not mean what she said; perhaps she was not quite feeling well last night.' "

"But she meant it," Violette said, bewildered.

"But a lady would never be reproachful. You must be kind, and above any such behavior. In the end, your elegance will prove that you are the real lady, and she the impostor."

"I think I understand," Violette said slowly. She began to smile. She liked the idea of out-ladying Joanna Feldstone. It occurred to her that if she had a doubt about what to do or say, she should try to imagine what Catherine would do or say. And she could not imagine Catherine ever responding to Lady Feldstone in anything other than a calm, civil way.

"As long as we are sidetracked, I wish to add something else about a lady's behavior."

"What is that?" Violette asked.

"A lady never leaves a fête or soirée, or a ball, with a gentleman. Not even a widow like yourself."

Violette tensed. "Blake sent me outside with Lord Farrow."

"That was incorrect. It was also incorrect of him, and you, Violette, to adjourn to the gardens alone together."

Violette blushed, recalling Blake's stunning kiss. Something twisted inside of her, hurtfully. And with the stabbing came fear. What if she had no chance to win Blake's love? What if her determination were not enough?

"Violette." Catherine's voice was kind, her eyes soft and sympathetic. "You must never allow a gentleman to kiss you, unless you wish to give him the impression that you are not really a lady and you are eager to be with him in a most unladylike fashion."

Violette bit her lip, nodding.

"The only exception, I believe, is if you love him and are marrying him."

Violette's pulse leapt. "I see."

"Good. Now, we shall share breakfast, but correctly." Catherine smiled. "A lady does not wear her hat to breakfast, Violette, but of course you did not know we would share breakfast today, so it is acceptable for you to leave it on." For a moment, Catherine studied Violette's bonnet, and she sighed. "We shall discuss fashion later. Now, you must wear a bonnet whenever you leave the house, and certainly you leave it on when dinner is taken outside the home, or at an afternoon tea. Gloves are *not* worn at breakfast, but they are worn at *all other times*, including at dinner and teas, outside the home. Inside the home, of course, you must always wear gloves, even for supper. You do know, of course, that you must expect to change your gloves six times a day." Catherine smiled. "A lady should own eighteen pairs of gloves, a dozen white kid, a half dozen white silk."

"Eighteen pairs," Violette cried, already confused.

"That allows time for laundering. A lady *never* wears dirty gloves, and a good rule to follow is this: If you are spending a day out of doors, a pair should be changed every three hours, in which case you will change your gloves more than six times that day."

"More than six times," Violette said, amazed. How could she remember all the rules about gloves? What if there were as many rules about everything else?

"And at a ball like the one last night," Catherine was cheerful, "you must have a pair to change into sometime before midnight. Dusty gloves are exceedingly unattractive, Violette. They are inelegant and unfashionable." Catherine's gaze strayed again to Violette's hat. Violette had the feeling that she did not particularly like it.

"I didn't have no idea," she said slowly.

"I know. And although we shall have our speech lessons later, it is 'any,' not 'no.' *I did not have any idea.* Please don't contract words like do and not."

Violette nodded, worried. "How can I remember all this?"

"Don't worry," Catherine said, patting her back. They walked over to the sideboard. "We shall go over everything again and again. You may take notes if you wish."

Violette hesitated. "I can't write."

Catherine whirled, eyes wide.

"I'm sorry," Violette whispered, shrinking a little inside. Blake had had the very same reaction—as if not being able to write were the most terrible crime.

Catherine recovered. "I am hiring a tutor. You shall have a

professional teacher to instruct you in speech and writing.'' She hesitated. "Can you read?''

"No," Violette whispered, flushed. "Catherine, I . . . I don't think I have enough money . . . ,'' she began.

"A lady *never* discusses her finances," Catherine said firmly. "And the word 'money' is not a part of a lady's vocabulary. The word does not exist.''

Violette nodded, her pulse hammering. "Then how am I going to pay for a teacher?''

"Violette, you are discussing finances!" Catherine then hugged her. "Never again. I shall arrange everything. Because we are friends.''

Violette blinked, amazed. "You would do that for me?''

Catherine smiled and looked at the floor. "Perhaps I am a romantic fool, but, yes, I would, and I will.''

Violette stared. Tears filled her eyes. Catherine was the kindest, nicest, most wonderful human being she had ever met. And then Violette decided that she had to succeed in what was beginning to seem like an impossible task. She had never wanted anything more, and she was not going to disappoint Catherine. Violette was determined.

And then, of course, there was Blake.

÷ *Sixteen* ÷

VIOLETTE'S lesson took place early in the mornings, so she could continue her employment at Lady Allister's. She not only had an instructor who was teaching her speech, reading, and writing, Catherine had also hired a dance instructor for her. Now the strains of a waltz filled the salon where Catherine played the pianoforte. Violette whirled about the salon in the arms of the slim, gray-haired Frenchman who had been teaching her the various dances every lady ought to know. For the first time since she had begun her lessons over a week ago, Violette was becoming relaxed. Dancing, she realized, was fun, once one stopped worrying about what to do and stepping on one's partner's toes.

Monsieur Montrail swirled Violette about and then the waltz ended. They stood together breathlessly in the center of the salon. Catherine slid around on the piano bench and, beaming, she applauded. "That was wonderful,'' she cried.

Violette slowly smiled. Her pulse was still racing from the physical exertion of the dance and the pleasure of having done it well.

"Madame Goodwin," Monsieur Montrail said, smiling very slightly under his iron-gray moustache. "You have outdone yourself. Today I am pleased."

"Thank you," Violette said, still breathless.

Montrail bowed at Violette and at Catherine. "Until tomorrow. And I think our lessons shall soon end."

Catherine rose, her daffodil yellow silk gown belling about her. "I believe you are correct, Monsieur," she said happily.

As Montrail left, Violette faced Catherine. "Do you mean that I have learned to dance adequately?" she asked.

"You were beautiful, Violette. Very graceful and you did not miss a step."

Violette beamed with pleasure. "I do like dancing, Catherine."

Catherine touched her arm. "You have been a brilliant pupil, dear. I had no idea our lessons would go this well."

"Really?" Violette was hopeful. Blake's image, always in her mind, loomed more strongly there.

"You can pass as a lady. No one would ever suspect otherwise."

Violette wasn't as confident as Catherine, for she did not feel like a lady, and she knew who she was. She would never forget growing up hungry, cold, dirty, and homeless in St. Giles. It remained an effort to walk and talk correctly, and she had to think carefully about all the etiquette she had thus far learned. Sometimes she could not remember a rule. And while she had mastered the alphabet, while she could now write her own name, she could not read, nor could she pen anything else. Perhaps my true colors will always show, Violette thought.

"What is wrong?" Catherine asked. "You should be thrilled to death, on top of the world."

Violette smiled briefly. "I might appear to be a lady, but the truth will never change, now will it?"

Catherine stared. "I am not sure of that," she finally said.

Violette sighed, walking away, her pale lavender skirts, trimmed only with a darker purple embroidery at the hem, floating about her as she moved. Catherine had done far more than teach her fashion, she had redesigned Violette's wardrobe, removing lace and beads, flowers and embroidery, and all sorts of trim from every garment Violette owned.

She stared out of the window at the street outside. A few coaches, carriages, and horsemen were passing by. It had begun to drizzle, and the single gentleman pedestrian had opened a black umbrella. "Blake will always know the truth," Violette said quietly without turning to face Catherine.

Catherine was silent for a moment. "Yes, he will."

Violette turned. "But you think that I can win him, anyway?" She desperately needed reassurance.

Catherine hesitated. "I think that when a woman has the kind of feelings for a man that you have for Blake, she must do everything in her power to win his love—or forever ask herself, what if."

Violette folded her arms across her bosom. "If this doesn't work, nothing will. This is my last chance."

Catherine was somber. "I would probably agree."

Oh, God, Violette thought, but she did not voice her unladylike thoughts aloud.

"You will have your first opportunity to impress Blake this Thursday night. Lord Pierce is having a dinner dance, and you are invited," Catherine said.

Violette stared, rigid. She finally inhaled hard and walked back to the window. She had never been more afraid of the future in her life.

Blake could not help himself. All week long he had wondered about what was going on at the Dearfield town house. He knew about Catherine's wild scheme. Every time he had seen her since the ball, she smiled serenely at him, as if she were keeping a huge secret to herself. It was Jon who had told Blake about the lessons.

He told himself he should stay away. What Violette Goodwin did or did not do was not his concern, but he failed to follow his own advice. That afternoon Blake's phaeton stopped in front of the Dearfields' London residence. As he stepped down onto the curb and quickly strode up the walk to the five-story brick town house, he had the distinct feeling that he was no longer in control of himself or his life. He told himself that he was being overly imaginative, a fool.

The butler met him in the foyer and told him that the Ladies Dearfield and Goodwin were in the salon. Blake thanked him, and, because he was almost family, he preceded Thompson to his destination.

But before Blake had crossed the threshold of the salon he

saw them and stopped, reaching out to silence the butler. Neither Catherine nor Violette, sharing a quiet tea, had heard him approach.

He signaled the servant to leave, staring at the two women. What a pretty picture they made. Catherine was beautiful in a bright yellow gown, Violette striking in lavender. In fact, his first glimpse of Violette had made him feel very much like he was being kicked in the chest by a donkey. He had forgotten just how lovely she was, or had she somehow grown lovelier?

Blake almost turned around to leave, but the women were animated, talking and laughing together, and he could not move. The day's earlier drizzle had passed and the sun was attempting to break through the clouds, rays of sunshine streaking through the windows upon them both. Violette said, "Lady Dearfield, you do tell the most amusing tales! Might I pour you another cup of tea?"

Blake's mouth dropped open. Her enunciation had been almost perfect. She certainly did not sound like, or appear to be, a shopgirl who had managed to marry far above herself.

"Thank you, Lady Goodwin," Catherine replied.

Blake watched Violette lift Catherine's cup and saucer and then the silver teapot. She gracefully poured the brew, set the teapot down on the silver server without spilling a drop or making any noise, and then she smiled at Catherine. "Sugar, Lady Dearfield? A single spoon, I believe?"

"Yes, thank you."

Violette added the spoonful of sugar. She placed the cup and saucer down on the table in front of Catherine, who thanked her. She then poured tea for herself.

Blake was frozen. He had to shake himself out of his amazement. Violette's diction was amazing, her manners quite flawless. In fact, now he noticed how elegant she appeared in her lavender silk gown. It was not cluttered with lace, ribbons, bows, fur, flowers, or any other of that horrible frippery she had so adorned herself with previously. Was this the same woman he had met in the York countryside? Or were his eyes and ears deceiving him?

Blake recovered with great effort, but he felt very uneasy and disturbed, though he could not understand why. He continued to stare, reminding himself that this was Violette Goodwin, not an impossibly beautiful noblewoman. She was an impostor—a terribly vulnerable yet clever young woman, one whom he was genuinely fond of and yet must remain distant from.

He sauntered into the room. Both women ceased conversation at once. Violette, in the midst of lifting the cup of tea to her mouth, set it down noisily in its saucer, spilling the liquid as she did so. Her blue eyes were wide, riveted on him.

And Blake felt an odd, savage satisfaction that he had disturbed her as much as she had disturbed him. "Good afternoon, ladies." He bowed.

Catherine stood, but Violette, correctly, remained seated. "Why Blake, how wonderful to see you," Catherine said, but she was quite anxious now and he knew her well enough to remark it.

Blake kissed her gloved hand and faced Violette, whose face was now flooded with hot color. She remained silent. "Lady Goodwin? This is a surprise. I did not expect to find you here," he said, a white lie.

Violette wet her lips. "I . . . I am delighted to see you, Lord Blake."

He could not help being amazed yet again. And, perversely, he was dismayed that this odd twist of fate was transforming her before his very eyes into a graceful lady—the kind of lady who would reign supreme this Season if Catherine gained her an entrée into their world, the kind of lady who could, just possibly, steal the heart of a rake like Robert Farrow. "May I join you?" Blake inquired.

"Of course," Catherine said quickly. "Thompson, please bring a fresh pot of tea, more cakes, and two more cups and saucers."

Blake looked at Violette's saucer, which was filled with the tea he had caused her to spill. Violette followed his gaze. Her hands, he saw, were clenched tightly in her lap. This was the very first time her gloves had been so pristinely white. More uneasy than before, Blake turned and pulled a third chair up to the small table. He sat down. His gaze shifted to Violette. She had become as still as a statue, as if afraid to move. Then he realized that he was as rigid.

It was completely inappropriate, but he suddenly recalled the torrid kiss they had shared at his mother's ball.

While they waited for Thompson to return, Catherine said, interrupting his thoughts, "I suppose you have heard about our lessons?"

"Actually, I do believe Jon mentioned something along those lines to me."

Catherine's smile was fleeting. Anxious. "Violette is a wonderful pupil. She has worked very hard," Catherine said, smiling. "She has been tireless, as I am sure you can see."

Blake eyed Violette, who was staring at him. He did not want to praise her, but he said, very low, "Yes, I can see."

Violette flushed with pleasure.

Catherine said in a rush, giving him an odd glance, "You should have seen her waltzing yesterday. Violette is one of the most graceful women I have ever known."

Blake would not be surprised. "Indeed?" He knew he was staring at Violette. It was on the tip of his tongue to suggest that they share a dance together at the next fête they both attended, but he refrained. That would be far too dangerous. This entire transformation was far too dangerous.

Violette gazed at him earnestly. "I'm learning to talk like a lady, to walk like a lady, even to dress like a lady. And I'm learning how to read and write." Her eyes were wide, searching. She did not smile. "I know the entire alphabet. I can write my name."

His heart flipped over. A part of him wanted to embrace her, hold her. It was painfully clear that his approval mattered to her, yet he did not want to be in this position. Yet how could he not approve? He had made a mistake, he should not have come. "What you have done is very admirable," he said carefully.

"Do you truly think so . . . my lord?"

Their gazes locked. Blake had to nod.

To break the tension, he faced Catherine. "Shall we ride tomorrow morning in the park?"

Catherine smiled at him. "Only if Violette can join us."

Violette gazed at Blake, her eyes shining. She was so hopeful.

Blake regarded her, hating himself. He was making matters worse. "Has Violette learned to ride as well?" he asked. If the answer was yes, he would not be all that surprised.

"No, Violette has not yet taken riding lessons. Blake is a superb rider," Catherine remarked, looking from Blake to Violette. "But I have a wonderful idea. Blake, why don't you teach Violette how to ride?"

Violette tensed, her gaze shooting to his face. He saw the expectation written all over it. It was on the tip of his tongue to agree, yet how could he? Especially since he was so damnably attracted to her? Various scenarios flashed through his mind, none of which had anything to do with horseback riding. "My schedule will not allow it."

Violette's face fell. Under the table, Catherine actually kicked him, hard, in the shin. He managed not to grunt.

"Violette has been invited to Lord Pierce's tomorrow evening," Catherine spoke into the suddenly strained silence. "Isn't that wonderful? It shall be her debut, so to speak."

"And how did you arrange that?" Blake asked. He would not go to the Pierces', even though he had been invited himself. Oh no.

Violette stared.

"I suggested it," Catherine said, a trifle annoyed.

"I suppose that you will next give her a letter of introduction?" Blake asked, feeling quite annoyed himself. With a letter of introduction from Catherine, the toniest doors in London would open to Violette. He did not like this, he did not like it at all.

"That is a capital idea," Catherine said as Thompson reappeared.

The teapots were exchanged, Violette's cup and saucer replaced, Blake given a set as well. Catherine said softly, "Violette, dear, will you pour?"

As Violette reached for the teapot, Catherine said, "Surely you shall be at the Pierces', Blake?"

Blake watched Violette lift Catherine's cup and saucer. The saucer rattled because her hand was shaking. "No, I have other engagements."

Her gaze flying to his face, Violette set the cup and saucer abruptly down. "You won't be going?" she said, stunned.

"You will not be going," Catherine corrected softly.

"I am afraid not," Blake said stiffly.

"Why?" Violette asked thickly, her gaze riveted on his. "Because of me? Because I'll be there?"

Blake's eyes widened. How astute she was. A new, terribly awkward silence fell over the table's three occupants. And before Blake could reply, Violette was on her feet.

"I beg yer pardon," she said, the slightest trace of Cockney slipping into her tone. "I am unwell. I am afraid I must use the cloakroom." Her face crumbled.

"Violette!" Catherine began.

But Violette rushed out of the salon.

Catherine stood. "What is wrong with you?!" She almost

shouted. "Did you come here to hurt her feelings?"

Blake was also standing, staring after Violette, who had now disappeared into the corridor. "Blast," he said, his jaw flexed. "I do not know." But then he faced Catherine, his eyes dark. "I could not stay away. What do you want from me?" he cried. "Bloody hell! What do you both want from me?"

It was a moment before Catherine replied. "You are a gentleman and her friend. Why do you not come to the Pierces' and help me launch her successfully into society?"

"The way I helped protect her at Mother's ball?" His reply was hard, automatic, absolute. "No."

Catherine stared at him.

Blake stared back. "What is all this about?" he finally asked. "I am not a stupid man, Catherine."

Catherine wet her lips. "This is about Violette being brave and brilliant. It is about her bettering herself, something we all should aspire to do."

"And what shall she gain from this self-improvement?" His tone was frigid. He knew what she wished to gain. "A second husband? Or myself?"

"How vain you are," Catherine said, her tone like the lash of a whip. "There are better catches in town than you, Blake."

"But not for Violette," he said coolly. Uneasily.

"No?" Catherine's hands found her hips. "How much do you wish to wager?" Their gazes clashed.

"I did not know you were fond of gambling, Catherine."

"I am fond of justice," Catherine said.

"And I am not?" Blake felt his spine stiffen. "My dear, you and Violette Goodwin may cook up whatever schemes you wish, as long as I am not included in them. And I wish the both of you good luck." Blake could not understand why he was so angry. An image of Violette with Lord Farrow was haunting him now.

"We do not need luck," Catherine retorted. "Because, if you have failed to notice how wonderful Violette is as a person, and how beautiful as a woman, why, I think you shall be the only one this Season." She must have read his thoughts. "I have no doubt that Lord Farrow will be most impressed with Violette's transformation."

"Good. I hope that he is," Blake said tersely. "In any case, I am late for an appointment." It was a lie. He had cleared his agenda until noon. He bowed.

"Coward," Catherine said.

He jerked. "I beg your pardon?"

"You heard me," Catherine said firmly. "I called you a coward."

Blake was incredulous.

Catherine smiled. "Yes, you are a coward. I shall tell you exactly what I think. I think you are besotted with Violette, smitten, and running as fast as you can because of all that you feel for her. And I do not think it is a matter of mere desire. How am I doing?"

"You are mad," Blake replied coldly. "Absolutely, utterly mad."

Catherine smiled sweetly at him. "I don't think so," she said.

Blake whirled and strode from the salon.

❖ *Seventeen* ❖

BLAKE was closeted with his brother and father in the library, advising them on certain investments they wished to make in a particular bond market, when they were interrupted. Tulley's face was impassive. "My lord," he addressed the earl, "there are two gentlemen here who wish to speak with you and they insist it is most urgent."

The earl stood up from behind his desk, annoyed. "Tulley, have them leave their cards or make an appointment with my secretary."

"My lord, sir, they are inspectors with the police, and they insist they must speak with you now."

Blake, who was seated, slowly stood. The earl, puzzled now, nodded. "Well, I cannot imagine what inspectors want with me, but send them in. I shall spare them ten minutes."

Blake had a very bad feeling. A moment later two gentlemen entered the room, both wearing dark suits, but holding their hats nervously. The earl stepped forward to shake their hands. They were Inspectors Howard and Adams.

"I am sorry, my lord, for the interruption," Inspector Howard said apologetically. Of medium height, he was heavily jowled and portly, and his eyes kept darting from the earl to his sons. "But a murder investigation cannot be delayed."

Murder, Blake thought, his insides curdling. "And whose murder are you investigating?" he asked with an easy smile, but he already knew. Jon had also jerked to attention.

"Sir Thomas Goodwin's," the second inspector said. He was tall and husky and sported thick, muttonchop whiskers. "A complaint has been filed. Our investigation is only preliminary. We are gathering evidence prior to deciding whether formal charges should be brought against the accused."

"We have not yet decided whether to exhume the body," Inspector Howard added. "If we exhume the body and find what we think we might find, then formal charges will have to be brought and, of course, there will be a trial."

Blake was sick. "Is it not likely that Sir Thomas, who was seventy years of age, died a natural death?"

"Of course that is possible and we continue to consider it. But Lady Feldstone, his daughter, is convinced that he was poisoned with arsenic," Inspector Adams said.

"So what is stopping you from exhuming the body even as we now speak?" Blake asked, standing with his father and the two inspectors in the center of the room.

"Exhumation is dirty work. An autopsy is laborious. And we don't disturb the dead unless we have strong cause to do so," Howard said, then he smiled quickly, nervously. "Might we ask everyone present about the evening of Sir Thomas's death?"

Blake began to speak, but the earl raised a hand, silencing him, while also giving him a quelling look. "Gentlemen, neither myself nor my sons saw Sir Thomas that evening. In fact, we saw Sir Thomas the day before when he called at Harding Hall to introduce us to his bride."

"We are aware of that," Adams said. "And what was your opinion of Sir Thomas's health that day?"

"Frankly," the earl said, "he appeared quite ill. My first thought was that he did not look as if he had very long to live."

"Would you swear to that in the Queen's Bench?" Howard asked.

"Of course."

"And you, my lords? What is your opinion of the last time you saw Sir Thomas?"

"I believe I speak for both of us," Jon said, touching Blake's arm. Blake was impatient, hardly able to keep his impulses in check. "We both thought he looked unwell, and we would both gladly swear to it in court."

Inspector Howard was now making notes in a small, leatherbound notebook. Adams nodded. "And the bride. Was her behavior odd in any way that day?"

Blake couldn't help himself. "Of course not." But even as he spoke he recalled that first meeting so clearly—and just how nervous and ill at ease Violette had been. He understood why she had been so anxious, but now all he could think of was how it could be misinterpreted.

"And what was her behavior like?"

Blake was silent, as was Jon. The earl finally spoke. "Actually, Lady Goodwin was not quite comfortable, having never been introduced to my family before."

Adams said quickly, "What do you mean, exactly?"

Blake grimaced, wishing his father had not spoken up.

"She was nervous, I believe. But rightly so. She is very young and unused to the kind of life we lead."

"How nervous was she?" Adams asked as Howard scribbled frantically in his notebook.

The earl glanced at Blake and sighed. "Nervous enough to almost break some knickknack on my wife's table."

"She was very nervous, then," Adams said.

"Perhaps," the earl conceded.

"Her being nervous about being introduced to the family does not make her a murderess," Blake said very smoothly.

"Perhaps not," Adams said blandly.

Inspector Howard had stopped writing. "We wish to interview the staff at Harding Hall. Might we have your permission, my lord?"

The earl nodded, while Blake, inwardly, cringed. "Of course. I will have my secretary write instructions for Neddingham."

Adams continued. "And the night of your dinner, the night of Sir Thomas's death. Lady Goodwin left her husband in bed, medicated by Dr. Crumb with laudanum. How did she appear that evening?"

Blake turned his back on the ensemble and stared grimly out of the window at the gardens outside. A taut silence now reigned. It was absurd to think that Sir Thomas had been murdered, wasn't it?

"My lord?" Adams prodded.

"She was somewhat nervous again," the earl said.

Blake turned to gaze at his father, but not with reproach. His father would always speak the truth and could not be blamed for doing so. But the earl seemed chagrined. And Blake thought that the investigation was already picking up speed, and set on a downhill course.

"How nervous was Lady Goodwin? In what way?" Adams asked.

The earl proceeded to reply. Blake listened, well aware that the conjecture might be enough to cause the inspectors to exhume the body. What if there was arsenic found inside of Sir Thomas's corpse? Blake recalled, too well, Joanna Feldstone's hurled accusation that Violette had purchased rat poison the day before Sir Thomas had died. And Violette had not said a word in response, in denial, in self-defense. Had she bought rat poison? Blake hoped not.

The inspectors finally finished, shaking hands with the three men. But before they left the library, Blake could not help himself. "What will you do?" he asked casually.

Inspector Adams cleared his throat. "Well, we are not quite at liberty to say." His glance darted from Blake to the earl and then to Jon. "And I do not think we have actually decided."

Blake smiled in a friendly manner. "As a favor to me, what do you think you shall do?"

Adams sighed. "Well, my lord, as a personal favor then, but this is privileged information, not to be revealed outside of these four walls. It seems impossible for us not to order an exhumation of the corpse."

Blake's jaw flexed. "Why not?"

"Because we have learned from the druggist in Tamrah that the day before her husband's death, Lady Goodwin purchased enough rat poison to kill a dozen huge rats."

Blake stared, a sick feeling welling up inside of him.

Adams shifted, hands in his coat pockets. "A dozen rats—or one frail, old man."

Violette did not want to remember her first ball at Harding House. But as she stood on the threshold of the ballroom at Rutherford House, butterflies seemed to wing their way through her stomach. Her hands were also damp. She had never been more nervous.

Yet a few nights ago she had been a success, according to Catherine. Violette also thought so. She had danced away the entire evening at Lord Pierce's. She'd had many offers for a stroll or a drive in the park. Violette had almost enjoyed the evening. Almost, but not quite, for Blake had not been there.

Violette hoped desperately that he would be present at the Rutherford ball tonight.

Violette surveyed the ballroom, searching for Blake. It was already crowded; she estimated there were several hundred guests present. She finally glimpsed Catherine, resplendent in a mint green taffeta ball gown, speaking with Jon. For one moment Violette watched them, remarking how striking they were, both being so beautiful and so golden blond. But if Blake were present, she failed to see him.

Hoping to appear elegant, and also hoping to hide any vestiges of anxiety, Violette finally descended the short flight of steps into the ballroom, which was larger even than the one at Harding House. She became aware of heads turning as she passed, working her way over to Jon and Catherine. She did not make eye contact with anyone. Although she had been graciously received at the Pierces', this affair was so huge that she did not know what to expect. Were the guests recalling Joanna Feldstone's accusations? Were they aware of, and recalling, her past?

Violette reached Catherine and Jon and warm greetings were exchanged. "You are even more stunning tonight than you were the other evening at the Pierces'," Jon said, kissing her hand.

Violette smiled, glad not to be alone, but glanced toward the threshold of the ballroom again. Farrow was just descending the stairs.

"You are lovely, Violette," Catherine agreed, following her gaze. "I am very proud of you."

Violette managed a thank-you and stiffened. Blake was just coming down the steps. She forgot to breathe. Her heart skipped a beat. Oh, God. He had come. This, then, was her big chance to impress him with her metamorphosis from an ugly duckling into a silver swan.

And his gaze instantly found hers, even across the distance separating them. For one single instant, their eyes locked. And then, instead of continuing directly forward, toward Violette and Catherine, he veered away, and, with his back to them, began chatting with a group of guests. Violette was crushed.

"Oh, dear," Catherine said, taking Violette's hand. She studied Violette's stricken expression. "Oh, dear. Perhaps we had better develop a new strategy."

"Is that Lady Cantwell?" Violette asked. But even from this distance, Violette recognized her. She was smiling at Blake, her gloved hand upon his arm. A silver-haired gentleman was beside her. Blake never once looked toward Violette.

"Yes," Catherine said, somewhat tersely. "And that is her husband, Lord Cantwell, with her."

Violette regarded Catherine, trying to decipher her expression. "Is she in love with Blake?" she asked bluntly.

Jon and Catherine exchanged glances. Jon said, gently, "She was once, a long time ago."

Violette flinched. "How long ago?"

Jon hesitated. "Eight years ago, to be exact."

"I don't understand," Violette said, gazing across the ballroom again. But Blake had wandered away from the Cantwells, and was now chatting with Dom St. Georges.

Catherine sighed. There was something in the sound that made Violette turn to look at the woman who had so suddenly become a dear friend, and, after Ralph, a best friend. The two women's gazes met.

"You would hear the story eventually, so you may as well know," she said. "Gabriella was a widow when she married Cantwell. And she married him only after refusing Blake."

Violette gasped.

Catherine touched her arm. "They shared a tendre for one another, Violette, but it was a long time ago."

Violette was far more than dismayed. "But . . . he said he didn't want to marry—not anyone."

Catherine was silent. Jon said, "That is how he feels now, Lady Goodwin. When my brother offered marriage to Gabriella, he was eighteen years of age."

Violette touched her moist eyes with her gloved fingertips. She was shocked by what she had just learned. And then it all, startlingly, clicked into place. It had been Gabriella with Blake that night at the ball eight years ago. And Violette recalled their embrace as if it were yesterday. She was frozen.

"Violette?" Catherine said. "Do not fret about the past. I know that Blake is very fond of you."

"I don't think so," Violette said miserably. She heard the hurt in her own tone. "Perhaps I should give up."

"If you are truly in love with Blake, then you should fight for what you want," Catherine said flatly.

Violette whirled. "Fight for what I want? What do you mean? You taught me to be genteel. Ladies do not fight."

Jon chuckled.

"I did not mean by coming to blows. What I mean is that it

is time for you to resort to the oldest trick in the book.''

Violette stared.

Jon murmured, ''I look forward to hearing this.''

Catherine ignored him. ''Make him jealous,'' she stated. ''Very jealous. Fill your dance card. Flirt outrageously. Act as if you are enamored with every man you dance with—act as if *you* do not care that Blake is even here. I suspect you shall get a reaction from him then.''

Violette turned to watch Blake. He was speaking with two older gentlemen whom she did not know. She searched the crowd for Gabriella Cantwell and found her instantly, for she was outstanding in her bronze brocade gown.

Violette had never felt less confident, but she said, ''I shall do it.''

Blake sipped a glass of champagne, eyeing Violette over the flute's rim, retaining his calm and his cool. She had been dancing for over an hour now; she'd had at least a dozen different partners, and not only had she been dancing, and gracefully, but she had laughed and smiled and flirted quite outrageously the entire time. Even with Lord Paxton, who was over eighty, and with Lord Lofton, who was twenty, and with everyone in between.

It was almost impossible to believe that she was the same woman he had met at Goodwin Manor just a month or so ago. Blake felt like truly setting Catherine down for her wild, crazy scheme.

For Violette was stunning in her silver ball gown, stunning and elegant, more so, Blake thought, than any other woman present that evening. And he knew he was not the only male to think so. She had been surrounded by admirers almost from the first moment Blake had arrived at the ball.

But did she really think he would become jealous by this ploy?

But before Blake could answer his own question, he stiffened. It was one thing to watch Violette dancing with Paxton or Lofton, or those other sots, but now Farrow was leading her onto the dance floor. Blake stared. Violette appeared mesmerized by whatever he was saying. But perhaps she *was* mesmerized. Farrow was handsome and gallant, women flocked to his side—and into his bed.

As they began to dance, Blake swigged down the rest of his champagne, then took another flute from a waiter passing by with a silver tray. Farrow did not have honorable intentions toward Violette, but it was not his business. He had already warned her twice.

"I approve," a soft voice he would never forget said from behind him.

Blake turned and met Gabriella's direct green gaze.

"Not that it is my place to approve of anything that you do," she said with a smile, "but I did like Lady Goodwin from the very moment that we met at your mother's ball."

It was odd, but Blake realized that his pulse was not racing with unnatural speed as it had been wont to do whenever he happened across Gabriella. "There is nothing to approve of," he said automatically.

Her smile faded. "Oh, Blake. Your feelings are so obvious—at least to me."

He stared at her, recalling the past—the warmth and friendship, the passion, the conversation, the love. He smiled. "You always knew me better than anyone," he finally said.

"Yes, I did," she admitted frankly. "Lady Goodwin suits you, Blake. She is strong, honest, and real."

He stared, not at Gabriella, but at Violette, who was still waltzing in Farrow's arms. His heart turned over as he watched them. "I have no wish for any entanglements," he heard himself say.

"Than you shall lose her to someone else, and it is all my fault," Gabriella said poignantly.

His gaze flew to her face. He was about to deny the truth of her last statement, but she cut him off.

"I still regret how much I hurt you, Blake, and I always will. I still regret being so afraid."

Blake looked at her, knowing her well enough to understand that she was being honest, nothing more. "I know," he said, and he touched her bare arm briefly.

She smiled and kissed his cheek. "Life is for the brave; I was a coward. But look at her." Her gaze found Violette, who was craning her neck now in order to regard Blake and Gabriella. "She is as brave as a woman can be."

Blake also regarded Violette, his gaze connecting with hers across the room. Oddly enough, Gabriella's words stirred up a sense of pride in him. "Yes, she is very brave."

And when he tore his gaze away, Gabriella was gone.

✤ *Eighteen* ✤

AS Violette finished a waltz with a baron old enough to be her father, she glimpsed Blake leaving the ballroom. He was alone—not that it mattered. She was devastated from having seen him converse with Gabriella.

She had not made him jealous. And she could not compete with the other woman, that was so very clear. Violette wanted nothing more than to go home.

The baron smiled at her. "You are a wonderful dancer, Lady Goodwin."

Violette managed to smile back, as the baron bowed and left her. Suddenly she was standing alone on the fringes of the dancers, for the very first time that night. Did Blake still love Gabriella? Violette was sick inside.

She glanced across the crowded ballroom, wondering if she could work her way unnoticed to the other side and then out of it. But before she could do so, one of her many admirers came quickly forward. He was her own age, wearing wire spectacles. He smiled eagerly. "Lady G-Goodwin, m-may I h-have the pl-pleasure of this d-dance?"

Violette scrambled to recall his name. "Lord Lofton, if you do not mind, I am exhausted." She could not even smile. "And my feet do hurt so. Might we dance a little later after I take a short rest?"

"Of-of c-course," Lofton stammered. "C-can I g-get you s-some re-refreshments?"

Violette knew from Catherine's lessons that she could not refuse. "That would be wonderful," she said.

Lofton dashed off toward the dining room. Violette pretended to watch the dancers, feeling as if she were on the verge of shattering into pieces. She did not want Lofton's, or anyone's, attentions now. And then she saw Baron Feldstone on the fringes of the crowd. Joanna was beside him.

Her heart sank. Violette darted out of a pair of doors that led into the main corridor. A few guests were ambling toward her from the foyer. Violette hesitated, then abruptly reversed direction. She fled down the corridor, not certain where she was going, wanting only to escape the noise, the gaiety, the crowd. She passed the salon where billiards and whist were in play, spying a pair of french doors. Immediately she opened them and stepped outside onto a terrace. She was relieved to find it vacant and she hurried to the far side where she sank down on a stone bench.

She had been a fool. To think that she could pretend to be a lady when she had been born in London's slums, to think that she might turn Blake's head when he was not interested in her, not at all. He had not looked at her even once that entire evening, but he had spent at least ten minutes speaking with Gabriella—and any fool could see how well acquainted they were. Violette now knew that they had once been lovers.

She did not want to love him, not anymore, not when it meant that she had to sufffer with this immense aching in her heart.

And Violette did not want to be a part of his world anymore. Especially not tonight. Her mind had been so full of dreams, her heart so full of hope. No longer. She wanted to go home to her flat in Knightsbridge, to seek the comfort of her bed, to pull the covers high up over her head.

But Ralph would be there in the barely furnished parlor, drinking a mug of ale, waiting for her. He would take one look at her and demand to know what was wrong. He would guess that a fiasco had occurred, as he had constantly predicted that it would. She would want to be comforted and consoled by him. Instead, he would say I told you so.

Violette wiped her eyes with her sleeve. Her future was clear. She would continue to work for Lady Allister, harder than ever before. She would save every penny that she made. In two years, perhaps even sooner, she would open up her own shop in some exclusive West End neighborhood. Her life would be the ladies she clothed and served.

And eventually she would forget all about Blake. He could have Gabriella, or any other woman that he chose.

Her eyes were moist and Violette rubbed them with her gloved fingertips, only to hear a cough behind her. She glanced up, dismayed, meeting Charles Lofton's concerned gaze.

He shifted ueasily. "Lady G-Goodwin? Are you all r-right?" He held two glasses of champagne. "I l-looked everywhere f-for you."

She could not smile. "I fear I am not well. I think I shall have to go home."

"Let m-me t-take you b-back inside."

"Thank you," Violette said simply.

They left the terrace, the beauty of the evening gone; a fairy tale shattered as easily as a crystal vase. Violette was acutely aware of Charles now, acutely aware of how her heart ached with wanting what she could never have.

Charles took her elbow as they entered the house. Violette fought for self-control, aware that his gaze kept returning to her face. It was searching.

In the foyer they paused. Other guests were going up the stairs, to where the men's and ladies' cloakrooms were, or coming downstairs, returning to the ball.

Charles gazed into her eyes. "I am so so-sorry th-that you are not w-well, Lady G-Goodwin," he said earnestly.

"It is just a touch of the flu," Violette said. She felt as if her fragile facade would soon crack, especially because Charles was being so kind. "I think I shall go upstairs for a moment." She needed, desperately, to compose herself, before returning home and facing Ralph.

"I see." He hesitated. "When w-will I s-see you again? C-can I take you for a drive in the p-park when you are b-better?"

Violette did not hesitate. "I do not think so, but thank you so very much," she said.

On the second landing Violette paused, one hand on the oak banister, the foyer directly below her. Charles Lofton had returned to the ballroom, but a few couples were beneath her, conversing amiably. She did not see Blake.

She did not know where the women's cloakroom was, but a door opened and several men came out of their cloakroom. Violette turned to the opposite door and swung it open. Several women were inside. Two ladies stood in front of mirrors, powdering their faces. An elderly redhead and a faded blonde were resting on settees with unslippered feet. The cloakroom became silent the moment Violette entered it.

Violette knew that no one wanted her there, but what had she done? Her own gender had treated her with suspicion ever since her marriage to Sir Thomas. Perhaps she was growing used to such treatment, because she felt numb now, and did not really care if she were somehow offending someone. Ignoring them all, she walked over to an ottoman and sat down hard in front of the mirror. She stared at her face. She looked extraordinarily pale, brittle, about to break.

She told herself not to think about Blake. For every time his image appeared in her thoughts, she wanted to cry.

Suddenly one of the women sitting in her stockings stood with a huff. "I think I shall leave. There are some things I refuse to accept, and an impostor from the slums is one of them."

Violette jerked, stunned.

"I will leave with you." The redhead slid on her slippers and the two women marched out without giving Violette a backwards glance.

Violette did not move.

The other two women ignored Violette as they finished their toilettes, as if they had not heard a word, but they also quickly left. And then Violette was alone.

She covered her face with her hands. She was worse than a fool, to think she could enter the Hardings' world. She had not fooled Blake, she had not fooled anyone. She was not an aristocrat, she was an impostor; she did not belong at Rutherford House or anywhere else in the West End. She was going home. Without Blake, there was no point in pretending anymore.

She stood and left the cloakroom. As she entered the landing, two gentlemen were emerging from the opposite withdrawing room. Violette intended to ignore them, but one of them whistled loudly and blocked her way. His breath smelled strongly of whiskey.

"Lady Goodwin, isn't it?" He grinned at her. He was a young, handsome rake. "I haven't yet had the pleasure, although I've heard all about you."

"We have not been introduced," Violette managed stiffly. He was standing so close to her that his knees brushed her skirts. Such a posture was rude. She started to move past him but he raised his arm, planting his hand on the wall by Violette's shoulder, barring her escape. Violette gasped.

"Oh, come. I do not think, in your case, we need stand on formality?" He grinned again. His grin was pleasant. His eyes were not. They gleamed and frightened Violette. "Stanhope. Name's Fred Stanhope."

"I beg your pardon," Violette said stiffly. "Please let me pass."

Stanhope did not remove his arm. "Maybe you should leave her alone, Freddie," the other man said. He was also young, but obesely fat.

Stanhope made a dismissive noise. "Why? Let's take a walk, sweetheart, just you and me," he said to Violette. "Or better yet, let's take a ride in my carriage. I know a quiet place. We

can share supper together. I shall make it worth your while."
His smile flashed.

Her pulse pounded. She was far more than alarmed. "Let
me pass—please."

"I don't think so."

Violette wet her lips. She darted a glance behind her and saw
two women coming up the stairs. She did not want to cause a
scene. "Please," she said again, with growing desperation.

The men's cloakroom door opened. Violette saw Jon emerge
and cried out. He immediately halted, his pleasant smile fading.
"What is going on here?" he asked.

Fred Stanhope reluctantly turned, dropping his arm as he did
so. But he did not move further away from Violette, keeping
her hemmed in with his body. "Hullo, Farleigh. I am making
the acquaintance of a beautiful woman."

"We have not been properly introduced," Violette said
hoarsely. "He will not let me go by."   •

Jon's expression tightened. "What in blazes are you doing,
Stanhope? Let the lady by."

"If she were a lady, I would have to agree," Fred said easily.
"But in this instance, I suggest you mind your own affairs and
leave me to woo where I choose."

Jon did not move. His blue eyes had darkened.

Violette wanted to die.

"Last chance, my friend," Jon said softly. Dangerously.

Stanhope made a dismissive noise.

And Jon reached out, grabbing Fred by the shoulder and
spinning him away from Violette, so hard that Fred crashed
into the opposite wall. Violette cried out. Fred recovered, re-
gaining his balance, while Jon faced Violette. "Lady Goodwin,
let me escort you downstairs." His tone was gentle, kind.

Violette was about to nod when she saw Fred rushing Jon
from behind. She screamed in warning.

But before Jon could turn Fred had barreled into him with
all of his weight and at full speed. The momentum of his ram-
page sent Jon flying across the landing—toward the banister.
Violette froze. Her heart stopped. All she could think about
was that the railing could not possibly withstand the force of
the two men.

Both men crashed into the banister. To Violette's relief, it
did not break. They nearly toppled over it, however. Below
them was the foyer on the first floor.

Instead, they fell to the carpeted landing, and quickly rose to their feet, wrestling. The heavy man shouted at them to stop, but neither Jon nor Fred appeared willing to listen. They grappled back and forth, the banister inches behind them.

Violette was terrified.

And suddenly Jon had Stanhope pressed backwards against the railing, and then their positions were reversed. Jon's hips were pressed to the railing, his back bent over it at an impossible angle—with Fred's expression so savage that it seemed as if he wished to push Jon over it and to the floor below. Jon's expression changed, becoming a mask of fear.

''No!'' Violette screamed.

The crack was loud. Splintering wood. The railing gave way. And with a cry, both men fell to the floor below.

PART THREE

The Murderess

⊰ *Nineteen* ⊱

THE doors to the library remained closed. The Hardings were inside, as was Catherine, the duke of Rutherford, his son, Dom St. Georges, and a physician who had been immediately summoned to attend to Jon. He had been carried there by his brother. Fred Stanhope was dead.

Violette stood hunched against the wall just outside of the closed doors, shaking violently, tears streaming down her face. She prayed desperately that Jon was not dead.

But how could any human being survive such a fall? And there had been so much blood.

The ball was summarily finished. The guests had left in pairs and clusters, speaking in hushed tones, aghast and shocked. Violette had not even thought about departing.

Anne St. Georges appeared, her face pale and set in grave lines. She regarded Violette as she approached. Violette inhaled, trembling visibly. "What is happening?" she whispered. "I must know!"

Anne touched her shoulder. "Shall we go inside?"

An image of Jon's face, etched in terror, just before the railing broke, seared Violette's mind. She was not ever going to forget that final, horrible instant just before both men fell to the ground floor below the second landing. In that moment, everything had seemed to happen in slow motion, a cruel, horrifying kind of torture. Violette had rushed forward, but too late.

And it was her fault.

That realization was so terrible that Violette shut her eyes, forcing it away. She felt so violently ill she thought that she might wretch, right there in the hall, in front of the marchioness. Anne was studying her out of grave blue eyes. Violette did not

want to go into the library where the Hardings were, where
Blake was. She was afraid to come face to face with Jon's
family. Yet she had to know that Jon lived. *Please, God.*

Anne smiled kindly and opened the doors. Violette looked
past her and saw Jon lying prone on the sofa, his face starkly
white, his eyes closed. A tall man in a dark suit bent over him:
clearly he was the physician. Jon's bloodstained jacket and shirt
lay on the floor. Blake knelt beside the doctor, holding Jon's
hand. Violette only saw his broad back, but it was easy to note
the tension in his stiff shoulders. The earl and countess stood
at Jon's head, the earl with his arm wrapped around his wife—
clearly he was supporting most of her weight. The countess
was white with shock and fright. She seemed dazed, clinging
to her husband. Catherine stood with them, apparently trying
not to cry, while Dom St. Georges and the duke were gathered
at the foot of the sofa, watching the examination with severe
expressions.

Violette found the courage to follow Anne into the room.
She did not hesitate. She moved immediately to Catherine. The
two women embraced and rocked one another.

"Dear God," Catherine whispered. "Oh, dear God."

When Violette pulled out of Catherine's arms she saw that
Blake had shifted so that he could stare at her. His eyes were
wide—and harsh and cold.

Violette stiffened, unable to breathe. She thought, *Blake will
never forgive me.* She had seen it in his eyes.

The doctor sighed and straightened, affording Violette a better view of Jon. His head had been bandaged. One side of the
bandage was pinkish-red. Violette saw his bare chest rising and
falling very gently and she began to cry again, this time silently,
in relief. *Thank God he was not dead.*

The earl moved forward. "You have not said a word. How
badly is he hurt?" His face was gray. He appeared to have
aged a dozen years in the past half-hour.

The doctor faced him, his expression somber. "I will not
mislead you and your family, my lord. It is very serious. His
back is broken. I am sending for assistants and more medical
equipment. We shall work through the night. If he is stabilized
by tomorrow evening, he can be moved to his home. A long
period of recuperation will follow."

"If he is stabilized?" the earl asked. "I want to know everything. He will recuperate?"

"He is young and he appears strong. As you know, he suffered a blow to his head when he fell, but that is not what concerns me. A broken back is very serious. He is currently in a physical trauma. Because he is young, though, and healthy, I do not expect him to expire."

"My son will live?" the countess cried softly.

"I expect him to survive this trauma," the doctor said quietly. "Those odds are quite good."

Violette gripped Catherine's hand. What was the doctor saying?

Blake stood. Voicing Violette's exact thoughts. "What are you saying? Precisely?"

"Assuming that he shall live, his recovery will be slow, painful, arduous. And possibly," the doctor cleared his throat, "incomplete."

"Incomplete," the earl echoed.

Violette looked only at Blake now, understanding his anguish.

"I am saying that he may recover fully, he may not. I must set his back so it heals properly, and that in itself is a very difficult operation. And even if set properly, we cannot know the extent of the damage to his spinal cord. There is a chance he may be capable of all normal physical functions. There is a chance he may not."

"What is the worst scenario?" the earl asked sharply.

The doctor hesitated. "If Jon has suffered extreme damage to his spinal cord, there is a possibility he might be paralyzed to some extent or another."

Blake was ashen. "Paralyzed? To some extent? What the bloody hell does that mean?"

Catherine released Violette and rushed over to Blake, putting her arm around him. Tears began to fall from her eyes, but she did not make a sound.

"I will not know until he begins to recover," the physician said. "He might be completely paralyzed, unable to do anything more than talk. Or he might be partially paralyzed, from the waist down. If the spinal cord was, miraculously, undamaged, he will be as good as new."

Blake stared. Everyone stared. The countess covered her face with her hands and began to weep softly. Violette felt the tears streaming down her own face, but she did not dare move. Even she could understand what the doctor had said. It would be a miracle for Jon to recover fully from the accident.

The earl went to his wife and pulled her fully into his embrace. Her face buried against his chest, her sobs grew louder. He held her hard.

And Blake suddenly turned his dark gaze on Violette. It was filled with bitter accusation.

And Violette could not stand it. She fled.

Two days later, Blake sat beside Jon, who was in his own bed. Bright morning sunlight streamed through the open, unshuttered bedroom windows. Dr. Braman had spent most of the first night with two medical assistants operating on Jon. The following evening Jon had been removed to Harding House. He had awoken several times, but had fallen instantly asleep. According to Braman, the fact that he had awoken already was a very good sign. However, if he had noticed anyone or anything, he had given no indication of it.

Blake had remained beside Jon ever since the accident. Now he stared at his brother's face. Two days' growth of tawny beard covered his cheeks and jaw, but his pallor was still very remarkable. Blake knew, with all his heart, that Jon would recover fully—that in time he would be as good as new.

Violette's image slipped into his mind. He stiffened, unable not to feel a rush of hot anger whenever he thought about her. Suddenly Jon's door opened. Blake looked up as Catherine glided into the room.

She smiled slightly at Blake but only had eyes for his brother. She sat down on the bed by Jon's hip; Blake had pulled up an ottoman. She reached for Jon's hand and held it tightly.

Blake reached out and brushed his knuckles over Catherine's face. She looked exhausted; dark circles rimmed her eyes. Since the accident, she had been haunting Harding House. Blake thought, but was not quite sure, that she had moved into a guest room on the third floor.

"He opened his eyes two hours ago and looked at me," he said quietly. His voice sounded unusually loud in the deathly silent bedroom.

Catherine's smile was fleeting and wan. "Did he recognize you?"

"I think so," Blake said. Then he hesitated. "I am not sure. Our eyes met, but only for a moment."

Catherine nodded tearfully, and Blake watched her lift Jon's hand to her mouth and kiss it. Then she held it in her lap. His own vision blurred. But he told himself for the hundredth time that Jon would mend completely. He just knew it. There just was no other possibility. He bent and brushed a kiss to Jon's forehead, just below the bandage, as if his older brother were a small child.

Suddenly Jon sighed. Both Catherine and Blake tensed.

Jon's lashes fluttered, and suddenly the lids opened. His irises were huge, the pupils mere pinpoints. And for the first time since the accident, the light in Jon's blue eyes slowly turned lucid. He was gazing at Catherine. Suddenly he smiled.

"Hello," he said. "I thought it was terribly inappropriate for a lady to be in a gentleman's bedroom—much less in his bed?" His words seemed a bit slurred, but no more so than if he had been terribly drunk.

Catherine clutched his hand to her breast, tears falling down her face. "My dear," she whispered. "I guess I am ruined."

"Mm." Jon smiled. "Does this mean I have to do the honorable thing?" A twinkle appeared in his eyes, one so familiar and characteristic that Blake felt his own eyes grow moist.

Catherine laughed, but the tears kept spilling down her cheeks.

Blake wiped his own eyes with his shirtsleeve.

Jon looked at him. "Why are you both crying?" Suddenly his smile faded. "Am I drugged? God, I feel drunk, high as a kite. What's going on?"

Blake gripped his shoulder. "You have been dosed with morphine, so yes, you must be high, higher than a kite."

"Morphine?" Jon blinked. "Am I floating? I can see the bed, but I cannot really feel it."

"You are in bed," Blake said, somewhat cautiously. "Do you remember the accident?"

Jon blinked at Blake, then at Catherine. His smile began to fade. "Good God. The damned second-floor railing broke. Stanhope and I went over it."

A silence greeted his words. "Yes," Blake said quietly. "You did."

Catherine continued to hold his hand. "Stanhope is dead. You are lucky to be alive, Jon. You suffered a blow to your head, which is why it is bandaged. But you also suffered a broken back, which is why you have been medicated."

Jon stared. No longer smiling. "A broken back," he repeated, appearing shocked.

"Don't worry," Blake said quickly, rubbing his shoulder.

"You are well on the way to recovery." He smiled brightly.

Jon stared at him, and then at Catherine. "Is a broken back not serious?"

Blake said, "Of course it is. Your period of recuperation shall be long and difficult."

Jon looked only at Blake. He did not say a word. He stared, grim.

A frisson of unease filled Blake, but before he could speak, Catherine said cheerfully, "How do you feel, Jon, all things considered?"

He turned his intense eyes upon her, and still did not speak. He failed to smile, too.

"Jon?"

Jon's face hardened. His expression turned strange and unfamiliar.

Blake quickly glanced at Catherine.

And she cried out. For Jon had squeezed her hand—Blake saw the whitened knuckles on his brother's hand and realized what he had done. "Jon?" he asked uncertainly.

Jon's chest began to heave. "I feel the pillow behind my head, and the bed beneath my back." His stare was wide.

"That is wonderful," Catherine began.

But Jon cut her off. "But I cannot feel my legs."

Blake froze. Catherine lost all the color in her face.

"Christ," Jon cried. He pulled his hand free of Catherine's and, staring down at what he was doing, he laid his hand on his thigh, rubbing it. "Oh, God," he said. "I have legs, but I cannot feel them—and I cannot move them. Blake!" he cried.

The stone floor was cold and hurtful beneath Violette's knees. In fact, Violette was numb. She had spent most of the past two days in the small twelfth-century church, praying for Jon's full, miraculous recovery.

She was exhausted. Dazed. Last night, between prayers, she had fallen asleep on the church's cold stone floor. Today she was so stiff that she did not know if she could actually stand up.

Violette realized that she had stopped praying, but for how long, she did not know. Jon's prone image remained engraved there, as did Blake's hostile, accusing gaze. Violette's stomach curdled. Last night she had had a horrible nightmare. She was homeless again, a beggar on the streets. She had been so cold, so cold and so hungry. And she had been alone.

And then Blake had driven by in his sleek black phaeton. Violette had screamed at him to wait, stop, take her with him, but he had stared at her with undisguised hatred and continued on by.

Her vision as she stared at the many white candles burning on the altar, seemed to darken, lighten, and darken again. She forced the memory of the nightmare aside and murmured the litany she had been repeating for the past two days. "Dear Father, who art in Heaven . . ." Her voice was hoarse.

"Gentlewoman, are you unwell?" a kind voice intoned.

Violette turned slightly without rising, and stared up at a black-frocked priest. "I am fine, Father," she said hoarsely. But she was not fine. She was sick and weak and faint. Guilt consumed her.

"Are you?" He was more than kindly, dapper and white-haired, his expression sympathetic, his brown eyes concerned. "Come, dear. You have been here far too long. You were here all day yesterday until late last night and first thing this morning. May I help? Do you wish to talk about it?"

Violette nodded as the priest helped her stagger to her feet. "Someone is ill. I am begging God not to let him die," she whispered, her thoughts full of Jon and Blake. "I am begging God for a full recovery. I am begging Him for a miracle."

"I shall say a prayer for your friend as well." The priest smiled at her. "But remember this: God has a reason for all that He does. And if your friend leaves this world, or fails to recover fully, it is God's will."

Violette was not reassured. "If you could pray for him, I would be so grateful," she whispered. She stumbled down the nave, her gray skirts almost causing her to trip and fall. She felt terribly disoriented. How many days had passed since the accident? She could not remember. Time was a blur. No, it had been two days and two nights, that was it, that was right. Today her bones hurt her, proof that she had slept on the church's hard, cold stone floor last evening.

She paused on the sidewalk outside. Her pulse seemed unnaturally loud and rapid and strong. It made her feel uncomfortable. A haggard mother in a faded blue dress with two children in hand passed by on foot. The mother was scolding them. A dray pulled by two bay drafthorses rolled down the thoroughfare. A pair of gentlemen left an apothecary's shop just across the street. The entire world to which Violette was a witness seemed unreal somehow, surreal. The day was gray and cloudy and quite cool. Violette realized she had no coat, no hat, no gloves, just when she also realized that it was beginning to drizzle.

She did not want to go home. But where would she go if she did not return to the flat she shared with Ralph?

She suddenly saw an empty hansom driving by. Violette raised her hand without another thought, calling out sharply to the driver. She rushed forward as he halted his cab. Violette opened the door and clambered in.

"Where to, me lady?" the driver asked.

"Harding House," Violette immediately answered. "In Mayfair." Her pulse pounded far more unnaturally than before.

Violette began to lose courage as she climbed the broad stone steps leading to the front door of Harding House. Her mouth was dry. Her breathing was shallow. She planned to inquire after Jon's condition from the staff. She was more afraid than ever to face any of the Hardings, especially afraid of Blake.

A footman she did not recognize led her into the foyer, where the butler, Tulley, immediately appeared. Violette searched his impassive expression and thought that it was more somber than usual. Her heart sank.

He paused in front of her. "Lady Goodwin, good day."

Violette clung to her reticule. "Tulley. How is His Lordship, Lord Farleigh?"

Tulley's expression was impassive once again, remote, impossible to read. "He is awake, but abed."

Violette nodded fearfully. "What does the physician say?"

"Dr. Braman has not seen him since he awoke this morning, but he has conversed with Lord Blake and Lady Catherine."

"Oh, God!" Violette gnawed her lip. "Does that mean he is on the mend, Tulley? Please, I must know!"

Tulley's expression softened with concern. "I would not know the answer to that, my lady, but we are all praying for His Lordship night and day." And Tulley said, "Lord Farleigh cannot seem to feel his legs, nor move them."

Violette's eyes widened and she stopped breathing. Then she reached blindly out for support. She wound up grabbing the butler's arm. "Oh God," she said. "What do you mean, he cannot feel his legs? He cannot move them?"

"Exactly that," Tulley said quietly.

Violette turned away blindly, her pulse pounding, tears filling her eyes. *He was paralyzed. What if it did not pass? It was all her fault.*

"What the hell is going on here?" Blake demanded.

Violette whirled as Blake came striding rapidly down the stairs and into the foyer, clad only in badly creased trousers and an equally wrinkled shirt. His face was etched in stone. His eyes were icy cold. He continued forward, toward Violette, who did not dare move.

"What are you doing here?" Blake asked grimly, his entire body rigid with tension.

Violette almost cringed. "I . . . I only wanted to know how Jon is," she whispered.

"I don't want you here," Blake said harshly. "No one wants you here, Lady Goodwin."

For one moment, Violette was frozen, incapable of either speech or movement. She could not tear her gaze from Blake's strained countenance, and he stared back.

"Blake," Violette burst out, "I'm sorry! I'm so sorry! Please tell me that Jon will be fine?" Her voice broke.

"My brother is not fine. He is paralyzed. From the waist down." He continued to stare. He did not have to verbalize the rest of his thoughts, for it was all too clear that he was blaming her for the accident.

Violette hugged herself. "I am praying for him," she said tremulously.

"As if that would make a difference," Blake said. "Good-bye, Lady Goodwin. I think it is time for you to return where you belong."

Violette flinched. And then she turned and ran out of the house.

⸙ *Twenty* ⸙

"WHAT is the prognosis?" Jon asked.

Dr. Braman straightened. He had just finished his first examination of Jon since Jon had awoken earlier that day. They were alone in Jon's bedroom. Jon had insisted that no member of his family be present.

"I will be quite honest with you, my lord," Braman said. "It is doubtful that you shall ever walk again."

Jon turned white.

"I wish I could tell you otherwise," the doctor said sincerely. "But you have no sensation at all in the lower half of your body. After a fall like the one you have sustained, with this kind of paralysis, I have never heard of an instance of full recovery."

Jon stared. His heart thundered in his ears. The doctor blurred before him. Jon turned his head to stare out of one bedroom window. Outside it was raining heavily, the windowpanes streaked with water. The sky was charcoal gray, almost black.

He was dazed. In disbelief. Time stood still.

And then his mind began to function again.

He was a cripple. Good God. *He was no longer a man.*

"My lord?" Braman gripped his shoulder. "You are lucky to be alive. Most men would not have survived that fall. Stanhope—"

Jon threw his hand off. "Do not tell me that I am lucky," he roared. The upper half of his body came off of the bed. "Damn you! Get out! Get out of this room this instant!" he shouted. The artery in his throat bulged. His face had turned red. His fists were clenched. And he felt the immensity of what the doctor had told him, of what his life had become, then.

His hopes and dreams, his wishes, everything, lost, gone, turned into nothingness.

As Braman hurried across the room to leave, the door swung open and Blake, the earl, and the countess started inside.

Jon's murderous gaze caused them all to falter.

"Jon," the earl began.

"Get out," Jon said, his chest heaving. "I wish to be alone."

Catherine appeared on the threshold, her face white, strained with concern. Jon saw her and stiffened. Then he snarled. "And her! Especially her!"

Catherine was frozen, shocked.

"Jon, let me sit with you," the countess said softly. "My son, please—"

"No." Jon turned his head away, his jaw flexed, his temples visibly bulging. *Everything transformed into death and hopelessness.*

"We should leave," Catherine whispered. Her eyes were moist. "My lord? My lady? Blake? Come, please. Jon needs to be alone."

Jon refused to look at them, at her—those he loved so much.

He heard them leaving. His pulse pounded. Inside he was sick. He heard the door close.

And he reached out and seized the porcelain lamp on his bedside table and threw it with all of his strength across the room, at the opposite wall. It smashed there loudly, shattering onto the floor.

A vase of fresh-cut flowers followed.

The earl sat with his face in his hands. The countess sat beside him on the leather sofa in the library, her hand clasping his knee. Blake stood staring out into the windswept gardens, beaten down by the pouring rain. Catherine had dissolved into tears on a chair. Dr. Braman had just left.

"I don't believe it," Blake finally said. His voice was harsh. "This is impossible. He will walk again."

No one answered him.

Blake spun around. "I shall do my own research. There are always exceptions to every rule. I am certain that somewhere in this world there is a recorded case of an accident like this one, where recovery was complete."

The earl looked up. "If you find such an instance, such a miracle, then do let us know." His tone was heavy, harshly bitter. He looked crushed.

Catherine wiped her eyes with a handkerchief. "He needs us now. He needs to know that our feelings for him have not changed. He needs to know that we still love him, admire him, honor him. He will survive this crisis, I am sure of it."

"He will walk," Blake snapped. He thought about Violette. "If only he hadn't come to Violette's defense," he cried.

"How could he not?" Catherine responded. "Jon is a gentleman."

"Damn her for her flirting," Blake snapped. "This is her fault!"

Catherine gasped. The countess stood and walked over to her younger son and placed her palm on his shoulder. "Blake, it was an accident. As hard as it may be, it is not just to blame Violette."

Blake stared at his mother, whose eyes remained red and swollen from all the weeping she had done in the past few days. He knew that she was right. Yet another part of him was determined to cast blame on Violette for her part in this.

An image of her stricken face, a recollection of her whispered *"I'm so sorry!"* came to him then. Blake walked away from his mother. In spite of everything, he regretted his cruel words to her. "She should not have been at the ball."

Catherine stood. "Then it is my fault, is it not?"

He whirled. "You invited her because of me. God!"

"I told her to make you jealous," Catherine said, on the verge of tears.

Blake moved to her, putting his arm around her waist. "You are *not* to blame. We are all to blame, I guess." He could not help but think that if he had attended Violette even a bit, the accident would not have happened.

The earl sat back with a heavy sigh. "Enough. Enough of casting stones. We must concentrate on what is best for Jon."

"Yes," the countess said softly, returning to sit by her husband's side. A movement by the door caused her to turn. "Yes, Tulley?"

"My lady," the butler said. "I have a message for Lord Blake."

Blake took the envelope, not particularly interested in its contents. He broke the seal and stiffened. His pulse suddenly raced.

"What is it, Blake?" Suzannah asked.

"It is from Lady Allister. Those inspectors are at her shop, waiting for Lady Goodwin to arrive. Apparently they wish to ask her some questions. Lady Allister is concerned." He stared grimly, thinking, *This is no longer my affair.* Jon was paralyzed, that was his affair.

But Violette was innocent of murder.

"Blake?" Catherine moved swiftly to his side. "Perhaps Violette needs a solicitor?"

"Dammit," Blake said beneath his breath. "Mother, Father, excuse me. I think I must attend this interview." And he was already striding out the door.

By the time Blake arrived at the shop, both investigators were already in the process of interviewing Violette. Lady Allister met him at the door—she was already open for business—her expression grim. She immediately ushered him into her private office behind the front salon. "It is a good thing you have come, Blake," she said in a low voice. "Lady Goodwin cannot possibly handle those two policemen."

The inspectors were standing; Violette was seated. Her face was so white her skin seemed translucent. There were dark circles under her eyes. The moment Blake entered the room

Violette looked over her shoulder and uttered a small cry upon seeing him. There was no mistaking her relief.

Inspector Howard came forward. "My lord, this is a surprise."

Blake smiled without feeling. "I am in a shopping mood. And as you know, Lady Goodwin is a personal friend of mine. I could not possibly allow another clerk to attend me."

Violette stared at him tremulously. "Blake. They're asking me all kinds of questions."

"Answer truthfully," he said simply.

"It is really not necessary for you to be present," Howard said calmly.

"Is there a law against it?" Blake returned in the same tone and with the same demeanor.

"Of course not. This is not a hearing." Howard faced Violette. Lady Allister also remained present.

Blake shoved his hands in his pockets and leaned against the wall. She was not a murderess, but this had already gone too far. And she had violated far too many rules, offending far too many nobles, by entering the world she had upon marrying Sir Thomas. Yet she was innocent, so surely she would not suffer the indignity of a trial. Perhaps it would be best if Sir Thomas's body was autopsied, proving that he had died a natural death.

And if he hadn't?

That possibility was distinctly disturbing.

"Let us continue, Lady Goodwin. So the night Sir Thomas died you dined alone at Harding Hall."

"Yes," Violette murmured, twisting her hands.

"I wonder why you would dine alone that particular night?" Howard mused. "Perhaps you had a reason for not wishing to be present at Goodwin Manor?"

"That is a terribly leading question, if it is even a question," Blake objected with irritation. "Nor do I think Lady Goodwin understands the point you are driving at."

"My lord," Howard said, "we are questioning Lady Goodwin, informally, and we would appreciate your cooperation in this matter."

"He wasn't feeling well," Violette burst out. "He hadn't been well for days."

"But you left him alone in order to share supper with the Hardings? Were you in the habit of leaving your husband alone when he was feeling poorly?"

"No, of course not." Violette shot an anxious glance at

Blake. "He told me to go and have a good time."

"And you went, eagerly," Howard stated. "Why didn't you stay at home with Sir Thomas if he was ill?"

"I . . . I had never been invited to supper with an earl before," Violette whispered, glancing at Blake again.

"Ah, yes. So now we arrive at another topic. How old are you, Lady Goodwin?"

Violette said, "Eighteen."

"And Sir Thomas was seventy-two," Howard said. "And how long were you married to Sir Thomas?"

"Six months, exactly," Violette said hoarsely. She shifted to gaze at Blake. Her expression was beseeching.

And Blake grimaced. He could guess where Inspector Howard was now leading. But he could not guess why.

"Where were you born?"

Violette hesitated.

"Lady Goodwin?" the inspector prompted.

Blake pushed off of the wall. "This is irrelevant." But it wasn't. It was far too relevant—and far too damning.

Inspector Howard ignored him.

Lady Allister touched his sleeve.

Violette bit her lip. "I was born in St. Giles."

"Who were your parents?"

Violette hesitated again. Tears filled her eyes. "My mother was Emilou Cooper. My father's name was Peter." She trailed off.

"Peter? Peter what?"

She swiveled and looked at Blake. "Peter Garret."

Blake stiffened. He hadn't known. He glanced at Lady Allister, whose expression gave nothing away of what she might be feeling.

"Were your parents married?" Howard asked, although he obviously knew the answer.

Violette shook her head, her eyes downcast. Blake had the urge to strangle the inspector. Thank God this wasn't a trial.

"And where did you live as a child?"

She licked her lips and shot a miserable glance at Blake, then at her employer. "A lot of different places."

"Which different places? Please, be specific."

"I can't remember."

"Surely you must remember one of your homes?"

Violette shook her head. "Me—my—mother died when I was three. I . . . we moved a lot, me and my father."

"Where does he live now?"

"He died. He died when I was a child."

"So you were an orphan?"

Violette nodded.

"And how old were you when you were orphaned?"

Violette darted a desperate look over her shoulder at Blake. He tried to reassure her with his eyes, but he was growing sicker by the minute himself. Two garish spots of pink color had now appeared on Violette's cheeks, standing out starkly against the pallor of her skin. "I was ten."

"Did you live with relatives then?"

"No." Her voice was hardly audible. "Me an' Ralph, we lived wherever we could find a place to stay for a while."

"Ralph?"

Violette blanched.

"Who is Ralph, Lady Goodwin?"

"A boy. We grew up together," Violette said, staring only at her hands, clenched in her lap.

"So you lived with this boy? When you were ten? Were you having relations with him?"

Violette was silent.

Blake was furious. "This is beyond decency," he snapped.

"My lord." Adams faced him. "If you cannot hold your tongue, we shall insist that you leave. This is not a trial. We are merely questioning Lady Goodwin."

"And to what purpose?" Blake challenged. "In order to see if you can break her down, here and now, sparing yourself and your lackeys any further work? Or the effort of finding the real murderer, if there has actually been a murder committed?"

"My lord, with all due respect, we are doing our jobs, nothing more," Howard interjected in a friendlier manner.

"Blake, let them finish," Lady Allister said softly. "So we can all go about our business."

Blake sighed, sharing a glance with Violette.

Howard faced her. "Did you have relations with this boy, Lady Goodwin?"

"I don't understand," Violette said.

"Did you have sexual relations with him?"

Violette gasped. "No! Gawd!"

Adams raised his hand, silencing her. "Give me an example of where you lived with this friend."

Violette covered her face with her hands.

"I think you have made your point," Blake said harshly.

Howard ignored him, facing the judge. "I wish for Lady Goodwin to answer the question."

Violette looked up defiantly, fearfully. "We lived in cellars, on stoops, in closed-up marketplaces—anywhere we could."

Silence filled the room.

"So you were vagrant, an orphan. And how did you survive? A child with no parents, no home, a mere boyfriend?"

Blake groaned.

Violette stared at him, not answering.

"Answer the question, Lady Goodwin," Adams said warningly.

Blake came forward. "I understand that you wish to establish a defamatory character for Lady Goodwin, but I shall not allow it. Lady Goodwin has said enough. If she cannot obtain a solicitor to represent her interests in this grave matter, than I shall do for her."

Adams ignored Blake. "How did you and Ralph survive?"

Before Blake could tell her not to answer, she lifted her chin. "I was a cross-sweeper, a match girl, a flower girl, I even held gentlemen's horses."

"Did you beg? Did you steal?"

Violette took a breath. The sound was loud and sharp in the silent room. Her mouth trembled. "I never begged, not a day in my life."

"Did you steal?"

"Violette," Blake began.

She looked down at her gloved hands. "Yes." Her whisper was barely audible. "We were so hungry and—"

"Lady Goodwin." Adams was triumphant. "Did you not buy rat poison the day before Sir Thomas's death?"

Violette began to shiver. Blake gripped her shoulder. "Do not answer that question, Violette."

"Did you buy rat poison the day before his death?" Adams demanded. "My lord, you are interfering with our investigation!"

Blake smiled coldly. "Then perhaps you wish to bring charges against me?"

Adams scowled. The two men's gazes locked. Then the tall inspector faced Violette. "Lady Goodwin, Howard Keepson, the druggest in Tamrah, has already given us a sworn deposition stating that he sold you enough rat poison to kill ten rats the day before Sir Thomas died."

Violette made a soft, choked sound. "We had a rat."

"One rat?"

She nodded. "It was big."

Adams made a scoffing sound. "Lady Goodwin, why do you not just come out with the truth? You married Sir Thomas for his estate. You killed him for his estate. How clever you were. After all, you waited six months in order to do so, biding your time. And the night of the murder you dined out, perhaps suffering from the slightest bit of conscience?"

"I didn't kill 'im!" Violette was on her feet. "We had a rat! Sir Thomas was my friend! 'E was good to me!"

Adams and Howard exchanged glances while Blake put his arm around Violette. "Do not say another word."

She met his gaze and nodded fearfully.

"Lady Goodwin." Howard smiled. "We have ordered a Coroner's Inquest. You are not allowed to leave London until this matter is concluded. Do you understand?"

"No," Violette said.

"They have ordered an autopsy of the body," Blake explained grimly. "When shall you have the results?"

"In a day or two, at which point Lady Goodwin shall have to appear before a magistrate."

Blake glanced at Violette, who was ashen. In front of the magistrate Violette would be formally indicted.

"Lady Goodwin, considering all the circumstances, and the severity of the possible charges, we have no choice but to place you in temporary custody now."

"Temporary custody?" Violette said.

"Because the possibility exists that you might flee the city, indeed, the country, we shall have to detain you, Lady Goodwin," Howard explained.

Blake shifted, his body coming between the inspectors and Violette. He had a horrific image of Violette being sent to one of London's infamous prisons. "I beg your pardon. That is not necessary. Lady Goodwin is respectably employed and—"

Adams cut him off. "Can you guarantee that she will remain available for any further proceedings, my lord?" His tone was like a whip.

"I most certainly can," Blake said flatly. "Remand her into the custody of myself or my father."

Adams and Howard shared a glance. Blake could tell that Adams was not interested in being fair. "I shall personally be responsible for Lady Goodwin," he said. "You have nothing to fear. If there is a magistrate's hearing, Lady Goodwin will appear."

"Very well," Adams said. "But know this. If Lady Goodwin does flee these proceedings, you shall be named an accomplice, my lord, and I do not give a damn who your father is."

Blake smiled. "I am sure that you don't."

❖ Twenty-one ❖

VIOLETTE was mortified. She had been stripped of all pretenses, of any dignity she might own. Her entire sordid past, her background, her antecedents, had been revealed. Blake knew the truth.

She was also terrified. Violette stared at her hands, which were tightly clasped in her lap. She was being accused of murdering a man she had been indebted to and so terribly fond of, a man who had saved and changed her life, a man who had given her everything she had needed, who had been more than a friend and like a father to her. She was innocent. Surely Blake knew that? Violette glanced up, stealing a look at him. He was staring out of the window of the coach. He had not said a word since they had left Lady Allister's shop. And Lady Allister had suggested that Violette take some time off, until this matter was resolved. Violette was afraid that she was going to lose her job.

Would there be a trial?

Violette had never been to prison, although the workhouse where she had spent nine months as a child had seemed very much like a jail. Yet growing up in St. Giles, she had heard all about London's prisons, about Newgate, about Fleet Street. They were horrible places where prisoners were worked and starved to death, or merely incarcerated until they died. "If there's a trial, I'll go to prison, won't I?" Violette blurted out suddenly.

Blake met her gaze. His expression was terribly grave. "Hopefully there will not be any trial. I shall obtain a solicitor for you this afternoon."

"Thank you," Violette said. She did not understand his generosity, but she did not mistake it for kindness. Not now, when Jon lay paralyzed because of her. "Blake?"

He glanced at her, remaining silent.

"I am so sorry about Jon. If I could do things differently, I would," Violette cried.

He looked away. "Unfortunately, we cannot change the past."

Violette stared at her hands. Blake despised her for the accident and it made her want to die. Well, perhaps she would. For Violette knew all about justice. Justice was for the rich, not for the likes of herself. And murder was a hanging offense.

"Lady Goodwin," Blake said, interrupting Violette's thoughts. "What about your *friend* Ralph?"

Violette hesitated. There was always something odd in Blake's tone when he referred to Ralph. "What about him?"

"Have the inspectors questioned him?"

"I don't know. He went to work this morning, same as me," Violette said.

Blake's gaze was unwavering. "Did Ralph kill Sir Thomas?" he asked coolly.

Violette gasped. "Ralph ain't no murderer," she snapped. "How could you say such a thing?"

"I have always had my doubts about that man," Blake said. "And did you not tell me that he was the one who suggested you both flee Tamrah so abruptly after the murder?"

Violette gasped.

"And that is the first thing I shall tell your solicitor," Blake said calmly.

Violette sat very stiffly, on the verge of refusing his help. "Ralph has a hot temper, and sometimes he's jealous, but he isn't a murderer."

Blake stared, unblinking. Finally he asked softly, "Do you give him cause to be jealous?"

Violette could not reply, especially when she did not quite comprehend all the meanings of Blake's question. Their gazes had locked. "I don't understand you," Violette said. "Why did you come to the shop today? Why are you helping me?"

Blake looked away. His profile was stark. "I don't know," he finally said. "I do not understand myself."

As it turned out, Blake took her to Harding House, not his own town home. Because of Jon's accident, and the murder investigation, Harding House was the very last place Violette wished to be.

Violette was shown to a third-floor bedroom by Tulley. Her eyes widened at the sight that greeted her. A huge pink and white room dominated by a pink and white candy-striped four-poster canopied bed. Violette was in awe. The carpet she stood upon was red. An entire seating area, arranged in various shades of pink and white, was in front of a white and gold marble fireplace.

"If there is anything that you need," Tulley said, "just pull the bell cord and a maid will appear. The family dines at seven."

Violette nodded, almost incapable of speech. And it quickly occurred to her that she could not join the family for supper that night—or any other one. They all must hate her.

Tulley said, "Lady Goodwin, is there anything I might get you now? Some light refreshment, perhaps? Have you had dinner?"

"No," Violette said in a whisper. "I'm not at all hungry."

"Have a good rest, then." Tulley smiled, turning for the door.

Violette nodded. The door closed behind Tulley. Violette eyed the bed again, hardly able to imagine sleeping there. Lace frothed out from under the coverlet. She finally lifted it. Underneath were ivory satin sheets.

She walked over to the cream-colored sofa in front of the hearth. She touched the arm—the fabric was damask. A huge landscape was posed over the mantel. Violette stared at the breathtaking sweep of lush green countryside, spires in the distance. She moved closer. The painting was signed by John Constable. Beneath it silver candlesticks stood on the top of the mantel with a small open box of potpourri. Two brilliantly red velvet armchairs were on either side of the fireplace. If this was a guest room, she wondered what the countess's apartments were like.

Sitting down, knowing she could not really rest, she thought about all that had happened that day, growing sick with fright again, and she thought about Blake, and his paralyzed brother. Had he left the house to find her a solicitor? Why was he helping her?

She rubbed her face. Alone now, she could really face her fear. Her life, which had taken on a wonderful fairy-tale quality, had been transformed into a kind of hell. She had the urge to run away, as far from London and those inspectors as possible, as far from Blake and the Hardings as possible. She could get passage on a boat, one bound for France. She still had thousands of pounds left from Blake's gift.

Of course, she could not run away. It would be so dishonorable. Blake had given his word, and if she fled, he would get into trouble with the authorities. Besides, soon there would be an autopsy, and she was praying now that Sir Thomas had died in his sleep. At least that would solve one of her problems.

Violette stiffened at the sound of a knock on her door. She hoped it was a servant, but instinct told her it was not. "Come in."

Catherine opened the door. "May I visit?" She smiled.

"Of course." Violette's heart filled with dread. Surely Catherine despised her now. She began to tremble.

Catherine entered the room and sat down beside Violette on the damask sofa. "Have you recovered from this morning? Blake told me all about it."

Violette flushed, wondering if Blake had described the horrible interview in detail. "I don't think so," Violette said, studying Catherine's face, trying to discern the other woman's feelings for her.

"I am so sorry that this is happening, Violette," Catherine said, reaching for Violette's hand. "It is terribly unfair."

Violette's tone became hoarse. "Aren't you angry with me? Why are you being kind? Don't you hate me?"

Catherine's smile faded. For a moment she did not speak.

Violette lowered her eyes. "I know Jon's accident is my fault. I know he does not wish to lay eyes on me ever again. Like Blake. I do not blame either one of them. In fact, I do not understand how you can sit there so calmly, and be so friendly, after what has happened." Violette dared to look at the woman who had become a dear friend and mentor in such a short time.

"Everything has happened so quickly. Oh, Violette." Tears filled Catherine's eyes. "I do not blame you, but I am so afraid for Jon, dear God." She started to cry uncontrollably.

Violette only hesitated a moment. She reached out, embracing Catherine, holding her as she cried. "Maybe he will get well," she whispered as Catherine wept. She had never wanted anything more, never hoped for anything harder. "Sometimes miracles do happen," she whispered, wanting to believe her own words.

"I pray that you are right," Catherine said, sitting up and wiping her eyes with her handkerchief. She blew her nose, somehow managing to appear ladylike and dainty as she did so. Finally she faced Violette. "Blake told me about what happened to you this morning. I am so sorry—and so worried, too.''

Violette stared. "You are worried about me?" she whispered.

Catherine nodded. "Could it be that you think, because of all that has happened, that we are no longer friends? I am not that way, Violette. I have come to love you. As far as Jon's accident goes, if anyone is to blame, it is me." She closed her eyes. "God forgive me."

Violette reached for her hand, gripping it tightly. "Catherine, you are not to blame! Not at all!"

"I want to believe that," Catherine said. She dried her eyes again with her handkerchief. "But I am filled with guilt."

"Now I feel even more terrible," Violette said miserably.

Catherine stood and walked across the room to one of the room's windows. "I suppose guilt will not help anything. It will certainly not help Jon."

Violette hesitated. "Catherine? When, in your opinion, could I see Jon?"

Catherine turned, startled.

"I have to see him. It will be the hardest thing I have ever done in my life, but it is he whom I must apologize to, on my knees if need be," Violette said, meaning it.

"Jon is distraught right now. He refuses to even see me, and I am his best friend. In fact, he has refused to see or speak to anyone since Dr. Braman's last visit." Her voice choked.

"Oh no," Violette whispered.

Catherine fought tears visibly. "But he is not a small-minded person. He has the most generous heart of anyone I have ever met. I know that he doesn't blame you for what happened." She paused. "He might not welcome you or me with open arms right now, but he is very brave, and in time he will. I am sure of it." She was very pale. "In time, things will return to the way they were, even if he cannot walk, I *am* sure of it," she said with desperation.

Violette wondered if she was right.

Blake could not shake his mind free of what had transpired that morning. Howard and Adams had so easily destroyed Violette's character. He shuddered at the prospect of a trial. In cases like this one, Violette's background, character, and purchase of the rat poison might be enough to decide her guilt—even though she was innocent.

He had already begun a correspondence with a solicitor. George Dodge was one of the best attorneys in London, and he worked with some of the best barristers as well. If Violette was formally accused of murder, Blake thought that Dodge could do as much or more for her than anybody.

Blake hurried upstairs to visit his brother before returning to his own house. He shoved aside all thoughts of that morning. Visiting Jon was terribly painful; it was no easy task.

He would do anything, including selling his soul, if he could achieve a recovery for his brother. If he could, he would trade places with him.

Jon was sitting up in bed, propped up against fluffy pillows, his head bandaged, wearing a fresh white shirt. He had one arm flung up behind his head, and he was staring grimly out of one of the bedroom's windows. He turned as Blake walked in, but he did not smile as he used to do.

"Hello." Blake smiled. "I am glad to find you awake."

"Unfortunately I cannot sleep all day," Jon said.

Blake stopped beside the bed, his own easy expression vanishing. "I know you do not mean that."

Jon's jaw was hard, and he stared past Blake, out of his bedroom window.

"You are bored," Blake decided abruptly. "As I would be, if I were you. Let me take you downstairs for a change of scenery."

"No," Jon snapped.

Blake froze.

Jon's smile was twisted. "I have no wish to be carried about like some infant."

Blake's heart pounded forcefully. "That is ridiculous. And until you can walk again, you need help in being moved."

Jon stared at him coldly. "Do not tell me that I am going to walk again."

Blake stiffened. "Of course you are going to walk again," he began.

Jon reached for the closest object he could find, a heavy book, and he threw it at Blake with all of his strength. Blake ducked but not in time and the book hit his shoulder. He straightened, staring at his brother in shock.

Jon was flushed. "Just get out."

Blake could not believe his ears. "Jon, please. I'm your brother. I want to help."

"Get out. Now," Jon said viciously.

Blake did not move. He had never heard his brother use such a tone, not even with a rival or an enemy. He was at a loss, not knowing what to do.

"Dammit," Jon shouted, "I cannot move, so I cannot throw you out, but I am asking you to leave, Blake, this very minute—damn you!"

Blake remained frozen for the span of several heartbeats. And then he turned, feeling sick, sicker than he had ever felt in his life, and when he reached the door, he said, forcing his tone to be light and natural, when he really wanted to cry, "I will stop by this afternoon."

Jon did not reply.

Blake left.

⚜ *Twenty-two* ⚜

BLAKE had found a solicitor to represent Violette. Breathlessly, Violette followed the servant who had been sent to fetch her down the two flights of stairs and into the library. Blake and an elderly gray-haired man were seated at opposite ends of a sofa when she entered the room. Both men stood up. Blake introduced the gentleman as Mr. George Dodge, attorney-at-law.

When everyone was once again seated, Dodge spoke to Violette. "Lady Goodwin, Lord Blake has informed me of all that has transpired thus far. I am happy to represent you. I work with some of the finest barristers in the country. If anyone has a chance to win this trial, should this come to trial—and I suspect it shall even if arsenic is not found in Sir Thomas's body—you may rest assured that I do."

Violette nodded, gripping her hands so tightly it hurt. Her fear was escalating. "Why do you think there shall be a trial?" Her tone was high.

"Because of the extenuating circumstances of this case. I shall never delude you. You are not gentry, and your background is damning. That alone would inspire most officials to prosecute."

Violette trembled. "I didn't kill him. That's not fair. I am innocent."

Dodge regarded her calmly. "That was going to be my next

question, although Lord Blake is also convinced of your innocence and has told me so himself.''

Violette darted a shocked glance at Blake, who remained impassive.

''Now, an important question. Did your friend Ralph Horn murder Sir Thomas?''

Violette was on her feet. ''No! Ralph is not a murderer!'' She turned an agitated glance on Blake. ''You told him that, didn't you?''

''Do calm yourself, Violette,'' Blake said.

Violette sat down, frightened and angry, beginning to panic. She could not shake Dodge's certainty out of her mind that there would be a trial.

''Are you certain, Lady Goodwin?'' Dodge asked. ''I am on your side. You must always tell me the truth or I cannot defend you successfully. Protecting your friend is not a good idea.''

''Ralph is not a murderer. I am not protecting him. Am I going to hang?'' Violette cried.

Dodge shared a glance with Blake. ''I am going to do everything in my power to see that you go free, Lady Goodwin.''

Violette was not reassured. She wrung her hands. Her temples throbbed. ''Is that a yes—or a no?''

''I cannot guarantee you a verdict of not guilty,'' Dodge said matter-of-factly. ''Lady Goodwin, panicking now will not help our cause.''

Violette nodded, close to tears.

''Listen closely to me,'' the solicitor said. ''We have a lot of work to do and probably little time in which to do it. These kinds of cases can go very quickly—in the blink of an eye. The coroner might very well deliver his report in a day or so. We could be facing charges as soon as tomorrow evening. I have seen trials result within a week or even less of an indictment. The good news is''—and he smiled—''we could have a verdict in less than a fortnight. But I do need your full cooperation.''

''A trial could go so swiftly?'' Blake asked, appearing grim. Dodge gave him a look. ''Yes.''

Violette felt that the two men were sharing unspoken thoughts, thoughts they did not want to share with her. But she could not dwell on that. All she could seem to grasp was that she might be charged with murder as soon as tomorrow night, oh God. And would she be a defendant in court as early as next week? Violette was shaking.

Blake spoke again. "Lady Goodwin. Mr. Dodge needs to ask you quite a few questions. Are you up to it?" His regard was probing.

Violette met his gaze. "I have a terrible headache," she whispered. It was the truth.

A few more minutes, please," Dodge said firmly. "I am very concerned with how the inspectors defamed your character this morning. I am worried about the nature of your relationship with Ralph Horn. Lady Goodwin, could you please describe that relationship to me?"

"We are friends," Violette said, stiffening.

"And lovers?"

Violette turned white. "No, we are not lovers." Her pulse was racing. She had to look at Blake.

Blake's legs were crossed. One foot swung. He did not meet her gaze.

"Have you ever been lovers?" Dodge asked.

"Never." Violette was shaking. She glanced at Blake again. This time their gazes met briefly before he glanced away.

"Were you faithful to Sir Thomas?"

Violette's eyes widened. "What does that have to do with Sir Thomas's death?" she gasped.

"Your character has already been painted a distinct shade of dark gray. Before the trial is over, it will be painted pitch black. I need to know all there is to know about you."

Violette's chin lifted. "I am not a whore. Just because I was born a bastard in St. Giles doesn't mean I'm a whore. I have always been faithful to Sir Thomas," she panted.

"No one even used that word," Dodge said. "I do apologize for upsetting you." But he appeared satisfied. "Well," he said, "I shall begin to prepare a defense, as I do strongly suspect a defense shall be needed. We shall speak again first thing tomorrow." He stood, reaching for his leather attaché case. "I do wish to interview your friend, Ralph Horn."

Violette did not respond. She was ill, shaken to the quick. How could this be happening?

Blake also stood. "That will be very difficult," he said.

"And why is that?" Dodge asked, his expression one of mild confusion.

Violette was also puzzled.

"Because I sent a runner to fetch him from his job. He never appeared this morning at the factory, and he is not at his flat.

In fact, he has not left a single personal possession there.'' Blake turned and stared at Violette.

Violette was on her feet like a bolt of lightning. ''What are you saying?!'' she cried.

''I do believe your friend Ralph has fled the immediate vicinity,'' Blake said. ''In plainer English, he seems to have disappeared.''

After that interview, Violette decided to plead exhaustion and take supper alone in her room. She could not possibly dine with the Hardings that night.

Violette remembered when her life had been simple. When Sir Thomas had been alive, it had consisted of eating all she wanted and dressing up in her wonderful new wardrobe and doing a tad of shopping every day so she could enjoy the freedom of spending her pin money. But even before she had married Sir Thomas, her life, while difficult, and even at times brutal, had been simple. She had not been in love with a man so many stations above her that he might as well walk in the clouds of Heaven while she dwelled on the mere Earth.

Violette could not sleep. Blake haunted her—as did her desire to be held safely, and at times passionately, in his arms. She needed him now. But she could not fool herself. He had obtained the solicitor, but they were not even friends. At this point, she could almost settle for mere friendship from him. Somehow she had lost that, too.

And she could not stop worrying about a trial. She could not stop worrying about prison, and hanging. And what about Ralph? Where had he gone? Violette knew that her lifelong friend and partner was incapable of murder. But it was terribly clear that Blake thought otherwise.

Violette did not want to lose her freedom, or worse, her life. She did not want to lose Blake. But she felt as if she had taken that first step off of a cliff. She was in the air, falling . . . only she had no idea of where she would land—nor when. And what if Blake was not there to catch her?

Eventually she slept.

Violette awoke, shivering from the cold. She was confused. When she had gone to bed last night a warm fire had crackled in the hearth and heated bricks had been placed at the foot of her bed. She had been toasty warm, the blankets heavy upon her.

Dread crept over her in stages. She was not merely chilled to the bone, but the mattress she slept upon was no longer soft and plush—it was hard and thin, barely separating her body from the floor. And what had happened to her silk and satin quilts? They were gone.

Violette's eyes flew open as her hand, flung off of the mattress, groped the floor. *The floor.* It was rough, uneven stone. She was not in bed, she was sleeping on a cane mat on the floor. She cried out.

And then Violette realized that the worst that could possibly befall her had happened. She did not remember leaving Harding House. Sitting up, she glanced wildly around—at a dark, narrow, dirty alleyway she recognized. It was the alley where she had grown up in St. Giles.

Violette wrapped her arms around her kees and gasped again—her beautiful nightgown and wrapper were gone. She was clad in torn breeches and a dirty, thin shirt. Her feet were bare—and black with dirt. She looked down at her hands, expecting to see clean ivory skin. Her fingers and palms were gray-black with dirt and grime. Trembling violently, she reached up, already knowing what she would find. Her beautiful hair was gone, hacked off at the nape.

Violette started to cry.

How had this happened? She had been alseep in that beautiful pink and white bedroom at Harding House. How had she awoken there in the streets of St. Giles?

She stood up, staggering slightly. A rat darted across the stoop. On other stoops other vagrants slept on makeshift mats, wrapped up in coats and blankets thrown away by the gentry and somehow salvaged from garbage piles. What *had* happened? She wept. Why had she left Harding House? Where was Blake? Had she been walking in her sleep?

Blake. She needed him desperately, she did, but what if he saw her like this? Terror immobilized her. Her mouth was bone-dry. If he ever saw her like this, she would never win his heart, not ever.

But hadn't that become an impossibility? She was about to be accused of murder.

And then she glimpsed his fancy black phaeton driving down the alley toward her. Oh God, was he searching for her? Why else would he be in that neighborhood? Violette stiffened, dread-filled, not knowing what to do. How she wanted to run to him, call his name. But she was prepared to flee. She could not let him find her like this!

And she heard him then, calling her name. "Violette?! Violette! VIOLETTE!"

Violette stepped back into the shadows of the overhanging roof, pressing her back to the wall, shaking, hiding. She wanted to run, but could not seem to get her legs to obey the summons of her mind. Her legs would not move. But whether she wanted to run to him, or from him, she did not know.

The phaeton stopped. Very slowly, in suspended motion, the carriage door swung open and a man started to step out.

Violette cringed.

The man stepped around the carriage door, becoming fully revealed. It was not Blake. Dressed all in black, hooded, it was the hangman.

Violette screamed.

Blake knocked uncertainly on Jon's door. It was early in the morning, the time they usually rode in the park. When there was no reply he shoved open the bedroom door. The bedroom was cloaked in shadows as the draperies had not yet been opened. Jon appeared to be asleep.

Unsure of what his reception would be, Blake crossed the room and opened the curtains, allowing the mild early morning sunlight to filter inside. He turned and saw Jon staring at him from where he lay in bed.

"Good morning." Blake smiled.

"This seems to be a violation of my privacy," Jon returned.

"I am sorry," Blake said, his heart sinking heavily. "But in the past I have roused you in order that we could share a ride before breakfast." He smiled again.

"In the past I could ride." Jon placed his hands behind his head, staring. "We are in the present."

"You will ride again."

"I doubt it," Jon said.

Blake's temper flared, but he tamped it down with an effort. "So you intend to just give up?"

Jon did not reply.

Blake turned and opened another set of draperies. "Let's take a walk in the gardens."

Jon flung his arm down; his hand landed on his thigh. "Christ," he said. "*I cannot walk.*"

Blake felt his pulse roar. "Have you tried?"

Jon was as angry. "You are not a doctor, Blake. Now, if you do not mind, I am going back to sleep."

"I am not a doctor, but I am your brother, and I do mind," Blake snapped.

The two brothers stared at one another heatedly.

"What the hell do you want from me?" Jon finally asked. "Do you not have enough on your mind with Violette Goodwin's troubles?"

So Jon knew about that. "I want you to come downstairs with me, take some air, perhaps a step or two, and then we can share breakfast with the family."

Jon glared. "I am not in a social mood."

"Than humor me, your brother."

Jon cast his gaze heavenward.

Blake walked to the door and shouted for Jon's valet. A moment later Potter appeared. "Jon needs to dress and then we are going downstairs," he said firmly.

"Yes, my lord," the stocky valet said.

Blake and Potter helped Jon to sit up. Even performing such a simple act broke Blake's heart. He avoided meeting his brother's gaze. Jon was flushed, with frustration, he thought, and embarrassment. The valet began gathering clothing from the armoire and chest.

"Let me help you stand," Blake said.

Jon's gaze, bitterly mocking, met his. "It is easier if I lie here while I am disrobed and redressed."

It was a moment before Blake could respond. "Your attitude will not help you to recover," he said.

"Do you expect me to sing and dance, Blake? To be happy to be in this condition?" Jon cried.

"I want you to fight this condition!"

"There is nothing to fight! I am not going to recover! Braman said so. He is the expert."

"Braman is an ass."

Their gazes locked. And Jon said, "Come here."

Blake walked over and, comprehending him, he stooped. Glaring at his brother, Jon flung one arm around his neck. Blake put his arm around Jon's waist and straightened, helping Jon stand on his bare feet. But the moment of triumph was short-lived. Blake was supporting Jon's weight entirely.

"We will walk together," Blake said.

Jon did not speak.

Blake stole a glance at his set face, wanting to weep. He was going to make his brother walk, goddammit. Holding him tightly against his side, he took a step forward—but Jon only moved with him because Blake dragged him.

"Stop," Jon cried. "Dammit, just stop."

"No," Blake said. "Try. Please try!"

"I am trying! *And I cannot move my legs!*"

Their gazes met. Jon's face was red, his blue eyes anguished, furious. And Blake felt it then, the loss of hope.

He helped his brother back to the bed as Potter brought over Jon's clothes.

It was a few minutes before nine when Violette came downstairs for breakfast. Having passed a miserable night, her lack of sleep, combined with the events of the previous days, had reduced her to a state of extreme exhaustion. She was hardly hungry, but she knew her body needed nourishment. It was either that or collapse.

She had donned a pale gray morning gown and had braided her hair into one thick rope that hung down her back. She thought that the men would have taken their breakfast earlier. Violette was hoping that no one would be present in the breakfast room that day.

But she stopped short as she crossed the threshold, because both the countess and Catherine were present, sipping tea and nibbling toast covered with jam. The countess looked up from the *London Times*. "Good morning, Violette." Her smile had faded. She appeared tired, her face showing signs of strain and fatigue. "Please. Come in and join us for breakfast," she said.

Violette summoned a smile and entered the small, bright breakfast room very hesitantly. She sat across from Catherine. "Good morning, my lady," she said to the countess. "Thank you so much for allowing me to stay here—especially after all that has happened. I am so sorry for my part in Jon's accident."

The countess sighed. "We are all sorry, but I remain convinced that my son will recover." She stopped. It was a moment before she could speak again. "You are not to blame."

Violette looked down at her place setting, because it was so difficult to regard the countess. Once her eyes had sparkled, had been so full of gaiety and joy, but not now.

"Jon and Blake are outside," Catherine said too brightly. "They are taking breakfast together in the garden."

Violette met Catherine's gaze and saw that she was anxious.

She wished that the breakfast room looked out on the garden where the brothers were, but it did not. But maybe that was for the best, being as she was not a member of the family.

"Please help yourself to the buffet on the sideboard," the countess said.

Violette rose and went to the buffet, filling up a plate with far more than she could eat. She returned to the table and tried to get down her meal, the countess returning her attention to her newspaper, Catherine repeatedly glancing out of the window. It was clear to Violette that Catherine wished desperately to see what was going on with Blake and Jon.

"You are not hungry, Violette?" Catherine finally asked.

"Not really," Violette said, knowing she could not eat a thing. And then she heard footsteps approaching from the corridor, heavy male footsteps, and she stiffened.

It was only the earl and she relaxed. Richard Blake entered the room, clad in riding clothes and Hessian boots. "Good morning, ladies," the earl said, taking his seat at the opposite end of the table from his wife. His smile faltered. "Lady Goodwin." He nodded.

The countess laid her hand on his arm, and when she spoke, her tone was low but eager. "Blake and Jon are taking breakfast together in the gardens, Richard."

The earl, about to reach for his cup, froze.

The countess smiled at him, her eyes on his.

"That is good news," he said quietly.

And Violette felt like an intruder. No one wanted her present. Even though they were acting as graciously as possible, she was only at Harding House because of Blake—because she was the prime suspect in a murder investigation. She concentrated on eating, forcing a forkful of eggs into her mouth. At least she would not have to face Blake this morning.

But a sixth sense made her look up slowly a few minutes later—right into Blake's eyes. He stood on the threshold of the room, his expression strained and grim. And he was staring at her.

He tore his gaze from her and went to his mother, kissing her on one cheek. "Good morning, Mother. Did you sleep well?"

"Not too poorly," Suzannah replied.

Blake patted Catherine's shoulder as he strode by her. He only inclined his head at Violette.

She wondered if he meant to hurt her. He had succeeded.

Violette gazed at her plate. Was he ever going to let her forget about her part in the accident?

He began helping himself from the sideboard, the earl joining him there. Violette wanted to flee the breakfast room, especially as they spoke in hushed tones—which she could overhear.

"How is Jon?" the earl asked.

"The same," Blake said abruptly.

"But he was with you, outside."

"I did everything but beat the hell out of him to get him to come downstairs," Blake said, slopping eggs angrily onto his plate.

The earl stared at him. "I want to talk to you after breakfast, before you leave," he said.

Blake nodded.

Violette was trembling as her gaze met Catherine's. The other woman's eyes were filled with dismay. Violette glanced at the countess and saw her disappointment as well. The men began to eat, neither one of them manifesting much appetite. Violette sipped her tea, wondering how she might gracefully escape the table and its occupants.

Tulley appeared in the doorway. He moved directly to Blake. "My lord," he said, "I am terribly sorry to interrupt your breakfast but you have a visitor and he says it is most urgent."

"What is this about?" the earl asked with some annoyance. "Tulley, we have both just sat down."

Tulley glanced briefly at Violette and spoke again to Blake. "It is Mr. Dodge, sir. He wishes a word with you privately—immediately."

Violette jerked. Her gaze slammed to Blake, who also stiffened, and then was on his feet.

By now everyone had laid their forks aside. The earl sighed, glancing at Violette. Blake was grim. "I am sorry, Father, Mother, do excuse me." He bowed. And with long strides he swiftly left the room.

Violette did not move. Why was Dodge calling at this hour? Dread incapacitated her. She clutched the table for support. She had to know what was going on. But surely they did not have a coroner's report so soon!

"Violette, dear," the countess said, unsmiling. "Do not fret. Blake will handle everything, I am sure. Enjoy your breakfast. Can I pour you more tea?"

But Violette could not even respond to the countess's inquiry. Suddenly she stood, dropping her fork. Every eye in the room was upon her. "Excuse me," she whispered, and she lifted her skirts and raced after Blake.

He was in the foyer, deeply engaged in conversation with George Dodge. Violette paused in the hall, straining to hear, no easy task with the way her pulse was racing. And Dodge was saying, "Didn't think it would be so fast."

Violette leaned suddenly, heavily, against the wall. It was so very hard to breathe. What was he speaking about?

"What has happened?" Blake demanded.

"I have a friend in the Coroner's Office. The inquest has been completed. The findings are not good, Blake."

Violette was vaguely aware of Blake cursing. She realized that she was shaking.

"Arsenic. Sir Thomas was killed with arsenic, his liver was saturated with the poison," Dodge said.

Violette was shocked. She must have cried out, because both men turned to stare at her. But all she could think of was that someone had killed Sir Thomas. Sir Thomas had been murdered after all. Dear God.

Blake looked at her, his face oddly white.

"I am afraid," Dodge said, "that Lady Goodwin is going to be charged today with Sir Thomas's murder, probably within the next few hours. And she will then be placed under arrest."

❖ *Twenty-three* ❖

VIOLETTE stepped forward. "They're going to arrest me?"

Blake immediately moved to her and put his arm around her. She sagged against him. How she needed his strength. "Do not panic now," he advised her, his eyes on her face.

She regarded him, riveted, terrified. "Am I going to prison? Am I going to hang? For something I did not do?!" she cried.

"You are not going to prison, nor shall you hang," Blake said firmly.

Violette gazed at him, trying to decide if she believed him or not. But she could feel her world falling apart, the earth crumbling beneath her very feet. Panic clawed at her.

"Violette, why do you not go upstairs and rest? And leave your defense to Mr. Dodge and myself." Blake smiled at her.

Violette could not reply.

*   *   *

Blake stood alone in the library, behind closed doors. Dodge had just left. They had spoken together privately, briefly. As soon as Violette was arrested, she would be incarcerated, and there was nothing he could do to prevent it. She would remain in prison until a trial had rendered a verdict.

Blake was shocked. He had not really expected things to go this far. And although he had never been inside any prison, he could not imagine Violette incarcerated in one. He had heard stories about the conditions in Newgate and Fleet Street. Who hadn't?

He thought about the other morning at Lady Allister's shop. The inspectors had raked Violette over the coals, simply, mercilessly. In a full-fledged trial it could only be worse. She would not be found innocent. Murder was a hanging offense.

And as distraught as Blake was over Jon's accident, he could not dwell on that now, not when Violette's freedom, her life, was at stake. Other images were haunting him now. The very first time he had laid eyes upon her in Harding Hall, when she had worn that ghastly magenta and lace dress. The solitary, grief-stricken figure she had made at Sir Thomas's funeral. Violette in her shabby bedroom, holding a dress up to her chest, a few hours after that. And Violette at his mother's ball. Spectacular in Catherine's pale blue satin dress, spectacular yet so vulnerable, being an outsider and an impostor in a world which had no wish to ever accept her.

She still trusted him. She trusted him to rescue her from a guilty verdict and death.

"What are you going to do?" Jon asked.

Blake whirled. He had not heard the door open, but Jon stood there, supported by two servants, flushed from exertion. For a moment Blake could not speak.

"Put me on the sofa," Jon ordered tersely.

Blake rushed to help, and after a moment Jon was seated on the sofa, his useless legs dangling over the edge. The servants left. "You are the last person I expected to see," Blake said.

"The servants gossip ceaselessly and I heard what happened. What will you do, Blake?"

Blake stared. "Why are you concerned? Lady Goodwin's fate should hardly affect you."

Jon shrugged. "She is not a murderess. I do not hate her. In fact, I do not even blame her for what has happened, how could I? She was being accosted, Blake. A woman being accosted is unacceptable. I am angry, yes, with everyone; with life, in general; but I would have no heart left if Lady Goodwin was hanged for a murder she did not commit.''

Blake sat down beside his brother. ''I guess I do not really blame her for her part in the accident,'' he said grimly. ''But I cannot let her hang, Jon.'' And the thought crept unbidden into his mind. Had he somehow come to care for her, far more than he had previously suspected? Why else would he be so upset, so sick, so filled with dread over the recent turn of events? Why else would he want to protect her and spare her from humiliation and harm? His determination was vast.

Jon stared at him. ''She will lose in the Queen's Bench, will she not?''

Blake rubbed his throbbing temples. It was impossible for him to analyze his feelings or motivations now. ''Yes. I think so. I believe that Dodge thinks so, too. Dodge says he has seen juries render a verdict within days in sensational murder trials like this one.'' He could see the headlines already. *East End Murderess Poisons Elderly Husband.*

''Then there is very little time,'' Jon said. ''A few days from now, Violette might be dead.''

Blake inhaled. ''Do not even think such a thing.''

''You could always launch your own investigation to try to find the actual killer,'' Jon said. ''If the real killer is produced, Violette will be freed.''

''I already have, with Dodge's help. I have also hired runners to locate Ralph Horn.'' Blake paced, raking his hair with one hand. ''I imagine, if Horn is the killer, he is long gone by now.''

''Those are my thoughts exactly.'' Jon's tone was dry.

''If only we had more time to find the real killer,'' Blake reflected, ''but we do not.''

''Perhaps you should marry her,'' Jon said.

Blake jerked. ''What?''

Jon was grim—and calm. ''You heard me. Give her the Harding name. Let's face it, Blake. With my downfall your power and prestige has increased vastly. Your son shall inherit this earldom. And the whole world knows it. If Violette is your wife, one day to be the mother of your children, she will be tried by her peers, in the Lords, and I do not think any of our peers would dare to convict her then.''

Blake stood. His mind was racing. ''When the bloody hell did you conceive this idea?''

''It was the obvious solution, especially as you have been

pursuing her since the two of you first met, in one fashion or another.''

"I deny that," Blake managed. He was shocked by Jon's suggestion. Gabriella's image immediately came to mind, but he shoved it aside; he had no time for such a diversion now. In a way, Jon made sense. For when Rutherford and Harding combined their power, most lords were afraid to go against them. Blake knew he could count on the duke and Dom St. Georges in this instance. But . . . he did not want to get married. He had decided against marriage a long time ago. Eight years ago, to be exact.

"You also *need* a wife and an heir." Jon stared, unsmiling—he never smiled anymore, it seemed. "You have a duty to perform now, Blake, a duty to me, to Father, to the family and the earldom."

Blake walked away from Jon. "That is premature," he finally said. His hands were shaking.

"I don't think so. Face it. I am crippled, I am not going to walk again, and I cannot sire a son."

Blake turned. "You are a coward," he shot. "To quit before you have even tried to get well."

"Then I am a coward," Jon said with a shrug. His eyes glinted. "That is my choice, is it not?"

"Not if I have any say in the matter."

"Well, you do not." Jon's gaze held his. "You have nerve, though, calling me a coward, when you are the cowardly one."

Blake was frozen.

"You are afraid to take that lovely woman to wife." Jon was cool. "Afraid you might actually lose your heart for the second time. Violette is not Gabriella."

"That is absurd. Clearly Violette is not Gabriella," Blake said tersely.

Jon glanced toward the door. "Call the footmen, please, I wish to return upstairs."

Blake hesitated. He looked at his brother. "You want me to marry her, don't you?"

Jon stared. "Actually, I do. I have always thought that eventually you would, anyway. So it shall be sooner rather than later. And with good reason."

Blake stared out of the window. His heart raced. Was he afraid? And was he insane? Could he marry Violette in order to give her the protection of the Harding name? To give her power, privilege, and a chance to beat a false verdict? Yet could he let her be imprisoned, could he let her hang? Of course, there was the slim chance she would get off if tried in the Queen's Bench. Could he take that chance? Could he live with himself if she were found guilty, if she were hanged? He could not.

"Good God," Blake muttered. He could not believe what was happening.

Jon stared at him. "I see you realize you have little or no choice."

"You are enjoying this," Blake said. "But God only knows why." He stalked to the door.

"Where are you going?" Jon called.

"I am going to speak with Violette—to propose marriage to her."

Violette could not stop shaking. She was going to be arrested. And charged with murder. She was going to go to jail. She was going to hang.

She gripped the windowsill of the guest bedroom. She did not see the gardens outside. She had the urge to open the window, climb out of it, shimmy down the elm tree, and run. Run as far and as fast as she could, as far away as she might go. *Run.*

Her instincts were shrieking at her.

But what about Blake? If she ran away, she would have to leave the country. She would never be able to come back, not unless the real killer were found. And that might never happen. She would never see Blake again. Blake, whom she loved. Still.

Grimly, she reminded herself that he did not love her. In fact, at times he seemed to hate her. Violette knew he would never really forgive her for Jon's accident. Just as she could never ever really forgive herself.

Choking on a sob, she sank down in a chair. But at other times he truly seemed to care. Like that morning, when Dodge had brought the terrible news. His expression had been shocked, distraught. *I am never going to understand him,* Violette thought, covering her face with her hands. And while she trusted him implicitly on a certain level, believing in his power, his strength, and his integrity, she had no faith in justice or God. She *should* run away. Now, before it was too late.

Before she was arrested, taken away.

Footsteps caused Violette to drop her hands and jerk at the sight of Blake, who stood on the threshold of her room. The door was open behind him, but Violette had closed it earlier when she had come in. She did not move.

He stared back at her. "I knocked, but you did not answer. I thought you might have fallen asleep." His expression was grave.

Violette gripped the arms of her chair tightly. "No. I don't think I shall ever be able to sleep again." She laughed slightly, the sound high and filled with mockery. She trembled.

A shadow flitted across his face. He entered her room, closing the door. "This will pass. One day you will look back on this crisis and be able to smile about it."

"I don't think so."

He regarded her, finally producing his handkerchief from his breast pocket, and crossing the room, he handed it to her. "Here. Wipe your eyes. Please, do not cry. All is not lost yet." He did not smile. He was so very serious.

"I'm not crying," Violette said. But she dabbed at her eyes, which were moist.

"You are very courageous, Lady Goodwin," Blake said.

There was something in his tone that made her hope. She searched his face, his eyes, but could not read what he might be feeling in his heart. "What is it that you wish to talk about?" she asked tremulously.

He hesitated, then pulled up an ottoman and straddled it. His expression very somber, he said, "I wish to discuss marriage."

Violette was motionless. She could not have possibly heard him correctly. And if she had, he could not have been referring to a marriage between them. And suddenly, so suddenly, all her fear and panic were gone, and in their place was hope, sheer, desperate, agonizing hope. *Please, God,* she thought, *let him be asking me to marry him. Let him realize that he loves me, too.*

"Violette?"

She focused. It was hard to breathe. "Blake? I . . . I don't think I understand."

He nodded. "I am very worried about this situation. You need protection. I believe that I can protect you, as can my family."

Violette still did not understand. "What does this have to do with marriage?" Her voice was almost inaudible.

"I want to give you my name," he said seriously.

Her heart leapt. "You want to marry me?" Incredulity—and hope.

He wet his lips. "Prince Albert gave me the title of viscount last summer for a very personal reason. You see he has been, like myself, building row houses for those less fortunate than ourselves. In fact, we have compared our designs, and dreams, if you will.'' Blake finally smiled at her.

"I am lost,'' Violette said.

"If I marry you, Violette, you become a viscountess. You become a peer.''

"I still do not understand.''

Blake rose to his feet. "A peer is tried by his—or her—peers. My family has great influence in the Lords. I want you tried in the Lords, Violette, not in the Queen's Bench, where a verdict would most likely be rendered against you.''

Violette stared up at him. Her emotions had become suspended. An inkling began, one too painful to comprehend. "Be . . . plain,'' she whispered hoarsely. She could feel all the color draining from her face. All but the last vestiges of hope draining from her heart.

"We should marry immediately, this very minute,'' he said. "Before inspectors Adams and Howard come to arrest you. I am not going to allow you to be carted off to Newgate like some common criminal.''

Violette levered herself upwards with difficulty. All she could think of was that she had never wanted anything more than to be asked by Blake for her hand in marriage, but it seemed, dear God, that he was only marrying her to save her, not for any other reason. And she prayed that she was wrong. Desperately, she prayed that he would tell her what she wanted so terribly to hear.

"Violette, we have no other choice. If we marry, I will insist that you remain here, in my father's custody, until the trial. And we shall do everything in our power to make sure the peerage returns a verdict of not guilty. What else is there to understand?''

Violette wet her dry lips. Trying not to hear the little voice inside of her head, screaming, *Fool!* "If I were not in this trouble, would you be asking me to marry you then?''

He turned white.

It was answer enough.

"Oh, God,'' Violette said, turning her back on him. What she wanted, she did not, could not, want this way.

He seized her arm. "We do not have time. We should perform the nuptials now. This moment, in fact.''

She shook her head, unable to speak.

His grip tightened on her arm. "Violette, you are not think-ing clearly."

She whirled. "I am thinking very clearly," she flung. "What will happen after the trial? If I am cleared? You will be saddled with a wife you never wanted. You will be saddled with me!"

He took a step back from her. "We will reach an understand-ing now," he said finally.

"An understanding?" Her tone was wild, bitter.

"When the hoopla has died down, we can annul the mar-riage, or seek a divorce, whichever is easier," he said.

❖ *Twenty-four* ❖

IT was, without a doubt, the worst day of her life.

Violette stood beside Blake in a small salon in Rutherford House. The doors had not just been shut, they were locked. The draperies on the windows had been drawn. The small yet op-ulent room was gas-lit. And Violette and Blake were not alone. Dom St. Georges and Jon were behind them clad in dark jackets and trousers and snowy white shirts. Jon was seated. Reverend Alcott faced them, an open Bible in his hands.

As the reverend performed the ceremony which would, tem-porarily yet legally, unite her and Blake as man and wife, Vi-olette fought not to cry. It was perhaps the hardest effort she had ever made in her short life. She stole a glance up at Blake's face.

His profile was perfect, yet set in stone, making it impossible for her to comprehend his feelings. Yet she did not need to see his expression for her to know how he was feeling, he had made himself so very clear.

Violette's pulse pounded with painful force. She felt dizzy, lightheaded, weak-kneed, and faint. It was only two hours ago that she and Blake had reached their *understanding*.

She clutched the small nosegay in her gloved hands. This was what she had wanted. To be Blake's bride, his wife. Yet she did not want Blake this way, after all. But she had had no choice in the end. She did not want to die.

"I do," Blake said firmly.

Violette swallowed, aching in every fiber of her being, ach-ing in all of her muscles and bones. The reverend turned to her. "Do you, Lady Violette Goodwin, take this man, Lord

Theodore Blake, Viscount Neville, to be your husband, in sickness and in health, in poverty and wealth, to hold and to cherish, to love for all time, until death do you part?'' he asked.

Until death do you part. Violette licked her lips. Her breathing was shallow. Blake glanced at her. ''I do,'' she whispered, wondering if she was crying yet. And her words were not a lie. She would love him until she died.

Maybe, if God were merciful, she would not have a long life. To see him eventually marry someone else—after their divorce.

''Then I now pronounce you man and wife. Lord Neville, you may place the ring on the bride's fourth finger.''

Violette held up her left hand. It was shaking so terribly that she was embarrassed. Blake slipped a gold wedding band studded with diamonds and rubies onto her fourth finger, over her white kid gloves. Violette stared down at the beautiful ring until her vision blurred. She had never owned such a beautiful piece of jewelry before. She would, of course, give it back to Blake when they divorced.

''You may kiss the bride,'' the reverend said, smiling.

Blake faced Violette squarely. She lifted her gaze to his. She was wearing a simple pale blue silk dress and a matching hat with a half veil, the net in darker blue, that covered her eyes and nose but not her mouth. Blake seemed to hesitate. Violette stared at him, aware of being more unhappy than she had ever been in her life, of being more hurt than she had ever known a body could be.

His jaw flexed. His eyes seemed hard. He leaned forward and brushed his mouth against hers for less time than it took her heart to beat once. Although his lips hardly touched hers, his kiss was strange—indifferent, cold.

Violette closed her eyes, pulling away from him, hugging herself. How she wanted to escape the room, escape Blake. Too late, she realized she had crushed the nosegay she was holding.

He was surrounded by the men. Dom hugged him. Jon finally smiled. Blake managed a grin, but his expression was strained. Violette regarded them all, unmoving. They were acting like this was a real wedding.

''Lady Neville,'' the reverend said.

It took Violette a moment to realize that she was being addressed. Lady Neville, the wife of Lord Theodore Blake, Viscount of Neville. Her heart beat harder now. She forced a smile to her stiff, frozen mouth.

His own kind smile faded. Reverend Alcott was in his eighties. According to Blake, he had known the family since his father was a small child. He had married the earl and the countess. He had baptized both boys. Alcott touched her elbow. "Are you unwell?" he asked with utter sympathy.

His concern might very well undo her. Violette stiffened her spine. "I am fine, thank you."

"Lady Neville, if you wish to ever speak with me, feel free, anytime." He smiled at her. His brown eyes were warm. "I am a wonderful listener. And I do consider myself family."

Violette nodded, unable to continue smiling. Jon was staring at her. Violette hesitated. Every time she saw him it hurt her terribly. If only he would get well.

Now it appeared that he wished to speak to her. Violette had not spoken to or seen him since the night of the accident. Afraid of what he might say, Violette moved to his side.

He studied her. "Welcome to the family, Violette," Jon said seriously. "I am pleased to have you as a little sister."

He appeared to mean it. Violette was in disbelief. He was paralyzed because of her. "How can you say that?" she whispered.

"I am saying what I mean," he said flatly.

She wished he would smile. She wished his eyes would light up the way they once had. "I am so sorry, Jon," she said. "So very sorry."

"Now is neither the time nor the place to discuss the past, which cannot be changed in any case."

Violette nodded. He was clearly so unhappy. But he was an extraordinary man. "Thank you," she finally said.

Dom St. Georges grinned at her, stepping between them. His amber eyes were bright. He took her gloved hand and kissed it very firmly. "I cannot resist," he said. "I have had a feeling about this since we first met."

Violette did not understand. He might have been speaking Chinese. Nor did she care to understand, for she was looking past Dom, into Blake's eyes. He was staring at her very gravely. Her heart lurched. She thought about the way he had kissed her just a moment ago. Brides often cried at their own weddings, but with joy and happiness. She did not dare allow herself any tears. Her sorrow would be all too apparent.

"Shall we go?" Blake asked.

She nodded, fighting for self-control. "Thank you," she said to everyone present, managing, she hoped, to smile. She had the feeling that she failed. Blake had taken her arm, but not proprietarily. He led her to the door which Dom unlocked. They had not even stepped into the corridor when voices could be heard in the foyer. Violette recognized the men who were speaking and froze, gripping Blake's arm. Very clearly she had heard Inspector Howard speaking with the Rutherford butler.

"Christ," Blake ground out. "What damnable timing."

"Better now than five minutes ago," Dom said grimly, moving in front of them. They all returned to the foyer, where Howard and Adams stood holding their hats and shifting their weight, breaking off the conversation with the butler. The servant appeared relieved.

"My lord," he addressed Dom St. Georges. "These two gentlemen were most adamant about being shown into the salon to see Lord Blake. Yet you gave me the strictest instructions."

"I did." Dom was cool. He faced the two inspectors. "The marquis of Waverly, gentlemen, at your service." He bowed. "What may I do for you?"

"We have a coroner's warrant here," Howard said, stepping forward. "For Lady Goodwin."

Violette was aware of Blake slipping his arm around her reassuringly. She leaned against him, unable to control her trembling.

Dom smiled. "You do mean Viscountess Neville, do you not?"

Howard jerked, he and Adams exchanging a quick look. "Viscountess Neville?"

"Lady Goodwin has married Viscount Neville, and what a happy day this is. Perhaps you wish to congratulate the bride and groom?"

For one more moment, Howard and Adams were stunned. Then Adams pushed forward, facing Dom, Blake, and Violette. "I can quickly guess the games being played here," he said angrily. "But we do have a coroner's warrant for the arrest of Lady Goodwin."

Blake said coldly, "Perhaps you had better go fetch a new warrant, one correctly addressed. In order to arrest Viscountess Neville—my wife."

A moment of silence reigned amidst generally hostile stares.

"If you truly wish to arrest a member of the earl of Harding's family," Blake said, smiling. It was not a pleasant smile.

For another instant Adams did not speak, but he was turning purple. "This is not the end of this investigation," he ground out. "Someone has committed murder, and charges will be brought—against your *wife*."

"Someone has committed murder, all right," Blake said, "but *not* my wife."

A moment later Adams and Howard were marching out angrily. Blake thanked Dom. Shortly afterward Blake and Violette were inside his phaeton and the carriage was rolling quickly down the street. Jon had taken his own vehicle in order to return to Harding House.

Violette sat facing Blake, avoiding his eyes. She continued to shake. She felt shocked. The day had become incomprehensible. First an utterly false marriage, and then the warrent for her arrest.

"Violette." He reached over and covered her gloved hand with his. "Do not fret. They can arrest you now, but they cannot try you in the Queen's Bench, which is a victory for us."

She met his gaze. It was no longer cold—he was concerned. "I am so scared," she confessed through stiff lips. "Why is this happening to me?"

He stared. "I do not know," he finally said.

She wanted him to pull her forward, into his embrace. He did not. But she had known that he would not. She pulled her palm free of his, and gazed down at her lap. Hurting, and so terribly afraid.

"I am meeting Dodge. We have much to discuss. I shall drop you at home."

She had to meet his probing eyes. "What? What are you going to discuss? What is going to happen now?"

"We shall try to avoid any charges being leveled at all. We shall suggest, very strongly, that every effort be made to find the real killer. And if the inspectors insist on bringing charges against you, we are going to arrange for you to remain in my custody, or my father's, until the trial. I am confident that we can arrange that."

Violette touched her heaving breasts. *Until the trial.* Oh, God. What if there was a trial? What if, even in the Lords, they could not win? And how could they, when she wasn't really one of them?

She could still run away. The thought crystallized instantaneously.

But then she would never see Blake again; Blake who was trying to protect her from the worst, had married her in order to save her; Blake, whom she loved so much that it hurt. She did not dare look at him now. If she did, she would probably throw herself into his arms, begging, weeping.

"Let me do the worrying," Blake said, breaking into her thoughts.

Violette had to meet his gaze. "I don't understand you. You are the kindest man I have ever met. You are still being kind to me."

It was a moment before he replied. "I do not want you to suffer," he said.

She inhaled and their gazes locked. Something was taut and tight between them. It made Violette afraid to move, filling her with a tension she had never before experienced. Silence abruptly settled between them. Violette gripped her own hands. Did he care, after all? Just a little, perhaps?

If only he would change his mind. If only he would decide to keep her as a wife. Then she would not even consider running away, even if it meant hanging.

"We are almost home," Blake said into the stillness stretching between them.

Violette closed her eyes briefly. *We are almost home.* Was he trying to kill her with his kindness, his choice of words? It was his home. Not hers. And they both knew it. Because this marriage was a sham, a pretense—just as she herself was a fraud, a pretender—not a real lady and not a real wife.

In that blazing instant Violette knew that she was not going to be able to survive and withstand this marriage, no matter how short a duration it was. Every moment passed as Blake's wife would crush her a little bit more, bleeding her dry, until she was so broken and spent that she ceased to exist. Maybe hanging was better than impossible dreams.

Blake's town home had been designed in the Italianate style. Four stories high, occupying a narrow space, it was built of whitewashed sandstone, the roof tiled. The front doorway was arched and domed, and Violette was met there by a butler whom Blake introduced to her as Chamberlain.

"Chamberlain," he said, "this is my wife, Viscountess Neville. Please attend her as needs be. Violette, anything you need, you may ask Chamberlain."

Violette was beyond words, so she did not speak. The white-haired, bushy-browed butler had not blinked upon discovering that Blake had returned home so suddenly with a wife.

Blake bowed. "I shall not be home for supper. Do not wait up for me."

Violette refused to look at him. If she did, she would cry.

He turned and strode down the walk, past the orange and lime trees, climbing into his phaeton. Violette watched it drive away. She watched until the street was empty, the phaeton having disappeared.

"My lady."

Violette's anguish was interrupted. She faced the butler, realizing that they both stood in the street. She could not smile.

He stepped back, giving her a wide entrance into Blake's home. Violette walked inside, glancing around with little interest at the spectacular foyer. The domed ceiling was three stories above her, adorned with the largest crystal chandelier Violette had ever seen. It had been painted in the rococo style, and a raven-haired Venus appeared to be rising from the sea above their heads, surrounded by numerous water sprites and fairy creatures. The floor which Violette stood upon was boldly marbled in black and white. As Violette's gaze lifted she caught a glimpse of her overly pale reflection in a mirror hanging over one ornate, gilded, claw-footed side table. She appeared to be a living corpse, a very desolate one. She had never looked worse.

"My lady," the butler said when she did not move or speak. "Might I show you to your room? May I bring you dinner? Perhaps have a hot bath drawn?"

Violette finally looked directly at Chamberlain and realized that, although his lined face was impassive, his eyes were brown, warm, and kind. Although she did not have an appetite, she nodded. "That would be fine." Tears suddenly filled her eyes. "If you could, I would very much like plum pudding."

"As you wish, my lady." Chamberlain bowed.

Violette was awake when Blake came home. It was the next day, early in the morning. The sun was finally out, and the day was bright and nearly cloudless. Violette was taking a solitary breakfast in the dining room, which looked out on Blake's back gardens, red and gold now with the advent of autumn. She was unable to force more than a single bite of food down, knowing that Blake had spent the entire night somewhere else. But surely, surely, he had not been with another woman. Violette was certain he would never do that.

She squared her shoulders and pretended to eat as he paused on the threshold of the dining room. "Good morning," Blake said after a moment of silence.

Violette laid her fork down, forced a smile to her frozen lips, and turned to look at him. In spite of the fact that he was wearing the same suit he had worn all day yesterday, he did not appear either disheveled or rumpled, not at all. "Good morning." She did not mean to ask the question, but it tumbled without prompting from her mouth. "Did you sleep at Harding House?"

He looked away from her as he went to the sideboard where he picked up a croissant and studied it. "Yes." He then set the pastry down without eating it.

Violette's heart skipped. There had been something odd about his reply. And she did not understand why he had not come home to his own house, his own bed. Was she a pariah, then?

He faced her, unsmiling. "I have many appointments today, so I am going upstairs to bathe and change. Including one with your solicitor." He paused, as if waiting for Violette to comment, but she did not. So Blake continued. "So far, there have been no charges filed, but our sources do tell us that there will be charges in spite of your new status as my wife. Dodge is prepared to take care of the custody issue, so you need not worry about going to prison."

Violette could not even manage a thank-you. She looked down at her plate. She knew that Blake continued to regard her. So she would be charged with murder after all.

And then she felt him approach. "You are having lemon meringue for breakfast?" he asked with some amusement.

She had been pushing her fork through the creamy custard pie. She felt like throwing a forkful of meringue in his face. Why hadn't he come home last night? Where had he been?

He cleared his throat. "I will leave an envelope in your room in case you have any shopping to do today." Still he did not walk away.

Violette refused to look at him. She shoved a forkful of lemon meringue down, where it stuck in her throat.

"We shall speak later," he said awkwardly.

She did not reply, but looked up after he was walking out of the dining room. When he was gone she began to tremble. It crossed her mind that he might very well have spent the night with another woman. She instantly dismissed the idea as absurd. But was it absurd? He had a reputation as a ladies' man. She was short of breath. She couldn't help thinking about Gabriella Cantwell, even though she had no doubt that the other woman was far too honest and elegant to carry on behind her husband's back. But society was filled with other women who would leap at the chance to be with Blake.

Violette stood abruptly. She had no appetite. She did not think she would ever have an appetite again. Not unless things changed—drastically.

"Chamberlain," she called.

The butler immediately appeared.

"Is there a carriage I can use?" She had to get out of this house.

"Of course," Chamberlain said gravely. "His Lordship has several conveyances. Would you prefer a brougham or a landau?"

Violette did not know the difference. "Whatever you suggest," she said. "I am going upstairs to get my hat and gloves. I wish to go out immediately."

Chamberlain bowed as Violette left the dining room and went upstairs. On the third floor she slowed down, her steps faltering, as she approached her bedroom. The freckle-faced maid she had been given, a young girl of perhaps fifteen, had already confirmed that Blake's suite—he had two rooms—were adjacent to her bedroom. His door was closed. But as she walked by, straining to listen, she knew he was inside. She thought she could hear him speaking to his valet, his words low and indistinct.

She was filled with grief. Violette moved into her room, opening the armoire. Her things had been fetched for her from her flat yesterday. Violette reached for a pale green cashmere mantle and a darker green hat, then paused. She could not help but stare at her reflection in the mirror. Her face was gaunt, somehow icy, her blue eyes appearing huge and so very hurt. Was this what Blake saw whenever he looked at her? She hoped not. She did not want him to know how much he was hurting her, how he was slowly, inch by inch, destroying her.

She turned away from the mirror, closing the armoire. She was too heartsick to go out. She did not have the desire, the energy. She had nowhere to go anyway.

She sank down on an ottoman and found herself facing Blake's door. Would he come home tonight? She did not think so. And she should not be hurt. Because he wasn't really her husband, he was only rescuing her from a murder conviction.

Violette covered her face with her hands.

She heard her door opening and dropped her palms instantly, looking up to see Blake standing on the threshold that adjoined their rooms. His eyes were wide, riveted on her face. Violette hoped, desperately, that she had hidden her grief before he could see it. She stood. "You didn't knock."

"I thought you were downstairs."

She stared, wishing he would go away—wanting him to stay.

He raised his hand and she saw the envelope. "The money is here. I hope it is enough."

She could not speak. She did not want any more of his generosity—he had done enough.

He bowed. "Good day, Violette." He hesitated. "I do not think I will be home for supper tonight." He stepped forward and handed her the envelope, then turned around.

Her pulse accelerating, she watched him exit the room, feeling sick inside. Of course he wasn't coming home to dine with her—why should he? She almost called him back, but somehow prevented herself from doing so.

Tears blurring her vision, she opened the envelope, expecting to find twenty or thirty, perhaps even fifty, pounds. But in it she found five hundred pounds and a blank bank draft signed by him. The cash and the draft slipped through her fingers to the floor. She didn't want his money. She wanted his love.

⊰ *Twenty-five* ⊱

BLAKE'S office was in his bank, which was on Oxford Street. He had arrived there a few moments ago, but he sat at his massive desk in the dark, his hands clasped in front of him. His expression was grim.

He knew that he had thus far hurt Violette, and that had never been his intention, not at all. He had married her against his will, to protect her, period. But he was beginning to wonder if that was his only reason.

Blake sighed, leaning back in his chair. He was very tired; he had passed a restless night, worrying about a trial in the Lords, suddenly losing confidence. He kept thinking about how easily the inspectors had dragged Violette through the mud, and they were not seasoned prosecutors. Worse, he kept recalling how she had looked at him that day at Lady Allister's, as if he were some kind of superhuman man, a hero who could slay all fire-breathing dragons in her defense. And he also kept recalling her expression when he had walked into the breakfast room that morning. Bloody, bloody hell. Her hurt had been written all over her too expressive face. He could read Violette better than any book.

And if spending a single night at his parents' had hurt her so, how would she deal with a divorce or an annulment when the time came?

He looked up at the sound of a knock on his door. His assistant, a young, enthusiastic bespectacled clerk, poked his head in. "Mr. Dodge, my lord."

"Send him in," Blake said, standing. In a way, he was relieved at the interruption. But his stomach also tightened with dread.

George Dodge walked into Blake's spacious, wood-paneled office, carrying his topcoat, hat, gloves, and cane, as Blake lit several gaslamps. The two men shook hands.

"Well, the game begins," Dodge said, placing his belongings on one large rosewood chair while taking the leather seat of its mate. "Lady Feldstone has filed charges against your wife, Blake."

Blake stared, slowly sitting behind his desk. He shook his head. "Lady Joanna filed. Not the police. Perhaps this is good news?"

"Perhaps it shows a waning of enthusiasm on the part of the officials. The Coroner's Inquest will be a part of the evidence, Blake."

"Has a date been set for the trial?"

"Next Monday."

Blake almost fell off of his seat. "That's six days hence!"

Dodge nodded. "We have a lot to do. However, I do have interesting news," he said.

"And what is that?"

"I have obtained a copy of the coroner's report. Do not ask me how, but I prefer being prepared," Dodge said with a smile. "The autopsy findings are very interesting. Sir Thomas had so much arsenic in his liver that there is no question he had ingested the poison for some time. I have showed the report to my own physician. He maintains that such a concentrated amount of poison had been administered for at least six months to a year prior to the victim's death."

Blake jerked, eyes wide. "Six months. Violette was married to Sir Thomas for six months. But if Sir Thomas was ingesting arsenic before their marriage, then someone else is obviously the murderer." And that would exclude the missing Ralph Horn.

"Yes. Of course, it is impossible to decide the date the ingestion of poison began," Dodge said. "It might have very well been within the time frame of the marriage." Dodge regarded Blake. "Are you certain that Lady Goodwin is innocent of the charges filed against her?"

Blake prickled. "I am."

"This does give us a chance to discover other suspects with other motives," Dodge said. "My assistants are compiling a list of anyone with anything to gain from Sir Thomas's death, focusing on those who knew Sir Thomas prior to his marriage."

Blake had stiffened. But before he could speak, Dodge added, "I can tell you this with real assurance. If Lady Goodwin was purchasing arsenic during the six months in which she was married to Sir Thomas, it was not in Tamrah or a nearby village."

"What about Horn?" Blake asked stiffly, his mind spinning possibilities—and conclusions—relating to what Dodge had previously said.

"If he was purchasing arsenic, he was not purchasing it in Tamrah, either. My runners are still interviewing druggists in adjoining towns. I prefer to be prepared, even in the Lords. Horn, by the way, has yet to return to his place of employment on the St. Catherine docks."

"And most likely, he will not," Blake said matter-of-factly. "Not unless Violette is cleared of these charges and the murder investigation is closed. He is a damnable coward. But"—and Blake smiled coldly—"I say good riddance."

"Why have you taken such a firm dislike to the man? Are you convinced he is the murderer?"

"No, I am not convinced he is anything other than an opportunist and a thief." And then he returned to the astonishing thought he'd just had. "I wonder," he said slowly, "is it possible that Lady Feldstone, who is shouting foul play the most loudly, is the actual criminal here?"

Dodge leaned back against his chair. "I was wondering when you would ask that question," he said calmly. "For it has been apparent to me for some time that Lady Feldstone is one of the parties who has had the most to gain from her father's death."

*   *   *

Blake had little time to ponder Dodge's revelations or the fact that the trial was just around the corner. His assistant announced the arrival of his parents.

"My lord," Christopher said, appearing in the doorway of the office. He appeared sheepish. "The earl and countess of Harding."

Blake looked past his clerk at his father, who wasn't smiling, and his mother, who was. He could guess what had brought them calling so unexpectedly. His mother did have the habit of stopping by his offices, but his father never did. He grimaced, raking a hand through his hair. "Good morning."

The earl walked into the wood-paneled room without a word, while his mother came forward to embrace him and kiss him warmly on the cheek. "How well you look," she marveled. "Blake, is it true? There is this wild rumor flying about town— your father was approached this morning in the park—and the rumor is that you have married Lady Goodwin."

He looked into his mother's surprised eyes. "And if I have?"

The countess shook her head. "My darling son. I have worried endlessly that you would never settle down, that you would actually remain alone for the rest of your life. I am surprised, but not completely. I certainly noticed the interest you have had for Violette and she for you. Of course, I am a little concerned because of your differences. Your marriage might not be easy. But I am your mother and I know you so well. You would never be content with the typical society debutante."

Blake wasn't really surprised by his mother's accepting attitude. She had always been as liberal as she was generous. But he was ashamed. He did not want to tell his mother the truth about his marriage—that it would exist for a limited duration only. Blake looked past his mother at his father, who remained somber. He regarded the countess again. "Mother," he said, "it does not really bother you that Violette has transformed herself into one of us—but that she was born Violet Cooper, that she is a product of the East End?"

"Blake, darling. Had you told me this story, had I never met Violette, I would be dismayed and frightened for you. But I have met her. I have watched her transform herself. What she has done is amazing, and should be lauded, not condemned." The countess's smile faded. "I only wish that Jon had never fallen over that railing, and that he could be standing here today with us, sharing this moment."

Blake ached. "We all feel that way. We cannot give up hope."

"I am not giving up hope," the countess said firmly.

The earl stepped forward. "I would have appreciated being informed of this monumental event in a more timely, and more elegant, manner."

Blake hesitated.

"And do not ask me if I approve, being as you did not bother to ask me for my blessings before the deed was done." The earl was rather sullen. "My approval is a moot issue, obviously. But do enlighten me. When did the nuptials take place?"

Blake hesitated again. "Yesterday morning."

"Was there a reason for such secrecy and haste?" the earl asked pointedly.

Blake did flush. "I have not misbehaved with Violette, if that is what you were asking," he said with some heat.

"Can you blame me for thinking the worst?" the earl demanded. "For thinking that she trapped you into marriage?"

"She did not," Blake said flatly. "But there was a reason for secrecy, and for haste." He glanced at his mother, whose gaze was questioning. "I must be honest with you both. Please, Father, Mother, do sit down."

His father ignored the heavy leather chair Blake gestured to, although his mother gracefully sank into the second of the pair, adjusting her wide skirts with ease.

Blake paced. "I am *not* in love with Violette." He cleared his throat, aware of how adamant he had sounded. He softened his tone. "I did not marry her because she was the most suitable candidate to be my wife and the mother of my children. Had I chosen freely, undoubtedly I would have found some young debutante whose family we are intimately acquainted with. Someone like Catherine."

"What are you getting at?" Richard growled.

The countess was silent.

"By marrying Violette, I have probably spared her the hangman's noose. Father, the venue of the trial has been moved to the Lords. The trial is next Monday." Suzannah turned white. "We must do everything in our power to see to it that there is a friendly verdict, although I hope we can somehow have the trial dismissed before we even come to that point."

The earl nodded, crossing his arms. "So you have taken it upon yourself to rescue her."

"Exactly."

The two men stared at one another. "Blake, I know you are a thoughtful man. But have you really thought about what you are doing? I am not blaming Violette for Jon's accident, but I cannot forget the part she had in it. And unlike your mother, I am more leery of her past. And now she is your wife. Yes, you were very noble to rescue her, but she is going to be the mother of your children."

"I could not risk a trial in the Queen's Bench. I could not let her hang," Blake said. Tension pervaded his entire being. He knew better than to respond to the subject of Violette having his children. His father would erupt if Blake told him that neither Violette nor any other woman was having his children because this marriage was a sham and he would not marry again afterward.

"That is very noble of you," the earl said, studying him.

Blake had the feeling that his father could see through him. "I need your help, obviously. Is there any chance we could lose a trial if there is one?"

"I shall call in a few markers immediately. I do not think my peers will convict your wife for murder, Blake. Not against my wishes. Not when we are all one hundred percent certain that she is innocent." His father was grim.

"Good," Blake said, relieved. But he had never doubted that his father would stand by him in this instance. The earl was a very just man.

The earl walked over to him, laying his hand upon his shoulder. "Have you told me everything, Blake?" he asked.

Blake could not lie, not to his father or his mother, but he was not about to tell them the truth. "There is not much more to tell. We are looking for the real murderer." He smiled.

His father did not smile back. The earl, Blake knew, was aware of a gaping omission. "You have taken a big risk, Blake, and perhaps made a big sacrifice. But I am sure you are aware of it. I hope"—his gaze skewered Blake—"that she is worth it."

Blake did not reply.

❖ *Twenty-six* ❖

VIOLETTE was told by Chamberlain that she had a caller. She had not left the sanctuary of her bedroom all day. Her eyes widened as her steps faltered. Ralph stood in the foyer, grinning at her. " 'Ello, luv.''

"Where have you been?!'' Violette cried, rushing to him. They embraced for a moment.

"I been up north." His smile had faded. "Wot's goin' on, Violette? Yew went an' married that 'igh an' mighty 'Ardin' bloke?''

Violette gripped his arm. "Come inside. We'll share dinner. Blake is not at home.''

Ralph narrowed his eyes as they entered the parlor. "I already 'eard from the stable boys. Yew married 'Is Lordship!'' It was an accusation.

Violette regarded him grimly. "I did. They were going to arrest me, Ralph! Arrest me for killing my husband! Where, may I ask, have you been?''

"I been up north to Tamrah, like I said." He glared at her. "Lookin' fer some answers on me own. Bein' as that fancy lawyer an' 'usband of yers ain't come up with the real murderer.''

Violette stared. She had been almost certain that Ralph would not abandon her.

"But did yew have to go an' marry 'im?'' Ralph demanded.

"Yes,'' Violette said. "I had no choice. I don't want to hang, Ralph. Now I am more than Blake's wife, I am a peer. That gives me rights—including the right to be tried in the Lords, where Blake and his family have friends.''

"Bah,'' Ralph spat. "Yew goin' to sit in the 'Ouse of Lords?!''

"What did you find in Tamrah?'' Violette asked, trying not to think about a trial. She kept wishing that in the end, there wouldn't be any charges filed against her, or any trial after all. Ralph was right. How could she, Violet Cooper, sit in the Lords?

"Sir Thomas 'ad the pox.''

"What?'' Violette gasped.

"Fer a few years now. That's why 'e was so sickly all the time. Remember those sores 'e 'ad?"

Violette stared, in shock. It was a moment before she could accept what Ralph had told her. "Could he have died from the pox?" she asked hopefully.

"Luv, 'is liver was filled up with rat poison." Ralph's gaze was cold. "Someone wanted to bury 'im, an' that's the truth."

"You didn't find anything else out?"

"I found out who's been buyin' rat poison this past year in Tamrah."

"Who?" Violette whispered.

"There one other buyer, Violette, luv. The Feldstone house-keeper."

"Lady Feldstone's housekeeper?" Violette repeated, shocked. "But, surely you're not thinking . . . that's absurd?!"

"Mebbe. Mebbe not." Ralph took off his crushed felt cap and tossed it onto a cream-colored silk sofa striped with green, red, and gold. He sat down hard on the plush couch. Violette rushed forward when she realized what he had done, grabbing his hand and jerking on him. "Get up! God! Before you get dirt and soot all over Blake's furniture!"

Ralph scowled at her and did not budge. "Wot a good little wife yew are."

Violette stamped her foot. "Get up, Ralph Horn, before I hit you as hard as I can."

"Yer such a lady, Violette," Ralph said.

Violette clenched her fists.

Ralph sighed and stood.

Violette was relieved that he had not left a single spot behind. But then she met his eyes and saw him staring at her. She could not look away.

"Yew look bad," he said baldly. "Like yew ain't slept or ate in days. Like yer real sad, like yew cry a lot."

Violette bit her lip.

"Wot's 'e done to yew!" Ralph exclaimed.

Violette managed to shake her head. "This isn't a real marriage, Ralph. He only married me to give me his name." Her voice caught. She turned her back on Ralph, walking over to a small table that was uncluttered in spite of the current fashion for bric-a-brac and knickknacks. She fingered an exquisite crystal panther.

"Yer not 'appy," Ralph said, from close behind her. His breath feathered her nape.

Violette jumped. She had not heard him approach. The table was behind her hips, Ralph so closely in front of her that his legs crushed her skirts in spite of the crinoline hoops she wore. "No," she whispered, "I am not happy."

He tilted her chin up with one finger; she dropped her gaze. "I told yew. 'E ain't fer yew. But now wot are yew goin' to do?"

"We'll divorce when the trial is over, or before that, as soon as it is safe to do so." She continued to avoid his eyes.

"But yew don't want t' divorce 'im, now do yew?" Ralph asked softly.

Violette whispered, not looking up, "I am a fool. I love him so much."

"I know," Ralph said harshly. He suddenly took her into his arms and held her for a moment. When he released her, he said, "I'll kill 'im if 'e 'urts yew."

Violette forced a smile. "That would be even worse." She sniffed once. "Are you staying at the flat?"

He shrugged. "Don't really 'ave no reason to, not with yew gone." His pale gray eyes were very direct.

"Do you want to stay here?" Violette asked.

Ralph's expression brightened. "Now that's a good thoughtful gel. I'm sure a room behind the barn would be nice an' cozy."

Violette stiffened. "I will not put you behind the barn! There are several guest rooms on the third floor," Violette said. She hesitated. Blake would not like Ralph staying with them. "I'll tell Chamberlain to ready one of the guest rooms."

His eyes gleamed. "Well, if you insist, luv."

Violette sat alone in her bedroom on the pale chintz sofa in front of the fire which crackled and danced in the hearth. She stared at the heavy clock on a table just past the mantel. The gold hands told her that it was nine o'clock.

She and Ralph had shared supper alone, for Blake had not yet come home. Blake's cook had presented them with a ten-course meal, and Violette, although she had eaten, had not tasted a single morsel of food. How could she? When she sat at Blake's oblong mahogany table opposite Ralph, a pair of huge silver candlesticks interposed between them? Ralph had not seemed to feel any qualms. He had eaten enough for three men, while drinking two entire bottles of Blake's red Burgundy wine. Chamberlain, who never said a word, was growing on Violette. He had, bless his professional soul, offered Ralph a third bottle, which Ralph had, fortunately, declined. Violette had heard him snoring just a short time ago when she had wandered down the hall.

She stood, a rose-colored satin wrapper belted tightly around her. Where was Blake? Would he come home at all tonight? Perhaps he was at some fancy affair, dancing with some incredibly elegant woman like Gabriella.

Her heart lurched hard at the notion. She began to pace the room. Could he have not, at least, sent her a note telling her whether he would return at all that night? Wasn't that the husbandly thing to do? But they weren't really married! In fact, he had no real obligations toward her at all.

Violette did not know what to do. But at that precise moment, she heard footsteps coming down the hall outside of her bedroom door.

She did not hesitate. Her feet bare, she ran to her closed door and pressed her ear against it, breathing far too rapidly. She strained to hear. Yes, it sounded like two pairs of footsteps, not one, and then she was exultant, because she heard the door on her right opening and closing. Violette darted back across the room to the door which separated her bedroom from Blake's sitting room. It was adjacent to the fireplace. She pressed her ear against the smooth wooden surface, wishing her foolish heart would quiet down.

And she was rewarded with the sound of movement inside— and the sound of Blake's voice, dismissing his valet.

His steps sounded closer now, and she stiffened, failing to breathe. Before she could wonder what he was about, the door she was leaning on opened. Violette cried out, falling forward— against Blake.

He caught her beneath her arms, hauling her upright. "What in the blazes are you doing?" he asked, but mildly.

Violette jerked free of him, stepping back into her own room, feeling a hot, telltale flush covering her cheeks. She reached down to make sure that her satin robe remained firmly belted. "I . . ." Her mind was frozen, inacapable of coming up with an excuse.

"Were you eavesdropping?" Blake asked, his gaze bright and penetrating. But he was not angry. He seemed, perhaps, amused.

Violette straightened. "Of course not. I was about to knock," she lied. "There are some things I wish to discuss with you."

He smiled at her, as if he knew exactly what she had been about. Then his midnight gaze slid from her eyes to her mouth and down the satin robe, right to her bare, curling toes. A liquid jolt went through Violette, a streak of red-hot desire. His smile had vanished. Violette suddenly realized just how undressed she was. The satin fabric of her gown had become a sensual caress with each intake of breath, each brief movement she made. Blake was not really her husband. He did not have the right to see her when she was clad like this, in nothing but a slip of a nightgown and a thin outer wrapper.

"May I come in for a moment?" Blake asked slowly.

Violette was shaken. Blake's gaze had slipped again, and even though only for an instant, she found it difficult to breathe. And although she should tell him "No," she nodded. She was riveted in place, as if nailed to the floor, as he moved past her, his body brushing hers. Violette had never been more acutely aware of anyone. She had never wanted to touch anyone more. But she did not have the right to go over to him and lay her palm on his cheek, her face on his chest, just as he did not have the right to look at her as if he were trying to see through her nightclothes.

She bit her lip as he turned. He had shed his jacket but not his trousers or his shirt, and his sleeves were rolled up to his elbows, exposing his strong forearms. His feet, like hers, were bare. There was something powerful and provocative in having him enter her bedroom while preparing for bed.

He paused in the center of the room, facing her, his hands slipping into the pockets of his fine wool trousers. "I am sorry I missed supper."

"Are you?" Violette heard herself ask, her tone on edge. Immediately she flushed.

He stared. "I would not say so if it were untrue. In any case, I have had a hard and busy day."

And a busy evening? Violette wondered silently, but did not dare say so aloud.

"I ate at the club. I hope your day went well?" Blake said politely.

Violette stared at him, biting her lip. Why hadn't he come home for supper? Where had he spent the evening? Had he really been at his club? Was it always going to be this way? Two strangers cohabiting—until the divorce?

"Violette?"

"Did you really sleep at Harding House last night?" Violette asked abruptly.

His eyes widened.

Violette could not believe what she had so unfortunately and impulsively blurted out.

"I beg your pardon?" Blake asked stiffly.

Violette straightened her spine. "I was just wondering . . ." She could not continue.

Two spots of red color appeared on Blake's cheeks. "If I am a liar?" He completed the sentence for her.

"No." How Violette wished she hadn't spoken up.

"What is it that you really wish to ask me, Violette?" Blake asked darkly.

Violette inhaled. "You did not come home last night. And . . . you have a reputation."

"I see. And do I appear to be a ruthless cad who would leave his bride at home in order to philander about town?"

"I . . . I am not really your bride."

Blake stared. A heavy silence ensued. "No. You are not really my bride."

She walked away from him, aware that her hands were shaking. "I want a divorce," she said harshly. Another spontaneous outburst. "Now."

He was frozen. "That is ridiculous. And impossible. Or do you wish to hang?"

"I don't care," Violette said, sitting down hard on the couch, facing the fire, Blake behind her. She tucked her toes under the satin wrapper, hunching over, wanting to cry.

She heard him move. He strode around the sofa and halted in front of her, staring down at her. "Our marriage is a pretense, and we both know it. But if it makes you feel any better," he said, regarding her closely, "I will make certain that I do come home every night for the duration of our marriage."

Violette finally looked up at him.

"And if you need company in order to dine, then you shall have it," he said.

It was a victory of sorts, but it did not feel like one. Violette shrugged.

"I do not want to hurt you," Blake said.

"It doesn't matter," Violette returned woodenly.

He sat down in a chair, shifting his body so he regarded her directly. "It does matter."

Violette did not reply.

Blake sighed. "We must talk about more pressing matters. I had a long meeting with Dodge today."

Violette met his eyes. "Can this not wait until the morning?" She knew she was going to have nightmares that night. If she slept at all. And dreaming about Blake being forever out of her reach was bad enough. She did not want any more anguish in her life. She did not want to know another thing about her legal predicament that night.

"No. I do have some good news." His gaze never left her. "The venue has been changed. To the Lords. The bad news is that there is going to be a trial in the Lords next week. Charges have been pressed against you, Violette."

Violette could not move. It felt like her heart had stopped. "A trial? Next week?" She forgot about the crisis that was their marriage. All she could think about was that the incredible had happened, that she had been charged with murdering a man she had truly cared for—and that she might hang for a murder she had not committed.

"You have been officially remanded into my father's custody, so little will change right now." He smiled at her and she knew he was trying to reassure her, but he failed. "For the next few weeks you shall live here, as if you are still a free woman."

She could not speak. She could not move. *As if you are still a free woman.* His words echoed. She was frozen with fear.

"Violette?"

Violette said, "Oh, God."

"My father, Rutherford, and myself are calling in all of our markers. We have many allies already, Violette. And of course, I am hoping to locate the real killer as soon as possible."

Violette was ill. She was trembling. She dreaded the idea of facing an assembly of powerful nobles, all of whom would rip her apart in order to decide if she were a murderess or not. "What happens in a few weeks?"

He shifted. "There will be a verdict, if the trial runs to its conclusion."

"A verdict."

"We will find the real killer," Blake said firmly. "And you are innocent."

"I don't think I can manage this," she whispered. "They will destroy me."

"You can. And you will." Blake's tone was firm. "We shall be there together. I shall coach you all week. You have nothing to worry about," Blake said forcefully. "Remember, you are now Viscountess Neville."

But it was a lie and they both knew it. So many lies. And Violette wanted to rush into his arms. To hold him, hard, press her face against his chest, and have his strong, powerful arms holding her. And perhaps, if she didn't love him so much, she would have leapt up and embraced him. But she did not move.

"Violette?" Blake was standing. "You are pale. I do not want you to worry. We have uncovered some interesting news. I have begun to wonder about Joanna Feldstone's involvement in all of this. As it turns out, her housekeeper has purchased quite a suppy of arsenic this past year."

Violette already knew that. She stared up at Blake, incapable of speech.

"I will be right back," he said decisively. Violette watched him return to his rooms. She dropped her gaze to her hands, which had become icy, in her lap. It had become difficult to breathe. She was short of breath. How could she go to trial in the Lords? Those men were not her peers. She was an impostor, a pretender, a fraud. And before the trial was over, they would all know it. Oh, God. She did not want to die. She was only eighteen.

Blake returned, carrying a snifter in his hand. "French brandy. Drink it." He handed it to her, his eyes on her face.

Violette stared at the amber contents. She was frightened. Very frightened. And filled with panic.

"Drink," Blake said, a command. "It will help you sleep." His tone softened. "You look very tired, Violette."

Violette glanced up at him, met his compelling eyes, unable to understand the sudden gentle light she saw there, and she obeyed.

But she could not sleep, not even after she had drank half the glass of brandy. Violette sat on the edge of her big bed, staring toward the fire, which was dying—staring at the door which adjoined her room with Blake's.

It felt as if her entire life were passing before her eyes. She was going to lose everything—Ralph, Blake, her new friends the Hardings, her life.

Violette hugged herself. Her life was at stake. If she were dead her marriage did not matter.

But Violette thought about the look in Blake's eyes when he had handed her the brandy. It was a look which made her believe, in spite of all logic, that he did care for her a little bit, that all that he was doing now was because of some fondness he held for her, and not just because he was such a heroic man.

She stared at Blake's door. She needed him now. Like never before. She needed to be held, touched, kissed. He could caress away her terrible fears. And she could express her love for him with her hands and her mouth. She did not have to be experienced to know that, because the urge was overwhelming. She might never have this opportunity again. A few weeks from now, she might be dead.

Violette stood and walked over to the table in front of the sofa. Her snifter sat there, the brandy catching the light from the fire. She bent to pick it up and took a long draught. Heat warmed her insides considerably.

She had to go to him. Because she needed him so badly and because if she didn't try, in this final hour of her life, she would never know what might have happened, what might have been. Wasn't it better to go to Blake, risking rejection, than to allow things to continue the way they were? Maybe they would share this one night together. Or two, or three, or even four or five, before the final verdict.

Violette caught the end of her braid with shaking fingers. She took off the red ribbon, then finger-combed her hair until it fell in rioting blue-black waves around her shoulders and down her back. Her heart beat now with alarming strength; her knees were weak. Violette found herself reaching for her sash and pulling it more tightly around her. She walked to the door separating their room and tested the knob. It was unlocked.

Violette turned the knob and opened the door, almost ill with desire that was far more than physical. She peered into the sitting room, which was dark. There would be no turning back now. There was no other choice.

And across the carpeted expanse she saw that the bedroom door was open, a light spilling out. Blake was still awake.

Violette entered the outer room, shivering. And before she could reassure herself that she was certainly the only one deafened by her heartbeat, she tripped on the tasseled edge of the rug. Crying out, she almost fell to the floor.

"Violette?!" Blake exclaimed from the other room.

Violette was standing when he appeared in the doorway of his bedroom, holding aloft a taper. His eyes widened. He stared.

Violette faced him, feeling her cheeks heat. She was at a loss for words, but not because she had been discovered in the act of entering his rooms. He wore nothing but a pair of silk drawers. She hadn't realized how broad his shoulders were, how muscular his chest, or that it was dusted with black hair. And when he moved, muscles rippled everywhere, dear God. Nor had she realized how flat and hard his stomach was. It was indented with sinew. She glimpsed his navel and forgot to breathe. Her loins had become alive in a shameful way.

"What are you doing?" he asked tightly.

Violette took a gulp of air, trying not to look at his thighs, which bulged with muscle above the knees. "I can't sleep."

His gaze swept over her. Violette realized her robe had opened, the sash loosened from her fall, and although the heat in her cheeks increased, she did not tighten it. Her behavior might be wanton, unladylike, but she felt wanton now, like never before.

And she knew with certainty that he found her beautiful. She could tempt him the way Eve had tempted Adam.

"Maybe, if you go back to your bed," he said harshly, "you can."

"I can't," Violette whispered, her tone odd even to her own ears. It seemed thick. "I'm too afraid."

His regard was unwavering.

"Blake," she said, low. "I can't stand the thought of facing the Lords. I am not afraid, I am terrified," she cried.

Blake's jaw flexed.

"I don't want to die," she added, her gaze glued to his face. "I don't want to die," she repeated. "I," she stopped. She had almost blurted out, *I need you. Please.*

"You are not going to die," he said firmly. "Come. Sit with me and we will talk about this for a while."

Violette nodded, her pulse skipping wildly, her legs almost failing her.

Blake moved past her and set the light down on a small side table. He gestured and she came around and sat down on the sofa. He hesitated briefly before sitting beside her, leaving an ample amount of space between them.

Violette stared at him. He stared back. It was hard not to

look at his left arm, because it was so starkly bare, or to let
her gaze wander to his shoulders, his chest, or his crunched-up
abdomen.

"You're shaking," he said suddenly. "I don't want you to
be afraid." His voice was hoarse.

"Help me forget," she whispered, a single tear slipping from
one eye.

He suddenly reached out and touched her hair, catching
strands of it in his fingers, weaving the strands there. "I'm not
going to let anything happen to you," he whispered. "I swear
to you, Violette."

She believed him then. His words were a vow, made from
the heart. She didn't mean to, truly she didn't, but tears slipped
down her cheeks. She wanted to tell him how much she loved
him—with all her heart, and then, somehow, impossibly,
more—but of course, she did not dare. Yet the words were
there, inside of her, a bubble bursting, about to explode forth.

"Violette, don't cry," he said, agonized.

She shook her head, trying now to stop, but it was impossible. Just as her love for Blake was impossible, just as the
crisis of her life was impossible.

Suddenly he gripped both of her shoulders with his hands.
Violette cried out and leaned against him; his arms closed
around her, hard and strong and warm and safe. She had found
her haven.

"Hold me, please, like this, Blake," she whispered, her lips
moving against the naked skin of his throat. "I need you so
much!"

"Violette." His tone was hoarse. His hands slid up her back,
beneath the heavy mane of her hair, then down, low and lower
still, past her hips. They remained there, splayed wide. "Violette. *I need you too.*"

Violette gasped. Their eyes met. His gaze was brilliant. Fire.

Violette did not move, knowing, hoping, waiting.

His expression changed. Suddenly fierce, he caught her face
in his two big hands, and seized her mouth with his.

❖ *Twenty-seven* ❖

VIOLETTE fell backwards on the sofa, Blake on top of her. His mouth took hers again and again. Violette clutched his shoulders, tasting the saltiness of her own tears as their mouths fused. He suddenly pulled back from her.

She gazed up at him and without realizing what she was doing, she touched his face, cupping his cheek. "Blake," she whispered, consumed with her love for him.

A brilliant light flared in his eyes. And abruptly he had her face in his hands and he was kissing her wildly, tugging on her mouth, devouring it, pressing it open, their tongues finally meeting. And then his arms were around her and her spine was pressed deeply into the soft again. Violette kissed his throat repeatedly, his collarbone, his shoulder.

He groaned, embracing her tightly, shifting his body so her thighs opened and his legs pushed between them. Violette gasped when the hardest part of his body, a shaft that felt like steel, came into contact with her sex. His arousal was rock-hard, massive, and feeling him there against her sent a fever raging through her veins.

"Violette," he said thickly against her neck. "I am trying very hard to think clearly about why we should not do this."

Violette ran her hands up and down his hard, naked back. His skin felt like velvet, his muscles tight and taut beneath it. "You feel so wonderful," she whispered. "Nothing has ever felt this good before." Her fingertips skimmed the waistband of his drawers.

Blake groaned, lifting himself up slightly so their gazes could meet. With one hand he suddenly anchored her face. "You are so very beautiful," he said. "So beautiful and so real. I have never met anyone like you before." And he kissed her hard before she could respond.

Her heart soaring, Violette found herself wrapping her calves around the backs of his knees. His manhood settled more intimately against her and she moaned into his mouth, thinking that this was what she had waited for her entire life without even knowing it. Blake slid his palm beneath her gaping wrapper, covering her breast. Violette whimpered as her nipple tautened beneath his fingertips. She was beginning to feel dazed.

He shifted so their eyes could meet, then bent, pushing the satin rose wrapper off of her shoulders. Through the lace panel, he tongued her nipple, causing Violette to jerk and gasp, stunned by the pleasure he had induced. He tongued it repeatedly, finally tugging the erect point between his teeth. Violette squirmed, gasping, her fingers buried in the hair at his nape.

"I think I am going to die," Violette managed in a queer tone of voice.

"No, don't die," Blake said hoarsely, sliding her lace straps off her shoulders, his hot gaze briefly holding hers. "Come with me instead."

Violette wanted to say yes, that she would go anywhere that he wished with him, but she failed to speak, it was impossible, as he slid the nightgown down to her waist. He stared at her heaving, ivory-hued breasts.

Violette wanted him to kiss her, taste her, again.

And he did.

And then he lifted her into his arms and strode across the sitting room, into his bedroom. Violette glimpsed a massive four-poster bed, the wood so dark it was ebony, the covers crimson and gold. As he laid her down in the center of the mattress, he said, "If you shall have any regrets tomorrow, then now is the time to tell me to stop, while I, just possibly, still can."

Violette lay in the midst of the bed; Blake stood by the bed's edge. She had never seen a man like this before, had never even imagined Blake this way. With his eyes burning so brightly for her, his entire body rigid with tension and desire, his manhood tenting his silk drawers. Violette tried to speak. To tell him she could not ever have any regrets for any time, brief or not, spent with him. But all she could do was wet her lips. "Please," she heard someone whisper; it was herself.

His jaw flexing, he stepped out of his drawers. Violette stared, mesmerized, drinking in the sight of him, for he was superb. He sat down beside her, his expression almost grave, cupped her breast, bent, and feathered his mouth to hers. It was a gentle brushing, and after the savage way he had kissed her earlier, the exquisite tenderness caused Violette to cry out. She no longer recognized her own body, it was on fire, about to explode from some very deep, inner core she had never before recognized or even known that it existed.

Blake pulled her wrapper off, tossing it to the floor. An instant later her nightgown followed. He inhaled. "God, you are so lovely. Violette . . ." He trailed off, his hand sweeping from her shoulder to her hip and then down her thigh, her calf, and to her foot. Giving her one very direct glance, he lifted her foot and pressed a kiss to the arch.

"Oh God," Violette thought, and realized she had spoken her thoughts aloud.

He smiled slightly, pressing a kiss to her navel. Violette arched up beneath him while his palm stroked up the inside of one thigh. "Blake," she whispered, half in protest, half in plea. The heat was building, she felt faint. She did not think she could stand too much more, yet she was not sure what awaited her on the other side of passion.

He kissed her nipple, suddenly palming her sex. Violette could not move. It had never occurred to her that Blake might touch her there, or that she would find such an intimate caress so exquisite and breathtaking.

His fingers separated her, slipped over her, found and caressed the most sensitive part of her. Violette could no longer think. Her hips began to shift wildly. She tried to look at him, but her vision was blurred—yet Blake was staring at her now with utter intensity while his hand continued its quest. Suddenly he bent and pressed her thighs apart. Violette did not know what to expect, but when his tongue touched her, she cried out.

He did not release her thighs. He began to suck on her, kissing her, laving her thoroughly. His face was buried between her thighs. Violette had stopped thinking long ago. She had the strongest notion that she was about to die and go to heaven. And if she did not, that would make her die, too.

A sob escaped her lips.

Blake moved on top of her. "Darling, come with me, now," he said hoarsely, but it was a command.

Violette blinked and met his bright blue gaze, which seemed to contain far more heat than the sun ever could—it was far more potent and far more blinding. "Please," she begged.

His smile was brief, fierce, and then he drove into her.

Violette had been experiencing the greatest pleasure she had ever known, and when he entered her she was completely unprepared for the sudden pain. She cried out.

Blake froze, eyes wide, the biceps in his arms bulging, his shocked gaze meeting hers.

But the pain was gone as suddenly as it had appeared, and Violette began to relax slightly. He felt amazingly hard packed there inside of her.

He pulled out. "Violette, Jesus, you didn't tell me!" His eyes remained wide and stunned.

Violette felt the tears gathering. His being joined with her, a part of her, had been so beautiful. "Don't leave me," she said.

"I'm sorry," he rasped, enfolding her tightly in his arms. She felt the stiff tip of his phallus quivering against her belly. He lifted his head to brush kisses to her forehead, her nose, her temples, and finally her mouth. "I am sorry. I did not know. I had no idea that you were a virgin. I never meant to hurt you; I never want to hurt you."

She gazed up at him, acutely aware now of the heat generated by his manhood on her pubis, equally aware of her thighs wrapped around his, spread achingly wide. She had comprehended his every word, wanted to reply, she truly did, but his body was having a definite effect on her again. She was open, vulnerable, exposed—and lacking. She wanted to tell him that it did not matter, that the pain was long since gone, but she only inhaled air. "Blake," she said, the sound strangled. She could feel the heavy weight of his testicles wedged against her own engorged sex.

He hesitated, his temples throbbing. "Slowly," he said. "This time slowly, gently, I promise." Their gazes locked.

And a brilliant promise was there. Violette nodded, feeling him as he pressed the engorged tip of his penis against her. It was slick and wet with her body's own secretions.

"If I hurt you, you must tell me immediately and I will stop," he breathed against her ear, kissing the lobe once.

"You're not . . . hurting me," Violette whispered.

Blake smiled slightly, briefly at her, bent, and began to tongue her nipple. As he did so, he rubbed himself back and forth slickly, wetly, over her sex. The pressure inside Violette quickly crested again. A feverish tightness reappeared, one explosive and filled with possibilities far too immense for her to grasp.

"Oh, God," Violette said.

"I agree," Blake murmured thickly, beginning to test and penetrate her.

Violette tensed, waiting for the sudden stabbing of pain. But as he slowly moved his length inch by inch inside of her, it did not reappear. Instead, the fever raged, hotter, brighter, than before.

"How does that feel?" he asked thickly, sheathed entirely inside of her.

Violette stared at him, unable to answer, unable to speak. She could feel him there, so tight and hot and deep inside of her, and nothing had ever felt so good, so right, so beautiful, so utterly perfect before. "Never stop," she managed. Tears suddenly filled her eyes as she held him tightly to her.

"Never," he said hoarsely, and he began to move.

Violette whimpered, purely in the throes of pleasure, holding onto him now, somehow knowing that heaven loomed before her again. Blake groaned, finding her mouth, driving faster now. With one hand he reached for her thigh and encouraged her to wrap it around his hips.

"Darling," he gasped, the sound raw. He searched for and found her lips again for another hungry kiss.

"Blake!" Violette gripped his back, pumping her hips up at him as his thrusting increased, her mind spinning, her chest choked. And then it happened. Stars exploding. Brilliant, bright lights. Death. A wonderful, wonderful explosive death. And Heaven.

Blue-black, star-studded, weightless, timeless, infinite, immense.

Violette was vaguely aware of Blake crying out, straining over her, while she floated slowly, bonelessly back to earth. He collapsed on top of her, cradling her tightly in his arms. His labored breathing was harsh but so wonderful against her neck.

Violette sank deeper into the mattress. She smiled against his face, joy welling up inside of her from the spring that could only be her soul. Who had ever known it could be like this? Could anything be more glorious than two people, a man and woman, in love, coming together like this? Oh, my. Still smiling, she stroked his sinewed back. Joyous.

She realized that he was lifting his head in order to regard her.

Violette smiled into his eyes. How blue and beautiful they were. She looked at every perfect, breathtaking feature of his face. Her heart was so very tight. So very full. The words were there, on the tip of her tongue. *I love you.* God, she did. But she said, "I had no idea."

His expression was grave. He did not smile. He continued to study her, then slipped onto his side. But he kept his arm around her. "I am sorry I hurt you," he finally said. "I did not realize it was the first time for you. I am an ass."

"You are not an ass." Violette's smile faded. "I should be

angry with you. Not for hurting me, but for thinking so little of me.''

Blake grimaced. ''You were married to Sir Thomas, Violette.''

''But he was an old man!'' she exclaimed. How could Blake have imagined her to have shared a bed with her husband—who had been seventy years old?

''But it is the way of the world, the way of men,'' he said. His gaze roamed over her face. Suddenly he cupped her cheek. ''God, you are so beautiful,'' he said, and he leaned forward to kiss her. ''And that''—he hesitated, unsmiling, intense—''was incredible.''

Blake watched Violette as she slept.

The sun was finally rising. He had not been able to sleep all night. Now soft, pink-hued light came through the windows—the draperies were open—and played over her sleeping form. She lay on her belly, her face turned toward him, a small smile on her face. Her black hair cascaded all around her. She was so very beautiful. And being with her was not like being with any other woman he had ever known. Being with her felt like that was where he belonged.

He stared up at the ceiling grimly. He tried now, very determinedly, to recall just how it had felt making love to Gabriella. Oddly enough, the memories were so dim now, so muted, so old, that he really couldn't remember. And wouldn't he be able to remember if he had had the same overwhelming sense of belonging?

Blake flung one arm up over his head. The past no longer seemed to matter. How could it, when he had just made love to Violette with far more than his body—with all of his heart, and maybe even his soul?

Yet he wasn't sure how last night had happened. He had been determined not to consummate their marriage. Determined not to become involved, not like this.

Blake turned to stare down at her again. He ached to touch her, hold her, kiss her, be inside of her. So much so that he wasn't sure he could refrain from making love to her again. But then what? He had intended a divorce or an annulment after a verdict of not guilty. But now their marriage was consummated, and Violette had been innocent of men.

He studied her perfect features, each one so fine and delicate, torn. Who would ever guess that she was from the streets of the East End? Perhaps, like in the romance novels he had caught Catherine reading, it would one day be discovered that her father was a duke. But Blake knew better than to believe that.

He returned his gaze to the molded ceiling. What was he going to do? He was so drawn to Violette. Worse, not only did he want to make love to her again, but he wanted to protect her from all harm. He could not recall when he had last experienced such protective instincts for anyone, man, woman, or child.

And then he wanted to explore every facet of her utterly original character, and watch her explore her life.

But dammit, he was *not* in love with her.

In any case, it was his duty, the honorable choice, he knew, the only choice, to remain married to her now.

Blake had to face his deepest fear. After all these years, he had to face the fact that he had allowed himself to love deeply, completely, once, and had suffered vastly for that mistake. Yet Violette was already his wife. Gabriella had refused him, marrying Cantwell instead. Violette already had his name, and she could neither refuse him or run away from him.

He was not comforted. Staring at the ceiling, he had the strongest feeling of walking way out onto a shaky tree limb. One more inch and the limb would break—and he would crash to the ground.

Blake slipped from the bed. He stared down at Violette—his bride. Could he not control his fear? Was it not time now to take another chance, to risk himself and his feelings again?

One thing was clear. Violette needed him, and he could not let her hang. And he needed her.

Blake suddenly bent over her, pushing aside the mass of her hair. Very gently, he kissed her nape. When Violette's eyes fluttered slightly, he pressed another kiss to the corner of her mouth. She sighed, smiling ever so slightly.

And Blake sank onto the bed, pulling her into his arms.

⚜ *Twenty-eight* ⚜

VIOLETTE lay in bed, cuddling her pillow, as Blake got to his feet. She watched him step into his drawers. She was smiling, enjoying the sight of his hard, muscular body, her own body gloriously sated, and joyously alive. She was deliriously in love.

Blake glanced at her. "I will be taking breakfast in half an hour." His gaze warmed as it slid over her; the covers were only pulled up past her hips, exposing her supple back, shoulders, and arms. "Do not rush on my account. Go back to sleep if you wish."

Violette smiled widely at him. "I am not in the mood to sleep."

He smiled slightly in return, inclined his head, and strode from the bedroom. Violette's happiness faded a bit. Surely there was not still conflict, questions, anxiety lingering between them? Not after last night!

Violette sat up, clutching the covers to her neck. All that had thus far happened hit her then. She stared across the room, at Blake's just-closed door. Now that they had made love, would they not have a real marriage? Didn't he love her, too? He had certainly made love to her as if he did. There was no possible way, she decided, that he would ask her for a divorce now.

But then she thought about the trial. It was next week. Blake's intentions might not even matter. Her heart lurched with dread at the thought.

But it did matter, she realized as she got up and walked into the bathing room, somber now. It mattered very much. Even if she were convicted for a murder she did not commit, she wanted Blake to love her the way she loved him.

Violette rang the bellpull for Margie. Worry had displaced her joy. She did not know what to do, what to think.

The little freckle-faced maid appeared instantly. "Mum?"

"I wish to bathe and dress and be downstairs in thirty minutes," Violette said.

The maid's eyes widened; she said, "Oh!" and rushed into the bathing room to pipe water into the bath. Violette watched her, and then she was suddenly seized with a memory of Ralph.

She did not have to be brilliant to know that Blake was not

going to be happy if he wandered downstairs and found Ralph dining in his breakfast room. Oh, God. She had to explain.

Violette, now regretting offering Ralph a guest room instead of a bed above the stables, wrapped only in a bed sheet, rushed into the bathing closet. "Margie! Where is Mr. Horn?"

"He has just come down for breakfast, mum," the little maid said, testing the water for warmth.

Violette's brow furrowed. Then, without another moment of hesitation, she ran to the door adjoining her room to Blake's. She rapped sharply on it.

Blake opened the door, his eyes widening, his valet moving in the room behind him. "Violette! What in the blazes are you doing?"

Before she could answer he had strode into her room, shutting the door abruptly.

"I'm sorry," Violette said, the words tumbling out. "But I have to speak with you!"

Some of his anger faded. "What is wrong?"

"Blake, please don't be mad at me," she blurted. "But yesterday, when I came home, Ralph was waiting for me on the street."

Blake stiffened. "Horn? He was here?"

Violette wet her lips. "He is here."

He stared. "What do you mean, precisely, by 'he is here?' "

Violette winced.

"Here? In *my* house?"

Violette opened her mouth, intending to explain, but found it extremely difficult to get any words out.

"Where the hell is he?" Blake demanded, turning red.

"I let him use a guest room."

Blake's brows shot up.

"And I think he is taking breakfast downstairs at this very moment," Violette cried.

Blake strode across the room and out of her door.

Violette ran after him, but halted on the threshold. "Blake! Why are you so angry?" she called after him—but he was disappearing down the hall and he did not deign to reply.

Violette whirled, dropping the sheet. Her maid, who had apparently been privy to the entire conversation, gaped. Violette ignored her, retrieving the rose wrapper from the floor. She threw it on, belting it tightly, and ran after Blake in her bare feet.

She raced down the stairs. "Wait, please, wait," she called after him, but he was an entire floor ahead of her.

As he hit the ground floor he stared up at her. "You cannot come down in that state of deshabille," he said furiously.

Violette winced but did not stop as Blake disappeared down the hall. She ran faster, hitting the ground floor landing at a run. The footman at the front door pretended not to see her. Violette heard Blake's voice, hard and angry as she raced down the hall and slammed into the breakfast room.

Ralph was sitting at the head of the table, in Blake's seat. He had, she was certain, done it on purpose. He had a plate in front of him piled with food, more food than any single person could possibly eat. He was sitting back in the chair, his arms folded across his chest, his expression insolent.

Blake was saying, "I wish I could say that your sudden appearance is a surprise, Horn. Get out of my chair."

Violette came forward. "Ralph, please do as he says."

Ralph did not move, although he looked at her—as did Blake. "Go back upstairs," Blake told her coldly. "This is not your affair."

"Not my affair?" Violette gasped.

"Get out of my chair, Horn, before I remove you from it myself," Blake said very tightly.

"Ralph, please!" Violette cried.

Ralph stood up. "Mornin', Yer Lordship. Sleep well?" His tone was mocking.

"And to think I was about to ask you the very same thing," Blake said. "Have you enjoyed my hospitality?"

"Certainly did," Ralph said. "Now I know why she did it. If I'd been 'er, I'd 'ave married yew, too." His smile was as cold as Blake's. "Couldn't pass up all these fine things."

"Stop it," Violette said, her pulse racing.

Both men ignored her. Blake stepped directly in front of Ralph. "So tell me, Horn, where have you been? I must say, I did not expect you to reappear until the murder trial was long over."

"Where I been," Ralph said, "ain't none of yer busyness, me lord."

Violette stepped between the two men, who looked as if they would jump at each other and attempt to strangle one another. "Please!" She put her back to Ralph. "Ralph was in Tamrah. Investigating the matter of the arsenic. He also found out that

Lady Feldstone's housekeeper was purchasing rat poison last year.''

Blake gazed at her. "You are lying to protect him?" he asked incredulously.

"I'm not lying!" Violette cried, aghast.

"You are lying to protect him," Blake ground out.

"I am not."

"You did not mention this last night," he said pointedly. "And whom, may I ask, gave you the right to invite this ... this ... man into my house?"

Violette was hurt to the quick. She lifted her chin, swallowing the lump of anguish. "I thought, after last night, that it is now *our* house," she said softly.

"Last night," Blake said, "changes little, if anything."

Violette inhaled. Had he struck her physically, he could not have hurt her more.

"Violette," Blake said, instantly reaching for her arm.

Violette flung him off, backing away from him.

"I am sorry. I spoke rashly, out of anger," he said.

Violette shook her head, too wounded to speak. She turned and ran out of the room.

Blake stared after her. "Dammit," he said harshly.

" 'Appy?" Ralph sneered.

Blake turned, fist clenched, and hauled back. Before Ralph could duck fully, he'd slammed his fist into Ralph's jaw, knocking him backwards into the opposite wall. Blake rushed forward, pulling him up to his feet by his shirt. "I don't like you," he said, "I don't trust you. In fact, regardless of the Feldstones' housekeeper's actions this past year, you are still the number one suspect on my list of possible murderers." He released him.

Ralph straightened from a crouch. "Yew can suspect me all yew want, Yer Lordship, but that won't change the facts. I didn't kill Sir Thomas, an' more importantly, Violette loves me the way she'll never, ever love yew."

Blake stiffened.

Ralph smiled. " 'Cause we're the same, 'er an' me, an' nuthin' can ever change that, not 'er new ways an' airs, an' one day she'll give up on yew an' yer fancy ways an' she'll come 'ome."

Blake stared. His expression had become unreadable.

*   *   *

Violette retired to her room. From her third-story window, she watched Ralph depart, clearly thrown out by Blake. And an hour or so after his departure, she saw Blake leave in his sleek black phaeton. She wondered where he was going. She tried not to care.

Her maid tried to coax her into accepting a light dinner in her room. Violette sent it all back, even the plum pudding.

She did not know how she had come to this impasse. To love a man who clearly had no real feelings, no love in return, for her. How cruel and hateful Blake was. Yet she did not hate him. If only she could.

She could not cry. Her tears were used up. But for the thousandth time she wondered how she could survive this marriage, especially after last night.

There was a knock on her door. Violette sighed and stood, opening it. Margie faced her uncertainly. "Mum," she said, and cleared her throat. "His Lordship wished me to tell you that you are dining at Harding House this evening at eight."

"I'm not going," Violette said flatly. And she meant it. She could not face the Hardings. She knew the earl and countess would be upset and dismayed to learn that their son had married her. It was entirely different than inviting Violette as a guest into their home.

But more importantly, she wasn't going anywhere with Blake—except, she supposed with a sinking sensation, to the Lords next week.

Margie's eyes were wide. "But His Lordship sent a note. I mean," she stammered, "he must want you to go out with him or why would he bother to send a messenger?"

"I don't care," Violette said, her pulse pounding. Roaring. "Tell him I am unwell when he comes home."

Margie's eyes were wide.

"I am serious," Violette said. "I am not feeling well and I am NOT dining with him at Harding House."

"Yes, mum," the maid said meekly.

Violette slammed the door.

Violette froze when she heard Blake's footsteps in the hall outside her bedroom door. She crossed her fingers and prayed that he would go away, but he did not. He knocked.

She debated pretending to sleep. But she was still fully dressed in her daytime clothes. A glance at the clock showed her it was just seven P.M., an hour before the Hardings' supper party. She gnawed her lower lip.

"Violette?" Without awaiting her permission, he pushed open the door and stepped inside her room. His gaze found hers. It was direct and piercing.

Violette stood in the center of the room, frozen. She did not move. She could not. He was the last person she wanted to see, yet he was the one her soul yearned for, always.

"So, you are unwell?" he asked, one brow lifting.

Violette hesitated. "I have had a headache all day."

"I did not know you suffered from migraines."

She thought about that morning. "Now you do."

"But you are not abed. Most women take to their bed when suffering so." His gaze was impenetrable.

"I can't sleep. Because of the pounding in my head," she lied.

He turned and shut the door, alarming Violette. When he faced her, he stared. "Chamberlain tells me that you have been in your room all day, and that you refused to eat dinner."

"I am unwell. I am not hungry," Violette said, a catch in her voice.

"Are you unwell? Or are you angry? Perhaps hoping to punish me childishly?" Blake asked. "By abusing yourself?"

She stiffened. "Why would I be angry with you? In order to be angry, I would have to care. And I do not." She flung out the words. Her fists were clenched.

"I am very sorry," he said softly, "about my terrible temper this morning."

She shrugged. Trying not to cry. "Ralph can take it."

"I am not talking about Horn. I am talking about you," Blake said.

Violette looked into his eyes and thought that she saw something soft and tender there. She whirled abruptly, giving him her back, clenching her fists so tightly that her own nails hurt her palms. "I don't know what you mean."

He came up behind her. "I never meant to hurt you. I am not a cruel man. Please forgive me for what I said. I was angry with Horn and . . . confused." He seemed to hesitate.

Violette did not move. She did not want him to be kind. She could suffer his cruelty far more than his kindness. "Do you like me at all?" she heard herself ask bitterly.

He did not answer.

Violette turned slowly around, dreading what she would see. But she could not read the emotions, if there were any, lurking behind the mask he wore.

"Of course I do," he finally said.

"But you only married me to rescue me," Violette said, holding his gaze.

His jaw flexed. He opened his mouth but no words came out.

"You don't have to answer. I know the truth. We both know the truth. I am not a real lady. I am a fraud. A beggar, a thief—possibly now even a murderess."

"Don't speak that way," he said sharply.

"Why not?" She walked away. "Or should I say, 'Wot not, guv'nor?' " She allowed herself to slip into the strongest Cockney possible.

He winced. "Why do we not try to make the best of what circumstance has handed us?"

Violette almost wept. She crossed her arms and hugged herself, unable to answer.

"In any case," Blake said into the tense silence of the room, "we are wed now, and that is a fact. Especially after last night."

Violette recalled his devastating words of that morning. "But not for very long, hopefully."

He stiffened.

She met his gaze. "I really do have a terrible headache, Blake. Please, allow me to beg off this evening's supper."

He stared. His face was now utterly, starkly devoid of emotion. "Very well. I shall also cancel. But plan to dine with my family tomorrow, Violette," he said. And there was a warning in his tone.

Violette finally crawled into bed a short while later. She could not sleep. She was too anguished, and dammit, her feelings for Blake would not turn into pure hatred. If only she could stop loving him. If only she could stop clinging to the most fragile thread of hope that somehow, one day, her impossible dreams would ripen into reality.

Violette covered her head with her pillow, wishing that she could stop her mind from thinking and her heart from feeling. But that was as impossible as stopping the blood from flowing through her veins, the air from flowing into her lungs. She loved Blake desperately. She had never loved this way before, would never love this way again. It was a rude, cruel comprehension.

His lovemaking haunted her. It was inexplicable. When he lay with her, it felt as if he cared, far more than a little. It was only an illusion, but it was a beautiful illusion, one Violette would gladly embrace again.

It was so tempting. To go to him, and find that illusion of love in the dark of the night.

Violette was a woman now, aware of her power. She knew Blake would not reject her if she crept into his bed. Yet in the light of the next day, Violette was afraid of the anguish, for she had not a doubt it would be far worse than what she was consumed with now.

Blake ate his supper alone. His dining room had never seemed so empty before. His oval table, which could seat twenty-four with added wings, had never seemed so vast. Before he had pushed away his second course he had finished an entire bottle of vintage Bordeaux. Yet he hardly tasted either the wine or his cook's meal, and it was clear that Cook was outdoing himself for the newlyweds. As he ate the glazed venison mechanically, he thought about the woman who had become his wife.

He did not understand her, not at all. Had he wounded her so badly that she now wanted the divorce he had decided against? That thought made Blake positively ill. What was happening to him? Was he in love? Who had ever thought that life could become so complicated so quickly and so effortlessly?

His life had not been the same since the moment he had first laid eyes upon Violette—and that was only two months ago.

He pushed his plate away, having taken merely a few bites, but asked Chamberlain to open another bottle of wine. He told himself that he did not care if she divorced him after the trial. It would be for the best. It was what he had originally wanted himself.

He did not feel very convinced.

"My lord"—Chamberlain appeared carrying an entire lemon tart—"Cook has made your favorite dessert. Shall I serve you?"

Blake stood abruptly. "I am in no mood for dessert, although you may tell Cook it appears lovely, and that supper was, as always, superb." Blake picked up both the wine bottle and his wineglass, but Chamberlain did not show the slightest degree

of surprise. Blake was not an excessive drinker and his staff
knew his habits exactly, as well they should. He was also aware
that tonight he was not quite sober. He did not care. "Good
night. And thank you, Chamberlain."

Chamberlain bowed. "My lord, may I say one thing?"

Blake turned, surprised. "Of course."

"Her Ladyship also refused her supper tray."

Blake was aware that he tensed. He kept his tone casual.
"Then I imagine she shall need a very large breakfast in the
morning."

Chamberlain nodded and left.

Blake walked slowly upstairs. Was Violette trying to make
herself ill? He was upset that she was not eating. And he was
positive that she did not have a migraine, that it was an excuse
to avoid his company.

At his doorway he paused, glancing at Violette's adjacent
door. He could not help but strain to hear, listening for God
only knew what. Her bedroom was silent, and he saw by peering at the crack where the door met the floor, that it was cast
in absolute darkness. She was asleep.

Oddly, he was disappointed.

He had no right to that disappointment.

Blake turned away and entered his own rooms. A fire blazed
in the hearth of his sitting room. He was wearing a smoking
jacket over his trousers, and now he kicked off his slippers,
setting both the wine and glass down on the side table by the
mint green sofa. He stared at the flames.

He thought about last night and that morning. If only he
could forget.

A noise made Blake turn. His eyes widened. Light was spilling out from under the door which adjoined their rooms. She
was not asleep, and clearly she had just lit a lamp. His pulse
raced.

He watched the door, sipping his wine, waiting for the light
to go out. But it did not. A new tension pervaded his body.

And then he made a decision. He quickly went downstairs,
down the halls, into the back of the town house—into the
kitchen. Cook, a short, plump Frenchman, was sitting at the
kitchen table as two maids finished cleaning up. The maids
stopped scrubbing the counters and Cook leapt to his feet as
Blake appeared in the kitchen—a place he had never, ever entered before.

"My lord," the Frenchman cried, wide-eyed.

"Monsieur Dupuis. I am sorry to disturb you. I wish to bring a tray up to my wife."

The cook turned and snapped out orders. Feeling somewhat foolish, aware that he was a little drunker than he had thought, and definitely aware of being an outsider in this particular domain, Blake watched a tray being filled with a delicate salad of field greens, cold poached salmon, the glazed venison, string beans and beets, potatoes, and finally, a generous serving of lemon tart.

The cook brought the tray to Blake himself. "My lord, shall this suffice?"

"Yes, thank you," Blake said. "Good night." He left the kitchen and returned upstairs. At Violette's door he noticed that the light was still on inside of her bedroom, and he was relieved. Balancing the silver platter carefully, he knocked on her door.

Without even asking who it was, she opened it immediately. Their gazes met.

Blake managed a smile. She was wearing the rose satin wrapper, tightly belted, and he knew damn well what was underneath it. He tried not to think about it. "I saw that you were still awake. Chamberlain told me you did not eat. Supper was wonderful. I thought you might be hungry now." His words came out in a rush in spite of his inebriation.

She stared at him. "Actually," she finally said, her tone somewhat hoarse, "I am hungry. Please, come in." She stepped aside.

Blake regarded her without moving. He had never seen a more beautiful, enticing woman, and suddenly the night, and his house, seemed achingly silent and terribly still around them. He could not lie to himself. He had never wanted any woman more. It was going to be very difficult to merely bring her the tray and leave. In fact, he did not want to leave, even though he knew he must.

And he imagined how empty his home would feel if Violette divorced him. It was a dreadful, stunning realization.

He managed a small smile and entered her room, acutely aware of her, placing the tray on the small table where she could dine. As he did so, he heard her closing the door. The satin wrapper swished slightly against her legs as she walked over to the table.

Their gazes locked again.

"Please," Blake said, gesturing to a chair.

She hesitated. "Will you keep me company?"

He froze, his eyes searching hers. She glanced away, purposefully avoiding his scrutiny, he knew. "Thank you," he said softly.

Violette sat, as did Blake. He watched her eating—and there was no question about it, she was very hungry. He smiled a little as he watched her. Suddenly she looked up.

His smile faded.

"Am I embarrassing myself?" she asked huskily.

"No," he said. "Not at all. Why didn't you accept a tray earlier?"

She dug into the tart. "I wasn't hungry then."

He had to smile because immediately after the tart she returned to the venison. He thought about her being a child in St. Giles, sweeping streets for gentlemen like himself to cross, holding horses for him and his friends for a penny or two, sleeping at night, in the rain and the snow, on open stoops. He no longer smiled. A fierce protective instinct he could not deny overcame him again.

She laid down her fork halfway through the tart. "You're staring at me."

"That," he said slowly, "is because your beauty takes my breath away."

She did not move. Her eyes held his.

And Blake no more meant to kiss her than he had meant to speak his thoughts aloud, but he leaned forward, wrapping his palm around the back of her neck. She remained motionless. His heart suddenly banging against his chest, Blake feathered her mouth with his.

He paused, pulling back so he could look at her. "Do you want me to return to my rooms?" he asked in a murmur.

Violette stared, her face flushed. "No," she whispered.

Blake moved. He stood, pulling her up and into his arms. She clung, their mouths fused.

Violette awoke at dawn.

She lay in Blake's arms. Her face was on his chest, one of her thighs hooked over and between his. He had his arm around her. Their faces were turned toward one another.

She blinked back sudden, burning tears. Recalling every moment of last night—he had made love to her twice. At first he had been wild, almost savage, but her passion had matched his. Had Violette not been so sad, she would have blushed, recalling her loud cries—and his. Afterward it had been tender, gentle, as if they were two lovers enamored of one another, destined to be together, and both fully knowing it; two lovers in a time-less, eternal dance of joy and love.

Violette shifted so she was even closer to Blake, an impos-sibility. She was in the throes of anguish.

Being loved by him physically one moment, and rejected coldly the next, was not a cycle she could bear. This marriage was killing her. Her hopes and dreams were killing her.

Because logic told her there was no hope.

Violette squeezed her eyes shut. There were only two op-tions. To remain with him, hoping for what would never be, loving him so intensely that her soul was filled with pain, or to leave. To leave him now, before she was incapable of ever doing so.

To leave him now, while she was still free to do so—still alive to do so.

Violette looked at Blake, and slipped out of his arms. Nude, she sat up on the edge of the bed. She began to cry.

Running away was going to be the most difficult thing she had ever done in her life. Even though she was terrified of facing the House of Lords, if she had his love, Violette knew she could withstand the murder trial, a guilty verdict, and the hangman. But she did not have his love. Her life was over even if she did not actually hang.

She wiped her eyes and got to her feet, the decision made.

PART FOUR

The Divorce

❖ Twenty-nine ❖

SHE had left that morning while he overslept, something he never did, a failure caused by the excessive quantity of wine he had consumed the previous night. It was teatime. She had been gone all day.

He did not understand. He was impatient, even somewhat worried. Blake had already questioned the servants, hours ago, but no one had the slightest idea of where she had been off to. And to make matters more confusing, she had left in a hired hansom, instead of in one of his vehicles. But she would certainly be home at any moment, and he intended to give her a good setdown for her thoughtless behavior.

Yet Violette, he knew, was not a thoughtless woman.

The day wore on. Blake worked from his home. He found it hard to concentrate. Simple sums refused to add up correctly, to multiply or divide. Violette did not return. Where was she? And why in God's name hadn't she taken one of his coaches? It made no sense.

Blake gave up trying to work. He paced and stared out of the windows and glimpsed a hired hansom approaching from down the street. He swiftly moved closer to the window, straining to see. He was certain it was Violette, finally returning home. He glanced at the clock over the mantel—it was half-past five. He intended to berate her for disappearing without a word to anyone about where she was going and when she would return.

The hansom stopped in front of his house. Blake felt himself smile. His heart skipped a beat. He was relieved.

The door swung open and Ralph Horn alighted. Blake froze, seared with disappointment, as Horn came up the block. The hansom, apparently instructed to wait, did not move away.

Blake strode into the foyer and flung open the front door before Horn could even use the knocker. He bit back his first choice of words, which were, "Where is Violette," saying instead, "Good afternoon, Horn." But he wanted to know what the hell Horn was doing there at his front door, and where the hell his wife was.

Horn's smile was insolent. "Guv'nor."

The two men faced one another on the stoop. Blake had no intention of allowing him inside. When Horn did not speak, but merely grinned, Blake said coldly, "Where is Lady Neville?"

Horn's smile broadened. "Aggtually, she asked me to bring yew this." Ralph handed him a folded piece of parchment. "I come fer 'er things."

Blake did not really hear him. Very puzzled, he opened the vellum, and quickly realized it was a letter. He knew she had been learning to write and he could see that the letter had been constructed carefully. It also appeared as if someone had helped her write it.

Turning his back on Horn, not going inside, Blake quickly read—and stiffened with shock.

Dear Blake,
You were right. A marriage between us is impossible, and I, too, want a divorce. I do not want you to think that I am ungrateful for everything you have done for me. I am very grateful. I only ask you now to start divorce proceedings so we may both get on with our lives. I will contact you with my new address when I am settled. I wish you great happiness, always.
Your friend, Violette.

Blake crushed the paper in his fist. For one instant he was blinded by feelings of utter treachery. Utter betrayal. Profound deception. Then he looked up, saw Ralph grinning at him. "Get out," he snarled, and an instant later he smashed his fist into Horn's nose.

She had left him, she wanted a divorce. If it weren't so unbelievable, so painful, he might have laughed at the utter irony of it all. But he was incapable of laughter.

He sat at his desk in his nearly dark library, his head in his hands. He was incapable of doing much more than feeling at the moment. *Violette had left him.* He did not know what time it was, or how much time had passed since the insolent, smug Horn had left the premises. He did not care. He had left orders with Tulley that he did not wish to be disturbed.

So when there eventually was a knock on the study door Blake was furious. He lifted his head and stared.

The knocking continued. And then he heard his brother's voice. "Blake, I know you are inside." The door swung open.

Blake was glaring as Jon appeared on the library's threshold, standing with the aid of two footmen. Jon was the last person he wished to see. And had he not been sitting in almost absolute darkness, he would have told him that he was working, and not available for any interruptions then. But such an excuse was obviously false now.

"Good God," Jon said. "Put on some lights, Blake."

Exasperated, Blake stood and lit the gaslamp on his desk. The single light gave the library an eerie, almost unholy glow. "This is a strange time for you to call, Jon," Blake said unpleasantly. He sat back down.

Jon was settled in a chair. The servants left, leaving the door open. "I heard what happened. Is it true? Your wife has left you?"

Blake was in disbelief. "How in bloody hell did you learn that?"

Jon stared, unsmiling. "I refuse to say."

The staff. He was going to dismiss them all, especially Tulley, Blake decided savagely. He was on his feet again. He gave Jon a cold smile and walked over to the sideboard, pouring two scotch whiskys. He handed one to Jon, who regarded him searchingly. Blake raised his glass in a toast. "To my freedom. Which is all I ever wanted anyway." He tossed down half the scotch, realizing that he should have had a drink hours ago.

"Crap," Jon said. "Violette was good for you, and you were in love with her. What happened?"

"I am not in love, nor was I in love," Blake said, his eye ticking. "Christ! What a romantic you are!"

Jon smiled grimly. "You are avoiding the question."

Blake shrugged. "She left. With Horn. She wants a divorce, as I do. We are in accord." He finished the scotch. "Completely."

"Like hell you are," Jon said. "Are you giving her a divorce?"

"Of course I am." Blake refilled his glass. "After the trial, of course." His temples throbbed. "What a stupid time for her to leave," he muttered. "She has no sense, none."

"Bring her back," Jon suggested. "You can't go to trial, Blake, while separated. This weakens her case."

It did. Terribly. But Blake told himself that he did not care. "I am not bringing her back. Dodge can coach her this week on what she must say at the trial, and how she must answer any questions. I am not bringing her back, and I am not speaking with her, period." Blake was firm.

"Oh? You are never speaking with her again?"

Blake felt like answering yes. Instead, he glared yet again. "Of course we shall have to speak. To discuss the divorce."

"You are a fool," Jon said. "Why are you letting her go?"

Blake slammed his glass down. "Are you trying to provoke me? Have you forgotten? I only married her to save her from a guilty verdict in the Queen's Bench. And that," he gritted, "is the truth."

Jon studied him. It was a moment before he spoke. "Perhaps I should go speak with her. Encourage her to return. I am certain this can be worked out if the two of you talk to one another frankly."

"Don't you dare!" Blake cried. But inwardly, a part of himself almost wanted Jon to do just that. To go to Violette, make her come home. "There is nothing," he managed harshly, "to talk about."

Jon sighed. "Except for the trial."

"Except for the trial." Blake drank. "And the divorce."

Dodge brought the worst possible news that next morning. Their meeting was prearranged. They had exchanged messages the day before. The solicitor had been unhappy to learn that Blake and his wife were currently living apart. He had insisted that they reconcile immediately; when Blake had told him that was not possible, he had insisted that they dissemble at the trial—Dodge did not want anyone to know about the separation. Blake was not pleased with the prospect of perjuring himself in the House of Lords. He almost cursed Violette for her utterly appalling sense of timing.

Blake was drinking extremely strong black coffee and trying to recover from another night of heavy drinking—sleep had been impossible. Finally Tulley appeared, Dodge behind him. "My lord, Mr. Dodge to see you."

Blake stood to shake Dodge's hand but faltered when he realized that the solicitor was frowning and disturbed.

"Blake, I have bad news."

"I can see that," Blake said.

"I went to Lady Neville's flat yesterday to urge her to make amends with you, at least for the time being," Dodge said. "No one was home, so I left. But this morning, just half an hour ago, I returned to Knightsbridge. Again, the flat was deserted—and it was not half-past nine."

Blake had become motionless.

"Blake." Dodge was grim. "She is gone."

It was a moment before Blake actually could grasp Dodge's meaning. "Gone," he repeated.

"Lady Neville is gone. The flat has been vacated and locked up."

Blake stared, stunned and disbelieving.

"This time I interviewed her neighbors. She and Horn left yesterday in a hansom, with half a dozen trunks." Dodge stared. "She is taking a trip, Blake—and it doesn't seem to me that she intends to come back."

He felt the comprehension slamming over him like a full-fledged blow from a battering ram, pushing him backwards, back and still further back, and finally ripping apart everything in its path, ripping him apart. One line from her note flashed through Blake's mind. *I will contact you with my new address when I am settled.*

"I was so very concerned that I interviewed, as quickly as possible, a series of her neighbors. One young boy told me he heard her and Horn talking about Paris, Blake."

Blake was speechless.

"She has, it seems, run away," Dodge said flatly.

Blake stared, not seeing Dodge. Left the country. Fled. To France.

"My lord," Dodge said, "I am afraid this is very serious. The trial is in five days, and we have no defendant."

Blake closed his eyes, trembling. He finally said, "There can not be a trial without a defendant, can there, Mr. Dodge?"

"No. And unless Lady Neville returns, or is found and forced to return, there will not be a trial," Dodge said. "But that is not a favorable turn of events."

Blake understood only too well.

"We had better find Lady Neville immediately—and make sure she is at the trial before anyone ever knows that she was gone," Dodge said.

Blake inhaled, hard. The rush of air into his lungs was ac-

tually painful. *She had run away.* Why? But did it even matter?
She was gone. And she was not, he knew, coming back.

"Blake," Dodge said sternly. "We all know that she is innocent of murdering Sir Thomas, but no one else does. And if
it becomes common knowledge that she has run away, it will
be almost impossible to ever convince anyone that she is not
guilty—making Lady Neville's future return disastrous."

Blake turned away. He did not have to be told the conse-
quences of Violette's behavior. She had run away, and no act
could be more damning.

And he cared, no matter that he told himself otherwise. Because he knew she had run away, not from the trial, but from
their marriage, from him.

❖ *Thirty* ❖

PARIS

THEY had arrived in Paris with all of their belongings and four
thousand pounds—every cent that was left over from Blake's
gift. It was Ralph who insisted that they flee the country. Violette had been too miserable to do anything but agree.

The crossing of the Channel had been swift. They had spent
their first night in Paris in a small brick-fronted hotel not far
from the Quai d'Orsay. Now she stood on the Rue de Rivoli,
one of the most fashionable streets in the city, or so the concierge had said, clutching her cashmere mantle to her. It was a
chilly November day. Although the sun was out, its rays slant-
ing over the Jardin des Tuileries on Violette's right, most of
the elms had turned, their leaves brilliantly red and gold, although the lawns were still verdantly green, and a cool breeze
seemed to be coming off the river just beyond the gardens.
Behind Violette, inside the shop, the clerks were opening draperies and displaying wares. On the street in front of Violette,
carriages and coaches passed, filled with elegantly dressed,
gayly chatting women. There was a boulangerie on Violette's
right, a brasserie on the corner. The aroma of freshly baked
pastries and bread, mingled with something spicier and more
tantalizing, wafted toward Violette, whose stomach rumbled.
She had hardly eaten in days.

Violette glanced at the shop. It was set in a small, square

stone building with a garreted rooftop. The big slabs of tawny
stone were freshly scrubbed, the two front wood doors gleaming with wax. The sign above the pediment read "Maison
Langdoc" in oversized gilded letters. As Violette studied the
entrance, a big, redheaded woman from inside the shop glanced
out of the window at her as she crossed the foyer.

Ralph was looking for a flat for them to rent, and Violette
was looking for employment. The concierge of the Hôtel
d'Eglise St.-Marie had told Violette that the Maison Langdoc
was one of the finest retail establishments catering to ladies of
quality in the entire city.

She shivered, staring into the window. The maison reminded
her of Lady Allister's. Two clerks were putting ready-made ball
gowns in the first oversized window. The gowns dripped lace
and intricate beadwork. But it was so very hard to think about
finding work when her heart seemed to have ceased functioning
the way a heart should—Violette felt peculiarly numb, almost
incapable of feeling, yet a deep misery pervaded her entire
being as well. But she and Ralph desperately needed an income.
Four thousand pounds could be gone in the blink of an eye—
or after a hard winter of unemployment. Neither one of them
had ever been to Paris before, neither one of them could speak
French, and Violette was afraid of what the future might hold
for them. She would, of course, learn to speak the language as
soon as possible. It would help her to keep her mind off of
Blake—and what would never be.

She had only left Blake in her bed two days ago. It seemed
like two lifetimes ago.

She wondered if she would ever see him again.

A big black coach halted on the street beside Violette. She
watched without interest as two fabulously dressed women exited the vehicle, the carriage doors opened by a footman, and
they were followed out by two waiting ladies. They passed
Violette with curious glances and entered the Maison Langdoc.

Violette turned, knowing she must go in, but she made no
move to do so. She had not said good-bye to anyone. Ralph
had not let her. She knew he had been right to insist they flee
immediately, before those inspectors might try to detain her,
but she had wanted to thank Catherine and the countess for
everything, and Lady Allister as well.

The doors to the shop suddenly opened and the stout redheaded woman stepped onto the street. Although she was quite
overweight, she was very attractive, her hair a dark, natural red,

her features classically handsome, and she was dressed in a stunning apricot-colored moirée gown. She gazed at Violette. *"Madame, qu'est-ce que c'est? Voulez-vous entrez chez moi? Puis-je vous aider?"*

Violette realized that the woman was speaking to her. She tried to smile. "I beg your pardon," she said very softly. "I do not speak French, although I shall learn, as soon as possible." To Violette's horror, all she could think of in that moment were her lessons with Catherine, and her hopes and dreams with Blake. Tears suddenly filled her eyes.

"Oh, *ma pauvre*," the Frenchwoman said, taking Violette's arm. "My poor one. Come, *venez avec moi*. Come." Her smile was kind, as was her melodious voice.

Violette dabbed at her eyes with her gloved fingertips and allowed the woman to lead her inside the shop. The floors were carpeted in red. The walls were wood-paneled, but mirrors were everywhere, making the interior large and bright. Huge crystal chandeliers hung from the ceilings, which were high, and various settees, ottomans, and chairs graced the room, all upholstered in shades of crimson and gold. The Parisian led Violette to a yellow damask sofa and encouraged her to sit. Violette obeyed, trying for another smile.

"May I bring you something to drink, *ma belle femme*?" the woman asked.

"I am not a customer," Violette returned, thinking the woman had misunderstood.

"So?" The redhead shrugged with a smile. "You are so sad, and you appear lost. *Café au lait* will help, *je le sais*."

Violette did not protest as the lady disappeared up the narrow stairs just to her left. She found her handkerchief, in case the tears should rise up again, while the patrons at the other end of the room began examining fabrics with exclamations and varying degrees of enthusiasm. It was hard to believe that she was in Paris. Violette hoped she had not made a mistake by leaving London—by leaving Blake.

The redhead returned, carrying a small sterling silver tray covered with an exquisite lace doily. The tray contained a steaming cup of coffee laced with hot milk, a porcelain plate filled with mouth-watering pastries, and a silver sugar bowl. "Thank you," Violette said as the tray was set down on the side table, the lady taking an ottoman beside her.

"How is the *café*?"

"Very good," Violette said truthfully. Her stomach rumbled

loudly now. It was the most delicious cup of coffee Violette had ever had.

"You are, how do you say, *famished*?"

"I guess I am somewhat hungry," Violette admitted ruefully.

"Eat. I am Madame Langdoc."

Violette started. "The proprietress here?"

Madame Langdoc smiled with pride. "*Mais oui*."

Violette hesitated, then picked up a croissant and ate, in spite of her hunger, careful of her manners. Madame Langdoc did not speak until Violette had finished and was sipping the *café au lait* again. "Do you feel better now?" she asked.

"A little," Violette said. "Thank you. You are very kind."

"What is wrong?"

The blunt question, accompanied by her probing, concerned brown eyes, startled Violette.

"You are very sad, and very beautiful. Is it a man?"

Violette felt her cheeks heat.

Madame Langdoc touched her palm. "*Ma pauvre femme.* You are in Paris, now. Of course it is a man. What else but *l'amour* could make you so sad and so lost on the street outside my shop?"

Violette glanced at her lap. "Yes," she whispered. "I am sad. I am lost." She wondered if she would ever find her way again through life.

"You love him very much," the Parisian said.

"Very much. Always." Violette closed her eyes over fresh, hot tears.

"Perhaps you should go to him and tell him so. A beautiful woman like yourself, one with a kind, good heart, I am sure that he loves you, too."

Violette met Madame Langdoc's gentle gaze. "He is divorcing me."

The Frenchwoman straightened. "*C'est incroyable! Le bâtard!*" Her eyes flashed.

"It is so complicated," Violette said. She sighed, the sound tremulous, shaky.

"Love is always complicated," Madame Langdoc said firmly. "But divorce, that is, how do you say, *insufferable*."

"No. He only married me to protect me. He never loved me." Violette forced a smile. Her vision blurred. She took a breath of air and forced a cheerfulness into her tone that she did not feel, would most likely never feel again. "Madame

Langdoc, the reason I was standing on the street outside of your shop is because I am in dire need of employment. Before my marriage, I worked briefly at an establishment like this one in London, at Lady Allister's. Do you have a position available?" Violette gripped her palms. Her gaze held the older woman's. "I am a very hard worker. I am eager to learn. I promise you I shall speak French passably within a few months. My life shall be my work, Madame."

Madame Langdoc stared. "*Ma pauvre*, I believe you. And although I was not looking for another employee, perhaps I can use you here. I have been thinking recently of working a bit less myself, you see."

Violette straightened. For the first time since she had left Blake she felt the stirring of interest, of eagerness. "Really?"

Madame Langdoc smiled. "*Ça c'est la vérité*. I am not so young, *ma belle*. And we are very busy here." And even as she spoke, the doors to the shop opened and a trio of finely dressed ladies entered the shop, a beaming clerk rushing forward to greet them.

Madame Langdoc rose. "You may start tomorrow," she said decisively. "And today, today I insist you eat a good meal and rest."

Violette also stood. She clasped the Parisian's two hands. "You are too kind. Thank you. You will not be disappointed, Madame, I promise you that."

Madame smiled. "I am a very good judge of people, *ma belle*. And I already know I will not be disappointed in you."

The letter, dated December 1, 1858, began:

My dearest Catherine,
    Paris is beautiful, perhaps the most beautiful city in the world. I do not think I have ever been happier. I have a flat in St-Germain-des-Prés in a charming little building built two hundred years ago. The concierge is an old man who insists on bringing me fresh croissants every morning from the boulangerie down the street. I can speak a bit of French, and am studying the language avidly. In fact, my first day in Paris I obtained employment at Maison Langdoc, the finest ladies' shop in the city. I love my job; my fellow workers; my employer, Madame Langdoc, who is so very kind; and my customers. How very lucky I am.

I am still studying English, of course. Every night, no matter how tired I am, I read and write, using the grammars and books you gave me. I am trying to read Shakespeare now. How difficult it is! And I wrote this letter myself (with a little help, of course).

I do hope Jon is much better; please give him and the earl and countess my regards. I also wish you the very best. I do miss you. I hope one day we can sit together like in the past and chat about old times.

Best Regards,
Your Loving Friend,
Violette Goodwin.

Catherine read the letter again, her hands trembling. No, there had not been a single reference to Blake, she had not even used his name, although there had not been a divorce, and Violette sounded as if she were truly happy. Was it possible?

Catherine folded the letter, not sure of what to think. More than six weeks had passed since Violette had run away. Catherine recalled with utter clarity just how enamored Violette had been. Had she gotten over him? If there were nuances to read between the lines, Catherine could not find them.

And if Violette were happy, that pleased Catherine, who did not want to see anyone suffer. But what about Blake? He did not have to wear his feelings openly, or speak of them, for her to understand him. She knew him too well, had known him too long. He had changed. He had been, she knew, far more than betrayed by Violette, he had been crushed.

How Catherine hurt for him. He had not deserved this. First Gabriella, and now Violette. Catherine did not think he would ever trust another woman again. If only Violette would return— but she was a fugitive now, a warrant still pending for her arrest, and if she ever did return, she would be imprisoned by the authorities and tried for Sir Thomas's murder.

Catherine slipped the letter inside the drawer of her small mahogany secretaire, but kept the envelope with Violette's mailing address. She had no choice now but to give Violette's address to Blake. Since Violette had fled the country, no one knew where she had gone, and this was the first time she had contacted anyone. Blake could have hired runners to find her, but he had refused to even consider doing so—shrugging off first the earl's and then the countess's suggestions that he learn her whereabouts, at least. In fact, hadn't he said, for all that he cared, the earth could have swallowed her up?

Catherine hurried downstairs and ordered a carriage. Her pulse raced. She couldn't help wondering what Blake's reaction would be to Catherine having finally received word from his missing wife.

Catherine had to wait outside Blake's office in the bank for several minutes while he finished a meeting with a client. Her coat on her lap, the envelope in her reticule, she sat impatiently in the small antechamber, ignoring the admiring glances of Blake's young assistant. Finally the heavy oak door opened and Blake appeared, ushering out a small, dapper gentleman clad in tweeds. Catherine smiled to herself, as always, admiring Blake's appearance. He was a very handsome man, and whenever she saw him she was reminded of it anew. No one was more dashing in a black suit. But he was also intelligent, forceful, and creative, and she was very proud of him.

He came forward, smiling. "What a pleasant surprise," he said, kissing both of her gloved hands.

Catherine's smile faded as she noticed the dark circles under his eyes. Again he appeared to have passed a restless night—or a late one. As Blake escorted her into his office, she said, "You seem a bit tired, Blake. Are you well?"

He closed the door. "As well as ever."

"Ahh," she said knowingly, keeping her tone light. "Someone must have passed an extraordinarily good night."

He flashed his dimpled grin at her. "My dear, you are fishing, and I have no intention of telling you what I was up to last evening."

She became very serious. "I am worried about you, Blake."

His easy expression vanished. "I hope you have not come here to harp at me."

"I do not harp."

"You most certainly do."

They stared at one another. Catherine sighed, and reached inside her reticule. She handed him the creased envelope. "I came because I have received a letter from Violette and I know you must want, or need, her address."

Blake was frozen. But only for an instant. His mouth firming, he read the return label. "May I keep this?" His tone gave little away, having no emotional inflection.

"Of course." Catherine studied him as Blake slipped the

envelope into the breast pocket of his ebony suit jacket. And then he moved behind his desk, although he did not sit. "What can I do for you today, Catherine?" he asked very formally—as if she were a client or a customer and not a dear old friend.

"Blake," she said softly, "don't you want to know what she has written me?"

"Not particularly." He stared. His expression was very hard.

"She sounds as if she is happy. She has a charming flat, and a wonderful job at Maison Langdoc—an establishment I have shopped at myself. She is speaking some French, and reading Shakespeare."

Blake lifted his eyebrows dismissively.

"I can't believe that she is happy," Catherine cried passionately.

"And I," Blake said slowly, "do not care."

"I don't believe that."

"Catherine, I cannot control your thoughts, or your beliefs," he said quite coldly. "If I am at all concerned, it is only because Violette is a fugitive from Her Majesty's law, wanted for murder, and unable to return to this country without standing trial— a trial she would now, undoubtedly, lose. Of course, were she not legally my wife, I would not even be concerned about that." His smile was as cold as his tone.

Catherine despaired. She finally said, "Will you write to her?"

Blake smiled, and it was a grim one. "No."

Outside the wind sent up twisting swirls of snow, miniature cyclones blasting any pedestrians who might be unfortunate enough to be out and about. Although it was only noon, the streets were quite deserted, most Parisians having apparently decided to stay indoors for the winter's first big snowstorm. Violette folded fabrics for lack of anything better to do, watching one lonely hansom approaching outside. Already the snow was fetlock-deep. There had not been a single customer in the shop since it had opened two hours ago.

The two other clerks were chatting in one corner of the salesroom, bursts of laughter punctuating their conversation. Violette had become friendly with both Paulette and Marie-Anne, two women her own age, but she was not in the mood to gossip about their suitors and the past weekend filled with parties and food and champagne. She could not imagine being happy like that.

"Violette, *ma belle*." Madame Langdoc came downstairs and smiled at her. "Stop. *Arrêtez-vous*. You have folded and refolded since we opened today when tout *c'est bien*."

Violette sighed. By now, Catherine had surely received her letter, as had the countess and Lady Allister. Every day when she returned to her flat, she checked for mail. So far, she had not received a single reply.

"I am going to close the shop today," Madame declared. "This is a waste of everyone's time, and later I will be worried that you girls shall not make it to your homes safely."

That was how Madame was. Big-hearted to a fault. Worried about her "girls." When Paulette had been sick a fortnight ago, Madame had spent hours at her bedside, arranging for the doctor to call on Paulette herself. Violette's insides tightened. "Perhaps you are right," Violette said, momentarily feeling ill.

But at that moment they both saw the hansom outside halting—right in front of the shop—and Violette was diverted. Its snow-covered door opened and a tall gentleman in a black greatcoat and brimmed hat leapt to the street. He seemed remarkably familiar, and as he strode directly to the front doors of the maison, Violette froze.

No, it was impossible.

He entered the shop, taking off his hat, his dark gaze piercing her immediately. It was Lord Farrow.

Violette did not move. She was stunned.

And he shook the snow from his coat, slowly smiling. "Lady Neville," he said. "On a wretched day like today, it appears that I am in the nick of time."

Violette suddenly smiled. She couldn't help it; it was wonderful to see someone from home, even if it was the enigmatic Farrow. She came forward, suddenly joyous—and she had not felt that emotion in so very long. "My lord, how good to see you. What a wonderful surprise."

He smiled at her, taking her hand and kissing it very firmly. Violette was not wearing gloves and the pressure of her mouth gave her a strange little jolt—one that made her pull her hand away instantly.

When he straightened, his gaze held hers. "I unearthed your whereabouts from Lady Allister, my dear. I was very afraid I would never see you again."

Violette's smile faded. Her pulse sped, with some alarm, and no small amount of surprise—both at her own reaction to his sudden appearance in her new life—and to his words. "This is not a coincidence?" she asked.

"No," he said flatly, "this is not a coincidence."

⊰ *Thirty-one* ⊱

THE brasserie remained open in spite of the falling snow, which was so thick now that the brick and stone buildings across the street could not be seen, but inside the intimate wood-paneled brass-trimmed restaurant a huge fire blazed in the stone hearth, and most of the small tables were occupied with wining, dining, animated patrons who lived in the neighborhood. Violette faced Farrow from across a small, square table set with a snowy white tablecloth and a centerpiece of dried flowers tied with a lavender ribbon. He had ordered them a carafe of red wine and two portions of chicken fricassé, a baguette and butter.

Violette was still amazed by his presence in Paris. She was still trying to absorb what he had told her—that he had come to Maison Langdoc to see her specifically.

"You are as beautiful as ever," Farrow said, pouring them both a glass of wine. "More so, in fact." He smiled at her, although his gaze was penetrating. "I have thought about you often."

Violette tensed. "You are too kind."

"No, I am honest." His regard was direct, his smile brief. He was an attractive man with a powerful presence and suddenly, painfully, he reminded her of Blake. "Violette, I would like to ask you something."

She looked up uncertainly. "Please."

"Why did you run away from London? Just days before your trial?" His gaze was searching.

"I did not kill Sir Thomas, if that is what you are thinking," Violette said softly. She could not hold his gaze, it was too disturbing. "I had to leave. It had nothing to do with the trial."

"I see," he said. His tone caused her to look up. "Blake?" he asked.

She nodded.

"Perhaps this will work out for the best," he mused. "I am very happy to be with you again, Violette."

She met his brilliant eyes. Her heart skipped. She was not completely immune to him, no woman could be. "My lord," she began carefully, "surely business affairs brought you to France?"

"When will you call me Robert?" he asked.

Violette felt herself flushing. "I am not sure that is appropriate."

"Because you remain married to Blake?" he asked softly.

Violette glanced away. "We are in the process of obtaining a divorce."

"Yes, I know."

Violette started. "How do you know, my . . . Robert?"

He smiled, clearly pleased that she had used his given name. "Most of London knows, Violette, that Blake has petitioned the courts for a divorce against you."

So he had begun the divorce proceedings. She found herself strangely frozen inside. Because she had left him, she had known that this was inevitable, since she had asked him to proceed. So why did it still hurt?

Farrow reached across the table and took her hands in his. "You will get over him, Violette. I shall make sure of it."

Violette met his brilliant brown eyes. He was far more than handsome, he was charismatic, and she could feel his intensity and his determination. But she was no longer flattered, or even thrilled to see him. Yet she hardly wished him gone. Instead, she was afraid.

"What is it?"

"I am not sure," she said slowly, "that I shall ever recover from loving Blake."

He stared, unsmiling, and released her palms.

She met his gaze. "Now I am the one being honest."

"Brutally so," he said. He took a sip of wine. She could feel him thinking, choosing his words, deciding what to say, and what to hold back. "Business affairs did not bring me to Paris, Violette. You brought me to Paris."

Violette had been about to reach for her wineglass, but with her hand extended, she froze. Their gazes locked.

"I am sorry you are hurt," he said finally. "I do think Blake had a tendre for you. But I am a man, and I have had a tendre for you since we first met. I am not sorry you and Blake are divorcing; I am glad."

She removed her hands to her lap. He was making himself very clear. She did not know what to do, or what to think.

Two steaming plates of savory chicken sautéed with tomatoes and herbs arrived. Farrow thanked the waiter. He did not pick up his fork. "I intend to spend some time in Paris this winter and this spring," he said very seriously. "I am looking for a house to lease."

Violette did not move.

"I promise," he said, "I will not push you. I can see that you need to recover from the past. For now, I would be happy if you would agree to dine with me upon occasion, accompany me to the theater, or stroll with me when the weather permits. Do not send me away, Violette. I do not think I can take no for an answer."

Violette wet her lips. This man had changed. He was very, very serious, and she had the strongest feeling that he had come to Paris, not in search of a mistress, but courting a bride. She almost told him, no, she could not see him, not ever again, because her heart belonged to another.

Instead, she heard herself say, her tone hoarse, "I would be pleased to accept your invitations when you choose to extend them, Robert."

A fierce light lit up his eyes and he reached for her hand, gripping it tightly.

Violette tried to smile but failed. All she could think of was Blake.

And outside, the wind howled, the snow swirling on the frosted windowpanes.

The snowstorm was still howling when Violette arrived home. Ralph was employed in a factory not far from the Bastille. He was welding tools, which he hated, but his employer did not care about the weather, and did not close his premises because of the storm. However, because Ralph left for work at dawn, he was home by five every afternoon, far earlier than Violette. Their neighbors assumed that they were brother and sister. She made it a point not to speak with anyone.

Today, however, he was anxiously awaiting Violette when she finally climbed the three flights of stairs to their flat. He swung open the door before she could knock or use her keys. "Where have you been?" he exclaimed. "Don't tell me Madame Langdoc stayed open this late in this weather."

Violette entered their cheerful flat. The salon had several windows, all facing north, which meant it was usually filled with sunlight, even on a winter day. Colorful fabrics in reds and pinks covered the furniture, and the rugs, though faded, were blue and green and gold, from Turkestan. The flat had been minimally furnished when she and Ralph had moved in, but Violette had acquired the rugs and some additional pink-and-white-striped chairs at several flea markets. It was charming and even roomy: Ralph had a room at the opposite end of the flat.

"She stayed open for a while," Violette said truthfully, taking off her snow-drenched overcoat. There was no point in telling Ralph about Lord Farrow. She knew what his reaction would be and she was not in the mood to reassure him when she could not even reassure herself.

"I brought us some beef stew for supper," Ralph said, eyeing her. "An' fresh bread an' a bottle of burgundy."

Violette of course was not hungry, but she was not going to tell Ralph that either. When she did not reply, he followed her into her bedroom. "Wot's wrong?" he asked.

She sat on her bed, atop a lovely pink and white handmade quilt, taking off her shoes. Her feet were now wet. "I am cold and tired," she said.

"Yer so sad an' I 'ate seein' yew like this!" Ralph cried abruptly. "I wish yew'd niver met that bastard!"

His outburst made her want to weep. "I'm just tired," she lied. Tired, confused, frightened . . . sad. So very, very sad.

He stared.

And she knew him well enough to now realize that something *was* wrong. "Ralph, why are you looking at me that way?"

He hesitated.

"Ralph?" Violette stood up in her stockinged feet.

"Yew got a letter. From London."

Violette forgot to breathe.

Ralph turned and left her bedroom. When he returned, an oversized envelope was in his hand. He gave it to her. "I didn't open it, but there's an address on the back. It's from Blake."

Her heart lurched. Her head spun. Violette sank back down on the bed, clutching the envelope. Oh, God. She was more than afraid to open it, she was terrified.

But a tiny voice inside of her head whispered, *What if? What if he wanted her to come home?*

Violette swallowed, breathing harshly now, and opened the envelope. She pulled out official-looking papers, some kind of contract, perhaps, or several contracts, and rifled through the large envelope again, looking for a letter from Blake. The envelope was empty.

Shaking now, she picked up the sheaf of papers, noticing the date on the first page, which was December 12 of last year. Both her and Blake's names were atop the page, which appeared to be a petition. She set it aside. It was followed by another document, dated January 18, 1859, which bore a wax seal on the upper-right-hand corner, and dear, dear God, the top of the document read, "Lord Theodore Edward Blake, Viscount of Neville, plaintiff," and she thumbed past and through, trembling in every limb, looking, desperately, for a personal letter from him.

"Wot is it?" Ralph asked.

There was no letter. Violette could not believe it. Just the petition, and the second, longer, terribly frightening document following it.

"Violette? What are them papers?"

Violette licked her dry, parched lips. Her heart beat inside her breast like a drum, painfully, loudly. She picked up the papers. She forced herself to see through encroaching tears. And she wasn't the most adept reader to begin with.

But she could read enough to understand what the documents meant. The first set of papers were a petition for divorce, filed by Blake on December 21 in the Court for Divorce and Matrimonial Causes, against her, the respondent, on the grounds of desertion and cruelty. Violette's hands shaked. She could hardly read further. Desertion . . . cruelty. *Oh, God. How could he!*

"Wot?" Ralph demanded.

And the second document, which was perhaps thirty or forty pages long, was the completed action of divorce. Today was February 1, but she and Blake had been divorced for three weeks now—and she had not even known it.

"He . . . He h-has divorced me," Violette said huskily.

"Good," Ralph spat. "Good riddance to 'im, I say!"

Violette burst into tears. Covering her face with her hands, she wept. Wracked by sobs.

"Gawd, I'm sorry." Ralph sat beside her, putting his arm around her, trying to hold her close.

But Violette flung him away, lurching to her feet, her face ravaged with grief—and hostility. "Now what will I do?!" she screamed.

"Violette, luv," Ralph began, standing, trying to touch her.

"No!" she shouted. And her face crumbled and she covered

her face with her hands again and wept, harder even than before.

Ralph cursed, helplessly watching, his fists jammed in the pockets of his stained gray trousers.

Violette finally dropped her hands. "I am pregnant, Ralph. I am pregnant with Blake's baby."

Ralph gaped.

It hadn't been this way before, but he hated returning home.

In the past, he hadn't minded the silence in his house, or dining alone. Now he minded very much.

Blake had finished supper, a meal that had probably been superb, except that he had not a clue, being as he hadn't really tasted anything on his plate. He returned to his study, intending to do some paperwork until he was tired enough to sleep. He wasn't sleeping well these days; he always seemed to be tired, a state of being which he ignored.

But the moment he sat down at his desk, he saw the envelope posted from France and froze. He paid little attention to the mail he received at home; everything of importance was sent to his offices at the bank. He had not a doubt whom the letter was from. But why in bloody hell would she write to him? They were divorced. They had been divorced for six weeks now. He hoped to never lay eyes on her again.

Blake hesitated, his gut telling him to ignore the missive, pretend that it did not exist. He tore open the seal and scanned the single paragraph.

He read:

> Dear Blake,
>   I have received notification of our divorce and I thank you for taking care of it so swiftly. I also wish to thank you for the generous pension, which I did not expect.
>   Best Regards to you and your family,
>   Violette.

He shoved the letter aside, aware that he was trembling and short of breath. What kind of letter was that? Why had she signed it in such a familiar manner? Why had the tone of the letter itself been so unfamiliar? She hadn't even asked how he was, clearly she did not care—just as he did not care—and why was he so upset? So angry? And had she thought he would divorce her and leave her in Paris penniless? He had settled a pension on her that left her spectacularly well off until the day she died. Unless, of course, she remarried.

He reached for the letter again and read every single word. This time he noticed her excellent script, her grammar and verbiage. Had she written this herself? Dammit! *He did not care.*

Blake abruptly, violently, ripped the letter in half, and then in half again. He reached for a file of papers, began scanning the profit-and-loss statement in front of him. Suddenly angry, he tossed the file aside. and stood, swiftly crossing the room. He poured himself a double scotch whisky, and, drinking, he stared at the small fire in the hearth.

All he could think was, *Damn her.*

His head was killing him. Blake strode up the steps to Harding House, angry with himself for once again drinking away half the night. Although he did not want to admit it to himself, he had been drinking heavily since fall. It was Saturday morning, and a ritual had long since been established of his taking an early breakfast with his family. These days, he also forced Jon to drive with him about town. It had not been easy to get his brother out of the house, just as it had not been easy to get him out of his bed in the first days following the accident.

Jon had shown no signs of recovering. By now, even Blake had given up hope.

"Good morning, Mother," Blake said, kissing the countess's cheek as he entered the dining room. His father, he saw, was not yet present. Too late, Blake recalled that they had had an early morning riding date which he had forgotten. Blast it.

"You have missed your father," Suzannah said, but without accusation.

"I will apologize. I overslept," Blake confessed. "Good morning, Catherine." She had become a fixture at Harding House since the accident, not that she hadn't been about frequently before that.

Catherine pulled back from him after he kissed her cheek, studying him. "How tired you appear, Blake."

He forced a smile. "It was a long night." As he moved to the sideboard Tulley appeared, spoke with the countess, who was told she was needed in the kitchen. Suzannah left. Blake put a single piece of toast on his plate and returned to the table, only to find Catherine regarding him with open worry. He sighed. "No lectures, please."

"You know me so well," Catherine said. "Blake, I am worried about you."

"We had this conversation a few weeks ago." He poured himself a cup of black cofee and took a sip, which was almost scalding.

"You do not look well. Were you drinking last night?"

Blake set his cup down. He hesitated. "Yes."

Catherine suddenly rose, came around the table, and sat down beside him. She put her arm around him. "You have been drinking a lot. I am not the only one who has noticed. Your parents are worried. Jon is worried. Why are you doing this to yourself?"

Blake rubbed his temples, which throbbed. "I do not know."

"I think we should talk about Violette," Catherine said.

Blake tensed, about to protest. But he looked into Catherine's compassionate green eyes, and the protest died before he could verbalize it. Violette's image was always there, in his mind, haunting him. "I have finally received a letter from her," he said harshly.

Catherine stiffened expectantly.

"No, not a letter, a two-line note." His jaw ground down.

"Oh, Blake, I can see that you still love her . . . ," Catherine began.

"I do not!" Blake shifted to face her, furious with her words. "We are divorced. I do not know why she had to write me at all, especially as she had nothing to say."

"Perhaps you should go to Paris and visit her," Catherine said after a moment.

His eyes widened. "Are you mad? Why would I do that?"

Catherine bit her lip and shrugged. Her eyes had become sheened. She finally smiled, sadly, and cupped his cheek with her palm. "Blake, I don't like seeing you like this," she said. "I do love you so."

Blake finally, grudgingly, smiled.

A cough on the threshold of the dining room made them both turn. Jon stared at them from where he stood, supported by two footmen.

Catherine dropped her palm. "Good morning," she began brightly. Too brightly.

Jon was flushed. "I can see that I am interrupting." His eyes flashed. "I will take breakfast alone in the library," he told the servants.

Catherine was on her feet, the color draining from her face. "Jon!" she cried. And not even looking at Blake, she ran after him as he was carried away.

Catherine found Jon in the library, regarding the gardens, which were dusted with frost. He did not glance at her as she walked in front of him. She wrung her hands. "Jon? You did not see what you think you saw," she said in a rush.

"Catherine." He smiled, but stiffly. "I am truly sorry that I interrupted a tender moment between you and my brother."

"Jon, you did not interrupt. You could never be an interruption."

He eyed her from where he sat in a heavy chair, then glanced away. Outside, the sun was shining through the bare branches of the oaks and elms. Acorns littered the bare, frosty lawns. "How kind you are," he muttered. "As always."

"Your tone is disparaging." Catherine sat down on an adjacent chair. "What do you think you saw?" She was a bit angry now.

He smiled at her, his beautiful mouth twisted cynically. "I know what I saw, my dear. You are a beautiful woman, and Blake is a man, one hardly blind."

Catherine blinked at him. "You are mad! Blake is in love with Violette."

Jon waved dismissively at her. "All the more reason for him to seek comfort from you."

"I will gladly comfort him," Catherine snapped, "but not in the manner which you are suggesting."

"Why not?" Jon's tone was dry, but his blue eyes flashed. "You are twenty-three years old, Catherine, and at the end of this month you will be twenty-four. Isn't it time for you to wed?"

"Wed?" Her eyes widened and she gasped. "Wed . . . Blake?"

"Why not?" Jon's gaze narrowed. "My brother is a bloody good catch. Rich, handsome, a heart of gold. And his son will be the heir to the earldom."

Catherine stared. Her nostrils, flaring, were pink now. "I don't understand, or even like, this conversation."

"But it makes sense, does it not? Why else would you have refused a dozen marriage offers these past few years—if you were not waiting for Blake?"

She could not respond immediately. Is this what he had thought all these years? When she spoke, her breasts heaved. "You are a fool."

"Really?" His tone was mocking, a tone she hated, had never heard before the accident.

"Really!" she cried, a shout. "Jon, I . . ." She faltered, aware of the immensity of what she wanted to say, was about to say. Inherent gentility made her stop. A lady did not declare herself to a man.

"You what?"

She wet her lips. But this was *Jon.* "I am in love with you. Not Blake. It has always been you," she said softly. Her heart was hammering so hard with expectation that she felt faint.

He stared. His expression did not change. He did not say a word.

And Catherine suddenly realized that all her dreams might go up in smoke, something she had never before even considered, for she had always known, since that first time upon the Yorkshire heath when she had met the brothers, that one day Jon would be her lover, her husband, her friend, her partner and helpmate in all things.

But Jon stared. "This is amazing," he said, after a very long and awkward silence.

Catherine knew she was going to weep. It was suddenly crystal clear. She was in a living nightmare. He did not feel for her as she felt for him. Oh, God. *He did not love her.*

"Catherine." He spoke flatly, his face impassive. "I am not ever marrying. I do not need, or want, a wife. Blake, on the other hand, needs you."

She wanted to tell Jon that she loved Blake like a brother. But her heart was splintering even as she had the thought, making it impossible to speak.

Jon smiled briefly at her. "Besides, I think of you as a sister, if you must know the truth."

Catherine heard a horrible sound, half a moan, half a sob. It had come from her. She turned raggedly away from him.

"Catherine!" he cried in alarm.

But she shook her head, incapable of replying, incapable of halting herself as she fled the room. Her life, it seemed, was over, before it had even begun.

*   *   *

Violette stood by the window, peering out from behind the cotton draperies, wishing he would leave. She also wished that Ralph were home.

But Ralph had quit his job months ago, or so he'd said (Violette suspected he had been dismissed), and while he was not working now, he was never home. He slept late in the mornings, then took off, only to return to the flat while Violette slept. He was strangely close-mouthed about what he was doing. Violette guessed that he spent his time on the streets with several Frenchmen she had recently seen him with, surly vagrant types she did not like, or in cafés, overindulging in red wine and brandy. She did not know what was bothering him, but she knew he was very unhappy. Their relationship had somehow become strained.

Below her flat, outside on the street, where the first green buds of spring were opening, Farrow paced, gazing around expectantly. Violette knew that he was waiting for her to come home. When he had knocked on her door ten minutes ago, she had not answered. He must have gone to Maison Langdoc first. He must have been surprised to find out that she was on a leave of absence. But Madame Langdoc would have never told him the truth, even though she seemed to like him very much.

She could not let him see her. Yet in a way, Violette was torn. In February and March he had courted her assiduously, taking her to supper, the theater, to the opera, and even to museums. In fact, Violette had become very fond of art and antiquities, just as she had become quite fond of him.

For, frightened and feeling very much alone, but acutely aware of the new life growing inside of her, Violette had come to look forward to his company. And why wouldn't she? He was handsome, intelligent, and while also, she suspected, bold, he had thus far been the perfect gentleman, treating her as if she were a real lady, which they both knew she was not.

But last week she had decided she could not see him anymore. Last week, she and Madame had agreed that she should rest at home until after the baby was born at the end of the summer. Madame did not think it correct for her patrons to witness Violette's condition. Especially as Violette was no longer wearing her wedding ring.

And her gowns were being let out for the second time. It was too obvious that she had put on weight—or that she was quite pregnant.

A knifelike pain stabbed through Violette's chest. Its source was not physical. Whenever she thought about the baby, due in four months, she thought about Blake. She wondered if it would always be this way—joy accompanied by anguish.

Suddenly Violette tensed. Farrow had turned abruptly to gaze up at the window where she stood. Violette ducked back behind the drapery, uncertain if he had seen her or not. But now her pulse raced.

How she needed a friend, but Farrow frequently crossed the Channel, and she must not let anyone in England know her secret. She was afraid Blake might learn the truth.

This time, he banged on her door. "Violette," he said sharply from the other side of the closed door. "I saw you standing in the window. Are you unwell? Please, let me in."

She was frozen, breathless.

"Violette?" he demanded again.

She wanted to let him in. She did not want to be alone. Of course, if he saw her pregnant, not only would he have discovered her secret, he also would never want to be friends with her again—or anything else. She hesitated; he banged again, shouting her name loudly enough to annoy her neighbor.

Quickly Violette pulled a large wool shawl off of a hook and draped it around her. She glanced in the mirror over the side table in the salon, checking her reflection both from the front and the profile. She breathed easier. She could deceive him if she did not let him in, if they spoke very briefly.

"Coming." She crossed the room and unlocked the door. As she opened it, he pushed it wide, and before she could speak, Farrow had marched right past her and inside of her flat. Violette's heart sank with dread.

He stared at her piercingly, fists on his hips. "Why did you pretend not to be home before? Were you sleeping? Are you ill?"

Violette nodded. "Yes, I was alseep, I have a slight flu."

He continued to stare. "I have not seen you in two weeks. You have avoided me. Why?"

Violette's eyes widened. She had not expected him to be this way. She clutched the shawl tightly. "I have been busy . . . ," she trailed off.

"No. I think you no longer want to see me. Is that true?"

She should tell him, Yes. She could not get the words out, because he was her last link to home, because she was unbearably lonely.

"What have I done?" he asked.

She shook her head, eyes downcast. "It is not you. It is I."

Before she could react, he had paced in front of her and was lifting her chin in his hand. He stared into her eyes, standing so close to her that she could see the gold flecks in his irises. Tears welled.

"Something is upsetting you," he exclaimed, releasing her face. He reached for her hands.

Violette clung to the shawl for another heartbeat, terrified as she realized what was happening, but he clasped her palms, forcing her to finally drop both ends of the mantle. It slipped off of her shoulders, to the floor.

"If I have done something," he began hoarsely, and then his gaze dropped, to her swollen breasts and protruding abdomen, and he froze, mouth open.

Violette inhaled. "You have done nothing," she said.

"Good God. You are pregnant." He had turned white.

"Yes, with Blake's baby." Tears fell down her cheeks.

He dropped her hands, took a step away, and continued to stare. "Does he know?"

"No." Violette rubbed her eyes with her fingertips. "And you mustn't tell him. He must never know."

Farrow stared. His color remained ashen. His jaw was flexed. "Is that the right thing to do?"

"I don't care!" Her voice rose. "Should I tell him about the baby, so that he can come here and take him away from me?"

Farrow was motionless. "If it is a boy, it is Blake's heir."

"Only until Blake has another, legitimate child." Violette was frightened now. "Why are you taking his side? Are you going to tell him?" she cried.

At first he did not answer. "I am not taking his side. That would be impossible, considering that I am in love with you."

Violette gasped.

But Farrow was grave. "But I am a man, a man without a son, a man in need of an heir. I can only imagine how I would feel if I were Blake, and that child, in these circumstances, were mine."

"Are you going to tell him?" Violette demanded harshly.

A moment ensued. "I do not know," Farrow replied.

Thirty-two

HE finally convinced Violette to walk down the block with him to a small restaurant which he had often mentioned, one always busy, filled with gay Parisians amidst flickering candlelights. Although it was late April, Violette took her shawl, hoping, he supposed, to disguise her condition. Farrow was still in shock. What did a man do when he was in love with a woman pregnant with another man's child?

They entered the small, intimate restaurant. A smiling proprietor ushered them to a window table that looked out on a centuries-old church dotted with pigeons. Farrow took a few moments to order them a meal. When he had done so, he looked at Violette and caught her studying him with a slight flush on her cheeks. She glanced away.

Should he tell Blake? He could not do so without losing Violette, he suspected, and not necessarily to the other man. But her silence was a deception, and it was not honorable, it was not right. He did not know what to do. "Violette?"

She looked up.

"What are your plans now?" he asked.

Her reply was cautious. "Do you mean, after my child is born?"

He nodded. "You must be in need of funds. I want to help you."

"That is too kind." She smiled at him. "I am not in need of funds." This was news to him. "Blake has settled a generous pension on me. Nothing will change. I shall return to work at Maison Langdoc four or five months after the child is born. I shall find a young woman to help with the baby."

He started, disbelieving. "Blake has left you a pension! And you have continued to work?"

She cocked her head. "I enjoy my employment. I am very good at selling to the ladies, and as it turns out I have a very good eye for what a particular woman can and cannot wear." She smiled. "Which does sound odd, considering how I used to dress myself."

"Why wouldn't you stay at home to take care of the child yourself?"

"I intend to stay home, as I said, for four or five or even six months. But Robert, I enjoy working at Maison Langdoc. I enjoy it very much."

He absorbed that, but had trouble with the concept. It was a unique proposition. Women belonged in the home.

"Actually," she said softly, her color having increased, "by the end of next year I am hoping to open my own shop."

He started.

She smiled at him. "I believe I can be a success. Do you think I can raise the money from a bank in order to start my own business?"

He knew he gaped. "You wish to open your own shop? Next year? After you have just had a child?"

She nodded. "I would do so now if I weren't in this condition. I believe I would need someone with means to sponsor me to the banks."

"Yes, you would," he said somewhat stiffly. He had to ask. "Violette, if you remarried, surely you would not wish to open a shop then?"

"Why not?" Her smile had faded. "You seem disapproving."

He sat back, staring. He could not imagine his wife being a shopkeeper. He supposed she could be persuaded to change her mind. "I do not approve. How can I? You have turned yourself into an extraordinary woman—a genteel, refined lady. You deserve all that life has to offer, Violette—a beautiful home in the city, a staff to attend you, a country place, silks and velvets, rubies and sapphires. But to continue to *work* after Blake has left you a pension? To become a shopkeeper after having a child?"

Her chin lifted. "I am sorry you do not approve."

He quickly reached across the table to clasp her hand. "But I approve of you. Wholeheartedly." He smiled at her.

She relaxed slightly. "You are a rake."

"Not anymore." He meant it.

She stared.

He hesitated. "As long as we are on the topic, painful as it is, I must ask you to consider what you intend."

She withdrew her hand. "Are we talking about my plans for a shop—or something else?"

"I'm speaking about keeping Blake in ignorance of your condition."

She looked down. "I am not telling him. The child is mine, not his." She had removed her hands to her lap, but not before he saw that they were trembling.

He sighed, torn, gazing at her. "Then I shall not say anything, if you feel this way," he finally said. It was not a decision he was comfortable with.

She jerked. "You will respect my wishes?"

"I have no choice, not if I wish to continue to court you, now do I?"

She stared. "Is that what you are doing?"

"Yes." He was grave. "I most certainly am."

"But . . . after the child?"

"The child changes nothing," he said flatly. "Not between us."

Violette regarded him with wide, unblinking eyes. "I think," she finally said, "that I am very lucky."

He wished she had said it as if she really meant it. He wished she still did not love Blake.

It was a beautiful, warm May day, the sun shining, the skies blue, a robin singing from the treetops, but Blake did not notice. In his office at the bank, he was immersed in his papers. He did not look up when his assistant poked his head into the room. "My lord?"

Still reading, Blake said, "Yes?"

"His Lordship, the earl of Harding, to see you, with your brother, Lord Farleigh."

That got Blake's attention. He looked up as his father walked into the room. Jon was being carried. He rose, moving around his desk. "This is an unexpected surprise."

"I am sure that it is," the earl returned with a slight smile. "We have a few matters to discuss with you, Blake."

Blake did not like the sound of that. He leaned one hip on his desk as the earl sat down, glancing at Jon. His brother smiled encouragingly at him. But there was the glint of steel in his eyes. "Do not keep me in suspense," Blake murmured. What could they want? He had not a doubt that they wanted something.

"Very well," Richard said. "You have been divorced since January, it is now May. And it is apparent to both your brother and I that you have not made a single attempt to find another bride."

Blake could not believe his ears. "I beg your pardons," he said stiffly—vastly affronted.

"Do not get all huffy," Jon said smoothly. "Blake, she left you six months ago. It is more than clear to everyone that you are very unhappy. It is time to get on with your life."

"*My* life," Blake said, not pleasantly.

The earl sighed with annoyance. "Blake, let us call a spade a spade. In a few years I will be seventy."

Blake snorted. "I would not call a decade a few years."

Richard ignored him. "Your brother is not recovering from the accident. His duty now falls upon you. You owe it to me, to him, to your mother, and to the earldom, to produce an heir. And that cannot be done without a wife. Therefore, we wish to know when you plan to remarry."

It was a moment before Blake could speak. He was very angry. "Actually, I have no plans to remarry."

"But you need an heir." The earl was standing.

Blake ground down his jaw, remaining silent with difficulty.

"Blake," Jon said with a brief smile that did not reach his eyes, "I know you have been hurt. For the second time. But you do have a duty to perform. So this time, you should choose for convenience' sake—wisely."

Blake stood and paced. A sick feeling had appeared from nowhere and it pervaded his entire being. He did not want to remarry, period. But he knew that his father and his brother were right. He had a duty to perform, one he could not deny. The thought formed instantly, out of thin air, inside of his mind. *Damn her.* Damn Violette. He never thought about Gabriella anymore.

"I need some time," he finally said.

"Why?" That from Jon.

Blake glared. "Because," he paused, "if I agree to this . . . this extortion, then at least give me the time to choose wisely."

"Actually"—the earl coughed—"we have the perfect woman in mind."

Blake halted in midstride.

"The perfect bride," Jon repeated, unsmiling.

It was a moment before he could find his voice. "Do tell."

"Catherine," his father said firmly. "It is more than time that she wed. I have already spoken with her father. He would be thrilled should you two become affianced."

Blake gaped. "Catherine? Catherine *Dearfield*?"

"Yes, Catherine," the earl said. "She is genteel, kind, the two of you are very close already, and she would, in short, make a perfect wife, a perfect mother, and I believe, a lifelong friend and partner."

Many images raced through Blake's mind. The first time he had met Catherine, a pretty little blond girl in pigtails astride her Arabian mare. Catherine's come-out, the pigtails gone, a shy but beautiful young lady revealed in an ice pink ball gown. Suddenly he looked at Jon. Jon had danced with her first that night, even before her father. The image was suddenly there in his mind as if it were yesterday, not three years ago. They had made a striking couple. Graceful, beautiful, and somehow inherently at ease with one another.

Of course, Jon was now confined to a chair or his bed. He would never waltz with her, or any woman, again.

Jon met his gaze. His face was impassive. "The two of you would do very well together, I agree. She would make the perfect wife, the perfect mother. And Catherine should marry, and soon. Otherwise she will be considered an old maid, and life will have passed her by."

He managed to speak. "Catherine is like a sister to me."

"She is not your sister," the earl said. "So why don't you get that excuse right out of your head?"

Blake bristled. "The two of you come here, and out of the blue, tell me to marry, and whom to wed, and I am supposed to come to heel like a well-trained hound?"

"Blake. We want what's best for you, what's best for her, what's best for the family and the earldom."

Blake sank into a chair. "I am sorry. I have been shocked." He rubbed his eyes with one hand. "I need some time . . . to think about this . . . to adjust my thinking."

The earl stood. "So your answer is not No."

Blake glanced up, into his father's eyes. "I will not shirk my duty, Father, that I promise you." Dread swept through him.

The earl smiled, pleased.

"But whether I will marry Catherine, that I cannot decide in a moment or two." And Blake turned to look at Jon.

Jon stared back at him.

Blake hesitated. He stood on the threshold of the drawing room at the Dearfield town house with the Dearfields' butler. Catherine sat at the secretaire, a quill in her hand, but she was not writing. She was staring pensively through the open french doors at the small back garden, which was a riot of yellow and white spring blooms. Her expression was far more than somber. It was sad.

"Lady Catherine, Lord Neville to see you," the butler intoned.

Catherine smiled as she turned, rising, hands outstretched. "Blake, dear, it is so good to see you." She sailed forward.

He smiled at her, unable not to really study her now. She was an attractive woman, although not his type. But he cared deeply for her, he always had. He took her hands in his and kissed her cheek. "Hello, Catherine. Have I interrupted you?"

"No, of course not. Come sit down. Thompson, could you bring us some tea and cakes." She smiled at the butler, who bowed and left. "Have you had tea yet, Blake?"

"No. I don't take tea at the office." He sat beside Catherine on the sofa, wondering why she was so sad. "Is something bothering you, Catherine? God knows, you have asked that question of me often enough. Now it is my turn." He smiled.

Her smile faded, she sighed. "Not really." She met his gaze and sighed again. "I guess I am a bit bothered." She smiled but it was forced. "I am lonely, Blake."

He tensed in spite of himself. But had he ever had a better opening? "Would you care to elaborate?"

She glanced down with a shrug. "I had always intended to wed, have children, to have a wonderful home and family, in fact. But now I just do not know."

His pulse raced. "You have refused a dozen good men, that I know of, since your come-out. Why?"

Her smile was fleeting. "I suppose I was waiting for a romantic hero. A knight in shining armor. A man who only exists in a woman's dreams."

He stared, because her voice had caught. He reached for her hand. "I did not know you were a romantic, Catherine." Suddenly he thought about Jon, who was also a damned romantic, as Blake had learned last year during the fiasco with Violette.

She smiled wanly. "Hopelessly so."

He hesitated. "Does the man you marry have to be a hero? Or can he be flesh and blood, hard-working, sincere?"

She gazed curiously at him. "I am not going to marry."

A silence ensued. "Not even me?" he finally said.

She gaped, eyes wide.

He managed a smile. "I botched that, I guess. How should

I begin? Catherine, I must marry. It has struck me that you and I would do very well together. We are already very good friends. I respect you, care for you deeply. Could I do better in choosing a wife? In choosing the mother of my children?''

Catherine stood up. "Oh, God," she whispered. "I cannot believe this. You want to marry *me*?"

He also stood. Fighting Violette's image. "Yes, I do. I have given it great thought." He had thought of little else all week. Jon and his father were, he had realized, right.

But she shook her head, staring at him as if he had grown horns. "I cannot marry you, Blake." She wet her lips. "Besides, you are in love with Violette."

"That is absurd," he snapped.

"Well, I still cannot marry you—it would not be right."

"I do not understand."

"I think of you as a brother."

He smiled. "My dear, I am not your brother."

It was a moment before she could speak. "Blake, it would not be right."

"Why not?"

She did not answer. She was distraught. "I can't," she finally said. "And what about Violette? She was—is—my friend!"

"Violette and I are divorced. Violette has nothing to do with this," he said harshly.

"But she loves you," Catherine said, hushed.

It was as if she had dealt him a physical blow. When he could respond, he said, "That is absolutely absurd—and irrelevant, too."

Catherine stared.

He stared back. Finally he said, "Catherine, is your rejection final?"

Her eyes widened. "I . . . I am not rejecting you, Blake."

He cut her off. "Good. Will you think about this? Carefully? As carefully as I have? You have said you do not want to be alone, that you want children, a home, a family. I am offering you those things, Catherine, and we are dear friends. My proposal merits serious consideration."

She was ashen. "Oh, God," she whispered again. "Very well. You are right. I will think about it carefully."

"Good." He smiled, but oddly enough, he was very shaken. He took her hand and kissed it, then quickly departed, wondering if, after all, he had done the right thing.

✦ Thirty-three ✦

CATHERINE knew that she could not marry Blake. It was impossible, immoral. For no matter how hard she had tried to cut her feelings for Jon out of her heart, she had not been able to stop loving him. Marrying Blake would be unfair to them both, even though she knew that he had not asked for her hand out of love.

She watched Blake striding away from the house, toward his waiting phaeton. Her heart hammered. There was no question about it. He was an impressive, wonderful man. If only she had never met Jon, had never fallen in love with him, then she would be the utmost fool to refuse Blake.

Blake's phaeton rolled away from the curb. Catherine walked away from the window, her hand skimming the back of a chair. Why did she feel so anguished?

The answer was suddenly crystal clear. Her entire being hurt her because the wrong man wanted to marry her for the wrong reasons. And because she hadn't lied to Blake. She had matured to womanhood believing that she would be a mother and wife—believing, deep in her heart and with all of her soul, that she would one day become Jon's wife, and the mother of Jon's children. Now, of course, it was obvious that she would grow old alone, but Catherine did not want to grow old alone.

Dammit.

Catherine could not believe that she would curse, even inwardly in her own thoughts, and was appalled at herself. But she could not dwell on the breakdown of her morals and conduct now. She rushed out of the salon. "Thompson!"

The tall, thin butler appeared. "My lady?"

Her pulse raced. "I need a carriage." Before he could nod she had dashed upstairs, skirts lifted above her ankles, well aware that her behavior was not genteel and that it was, indeed, remarkably odd. But she did not care what the staff—or anyone else—might think. She ran down the hall and into her bedroom, where she donned the first hat she grabbed, one black and feathered. White kid gloves followed. Catherine flew back downstairs.

Thompson was wide-eyed. "My lady, er . . . is there an emergency?"

"No. Yes. I don't know!" Catherine cried. "But I am going to Harding House." Her heart leapt. She had not seen Jon in a month. She had stopped visiting the Hardings at home after his cool rejection of her and her feelings. She was a fool, to both dread and anticipate seeing him now.

The carriage ride across the neighborhood was endless. Catherine did not dare think too closely about what she was doing. She intended to refuse Blake. She had no choice in that matter. But she absolutely had to speak with Jon about this. Her every instinct told her that.

Tulley beamed when he greeted her in the foyer. "Lady Dearfield! It is so good to see you, my lady."

Catherine managed a smile, wet her lips. "Lord Farleigh?"

"He is in the gardens, my lady, taking a bit of air and some sun."

Catherine nodded and hurried through the house. She saw him through the open french doors as she crossed the huge, silent ballroom, knowing from habit just where he would be. Her steps faltered. Seated under a tree on a blanket, clad in dark trousers and a fine white shirt, he was engrossed in a book. It did not matter to her that he could not walk. He was by far the most stunning man she had ever laid eyes upon, and, more importantly, in spite of his feelings for her, seeing him brought a wave of joyous anticipation cresting up inside of her. She had missed him. Terribly.

She paused on the threshold of the terrace. "Jon?"

He glanced up. For one blazing instant, his expression was animated—as if he were as glad to see her. But then his face changed, becoming impassive, impossible to read. Casually he closed the book.

Catherine crossed the terrace, coming down the three flagstone steps to the lawns where he sat. "Hello."

"Forgive me for not getting up," he drawled.

"Oh, please," she said.

He shrugged, staring.

"We have not chatted in a very long time," she began hesitantly. "May I join you?" Over their heads, sparrows pecked at insects and leapt about, twittering.

"You are always welcome," he said stiffly, gesturing.

She sat down on the plaid blanket, by his feet. She smiled at him. He did not smile back. "How are you?"

"As well as can be expected. I am going to Europe next

week. To mud baths near Geneva. They are supposed to do miracles.''

Catherine wanted to tell him that if they did not perform miracles, it would not matter to her. Instead, she was silent, smoothing the folds of her green print skirt.

"And you?" he finally asked. "How are you?" His gaze skimmed over her, lingering on her hat. "Is black now fashionable in the summertime?"

She glanced up, mesmerized by his penetrating blue eyes. And suddenly realized that her black hat did not complete her green and white ensemble. "Oh." She began to remove the hat.

And he finally smiled, slightly, at her.

The hat beside her, she blurted, "Your brother has asked me to marry him."

Jon did not blink. "Will you accept?"

Catherine was riddled with tension. "Are you not surprised?"

"Why would I be surprised? Blake must marry. You are the perfect choice."

Her tension grew worse instantly. "He is in love with Violette and we both know it. He has been terribly hurt by her."

"She left him. They are divorced. He is a proud man, and he will never take her back. He will recover, Catherine; all men do." Jon suddenly fell silent, his mouth twisted. "In any case," he added, "you can help him forget her."

"I cannot marry him," she said.

His regard was piercing. "Whyever not?"

She was in disbelief. Didn't he recall a conversation they'd recently had, in which she had declared her feelings for him? "It is not . . . appropriate."

Jon's upper body straightened. "It is very appropriate. You will not receive a better offer, Catherine, if that is what you are thinking."

"That is not what I am thinking."

"You are twenty-three. It is time for you to marry, and to marry well. Surely you will accept?"

"You *want* me to marry Blake?" Her tone was high, sounding to her own ears like a shrill screech.

"Of course I do. I should enjoy being the uncle to your and Blake's children." His smile was stiff. "You are practically a Harding already anyway, Catherine."

Catherine was frozen.

Jon was bland. "In fact, I have encouraged Blake in this matter. We discussed it recently."

She found it difficult to breathe, to move, but she could not remain in the gardens with Jon now. She had been a stupid idiot to come.

"Catherine? Do not be a fool. Blake would make a wonderful husband, and you would be the perfect wife."

She was standing. How she had managed to do so was beyond her comprehension. She was incapable of speech.

"Have I upset you? I am sorry," he said, his gaze hard, steely even, and very unfamiliar now, "but I am in favor of this match. Everyone is. You *must* accept."

Catherine could not speak, because the very last shreds of hope had just been unraveled, and were disintegrating as if before her very eyes. All her dreams, up in smoke. Numbly, she shook her head.

And then she turned and fled.

"Yer goin' to the thee-at-er like that?" Ralph was disbelieving. He was also drunk.

Violette was very pregnant now, and the lavender silk gown she wore had been let out three times already. But oddly enough, she had never looked better. Her skin had taken on an incandescent glow, and her eyes were very bright and very blue, but she was obviously with child. Most ladies, she knew, stayed home in such an advanced condition. "If Lord Farrow does not mind, then why should I?"

"But it is scandalous." Ralph mimicked her very words to Farrow many weeks ago.

She had just picked up her small beaded reticule, and now she flung it back down. "What did you do today, Ralph?"

His gaze narrowed. "Wot yew mean?"

"You know exactly what I mean." Her hands found her now ample hips.

He glowered. "Did a bit of walkin'."

"I think you spent the day in some gin mill!"

"An' wot's it to yew, luv?"

Violette stared. Ralph had become a stranger to her. He had become bitter in his unhappiness. She hardly ever saw him, and when she did, he was with his new friends, whom she despised. They were rough and gruff and menacing in appearance. "Is it Paris? Is that it?" she asked. "Are you yearning for home?"

"I ain't fond of the Frenchies, but this town's all right," he said, jamming his hands in his pockets. They both ignored the knock on the front door, which would be Farrow coming to escort her out for the evening.

"Is it the baby?" she asked quietly, but her hands had begun to tremble.

He stared. "Yeah. It's the baby, an' it's 'im." He jerked his head at the door.

Violette hesitated. "I'm sorry you do not want me to have a life," she said. She moved toward the door.

"We 'ad a life. Yew an' me. Until yew decided to become some fancy lady," Ralph said grimly.

Violette did not answer him.

" 'E's like the other one. Like 'Is Lordship, Blake. 'E'll cut yew in two, Violette," Ralph warned. "Use yew an' throw yew away like some old, leftover mutton bone."

Violette stiffened and opened the door. But Farrow was there, smiling at her, pleased to see her, and she smiled back. He kissed her cheek as he came inside. "You are so beautiful tonight," he said.

She knew, by now, that he meant it. "Thank you."

He nodded indifferently at Ralph, who did not leave the parlor. "Ready?" he asked.

Violette was about to nod when Ralph came forward, extracting a letter from his breast pocket. "This came earlier," he said coolly.

Violette immediately realized that the letter had been posted in England, and as she turned it over, she saw that it was from Catherine. Her pulse raced. "It's from Catherine Dearfield." She smiled eagerly. Then, "You've opened this! You had someone read it to you!" she cried to Ralph.

"It was a mistake," he said. They both knew that he lied.

Violette decided that Ralph had gone too far, but she could not worry about the miserable state of their relationship now, or what to do about it. She asked Farrow if he minded if she quickly read the letter, and when he said that he did not, she began to do so. It was easy for her to read letters and even newspapers now, but as she scanned the page, her smile vanished. An incredible knifelike pain pierced her breast. Suddenly she was lightheaded, short of breath.

"What is it?" Farrow exclaimed, reaching for her elbow, steadying her.

Violette blinked at him. "Catherine is marrying Blake."

Farrow hesitated. "I know. I heard. I . . ." He stopped. "Violette?!"

The blackness that swept over her was a relief. She sank into it, embracing unconsciousness, and nothingness. She hoped she was embracing death.

When Blake entered the library of his club, heads turned. He espied Dom St. Georges immediately, seated by the vacant hearth, the *London Times* in his hands, which he was reading. As Blake crossed the room, he was stopped constantly as his friends and acquaintances offered him congratulations on his recent engagement to Catherine Dearfield, which had been published in the papers. He finally took the chair opposite Dom.

St. Georges laid his journal aside. He had just returned with his wife and the twins from the Continent. He immediately gripped Blake's shoulder. "What news." He smiled, but his gaze was searching. "I suppose I should not be surprised. I suppose your marriage to Catherine was inevitable. Congratulations, Blake."

Blake avoided Dom's eyes and smiled slightly. "Inevitable. A good choice of words."

"Was it?"

Blake glanced up and was again made uneasy by his best friend's probing regard. "I know Catherine almost as well as I know myself, perhaps even better than I know you."

Dom nodded. "I am aware of that. And how is Jon?"

Blake's expression tightened. "He is not going to recover, Dom. Numerous doctors have confirmed that."

"I am so sorry," Dom said.

"He is unhappy. Bitter. God, how he has changed. I do not know my brother anymore. He rarely comes to the club, or drives in the park. He does not attend any fêtes. He is talking now about retiring to Harding Hall, and spending most of his time in the country. He is turning himself into a recluse, purposefully, and it hurts me very much."

"Don't let him do that," Dom said quickly. "He may have lost the use of his legs, but his life is not over, not by a longshot. He is an intelligent, warm-hearted, charming man. He must be encouraged to live life as fully as possible again."

"I am in complete agreement with you," Blake said grimly. And he thought, *I want my brother back.*

"In fact, in time he can marry. He is still the Harding heir, he is vastly wealthy, politically and socially powerful, and I have not a doubt that there are many beautiful women who would be eager to marry your brother.''

Blake stared. ''He can't have children.''

''Some women would not care. And Jon would make a wonderful stepfather, and there is always adoption.''

Blake remained motionless. He finally said, ''Jon would not agree.''

''Perhaps you and I have a project to take on,'' Dom said with his easy smile. ''To get him out and about and find him the right woman.''

Blake gripped his arm. ''You are a very good friend.''

Dom shrugged.

''So how was the south of France?'' Blake asked.

''Warm.''

''Is that all you are going to say?'' Blake was amused.

Dom did not smile. ''We spent the weekend in Paris before returning home.''

Blake stiffened. Violette's image flashed through his mind. He couldn't help wondering if Dom had run into her. He wondered what she was doing. Not that he cared.

''We bumped into Farrow on the Avenue des Champs-Elysées.''

''Farrow?!'' Blake sat up straighter, aware of his racing heartbeat. ''Farrow, in Paris, in the middle of the summer?''

''Apparently,'' Dom said, his golden eyes boring, ''Robert leased a house there last winter. He told me that he only returned once to London to take care of his affairs for a fortnight. He has, he says, been enjoying Paris inordinately.''

Blake did not believe in coincidences. ''Was he with my ex-wife?''

''No, he was not, but my wife did ask if Farrow had seen or heard of Violette.'' Dom stared. ''He became very reticent, very suddenly, Blake. He said yes, he had seen her, and that she was well. At which point he was most eager to depart the avenue and our company.''

Blake sat very still, his pulse pounding, even roaring, in his ears. Robert Farrow was living in Paris—where Violette now was. He could not believe it. And he did not think, for one instant, that it was a coincidence.

Not that he cared.

But dammit, he did.

"Blake?" Dom queried. "Are you all right?"

Blake stood. "No." He was grim. "Call me a fool, but I am going to Paris."

And Dom grinned.

⊰ *Thirty-four* ⊱

CATHERINE'S hand was shaking as she opened the envelope that she had just received. It was from Paris; it was from Violette.

They had not kept up any kind of genuine correspondence, but Catherine had finally sent Violette a short, chatty letter, telling her about her engagement. She had felt compelled. Now Catherine was afraid of what she might find written in the letter, so for a moment she held the folded vellum to her breast.

She was so confused, so distraught. She was engaged to a wonderful man; she should be ecstatic. Instead, she was close to being as miserable as a human being could be. She still did not quite know how the engagement had happened. She still knew it was wrong—a terrible mistake, an ultimate irony.

But the countess was already planning the most spectacular wedding London had ever seen. Blake had asked her if a date in December was acceptable, and Catherine had agreed.

Trembling, she decided she must not think about the wedding now—or about breaking off the engagement. Very unhappily, she unfolded the letter.

Violette had written:

> Dear Catherine,
>
> I have recently received the most wonderful news that you are engaged to Blake. I am so happy for you. No one deserves a man like Blake more, and I always thought the two of you perfectly suited for one another. Congratulations.
>
> All is well with myself here in Paris. I have taken a brief leave from my employment at Maison Langdoc, but plan to continue there shortly. And I suppose that I have news of my own. Robert Farrow has been courting me since last winter with, I believe, the most honorable intentions. I think he is going to ask me for my hand. I think I shall accept. Isn't that wonderful? I do not think I have ever been this happy.

Please send my regards to everyone.

Affectionately, Violette.

Catherine had to reread the letter to make sure she had understood it correctly. And then she read it a third time, trying to read between the lines. The last thing she wanted to do was to hurt Violette in any way, but Violette seemed genuinely pleased with her engagement to Blake. Was that possible?

Catherine did not think so. When a woman truly loved a man, that love did not die, it went on forever, against all common sense, all logic, all sanity. Catherine knew that herself firsthand.

"Catherine?"

She started at the sound of Blake's voice, clutching the letter and leaping to her feet. He stood in the doorway of the drawing room, regarding her intently. She managed a smile. "I did not expect to see you today," she said uneasily.

He came forward and kissed her hand—not her cheek, as he had used to do. "Is the letter bad news?"

She wet her lips. "No." Her heart hammered, sounding like blasts of thunder in her own ears. "It is just a letter from"—she faltered—"from Violette."

He stared. A slight flush appeared on his cheekbones. "I see. And what does she have to say?"

She knew she could not let him read it, for she knew he would be hurt. She held it against her skirts. She was incapable of lying, or even of deception, but surely she could omit some of the truth? "She . . . she asks after the family, sends her regards. She is happy in Paris."

"That is all?"

Catherine felt her cheeks burning. "That is all I wish to tell you," she finally said. And realized she might as well have thrown a red flag at a bull.

His eyes darkened. "There is more. Does she know about our engagement?"

Catherine's eyes widened.

"Well?" he demanded.

"Yes. She sends us felicitations." She bit her lip. She was not going to tell him about Farrow, absolutely not. "I do not know if she means it or not."

"May I see the letter?" he asked calmly.

Catherine froze, in disbelief. She finally said, "I beg your pardon?"

He held out his hand and repeated the question.

Catherine wanted to say no. "Blake, this is very unseemly . . . ," she began.

"What are you hiding from me?"

She handed him the letter, dismayed, and watched him read it. She knew him very well, so she saw his jaw tighten, his temples pulse. But otherwise, his expression did not change. He returned the letter to her. "Thank you," he said.

"Are you all right?"

"Why would I not be all right?" But he did not smile, and his tone was cold.

"You are angry."

"I am not angry. Why would I be angry? I am marrying you. She is marrying Farrow. How perfect the world is."

Had she detected a trace of bitterness in his tone? "Blake," she said in a rush, "perhaps this is the time for us to talk about our engagement."

He suddenly pulled her close and feathered her mouth with his—the first time he had ever kissed her in an unchaste way. His lips brushed hers very briefly. "We will talk about the engagement another time. I came to tell you that I am leaving town for a week." His gaze held hers. "Actually, I am going to Paris, and I am going there to see Violette."

Catherine stared. "You are going to see Violette?" Her mind raced.

"There are some financial matters I wish to discuss with her. Now that we are marrying, I do feel I should make certain Violette's circumstances are adequate. Of course, if she marries Farrow, she will not receive a pension from me. But until she has remarried, I think it is important that I make certain she is provided for in a satisfactory manner."

"Of course," Catherine said, her pulse—and her hopes—suddenly lifting. "I think it is a very good idea for you to go to Paris, Blake," she said.

Blake stood on the Rue Bellepasse, a very small, cobbled street lined with stone buildings containing small shops, including a bakery, two cafés, a bookseller, shoemaker, and a lively brasserie. The street was clean, pleasant, and shady, for old leafy oaks stood sentinel there. Above all the shops were residential flats, many with wrought-iron balconies, and Blake stood outside the entrance of No. 42 Rue Bellepasse, which was where

Violette lived. He was sweating, in spite of the fact that it was a pleasant midsummer day.

By now he was beginning to think that he was mad to have come all the way to Paris to discuss Violette's finances with her. Completely mad. He could have easily corresponded with her, either by himself or, preferably, through his lawyers. Perhaps it was not too late to change his mind, go to a hotel, and from there return home on the morrow.

He hesitated. His pulse was racing. And he had never before been an indecisive man.

Then he thought, *Christ*. He was already there, at her doorstep, and they had been married, even if very briefly, and he was supporting her, so he had every right to discuss what he wished to discuss with her. And he would not, of course, tell her that he had made the journey to Paris solely on her account.

His mind made up, Blake began to stride toward the weathered door of the tenement. But amidst all the traffic on the street, he suddenly saw a very elegant, open black carriage with plush red leather seats turning the corner, a stark contrast to the drays and dorries, carts and hansoms, he had thus far noted. Instinct made him pause. The carriage, pulled by two sleek black geldings, contained a couple. And even as Blake recognized the occupants, he also recognized the coat of arms embossed on the low-slung doors.

And Violette was leaning close to Robert Farrow, laughing, he saw now, at something he was saying. His heart turned over, he could not move. The carriage paused. Blake could not tear his gaze away from her. He had forgotten the effect she had on him, the impact. How he had entirely forgotten.

And Violette saw him. Her laughter died. She continued to clutch Farrow's arm, losing all of her color, turning a ghostly shade of white.

He recovered first. It took a supreme effort. Steeling himself for God only knew what, feeling as if he were going to war, he walked toward the carriage, his strides stiff with sudden tension. As he did so, he noticed that Violette had gained weight. And then he reached the curb and realized that she was heavily, shockingly pregnant.

Blake imagined that he himself turned even more ghostly than she. He stared, disbelieving and stunned, incapable of thought or speech.

Farrow reached past Violette to open the carriage door.

"Blake. This is unexpected." He did not smile as he climbed down, turning to offer a hand up to Violette.

She did not move. Her gaze was locked with Blake's, her blue eyes impossibly wide.

He forced his lips into a smile. "Lady Neville." He inclined his head. His heart was pounding now. He had one thought. Was the child his? And if so, why the hell hadn't she told him? Or was it Farrow's? He was extraordinarily good at numbers. It was late July. She looked ready to deliver at any time. He rapidly calculated when she had conceived, and realized that the child was definitely his.

She opened her mouth to speak and failed.

"Violette," Farrow said gently.

She flinched, glancing briefly at Farrow, then back at Blake. "Blake, I . . . What are you doing here?" she whispered.

Blake moved past Farrow. "Do come down, Lady Neville. We have matters to discuss." His tone was frigid, but so was he.

She was frightened and it showed. "I . . . I don't understand."

"No!" he snapped. "I do not understand." It was a snarl. He reached for her, caught her wrist. She had no choice but to step down from the carriage, caught in his viselike grip.

"You can't handle her like that in her condition," Farrow protested.

Blake turned a murderous gaze on his rival. "Do not tell me how to treat my ex-wife. Not unless she is already *your* wife."

Farrow stiffened. "Violette is tired. She wishes to rest. Why don't you come back another time?"

"Also, do *not* tell me what to do," Blake said, very low. His fists were clenched. He was ready to hit someone, preferably Farrow.

"Please, stop," Violette whispered. "Robert, I had better speak with Blake. I will be fine."

Farrow did not move. "I don't like this."

"That is neither here nor there," Blake said coldly. He took Violette's arm.

"I will wait here in the carriage, then," Farrow said abruptly. "If you need me, call.

Violette nodded, which infuriated Blake even more. Holding her tightly in case she tried to bolt, but acutely aware of her condition, he led her to her door and waited very impatiently while she unlocked it. Her hands, he saw with satisfaction, were trembling; she appeared terrified.

She did not look at him as she preceded him up the narrow, steep flight of stairs. He was instantly appalled. She was climbing up and down these steps every day in her condition? "Haven't I given you enough funds to live decently?" he asked harshly.

On the landing she paused, unlocking the door to her flat. It was a moment before she replied. "I like this apartment, this block, this entire neighborhood, in fact. And when I am working, I can walk to Maison Langdoc."

He was breathing raggedly. He followed her inside. The apartment was charming, if not utterly middle class. The salon was spacious, brightly sunlit, cheerfully papered, the ceiling high, and the two broad windows looked out onto the quiet street below. The furnishings were comfortable, clean, and pleasant. He almost relaxed.

She faced him slowly, still ashen.

"Is it mine?" He knew he was being cruel, but she deserved it.

She flinched. "Of course it's yours."

"And when is it due?"

She wet her lips. "In a few weeks."

"I see." He smiled unpleasantly. "And when, pray tell, were you going to tell me?"

She stared, not answering.

He wanted to hit her. He did not. "You weren't going to tell me," he cried. "You were never going to tell me!"

"No," she shouted back. "No, I was not!"

They stared at one another, anger sizzling between them, so much anger, months and months of it. And then Blake turned away, cursing, pounding his fist on the wall once. He wanted to smash the plaster into pieces.

"Blake, stop!" Violette cried. "You will break your hand!"

He froze. He did not know why he felt like weeping, but he did. He could not stop recalling the day he had realized that Violette had left him. Could not stop remembering waking up alone in her bed. "You have betrayed me," he said hoarsely. "Again."

"No. That was not my intention," she whispered to his back.

He whirled. "Then what, may I ask, was your intention?"

Her chin was high. But tears filled her eyes. "To keep my baby. That is all."

"I fail to understand."

The tears fell now, streaming down her cheeks. "Are you going to take my baby away?"

He stared at her, the loveliest woman he had ever seen, a woman he could not comprehend. In fact, looking at her now, he almost felt that he was gazing at a stranger, a lovely, genteel stranger, for she had changed so much. In spite of the flat where they confronted one another, she was no longer Violette Goodwin, a waif from St. Giles who could not speak without a Cockney accent, who could not maneuver her skirts without knocking over side tables. She had matured into a breathtaking woman, and, had he not known the truth about her antecedents himself, he would have found it impossible to believe that she was anything other than Lady Neville—that she had ever been anything other than Lady Neville.

"Are you going to take my baby away?" she cried, gripping her own palms.

He looked at her, then looked around at the flat where she lived. He thought about his own lavish town house in Belgravia, and then about Harding House and Harding Hall. "I do not know," he finally said.

She cried out.

Blake could not leave Paris, not with the baby due in a few weeks—three to be exact. He was still in shock.

He paced the suite that he had taken at the Hôtel Jérome. He had been pacing the Oriental rugs all afternoon. How could she have deceived him this way? He was sick, furious; he wanted to punish her for what she had done. Yet he recalled her tears. Violette was no actress. She was afraid he was going to take the baby away from her.

As well he should. His child was a Harding. He intended to adopt the boy, or girl. And if it was a boy, his son would one day succeed to the earldom. Blake could provide his child with the finest tutors, the finest care, the finest lifestyle. To leave his child in Violette's care, should she remain unwed, was insane. Of course, it did not seem that she would remain unwed for very long.

Blake slumped in an oversized chair. He remained oblivious to the lavish furnishings surrounding him—to the master paintings on the walls, to the gilded and lacquered antiques filling all the rooms. He did not know what to do. He only knew that he was incredibly unhappy, and that the cause of his unhappiness was Violette. And if he were truly honest with himself, he might even admit to being jealous of her relationship with Farrow. But he was too overwrought, he could not admit such a thing.

One thing remained clear. He would remain in Paris until after the baby was born. And then he would return home—but whether or not his child would accompany him, he could not say.

Violette could not sleep. That, her physician had told her, was very common among women in her condition, but tonight she knew her restlessness had nothing to do with the life inside of her. It had everything to do with Blake. She was terrified.

Terrified that he would steal her baby from her, and terrified of the feelings he still aroused within her. When she had seen him standing on the street earlier, had realized in a heartbeat that it was him, the world had seemed to stop and congeal. Before the fear, there had been nothing but joy.

Her happiness had been short-lived, of course, because of her deception. And now he knew. What should she do? Run away again?

Violette thought that he would probably follow her all the way to China now that he knew she carried his child. How could he not take it away?

Violette got up at sunrise, knowing that if she hadn't slept by now she never would. As she brewed coffee, she stared out of the window, watching her neighborhood coming to life, the baker opening his shop, two of her neighbors going to work. She was vaguely aware of the fact that Ralph had not come home for three nights now. She should be worried, but, actually, she was relieved.

And she wondered when she would see Blake again. He had left very abruptly, not telling her whether he was staying in Paris or returning to London. His anger also frightened her.

She knew, from a lifetime of experience, what angry men were capable of.

Violette dressed mechanically. It was hard to admit, but if Blake left she would not just be relieved; she would be dismayed as well. This made no sense. She had thought she had gotten over him by now. It occurred to Violette that she should marry Farrow as quickly as possible, as if that might strike her feelings for Blake out of her heart. Robert, of course, had not yet proposed. Maybe, she thought dismally, she was wrong about him the way she had been wrong about Blake.

A knock at her door made her jump. She had not buttoned the back of her dress, too late realizing she had chosen a garment she could not close without help. She put on a lightweight shawl and crossed the salon. It was early morning, the sun barely up. She was not expecting anyone, but sometimes Madame Langdoc or one of the clerks from the shop called to see how she was doing while on their way to work.

She opened the door and came face to face with Blake.

He nodded at her, unsmiling, his gaze skimming over every feature of her face in a way she knew so well, had thought she had forgotten. She took a step backwards nervously, her pulse soaring. "Good morning," she said, a croak.

Blake finally smiled at her, not naturally. He looked as if he had also been up all night. "May I come in? I left so abruptly yesterday that we did not have a chance to finish our conversation."

She stiffened, panic coursing over her; he was going to tell her he was taking the baby, she just knew it. Her heart hammering now, making her feel ill, she managed a nod and allowed him to step inside. She shut the door after him, bolting it, and faced him, twisting her clammy hands.

He looked at her palms, then into her eyes. "How have you been feeling?" His tone was gentle.

Violette started. She had not been expecting this. "Fine."

"I am serious." His gaze, brilliantly blue, was searching.

"So am I." She suddenly felt the strength of his magnetism. She had also forgotten how very attracted she was to him. Today, in a calmer moment, there was no denying it.

"And your doctor? Do you have a good one? What does he say?"

"I have a very good doctor. His name is Jean Aubigner. He says that I am as healthy as a horse, and undoubtedly my baby is the same." She smiled slightly.

And so did Blake. He shoved his hands in the trousers of his charcoal gray trousers. "You speak beautifully now," he said seriously, his gaze holding hers. "Naturally, without the least trace of an accent."

She flushed, suddenly aware of the pleasure his praise had generated inside her breast. "I am reading and writing now, too," she heard herself say.

"I know. Catherine told me." His expression changed.

Violette also stiffened. She wet her lips. "I heard about the engagement. I am very happy for you both."

He did not say a word.

Violette said, in a rush, "I always thought the two of you perfectly suited to one another." She forced a smile. It felt lopsided.

"Yes," Blake said. "Perfectly suited—that is what everyone says."

"How is your mother? Your father?"

His regard was unwavering. "They are very well."

"They must be pleased. About the engagement, I mean." But now she was thinking about his brother.

Blake nodded stiffly. "We have chosen December the fifteenth as the wedding day."

Violette forgot all about Jon. She thought she might throw up. "How wonderful—a Christmas wedding." She hurried past Blake. "Let me make some coffee. Do you like croissants?"

He followed her into the small whitewashed kitchen. Cheerful yellow drapes adorned the room's two windows. A sprigged tablecloth covered the kitchen table. "And you? When shall you and Farrow do the deed?"

Violette busied herself putting a kettle of water on the stove. Meticulously, she began measuring coffee. She felt her shawl slipping. "Actually, I do not know. He has not asked me yet." She did not look up.

"And when he does?" Blake walked closer. "Will you accept his suit?"

"Of course I will!" She laughed, and it sounded forced. "He is a noble, caring man."

"Than he has changed," Blake said flatly.

Violette turned, not realizing that Blake had come up behind her and was standing so close, and suddenly she was face to face with him and practically in his embrace. She froze. His gaze skimmed her face, lingering on her mouth. "You are far more beautiful than before—and that is practically an impossibility," he murmured.

His tone was soft and sensual. Violette stared into his eyes. Daring to remember what his kisses had felt like, tasted like.

She could hear his breathing. It seemed labored.

She darted past him. "I am a cow. Fat, like a washerwoman."

"That will change," he said roughly.

"I hope so."

"Are you still mad about desserts?" he asked.

She had to smile, and glancing at him, saw that he was smiling a little too. "Yes, but we have no plum pudding here."

His smile faded as their gazes locked. "But they have the finest pastries in the world in Paris," he said slowly.

The kitchen was far too warm for comfort. "Yes," she whispered. "They do."

Neither one of them moved.

And then the kettle on the stove began to sing. Violette jumped and rushed forward to remove it from the flame. She forgot to pick up a cloth; she touched the handle and cried out. Blake rushed to her side.

"I am fine," she cried, stepping away from him, thoroughly out of breath. But she had burned her hand. She went to the pump over the sink and began to work the faucet. This time Blake kept his distance. "It is nothing," she said, almost panting. She wanted him to leave.

She wanted him to stay. God, she did.

"You must be more careful," he returned gravely. "Your dress, it is not buttoned."

Her shawl had slipped. Violette was shaking as she turned to face him. She was, she realized in despair, as in love with Blake as she had ever been. "I chose the wrong gown. I can not button it entirely myself."

Their gazes held. After a moment, Blake said, "Do you wish for me to button it for you?"

Violette stared. It was very hard to breathe. She nodded.

Blake approached, his gaze on her face. Violette could not glance away. She wondered if he could hear her pounding heart. In her own ears, it sounded like a jungle drum.

"Turn around," he said.

Violette obeyed, aware of flushing. His hands skimmed her shoulders as he removed the shawl, placing it on the back of one of the kitchen chairs. And as he began to do up the buttons on her dress, his fingertips skimming her skin, Violette was seized with the most intense desire she had ever known. If Blake kissed her now, she would whirl, embrace him, fuse their lips—perhaps never let him go.

But he did not kiss her. His hands stilled, remaining placed lightly on her back. And then he stepped away from her.

Violette remained motionless, overwhelmed with yearning—and disappointment.

"Why are you here?" she asked imploringly, eyes closed.

He hesitated. "I am staying in Paris," he said, "until the baby is born." His gaze darkened. "Until *our* baby is born," he amended.

She faced him, wide-eyed. A part of her was joyous. Another part horrified. Finally her instincts as a new mother won out. "And then?"

His expression hardened. "And then I have no choice."

Violette gripped the edge of the sink for support. "What are you saying?!" she cried.

"I thought about it all of last night. It is best, Violette, that I raise our child in London as a Harding."

Violette could not move. Panic and dread warred for pre-eminence within her. She wanted to protest. But the very worst part of it was that she knew, deep in her heart, that his decision was the right one, the only one.

When she could speak, she said hoarsely, truthfully, "Then you shall kill me. A second time."

He stared.

❖ *Thirty-five* ❖

"WHAT do I have to do," Violette asked desperately, "to get you to change your mind?"

Blake gripped the back of one kitchen chair. Although he was certain he had made the right decision last night, then he had been alone—not confronting a distraught mother-to-be—not confronting Violette. Violette was, he saw, shaking visibly. "I can give our child all that you cannot," he said softly.

Violette trembled. "But if I marry Farrow . . . ," she trailed off.

He hesitated. His decision had become so painful. "I wish to adopt the child."

"You wish to take my child away from me!" she screamed. "The child is mine!"

He inhaled. Violette began to cry, but silently. He had wanted to punish her yesterday for her treachery, for her deception, and mostly for her having left him. But he did not want to hurt her now. Not like this. And deciding to adopt their child had not been meant to be a punishment—or had it? He heard himself say, "Paris is so very far away."

She stiffened. "I have plans, plans to open my own maison. But I will change all of that. Just do not deny me my child, Blake. Please."

"What are you saying?" he asked, his gaze on her face.

"I will go back to England with you. You can adopt the child—just let him stay with me. I won't marry, not if you do not wish me to."

His heart turned over, hard. It was a moment before he could speak, even though a part of himself was inwardly exultant, about to accept her incredible offer. "Violette, I would never allow or disallow you to remarry; this is a free world, and you are an independent woman, extraordinarily so."

She began to cry again.

"Please don't cry," he said hoarsely.

"But if I return to England? So you can see the child whenever you wish?"

"You cannot return to England. You are a fugitive from the law."

She froze, her face pale, tears shimmering on her cheeks.

Blake sat down on one of the kitchen chairs abruptly, his head in his hands. His temples throbbed. He felt as if he held Violette's life in his hands—a responsibility he did not want, one which was overwhelming. One thing was becoming clear. He could not hurt her, no matter how she had hurt him. And he accepted that realization now—for the very first time in nine long months. Dear God, she had hurt him, because somehow he had fallen in love with her against his will and all reason, against all odds.

He looked up. "I have changed my mind."

Her eyes widened.

"I will adopt the child, but he, or she, may live here with you."

"Blake," she whispered, moving toward him.

He lifted a hand, warding her off. She halted in her tracks. "I will buy you a house, hire you staff, a nurse, a nanny, all that you need." He found it difficult to speak, but somehow continued. "You will not live here, like this, with our child. I will have a contract of sorts drawn up."

Violette nodded, her eyes huge and luminous and trained upon him. "I do not know how to thank you," she said.

Blake stood. "I must leave. I am late." It was a lie. He was afraid he himself might burst into tears if he stayed another moment. He left the kitchen, his strides rapid, aware that she followed him. At the front door he paused. "I am staying for the baby's birth, but as soon as he or she is born, and I know you and the child are healthy, I am leaving."

Violette swallowed. "I understand."

He opened the door and suddenly she seized his arm. He turned, met her gaze, which was sheened again.

She smiled tremulously at him, stood on tiptoe, and brushed her mouth to his cheek.

Blake was frozen. Her lips affected him so powerfully that he could not move. His heart lurched, his blood raced, and the feeling of her tender kiss lingered on his face. It struck him then. Nothing had changed, in spite of all the time that had elapsed. He still wanted her the way he had never wanted any other woman. He was still in love with her.

Blake managed to stay away for the next four days. It was a very difficult feat. Although he occupied himself by hunting for an appropriate residence for her, which he found in the Faubourg St-Germain on the third day, and by interviewing staff, Violette haunted his thoughts constantly. He wondered if she kept time with Farrow now, was green with jealousy at the thought. Even as he hired an English-speaking butler and a chef, he worried now about her delivering the child safely. In spite of this age of modern medicine, women did die in childbirth. He had a private interview with Dr. Aubigner, who assured Blake that he did not expect any problems.

On the fifth day Blake again called at 42 Rue Bellepasse. He had gone to bed the night before knowing he could not put it off, for Violette must hire her own maids and nurse. Anticipation which he did not wish to feel had made a good night's rest impossible.

He was calling in the midmorning, far earlier than was customary, but he did not want to miss her. She greeted him at the door bleary-eyed, in a blue silk wrapper trimmed with exquisite ivory lace, her ebony hair loose and streaming over her shoulders. Blake stiffened.

"I'm sorry. Have you been knocking for a very long time? I was asleep . . . What time is it?" she asked huskily.

"No, I apologize, I will come back later," he said, trying to keep his gaze on her face. But it was impossible. Her breasts were swollen and ripe, he could see the shadows of her aureoles through the fine layers of silk, and her stomach was huge, just inches from him. He wanted to touch her. Ached to touch her.

Both her hard swollen abdomen and her equally swollen breasts.

"No!" She smiled then, but uncertainly. "I will brew us coffee and dress while it brews. Please." She stepped aside, opening the door.

Blake entered hesitantly. Violette shut the door and moved into the kitchen. He watched her from behind, not following her—her nightclothes left little to the imagination. Although he had seen her naked before, then she had been slim and slender, not lush and ripe and carrying his child. He should not have come, but he had a list of possible nurses for her to interview.

"How have you been?" she asked from the kitchen as she put a kettle on to boil.

He gripped his hat in his hands, glancing reluctantly, with fascination, toward her. He watched her take a loaf of bread out of the breadbox and begin to slice it. "Well. I have found a house for you on the Rue St-Dominique. It is furnished, and beautifully. I have hired a butler who speaks fluent English, and a chef who does not, although he claims he does." Blake smiled briefly. "I have selected several nurses for you to interview, ones with impeccable recommendations."

She froze, a crock of jam in hand. She set it down and left the kitchen, coming to stand on the threshold of the parlor. Her eyes were wide and no longer the least bit unfocused.

Blake shifted, finding it impossible to breathe normally. She was all woman, Venus, in her pregnant state, in her current deshabille. It was unnatural, fighting this kind of desire, this kind of compulsion.

"I . . . of course I will interview whomever you wish," she said huskily. "I hadn't realized you would act so swiftly on what you said the other day."

"I am a man of my word."

"I know that." She stared.

He could see that she was suddenly aware of the currents sizzling between them. Her cheeks were turning pink, and her breasts were rising and falling a bit more rapidly than was usual—although it was an extraordinarily warm day out. Later it would probably be scorchingly hot.

The kettle sang and Violette quickly turned away. This time Blake left the salon, but only went as far as the doorway of the kitchen. He watched her reach for the kettle. "Be careful," he said. Her breasts moved freely beneath the silk gown and wrapper, swinging like suspended globes.

She glanced briefly at him with a small smile, saw where he was looking, and her smile died. Her jaw tight, she poured the hot water. "Just a few more minutes," she said, her tone unnaturally low.

But he recognized it instantly. Now she placed the crock on the kitchen table, along with the sliced bread. She returned to the cupboard for two blue and white porcelain plates. Blake realized he had never watched a woman in the kitchen before. It was mesmerizing.

He stood in the doorway; she stood behind one of the chairs at the table, her hands gripping the carved wooden back. Outside of the open window, a robin watched them from the heavy branches of a leafy oak, as silent.

"Blake, I am already indebted to you," Violette said slowly. Her knuckles were white. "I want to thank you again."

The kitchen seemed small and airless. "You are not indebted to me."

"But I am. First in England, where you rescued me repeatedly, and then with your very generous pension," she broke off. He watched her color increase as she stared at her hands, clasping the back of the chair. "And now this. So very gracefully allowing me to raise our child with your lavish support."

His heart hammered against his ribs. He did not know what to say. And Violette astounded him. She was the graceful one present, and not just in manners and behavior.

Abruptly Violette turned to pour two steaming mugs of coffee. Blake was at a loss for words. Her presence, her beauty, her sensuality, and her integrity had all combined to make it difficult for him to think clearly. He tried to shake the cobwebs from his brain, but small conversation was eluding him. "Do you like Paris?" he asked finally.

"Very much." Blake held out her chair and she sat down.

He joined her at the small table. "I see." He also liked Paris. "Is it not difficult being a foreigner here?"

She met his gaze, her regard direct. "Sometimes. I like the life I have made here for myself." She hesitated.

He understood. "You are lonely?"

She flushed, the mug of coffee in her hands. "Sometimes. But I have Ralph, although I rarely see him now. We seem to have drifted apart. And Madame Langdoc has been very kind." Her gaze was on the tablecloth. She clutched the mug with both hands.

"And you have Robert," he said.

"He has become a good friend," she said, glancing sideways at him.

He could not stand the thought. And suddenly he was savagely glad that she was with child, because that would keep Farrow out of her bed. He said carefully, "I am glad for you."

Her lashes lowered, but he had glimpsed her eyes. Was she disappointed? But what did she expect him to say? That he was angry, upset, jealous? That he wanted her back? She had left him. He would never ask her to come back. Besides, she had said she intended to accept Farrow when he proposed. Blake could only assume that she loved him.

But did she?

Once, a lifetime ago, she had loved him.

"After the child is born, I intend to visit as often as possible," he said.

"That is fine."

"And I would like to take him home with me for Christmas and Easter. I want him to know my family."

Violette nodded. "I agree with you completely."

Again, she amazed him. Blake finally reached for his coffee. He couldn't help but wonder what it would be like if Violette had not run away. If she had remained in London, been tried in the Lords and found innocent, and now carried his child— in which case they would be sharing coffee in his house in Belgravia, not in this small Parisian flat, after a night spent making love.

Not liking the train of his thoughts, he said, "Tell me about this shop you wish to open." He met her gaze.

She was startled. "I won't do that now. But I had hoped to open up my own shop after the child is born. A ladies' shop like Maison Langdoc and Lady Allister's."

He watched her as she suddenly smiled. "I happen to enjoy my employment at Maison Langdoc, just as I enjoyed it at Lady Allister's. I have learned so much. I know that I once had horrid taste in fashion, but I have become quite good now at selecting styles and fabrics for my customers. There are some very powerful, wealthy women who have begun to ask for me now when they do their shopping." She became silent. "I suppose it is a hopeless idea."

He stared at her perfect profile. "I am not surprised that you have excelled at what you chose to do."

Her head shot up, eyes wide.

"I am not surprised at all," he said softly.

Flushed, she stood abruptly. "I'll get more coffee."

"You haven't even touched your coffee." He covered her hand, which rested on the table, with his. "And I think it is a very good idea. There are only a handful of topnotch ladies' retailers in town. I have always admired originality and initiative. I will help you get your business started if you wish. I have a sense that this could be a big success."

She stared at him, unmoving. "You would help me open my own shop?" she whispered.

He nodded, suddenly aware of how much it meant to her, and because of that, how much it meant to him.

"Blake. I am already indebted . . . I couldn't. And what about the baby?"

"You will have a nurse and a nanny. Bring the baby to work with you. You could certainly make one of the back rooms into a nursery. I will loan you the money, Violette, in order to get started, with interest, but with very favorable terms."

She was speechless.

"Are you going to cry?" He would not allow his gaze to wander now. Her wrapper had begun to stick to her flesh in tantalizing places.

She shook her head, fighting tears. When she could finally speak, she said, "It is the baby. Dr. Aubigner says most women get very emotional when in this state."

"So I have heard," he said wryly.

"I don't know how to thank you," she said, folding her arms above her abdomen and under her breasts.

He stared, averted his eyes. "I think I have imposed on you long enough," he said roughly. Suddenly he was standing. "Thank you for *le petit déjeuner*." He strode out of the kitchen, knowing if he did not leave now his self-control might snap. And then what? They were divorced; he could not stand another rejection. And he was engaged to Catherine.

She raced after him. "Blake, you did not eat a thing. You did not even finish your coffee."

He halted at the front door, his hand on the knob, shifting to face her. His gaze roamed over her delicate features.

She stared into his eyes, her pupils dilated. "And what about the nurses?" she whispered.

"The nurses," he repeated. He clenched the doorknob. "The nurses."

"Let me dress quickly, and then we can begin interviewing them together this afternoon," she said in a rush of words.

He could not reply. He found himself staring at her mouth, which was just slightly parted, and at her ripe breasts. The wrapper she wore, clinging damply to her flesh, had parted. Blake was frozen. It was clear that she was not wearing a single thing beneath it.

"Blake?" She suddenly realized why he was staring and she jerked the thin satin robe together, flushing. "It was so hot last night," she began.

Blake met her eyes. "Nothing has changed," he heard himself say roughly. "Nothing."

Her mouth parted, trembling.

"God," Blake said, and his palms closed on her shoulders, the satin wet beneath his hands. She moaned, immediately swaying toward him—but he had already stepped forward unthinkingly. Her swollen belly pushed into his. He was fully erect.

Violette reached up and covered one of his hands with hers. Holding his gaze, she moved it down, to where he'd ached to place it all that morning, on her wonderfully huge, hard stomach. "Feel our baby," she whispered.

And Blake caressed the mound that contained their child, eyes squeezed shut, tenderly. She stood utterly still.

He wanted to tell her how beautiful she was, especially now, he wanted to tell her how much he needed her, and how much he loved her, but he could not speak. He pressed his mouth against the side of her throat, a single small kiss, still exploring her belly, aching now to slide his hands even lower, to touch her sex. Instead he kissed the spot where her neck joined her shoulder. She whimpered, covered his hand with hers, and moved his palm up and over one breast.

Blake choked on a groan, cupping both of her breasts now, inside of the wrapper. A red haze filled his mind, wiping out almost all coherent thought. He wanted this woman so badly, in spite of how much she had hurt him.

The wrapper fell open. Blake, rolling her large, erect nipples between his fingertips, paused. Violette's eyes opened, their gazes locked. "You are so beautiful like this," he said.

She reached forward, gripped his hips, pulling him toward her until his hard arousal pressed into her own loins.

And he knew. This, today, was inevitable. Their gazes locked. They meshed. She in his embrace and his mouth on hers, hard and hot and hungry. She clung to his shoulders, pressing her body against his. His thigh jammed between hers, until she rode him.

It was a long, hungry, passionate kiss, one filled with nine endless months of separation, desperation, and a desire for one another that had not died, but somehow, instead, had inexplicably grown.

They sank to the floor. Braced on his hands and knees above her, Blake covered her face with kisses while she delved into his trousers, stroking deep and deeper still. He rained kisses on her throat and chest. He took one large nipple into his mouth and suckled on it. He reached down and cupped her sex, not roughly, but possessively. Violette gasped.

And thrashing, she finally touched his massive, rock-hard organ. Her hand closed around him.

His mind snapped. He arched into her palm, nearly insane with wanting this woman whom he had missed so much, so long. Violette pulled him toward her and he understood completely. For one instant he straightened and kicked off his trousers and drawers.

Yet with the back of his mind he was vaguely aware of the limiting factors in their lives, which he did not want to think about now—factors like the divorce, like Catherine, like Farrow.

Violette whispered his name, slid her hand down his belly, touched him, then suddenly slid down beneath him on her back. She kissed his abdomen just above his raging sex, again and again. Then her lips somehow pressed against him.

Blake cried out, all thoughts forgotten. He reared up over her, distended as never before. He had only one concern now. He did not want to hurt her or the child.

"Blake," she called, rubbing his shoulders urgently.

"Violette. Are you certain? I don't want to hurt you," he said thickly, ready to explode.

"You won't hurt me," she cried, her nails suddenly raking down his arms. "Blake, please!"

He rolled her onto her side and moved behind her, taking her into his arms, his phallus pressed up hard against her buttocks. He shifted, pressing himself between her warm, soft thighs. Blake caressed her belly, her breasts, then her thighs and finally her hot, wet sex. Violette bent one knee, moaning, an invitation he could not refuse.

He was there, poised against her entrance. Holding her hips, he tested her, using every ounce of self-control he had ever possessed. She cried out as he slowly, inch by inch, pressed his long, thick length inside of her. And then their union was complete.

He moved, thrusting rapidly, Violette meeting him as wildly. She panted, gasped, took his hands and placed them on her breasts. "Oh, God," she said, the sound strangled. "God, Blake, God!"

He felt her explosion. His hands slid to her abdomen and he thrust harder, deeper, as she continued to cry his name. He felt the peak approaching. A whirlwind of ecstasy, mind-numbing, cresting, explosive. His arms tightened around her. This extraordinary woman, a Venus, the mother of his child, whom he had missed so much, would always miss. "Violette!" he gasped.

And it was there in his mind, on the tip of his tongue, as he came. *I love you, I need you, come back.*

But he did not say the words aloud.

Blake held her in his arms, sanity returning to him. She was warm and wonderful in his embrace, a part of him never wanted to let her go, to have this moment end, but he was in a state of growing disbelief. She was about to deliver a child, for God's sake. Had he hurt her?

And they were divorced. He was engaged to another woman. She was in love with another man. What had they done?

He knew she was suddenly as shocked and stunned as he. Her relaxed body stiffened. Her tension felt as if it matched his exactly.

There was so much that he wanted to say that he did not know where to start, or if he could even speak. He swallowed, violent emotions warring with one another within him. "Violette, I beg your forgiveness. Have I hurt you?" He was more than anxious.

She shook her head.

He sat up and, looking down, saw her eyes squeezed shut. He reached for his pants. "Please do not cry now," he begged.

She shook her head again, gulped air. When she opened her eyes and their gazes met, he saw how upset she was. He helped her to sit up and slid her wrapper up over her shoulders. He pulled it closed, belting the sash. As he reached for his trousers, he heard her choke on a sob.

"I am terribly sorry," he began, and stopped. She was absolutely pale, except for her eyes, which were red. And in a way he wasn't sorry at all. Being with Violette was heaven on earth, and he was experienced enough to know that it would never be this way again with another woman. But she was not his for the taking. Their paths, once converged, had forked. Soon she would marry someone else.

He almost doubled over with the stabbing pain. "Did I hurt you?" he asked again, huskily.

Her tone was unnaturally high. "You do not . . . have to apologize."

He was about to argue, but sensed that if he did she would burst abruptly into tears, and he nodded instead. "Very well," he said cautiously.

"It takes two," she said hoarsely. Tears filled her eyes.

"Please," he said, touching one tear with the tip of one finger. *Do not hate me*, he wanted to say. He remained silent.

She brushed his hand away. "I am fine. You did not hurt me. Or the baby." She got to her knees and he realized she was trying to get up, no easy task in her awkward state.

Immediately Blake put his arm around her and helped her to stand upright. "Shall I run you a bath?" he asked quickly. He was wishing, desperately, that she had a maid. And almost wishing, as desperately, that this had not just happened.

"I can manage myself," she said, squeezing her eyes closed. Her expression was strained with anguish. He could not look away.

He knew he had to speak. But say what? Everything had become so complicated, so confused, beyond repair and solving, it seemed. Anguish overwhelmed him, too. Was she regretting their passion—because she loved Farrow? "You need a maid now," he said grimly. "And I want to take you to see Aubigner immediately."

"My appointment with the doctor is next week." She turned her back on him, hugging herself. And then she gasped, staring down at the floor.

"Violette? What is it?" he cried.

And he saw where she was looking, at the puddle of clear fluid on the floor, her body's water streaming down her legs.

For one moment he did not understand. But she whispered, swaying against him, gripping his arm, "My water has broken. Blake, Dr. Aubigner told me when this happens the baby will come very soon!"

When he realized what she said, he was terrified.

And her eyes were wide with sudden, uncontrollable excitement.

Violette was covered with sweat, her pale cotton gown sticking to her body like a second skin, so exhausted that she could not move, but she was beaming, her arms somehow outstretched, as Dr. Aubigner handed her the tiny, swaddled baby girl she had spent eight hours delivering. From across the private hospital room, one Blake had insisted upon, Blake stood, staring at them, his face drawn.

"You have a beautiful daughter, madame," the smiling, dark-haired doctor said. "A job very well done."

Violette felt her heart turn over as she felt her baby in her arms for the very first time. She brought the tiny child against her body and gazed down in rapture at her. The baby's blue eyes were wide open and seemed focused, although Violette was not sure that was the case. She had a chubby face, one blotchy in places with redness, but her eyes were wide and almond-shaped, and she had a tiny nose and a perfect pink rosebud mouth. Although her head seemed a funny shape, pointy in places and indented elsewhere, Violette thought she was the most beautiful child she had ever seen, the most beautiful child, surely, in the entire world. "Welcome to the world, darling," she whispered.

The baby stared unblinkingly up at Violette.

Violette laughed and hugged her gently, aware of an intense feeling of completion in her heart, her body, and her soul. How she loved this tiny human being. In that moment, she had never loved anyone or anything as much as she did sweet, sweet Susan, her daughter.

She became aware of murmured male voices and looked up to see Blake and Aubigner in a quiet conversation on the other side of the small room. From Blake's grim expression she knew he was asking about the child's health—did she have ten fingers and ten toes, her eyesight and her hearing? Violette laughed to herself. How silly men could be. Susan was perfect, just perfect, and she knew it without having to be told.

She gazed from her tiny, cherubic daughter to her child's father and felt her heart swell even more, impossibly so. How she loved Blake. All that had happened had changed everything, she realized. Not only had their lovemaking been glorious, in spite of her fears of his leaving her afterward, but he had stayed with her through the entire birthing, an exhausting and painful ordeal that had lasted eight long, at times agonizing, hours. Violette remembered holding Blake's hand so hard that he had actually gasped. He had not left her side even once, not until after Susan was born and in Aubigner's hands.

And she was naming the little girl Susan, after Blake's mother. Had it been a boy, she would have named it Richard, after Blake's father.

Violette smiled at Blake from across the room. He would not, could not, leave her now. Surely now they would reconcile. Surely he knew that as positively as she.

But he stared at her, unsmiling, his expression terribly strained and terribly grave.

And Violette's heart fluttered with unease even as Susan cooed happily. She stopped smiling herself. "Blake? Come. Come see your daughter. She is so beautiful. Please."

He walked over slowly, reluctantly. His hands were deep in the pockets of his gray trousers. He had shed his jacket and waistcoat long ago and his sleeves were rolled up to his forearms. Violette now noticed the scratches on his wrists and her eyes widened. Had she done that?

He stared down at them both.

"Do you want to hold her?" Violette asked, smiling again, but now uncertainly.

Blake's gaze was on his daughter, now it shot to Violette's face. He was gray beneath his healthy golden tan. He shook his head.

Violette was confused. She tried to sit up straighter, holding Susan more tightly now, enough so that the baby whimpered. "Oh, sorry, darling," Violette whispered, kissing her daughter's blond, downy head. She held the child out. "Blake? Come. Hold your daughter. Surely you are not afraid?"

Blake's chest seemed to swell. "No." It was one word, emphatic, final.

Violette did not understand.

And Blake inhaled. "Good-bye." He nodded abruptly. And then she saw it, before he turned, the tears filling his eyes. Violette was stunned.

And he was striding across the room, away from her, away from them, out of the door—out of their lives.

Violette sat up. "Blake!" she shouted. "Blake!" she screamed.

But he was gone, his footsteps rapid and hard, at first loud, but too quickly fading as he rushed down the hall, as he rushed away.

And only silence remained in the corridor outside the room.

PART FIVE

The Bride

⚜ *Thirty-six* ⚜

SUSAN lay in her brand-new cradle, one painted a pleasing shade of ivory and beautifully adorned with carved vines and flowers, rabbits and birds. She was sleeping in her little white lace nest very peacefully beside the large four-poster canopied bed in the master bedroom of the house Blake had bought for Violette in the Faubourg St-Germain. The nursery, quite stupidly, Violette thought, was on the floor above. It was unused. The moment she had come home from the hospital, Violette had decided that her baby would sleep in her room with her. The nurse slept in the adjoining bedroom—a room originally intended for the master of the house's wife.

Now Violette continued to pack a medium-sized leather trunk with her wardrobe. As she folded lacy chemises, beribboned corsets, silk drawers and petticoats, she kept glancing at her sleeping child. Susan was twelve weeks old. She was so beautiful, as blond and pink-cheeked as any angel, with her perfect, tiny rosebud mouth. Every time she looked at her daughter, Violette felt such an anguish she thought she might collapse and die. Dr. Aubigner had said that Susan could travel once she was three months old. Tomorrow they would cross the Channel.

Violette wondered if she could go through with what she intended to do.

One of the house's many maids appeared, wearing a black uniform and an apron, carrying an armful of newly ironed gowns. "Madame?"

Violette sat down heavily on the bed beside the open trunk, exhausted. "*S'il vous plait*. Please. And when you have packed my gowns, make sure I have stockings, hats, gloves, et cetera, all that a lady needs for a brief stay abroad.'' She could not really care about what clothes she took with her.

"*Oui, madame.*" The petite brunette began to pack each gown carefully amidst much tissue paper. Violette watched for a moment, wondering just how brief her stay would actually be. She only intended to remain in London for a few short days before returning home to Paris. And once home, she would focus all of her energy, all of her attention, her every waking thought, her every waking moment, upon opening a ladies' shop and making it a success. Blake had been good to his word. He had transferred a huge sum of money into her account, a personal loan with which to begin her new business.

Tears filled Violette's eyes. She could not stand it. She walked over to the sleeping baby and wondered how often a woman's heart could break. She had lost count long ago of the many times her feelings had been irreparably shattered, damaged, destroyed. "I think I might die without you," she whispered to Susan.

Susan sighed in her sleep.

Of course, Violette thought grimly, she might very well die in reality, because she was a fugitive from Her Majesty's law, wanted for a murder she had not committed. But surely if she entered London without any fanfare, and left as secretly, she would not be caught and arrested—she would not be caught, tried, and hanged.

But did it really matter? Perhaps death would be far easier to bear than the kind of existence the future held for her.

Then she shoved such morbid thoughts aside. She might be Lady Neville now, but a part of her would always be Violet Cooper, and she would never accept hanging, oh, no. She would never accept a living death.

Footsteps made her look up. She recognized them before she even saw Ralph, who came and went freely in her house, sleeping over when he pleased and taking most of his meals there. But he had not moved in. Violette had not asked him to, and he had not asked if he might. Sometimes she found herself hoping that, one day, he would just not return. The tension had never been worse between them. Violette knew that Ralph disapproved of all that Blake was doing for her. Sometimes she wondered if he was jealous of what might appear to be her good fortune.

Ralph stared at Violette from the threshold of her bedroom.

"I 'eard the maids downstairs. Said yer packin'. Where yew goin', luv?"

Violette gazed wearily at him. "You are dirty," she said, "and you are drunk."

He scowled at her. "An' yew such a grand lady, now ain't yew! I asked yew where are yew goin', Violette." His tone had become rough and harsh.

Violette reached down to stroke Susan's cheek, just once. Her skin was as soft as silk, downy. She wasn't sure she liked Ralph anymore. That hurt, too. "I am going to London."

Ralph stared. "That's wot they said! I thought them wrong! Are yew insane? To go back there?"

"I am going." Violette stood. She felt lightheaded, but she hadn't eaten a single thing all day. Perhaps she should have a croissant, or some soup. Violette was aware of the fact that her old gowns were all too big for her now, hanging off of her impossibly small frame.

"Yew are chasin' 'im!" Ralph accused. " 'Is Lordship!"

Violette shook her head in defeat and utter resignation. She even smiled slightly. "No. No. I am not chasing Blake. I would never be such a fool. In fact, I am going to London with an escort—with Robert Farrow." Her heart lurched. Robert had been wonderful these past few months, trying to lift her spirits, calling on her every day, bestowing fabulous gifts upon her—gifts she had refused to accept. He was very worried about her, she knew, but he approved entirely of what she intended to do.

Now Ralph gazed at her suspiciously, no longer quite so drunk. "An' the baby? Yew takin' 'er? Yew niver leave 'er alone fer a minute."

Violette pursed her lips, afraid she would burst into tears, something she did constantly, ever since the baby had been born. Aubigner said that some women suffered from a deep melancholia after giving birth, but Violette knew the cause of her grief had nothing to do with birthing Susan—that had been a cause to celebrate, a cause of joy and hope. Her melancholia was far more severe, more complicated, and so deeply rooted she knew she would live with it until she finally passed away. "Yes. I am taking Susan." It was hard to breathe. For Susan's little leather trunk was already packed with every single item Violette had purchased for her. Nothing was being left behind. Even the cradle was coming with them.

"Why are yew goin' back there? So they can hang yew? I

don't understand," Ralph said, his tone no longer hostile. "Don't go, Violette."

Violette rubbed one fist across her moist eyes, wondering why he even cared—when she did not. "I have to go."

"Do yew want to 'ang fer a murder yew didn't commit?" Ralph exclaimed.

Violette looked up at him. "If you are so concerned, why don't you return with me."

He stared, not replying.

And Blake's suspicions about Ralph filled Violette's mind. But she had shared a lifetime with Ralph, and she knew him so well, and the one thing he was not was a murderer. She was certain—wasn't she? "I am taking Susan to Blake," she said.

When Ralph continued to gaze at her, clearly not fathoming her meaning, Violette added, "And she is not returning with me when I come home." Her voice caught. "I am leaving her with Blake, where she belongs."

Several hours after arriving in London, the coach Violette had hired approached Harding House. Violette sat in the forward-facing seat, as ladies should do, clutching Susan to her breast. Susan was nursing contentedly.

Her face was set in steel, as was her heart. She dared not think. She must only do. She must only breathe in and out, get up, get down, walk up those stone steps, enter the front door and ask for the countess.

Violette knew she had no choice. Shortly after Blake had left her, she had realized that she could never give Susan what she truly wished for her to have, which was respectability. Blake might adopt her, but if Violette raised her she would be a shop-keeper's daughter, worse, she would be Violet Cooper's daughter. If Blake raised her, she would be a Harding.

Violette shut off the rest of her thoughts. She was shaking.

"Oh, madame," the baby's nurse said. She sat facing Violette, a heavyset, elderly woman with a kind face whose name Violette could never remember in spite of the fact that the nurse was so wonderfully sympathetic to both her and the baby. Seated beside the gray-haired nurse was the wet nurse Violette had hired several days ago, a young, red-haired girl from a small village a few kilometers north of Paris.

The coach had become small and stuffy, airless.

Violette stared out of the window as the magnificent facade of Harding House appeared at the end of the block. She felt ill, violently so, even though she'd eaten nothing but toast that morning, many hours ago. She had not even contemplated going to Blake's Belgravia home. It was past tea, he might be home—she had no wish to see him.

Did not trust herself to see him.

The coach halted. Susan had stopped suckling and Violette hugged her once, then disengaged her from her breast. The nurse reached out for her, but Violette shook her head, shaking now, and managed to close her bodice while holding Susan on her lap. She knew that all too soon she would hand Susan over to the countess.

Violette cuddled the baby to her breast so hard that Susan woke up with a cry. "Sorry, sorry, darling," Violette whispered, her face pressed to her daughter's. How could she go through with this?

But she must. *Do not think anymore*, she told herself.

"My lady?" the coachman intoned, holding the door open for them all.

Violette got unsteadily to her feet, very faint now. Refusing to release Susan made it all that more difficult to descend from the coach's single step, but the servant gripped her arm firmly as she came down. Violette inhaled deeply on the curb, waiting for the nurse and wet nurse, shaking, holding Susan as tightly as she dared. "Please wait," she said to the coachman, her tone low and thick. "I shall be but a few moments."

They marched up the wide, low front steps and paused at the heavy paired doors of the mansion. The two liveried footmen standing on either side of the wide doors did not stir or blink. Violette recognized the one and memories crashed over her, memories she did not want to face, not now, not ever. Of the first time she had seen Blake at Harding Hall in York, and how magnificent he had been, how he had appeared a prince among men, even then; of his holding her upright at Sir Thomas's funeral when no one present would come near her, how he had whispered in her ear that she should feel free to faint if she must; of his walking in on her in her bedroom at Goodwin Manor later that day, ordering her to consume brandy, as Violette stood there half undressed, much to Catherine's shock and chagrin. The memories came more rapidly now, as tears seemed to burn the back of Violette's lids. As if it were yesterday she recalled being in his hard embrace, she recalled the taste and texture and passion of his first kiss in the gardens behind Harding Hall. And finally, she remembered standing just where she stood now, desperate to find him, madly in love, so afraid and alone but somehow knowing he would help her, rescue her, once again. And then she had barged into his club.

Violette could see herself so clearly, a young, awkward girl from the streets garishly dressed in purplish-blue, huge roses on her bodice, birds and flowers on her hat. She could even hear herself as she had sounded then, saying "ow" instead of "how" and "me" instead of "my" and the memories made her wince herself. She must have been mad, chasing after Blake, thinking to seize a star, a shooting star, holding onto impossible, out of reach dreams. Utterly mad.

Oh, Blake.

Suddenly Violette found herself facing Tulley. His eyes widened and he gaped at her and the infant. Immediately he beamed, crying out, "Lady Neville! How *wonderful* to see you again! Do come in!"

Violette trembled more noticeably than before. She stepped inside silently, not trusting herself to speak, the nurse and redhead following as quietly. Tulley shut the door. He smiled at the little baby. "His Lordship's?" he asked.

So they knew, it was no secret, everyone knew. Violette nodded.

"How beautiful she is," Tulley said, reaching out to touch her blond curls. "And she looks just like you, if you do not mind me saying so, Lady Neville."

Violette fought for control, and to find her voice. "She is blond."

"Like Her Ladyship," Tulley nodded, referring to the countess. "Of course, children change. She might have hair as black as midnight like you and His Lordship, my lady."

Violette could not respond. She hugged Susan harder, and the baby squeaked. Finally she found her tongue. "Is the countess at home? I w-wish to see her."

"She is in the drawing room with Lady Dearfield," Tulley said.

Violette froze. She could not breathe. She did not want to see Catherine, not now, not like this. Of course, if Tulley knew, then Catherine surely knew about the baby, too. But in a few more weeks Catherine and Blake were marrying. In fact, Violette realized that she and the countess were probaby finalizing the last-minute wedding arrangements right now. She bent and quickly kissed Susan's forehead and tasted a tear at the corner of her mouth. Her own tear, which had somehow escaped to trickle down Violette's face.

Violette told the nurse and the red-haired girl to wait in the foyer, and then she followed Tulley down the hall. Every painting she passed, every light fixture, every gilded chair and side table, seemed to cause a stabbing in her breast. Too late, she realized that coming to Harding House had been a terrible mistake. She should have summoned the countess to her hotel suite.

Tulley announced her on the threshold.

The countess and Catherine were seated on one sofa, speaking quietly, some lists spread out on the low table in front of them. Violette thought that she had been right, they were finalizing wedding plans for Catherine and Blake.

Both women stared at her, wide-eyed, and then at the baby. It was the countess who recovered first, rising swiftly to her feet. She quickly crossed the room, neither smiling nor unsmiling. But her arms were outstretched. "Violette!" she said, her tone thick and hoarse.

For one moment Violette thought that the countess knew why she had come, and that she wanted Susan now. Violette was mentally preparing herself to give Susan away, but reflexively held onto her more tightly. The countess, however, did not even reach for the baby. Instead, she embraced Violette even as Violette held the infant.

The tears began then, impossible to stop, but slowly, a stream.

The countess pulled away. Their gazes met. "I have thought about you so often, my dear," Susannah said. "Blake has told me how well you are, how well you are doing, and I have been so glad for you." Her gaze moved to the baby. "Oh my Lord," she said softly.

Violette's heart was bursting with anguish. "Your . . ." She found it impossible to speak.

"My granddaughter," the countess whispered, her eyes shimmering and steady upon the sleeping child.

Catherine had stood up, but she did not approach. She seemed upset.

Violette could not even look at her, knew she had to. She did. "Hello, Catherine. Congratulations," she managed in a husky whisper.

Catherine seemed on the verge of tears. She nodded, not even saying hello.

Violette looked away, hurt in spite of it all, that Catherine would not even speak with her. She cradled Susan to her cheek, choking on a sob.

"Violette, dear, you must be exhausted," the countess said, placing her hand on Violette's back. "Please, come sit down. And tell us all that you are doing, and all about your beautiful daughter."

Violette rocked Susan, beginning to weep. She shook her head, unable to speak.

"Violette? What is wrong? What can I do? Tulley—a brandy!" the countess ordered. She placed her arm around Violette.

Violette fought for the strength and the will to give her daughter away. She raised her face. "She is," she began, "she is a Harding. A lady. A true lady, always, not . . . not like me." She could not wipe her face, which was drenched with tears, because she was holding the baby and her arms were not free.

"I know that, my dear," the countess said gently, her arm still around Violette. But her eyes were wide, filled with alert intelligence, as if she sensed what was coming. She did not move. "Come sit down and let me lend you my handkerchief," she whispered.

"No. You don't understand. I'm a pretender. I'll never be Lady Neville, just like I was never Lady Goodwin, only Violet Cooper. Blake said"—and Violette stopped, panting, unable to continue. Her grief was overwhelming.

"What did Blake say?" the countess asked grimly.

Violette swallowed hard, knowing she had to continue. "He said he'd adopt her. I want him to. I want you to raise her as a Harding. She will be a Harding from this moment on, and no one will ever laugh at her or call her names behind her back because her mother was Violet Cooper, a bastard and a beggar from St. Giles. I want her to have plum pudding every night, a puppy, a pony, ribbons and bows, and when she is older, the prince of all of her dreams. I want her to have everything I never had. I want her to have respectability." Violette choked. "I want her to be a real lady, not a fraud."

Silence filled the drawing room.

Violette suddenly shoved Susan into the countess's arms. "Good-bye," she whispered, and then she turned and ran, stumbling out of the room, down the hall, and through the foyer. She wrenched open the front door herself. And as she fled down the steps to the waiting coach, tripping many times, her own words echoed in her ears, again and again, in tandem with her tears.

A real lady, a real lady. Good-bye.

It had been a routine day, and Blake did not like routine days. He never really had, for he had always been the kind of man to thrive on excitement, but in the past few months, his tolerance for the mundane had become far worse. He thrived, it seemed, on insurmountable problems, on challenges, conflicts, and stress. This was why he had expanded his shipping operations into the very risky waters of the Philippines, had decided to build his controversial row houses in Bristol and Liverpool, and was considering a foray into livestock production in Australia or the American West. The mundane was far more than boring; it gave his mind time to think, to wander and to dwell on a topic he now considered forbidden, taboo.

The topic of his ex-wife and daughter.

Blake handed Chamberlain his hat, gloves, and cane. "Good afternoon, my lord," the butler said. "The countess and Lady Dearfield are in the salon."

Blake had been about to stride down the hall toward his private domain, the library, where he was anticipating a stiff, before-supper scotch. He stiffened, glanced at his pocket watch. It was seven, a time of day when his mother and fiancée should be at whatever dinner party they were attending that evening. "Have I missed something? Am I having company for supper tonight?"

His butler actually smiled. "No, my lord, we have no such plans."

For a moment Blake stared at his smiling butler. Chamberlain was never so friendly, in fact, he was usually as friendly as a board, and now there was actually a twinkle in his eyes. What was afoot? "In the salon?"

Chamberlain nodded.

Blake turned and walked a few steps down the hall. The salon doors were open. Catherine and his mother were on the sofa, something white, a bundle, between them. They were chatting and laughing and making funny sounds, like "ooh" and "ahhh." And they were not alone, because a heavyset elderly woman in spectacles sat on a chair, watching them benignly. What the hell was going on? He strode into the blue and white room.

His mother and Catherine looked up simultaneously. They

were wreathed in smiles. The countess bent, picked up the bundle, and stood. "Blake!" she cried happily.

And Blake saw the baby. He saw big, wide blue eyes and a chubby ivory face and silky blond curls. He froze. The grief he had lived with day in and day out ever since he had walked away from Violette and the baby in the hospital in France crashed over him now. He could not move.

"Blake, it is Susan, your daughter," the countess cried, rushing over to him.

He felt as fragile as a child himself, about to burst hysterically into tears. He stood stiffly as his mother paused in front of him. "How beautiful she is! She has eyes just like you, and your jaw, I think, but otherwise she resembles Violette!" Susannah was excited, gushing. "And her name is Susan." She stared at him. "She has named your daughter after me."

Briefly Blake closed his eyes, thinking about the fact that Violette had named their child after his mother. He focused again, instantly, devouring his daughter greedily with his eyes. How beautiful his tiny daughter was. How spectacular. But Blake did not reach for her. He managed to rip his gaze from his daughter's, which had been trained upon his face as intensely. In fact, she reached up now, waving one plump hand with five plump, wiggling fingers at him. She cooed. He thought he heard, "Da."

His heart seemed to shriek to a stop. "God," he managed, all he was then capable of.

He glanced at Catherine, who was standing, still smiling, but uncertainly, and looked around the room. As if he might find her hiding behind the sofa or the draperies. But of course she was not there. Surely she was in Paris, and had sent the baby to London itself. "Where is Violette?" he heard himself ask.

His mother was no longer smiling. "She has left."

"Left?" he echoed, hardly believing that she had come herself—risking her very life in the process.

Susannah nodded, cuddling the baby, giving her a fingertip to suck on. "She left—in tears. And she was very explicit. She wants your child raised as a Harding, adopted by you. She wants your child to have everything she should have, everything the family can give her, all that Violette cannot." The countess looked directly into his eyes. "It was the most magnificent gesture I have ever witnessed in my entire life."

Blake was breathless, shocked. "She said that?"

His mother nodded. "She said, Blake, that she wants your

daughter to be respectable, a real lady, and not a fraud."

Blake looked down at his tiny daughter, the single being most precious to him in this world, not including the woman he could never have, even though he had left her with her mother three long aching months ago, and he felt his eyes grow hot and wet.

"She meant every word, Blake."

Blake finally reached for his daughter and, for the very first time, took her into his arms. He cradled her against his chest, pressed his face to the top of her soft head. "I know," he said.

"I am glad you are still here," Blake said to Catherine as he entered the salon.

She sat alone on the sofa, an unopened book by her side. She smiled slightly at him. It was uncertain. "You asked me to stay."

"Indeed, I did." He crossed the room.

"Is Susan settled?"

"Yes. In the nursery with her things, the wet nurse and Madame Begnac." Blake glanced up at the ceiling, recalling the sight he had just left, of his tiny daughter suckling at the wet nurse's breast. He had never thought to see this day. To have his daughter returned to him, to have her there in his home, a part of his household and his life. He knew without having to be told what it had cost Violette to make this sacrifice. Just as he knew he could give her the one thing Violette never could—respectability. That money could not buy. As the countess had said, it had been a magnificent gesture—a gesture of inherent elegance. The gesture of a genuine lady. How ironic it was.

"Blake? I assume there are matters you wish for us to discuss?" Catherine said quietly.

He turned to look at her, a woman he loved . . . like a sister. The woman he loved the way God had intended a man to love a woman since the very dawning of time was out of his reach, even now, he guessed, bound for Paris and life with another man. Blake nodded at Catherine and sat down beside her. He reached for her hand.

"Before you begin, I want to tell you that I am so happy that your daughter has been returned to you," Catherine said softly.

He looked into her sincere green gaze. How could he tell her that he could not go through with their marriage? How could he humiliate her like this? But he could not marry her. He could not cheat her of her due, for she deserved more than he could give her. Just as he could not bear to be married to anyone ever again. And he was never going to marry again. Even though it meant that he would forsake his duty of providing the Harding family with a male heir. Never.

"Blake?" Catherine touched his face. "You are so distraught. I understand."

He started. "I don't think so. What I am about to do is insufferable, reprehensible in the extreme, beyond forgiveness. But I do care about you, Catherine, I always have."

She actually smiled at him. Her eyes were wet with tears. "And I do love you," she said, making him inwardly wince. She smiled again. "But as a brother, Blake. I cannot love you as a wife loves a husband, it is an impossibility."

He stared, stunned.

"And I know you do not love me that way, either, nor do I mind. In fact, I am relieved."

He could not believe their conversation. He clasped both of her hands. "Then you will not hate me if I break off our engagement?"

"If you do not break it off, I shall do so." Tears trickled down her cheeks. "I can't marry you, Blake. Because I am still in love with Jon."

It took him a moment to grasp what she had said. "Jon?"

"Your brother."

She was in love with Jon. Suddenly he recalled many little moments, the three of them together, astride their horses, or at a party, or even at supper at the Hall. And in his recollections he could now see shared looks he had not been a part of, looks of total comprehension and mutual understanding. "You have always loved him," he whispered. Remembering her first dance at her debut—with Jon. How golden and glowing they had both been.

She smiled through her tears. "Always. And I always shall. He, of course, has refused me very adamantly, before you proposed, but it does not matter now. I have decided to remain unwed. I cannot marry, Blake," she said simply. "Not you, not anyone."

How he understood. And he was suddenly angry. "Jon is a fool! I am going to thrash him for his stupidity! Beat some sense into him!"

"No." She gripped his arm. "Do not say a single word, you cannot, must not, for then I shall never forgive you."

She meant it, he knew. He finally, reluctantly, nodded.

She smiled and hugged him, hard. Then she gazed into his eyes. "I think you should go see Violette, Blake. I think it is time."

He stared, wanting to agree, knowing he could not—yet terribly torn.

⁙ *Thirty-seven* ⁙

THE Hotel St. James had a renowned restaurant filled with polished mahogany and gleaming brass, as popular with London's elite as it was with visiting Europeans. Violette had made plans to take supper there with Robert. But she was consumed with her grief. She did not have the strength or the will to lift herself up from her bed, much less dress for the occasion. How she missed Susan—as if her tiny daughter was dead.

But she kept telling herself that Susan was not dead, and that she had made the right decision, the only decision, offering Susan a life that she herself could never provide for her. Violette was wracked with anguish. She never did send Robert a message canceling their supper.

So at the first sound of a knock upon the door of her suite, she thought it was a hotel maid. She wanted to shout, "Go away, leave me alone, goddammit!" but instead, she forced herself upright. "Please. I do not wish to be disturbed," she called from the bedroom.

"Violette, it is I, Robert," Robert said loudly from the other side of the door to the sitting room.

Violette was briefly stricken—and she glanced at the clock on the mantel in the bedroom. He had been waiting for over three-quarters of an hour for her. She stumbled to her feet and across the sitting room, opening the door.

Robert stood there in his tuxedo, staring grimly at her. "I was afraid of this. You are distraught, terribly so. May I come in?" he inquired.

Violette nodded, realizing she must appear disastrous, with her hair coming loose, her face blotchy from weeping, her eyes swollen and red. She allowed Robert to enter. "I am sorry. I meant to send you a note canceling our supper but . . . ," she trailed off, unable to continue, stabbed with a heartbreaking pain.

He immediately turned, arms open, and embraced her. He had kissed her on several occasions, before her pregnancy had become obvious, but he had never embraced her, and certainly not like this, with the intention of comforting her. And Violette desperately needed comfort. She allowed him to hold her and stroke her back. She had no more tears left or she would have sobbed wildly in his arms.

Finally she knew their position was unseemly, for many minutes had passed, and she broke away from him. Knowing he watched her, she crossed the suite and sat down on a plush moss-green chair. "I am sorry," she said flatly. God, she was sorry, sorry for everything in her life.

He came over, pulling up an ottoman, sitting facing her. He reached for one of her hands and caressed it. "You have done a noble, selfless thing, and the Hardings can do far more for your daughter than you ever could." He smiled slightly. "A child does belong with its father, Violette, that is an accepted fact."

Violette wanted to protest. A child belonged with its mother, always and forever. *Oh, God.* "It feels like she is dead, even though I know she is not."

"No. She is not dead. And she will grow up being one of the most sought after debutantes in the land, perhaps one of the most sought after heiresses," Robert stated firmly.

"She will be respectable. A real lady," Violette said in a monotone. "She will have anything and everything a real lady should have."

"Yes," Robert agreed.

"I miss her so much!" Violette cried.

Robert did not reply.

A part of Violette's decision had been to never see her daughter again. How could she? Seeing her but not being able to be a mother to her was far too painful, and Blake's pull on her too potent, too dangerous, too damaging. "I have never felt so alone in my life," Violette whispered.

"You are not alone." Robert hesitated. Suddenly he had a small jeweler's box, one royal blue and velvet, in his hand. He held it out to her. "Violette?"

She stared at the box. Her mind was oddly numb. She watched him study her, then flick it open. A huge ruby ring sat there, surrounded by dozens of small diamonds. She did not move.

She had known that this was coming, of course. And she

would refuse, of course. Her heart belonged to one man, and one man only.

"Violette?" Robert cleared his throat, as if he was nervous. "I have wanted to do this for a long time, but then I learned of your condition, and there was no opportunity. I know that now is probably a bad time as well, but you need me and I am aware of it. My dear, I can comfort you, take you away from all of this, make you happy—I am so certain of it." His brown gaze was penetrating.

Violette stared at him, clawing the arms of her chair. She did not want to be alone. And she had never felt so alone, so miserable, or so frightened, before. She was tired of being alone. She wanted to be held, to be cherished, to have someone take all the pain away. She wanted to be loved.

"Violette. I am deeply in love with you. Please, do not refuse me. At least consider my offer."

Violette stirred. Her life at this point was over, in spite of the shop she was opening after the new year in Paris. But Robert Farrow was offering her a chance to begin a new life, and somewhere deep in her soul she was a warrior, a survivor who did not want to give up, give in, quit and die. A child as tough as she was fragile, who did not want to be alone, not ever again. Farrow, in many ways, was so much like Blake. Dashing, noble, and strong.

"I will marry you," she whispered thickly, Blake's image searing her mind. One day, she prayed, he would stop haunting her. One day he would leave her mind and her heart alone.

Farrow's eyes widened. And then he beamed, pulling her into the circle of his arms, holding her tightly. Violette closed her eyes, thinking that at last she was loved.

Thinking, *Oh, Blake.*

Blake paused, watching Jon who sat at the earl's desk in the study at Harding House, apparently balancing estate accounts. He had realized that he could not keep silent on the subject of Catherine's feelings for his brother, in spite of what he had promised her. He cleared his throat.

Jon looked up. "Running late today, Blake?" It was already midmorning, a time Blake should be ensconced in his offices at the bank.

"Actually, I have some errands I wish to do before going to work," Blake replied, immediately thinking of Violette. His thoughts made him begin to perspire. "Am I interrupting?"

"Yes, but happily so." Jon closed one huge, leather-bound ledger. "What is on your mind?" He folded his arms.

Blake entered the room and sat down in a chair facing Jon from across the massive desk. "I wanted to tell you first, before I tell Father and Mother. Catherine and I came to a mutual agreement last night."

Jon's grim expression became oddly implacable. "And?"

"We have broken off the engagement."

Jon stared, his countenance unreadable. He finally leaned forward. "Why? Why would the two of you, so perfectly suited for one another, call it off? Blake, has it not occurred to you that you need Catherine now more than ever? She would make a perfect stepmother." He seemed angry. His blue eyes were dark. His face was hard.

"I love her, but as a sister and a dear friend. And she feels the same way about me," Blake said.

"Christ," was Jon's only reply. He ran his hand through his tousled golden hair. Blake thought his palm was shaking ever so slightly.

"She told me that you rejected her," Blake said.

Jon froze. He had paled. "Good God! You don't think that she and I were up to something behind your back? That was well before you proposed to her, Blake. I believe you were married to Violette at the time, or on the verge of marrying her."

"She is in love with you," Blake said flatly.

Jon was motionless. He finally smiled, unnaturally. "That is absurd. I am half a man. She needs you—or someone like you."

Blake stood, furious. "Dammit! Damn you with your self-pity! You are not half a man, Jon, and your life is not over—it has hardly begun!"

Jon leaned forward, gripping the desk. "Damn me? Damn *you*! Who are you to tell me about my life!" He was shouting. "*You* can walk, *you* can make love to a woman, *you* can sire children. Do not tell me about my life, Blake!"

"You are a coward," Blake shot back. "And to think that my entire life I admired you, wishing, secretly, to be more like you! A small accident and you have given up all your dreams, becoming content to do nothing. You fool!"

Jon's fist hit the desk. "Do not throw my dreams in my face. Dammit! *I have no dreams!*"

"So what will you do then? Spend the rest of your days in this study, your nose in estate ledgers? Spend the rest of your life in the company of your valet? Slowly grow old, without joy, without children and grandchildren, without love? Why not just call it the end right now? Commit suicide? After all, you have practically done so as it is. Have you not already sentenced yourself to death?"

Jon's hand swept out. He sent every item on the desk crashing to the floor. Books, ledgers, files, folders, inkwells, and paperweights. "Get out! Get out of here, dammit, before I do something I will regret."

Blake did not know what possessed him, because he had never seen his brother angrier, and he himself had never been angrier—or had he ever loved Jon more. He strode closer to the desk instead of leaving, leaning down upon it until his face almost touched his brother's. They were eye to eye, nose to nose. "You are a coward," he said.

Suddenly Jon, who could not use his legs much less stand, levered himself upright, onto his feet. And for one split instant he was balanced that way. His fist shot out, landing hard in Blake's face, on his jaw. The impact of the blow sent Blake reeling backwards and crashing against the chair. Jon himself tottered over and collapsed to the floor.

Blake rose and rushed around the desk to help his brother.

"Do not touch me," Jon warned, already pushing himself up and into a sitting position. The muscles in his shoulders, back, and arms bulged.

Blake, about to reach for Jon, froze.

Growling, panting, Jon grabbed the legs of the chair and pulled himself closer. Then he seized the two arms. Still making animal-like sounds, fiercely determined, he began to pull himself upwards. Blake watched, wanting so badly to help, yet witnessing a miracle, and silently shouting encouragement. Using only his upper body, his white poplin shirt beginning to stick to his chest with sweat, Jon hauled himself upward slowly, inch by agonizing inch. When he was halfway into the chair, his hips level with the seat, he paused, sweat pouring down his face. Blake did not move. Jon grunted and pushed himself up higher, high enough to collapse into the chair. Blake exhaled.

The brothers' eyes met, Blake's shining, Jon's flashing. "Get out," Jon said.

Blake turned and left.

* * *

He would tell the earl and the countess about the broken engagement last. Before Violette left London, as she must soon do, before she heard the news as gossip, he would tell her himself, while thanking her for Susan, and reassuring her that she could see their daughter anytime. He stood outside of her hotel suite, loosening his cravat and collar. His pulse raced wildly.

But why was he so nervous, so afraid?

Blake closed his eyes. The last time he had seen her she had been covered with perspiration, in a cotton gown in a hospital bed, holding their newborn baby to her breast. The memory no longer caused him untold anguish. It was a memory he was beginning to cherish.

He expected a servant to open the door when he knocked. Instead, Violette opened it herself.

And even though he had known how great a sacrifice she was making in giving up her daughter to him, he was not prepared for the sight of her, so small and thin, her face bony, huge circles beneath her puffy eyes. Her appearance was devastating to him. He was so stricken he could not even bow and say good morning. He forgot to remove his hat.

Her eyes were huge. "Blake?" And then she looked behind him, eagerly, as if expecting him to be accompanied by someone. Disappointment covered her features.

He suddenly realized that she was looking for Susan. He hadn't thought to bring the child, how stupid he had been. "Good morning." He took off his hat.

She inhaled, met his gaze again, then quickly looked away. "Do come in," she whispered.

He entered the suite and waited for her to close the door. She faced him, arms folded tightly across her body. Why was she so thin? Most new mothers were lush and plump. He wet his lips. "Violette, what you have done is more than wonderful, it is generous and noble and selfless. I came to thank you, to. tell you that Susan will lack for nothing, that one day she will be a reigning woman in this land. There is nothing I will not do for her."

Violette nodded, her eyes huge and luminous.

He was ready to give the child back. But Susan was no ball, to be tossed around at whim. "I also came to tell you that you may see Susan, or have her brought to you in Paris, anytime."

She stared at him, appearing ready to weep, not saying anything.

"You are so upset," he said, a heartbeat away from going to her and holding her tightly, so tightly, against his chest.

Her mouth was tightly pursed. Another moment passed before she finally spoke. "Is she . . . all right?" she asked hoarsely. And she touched her chest with one hand, as if covering her wounded heart.

Blake could not reply. Her left hand covered her chest, and on her fourth finger was a huge ruby ring surrounded by rows and rows of diamonds. It was an engagement ring.

"Blake?" she cried in alarm. "Is Susan all right?"

He jerked, in a state of disbelief—he was too late. "Susan is fine. A beautiful, happy child." He could hardly get the words out.

She sank into a chair. "I am returning to Paris this afternoon," she said. "Take care of her, Blake."

He stared at her hand on the chair's thick, rolled arm, stared at the glinting ring. "Congratulations," he heard himself say stiffly.

She started, meeting his gaze. And then she saw where he was looking. She was already pale, but now she turned the stark shade of a newly laundered sheet.

"When do the nuptials take place?"

She wet her lips. "Robert wishes for us to wed as soon as possible, in Paris, of course." Her smile was brief and forced.

"As soon as possible," Blake said. "So Robert shall live in Paris now?" He could not believe this conversation was taking place, that he was acting so casually, so indifferently, when he felt his entire being disintegrating fiber by fiber and piece by piece. *She does not love you*, he thought. *She loves Farrow after all.*

She nodded, looking at the floor. "Perhaps next month."

"Next month," he echoed. He finally recovered some self-control. "Again, congratulations." He made a show of looking at his pocket watch. "I am late. Please, feel free to visit Susan before you leave."

Violette did not reply.

He stared at her—she stared back. Silence and tension pervaded the room. Only the ticking of the pendulum clock in the corner broke it. How loud it sounded, how deafening. He finally walked to the door. "Good-bye, Violette." Had he not said those exact same words once before? But this time, he meant them. This time, it was truly over.

She was giving herself freely to another man.

"Good-bye, Blake," Violette whispered to his back.

He did not turn to take one last look at her, he did not have to. He was never going to forget her, did not even want to, in spite of the pain. He opened the door.

And Inspector Adams met his gaze, beside a smiling Inspector Howard. "Good day, my lord," Howard said.

Adams walked into the room. "Lady Neville. You are under arrest," he said.

⊰ *Thirty-eight* ⊱

THE cell door slammed. Violette leapt back, against the stone wall of her prison. The guard, burly, bearded, and distinctly malodorous, a man missing several teeth, leered at her and turned and walked away, disappearing into the shadows.

The inmates began to laugh, screeching at her. They were all female. " 'Ey, luvey, not so 'igh an' mighty now?''

"Look it the foin lady! C'mere, me lady, 'ow's about a kiss fer ole Bessie?''

"Aw, aw, aw, aw!" Someone else laughed violently.

Shrieking seemed to fill up the prison.

Violette was motionless. Eyes wide, she stared at the pale, contorted faces framed by stringy, greasy hair peering, gawking, gaping at her from the surrounding cells. She had been incarcerated in the Fleet Street Prison. She was on some lower floor, inside the bowels of the earth, in the women's section. But these women all seemed mad, animal-like. And the air was still, dank, and fetid. It was dark inside, for there were no lights, just a few burning torches set on the walls, and Violette could could hardly see through the gloom. Inmates kept calling to her, laughing at her, screaming for her attention.

But she had her own cell, most of the other women prisoners did not. Her guards had told her that murderers and murderesses were jailed separately, just in case they decided to kill another time.

"Honey," an old crone squawked, "you gimme a nice fiver an' I'll get you wot you want—tobacco, gin, a nice hard man, anythin' ol' Remie can do."

Violette met the old woman's piercing, soulless eyes. Remie burst out laughing. She had the adjacent cell, and one of her hands was extended through the bars, fingers spread, clawlike. Violette realized she was tugging on Violette's skirts. She leapt away from the madwoman, only to crash into the opposite side of her cell, and into another pair of groping hands. She met a pair of burning gray eyes, a face framed by strawlike hair. Crying out, Violette shrank against the back wall of her cell, which was stone. Remie continued to offer her objects and services, still reaching into Violette's cell, but Violette stopped listening, too numb with fear. The other prisoner, whom Violette now realized was very pregnant, was gripping the bars of Violette's cell and shaking herself on them. Her huge stomach wobbled with her intense gyrations. Violette felt her knees give way.

She sank to the floor only to recoil in horror as her hand slipped on human feces. She choked on a sob, on her feet again, cowering in a corner. She had nothing to wipe her hand on except for the hem of her dress, which was already soiled. The wall she leaned against smelled suspiciously like urine.

Violette inhaled hard, fighting the numbness, the shock which was choking her mind. She wasn't a murderess, she had not murdered her own husband, dear Sir Thomas, and, God, hadn't she suffered enough? She had lost Blake, she had lost her own sweet daughter, and now this? Oh, God.

She planted her back against the wall, panting, staring back at the pale faces grimacing and grinning at her. Was everyone here insane? Is this what prison did to its inmates? She wasn't a murderess! Why was she here? She had to get out.

God, Blake! she thought, panic overwhelming her. *Please, get me out of here!*

She squeezed her eyes closed. That wasn't going to happen. Blake might be a Harding, but even his father, the earl, could not remove her from this horrible place. Not until the trial was over, not until she had been judged innocent.

And there would be a trial, in the House of Lords, dear God. And she would be judged innocent, because she was innocent— wouldn't she?

Violette gulped in the fetid, sour air. What if she were found guilty of murder by some monstrous mistake? How could she be found innocent after all that had happened? She had run away, she knew how it seemed. No one would ever believe that she had been running away from Blake and not from the trial and the verdict.

And she was a fraud. The Lords would realize that immediately. All too soon she would be exposed as Violet Cooper, the bastard orphan, a beggar and a thief, born and raised in St. Giles. Whom was she fooling? She would not be found innocent. She was going to hang.

"The countess will be down shortly, my lady," Tulley told Catherine.

Catherine nodded, wringing her hands anxiously. She considered the countess far more than a friend. Having lost her own mother when she was but a child, the countess had always been a surrogate of sorts. Catherine knew Blake intended to explain their broken engagement to both of his parents, but she had to speak to the countess herself. "I will wait in the red salon," Catherine said, referring to the smaller of the two entertaining rooms.

Tulley hesitated. "Perhaps you wish to wait in the gold salon, Lady Dearfield?" He gestured to the pair of doors which opened onto the huge parlor where the Hardings entertained. "Lord Farleigh is in the family room."

Catherine froze, but only for an instant. Then her heart thudded wildly. When was the last time she had seen Jon? That day in the gardens, when he had told her, so cruelly and callously, that he had hoped she would marry his brother. She should hate him, but she did not. She missed him terribly. Him and that special rapport they had shared—even if it had only existed in her own mind.

Catherine did not know she could be so brave. She smiled at Tulley. "How wonderful. Then I shall have some company while I wait for the countess."

She left the butler behind before he could protest or tell her that Jon did not wish to be disturbed. Her heart pounded with alarming strength now. She felt faint with nervousness, with anticipation.

The salon doors were closed. Catherine paused, reaching for a knob. Immediately she heard a strange sound coming from inside of the room. A soft squeaking accompanied by a grunt. Confused, she pushed open the door.

Catherine bit off her gasp. Jon was in the strangest chair she had ever seen. Although made of wood and having both a cushioned seat and back and arms, it had no legs—it had wheels instead. The kind of wheels one might see on a donkey cart or a victoria. And the chair was in motion. Jon was pushing the wheels, turning them actually, with his own bare hands. The chair was speeding toward the opposite wall.

In that instant, Catherine realized what was about to happen and she made a sound—just as Jon also realized his predicament. He had been flushed from exertion, now he whitened and cursed. With his hands he tried to stop the wheels, too late. The chair crashed into the far wall, crushing Jon's knees.

"Dear God!" Catherine flew across the room.

He jerked, swiveling his head to look at her, and his cheeks turned red again. Catherine's steps faltered as she reached for the chair. "Are you all right?"

"I am fine," he said gruffly.

"Your legs," she said, pulling the chair away from the wall.

His jaw flexed. "I have no feeling in my legs, Catherine— or have you forgotten?" His tone was not quite as mocking as it had been in the past year.

She met his gaze. And in that instant, it was like being in the past, for she was lost, swept away, dangerously, deeply connected to this man. She shook herself free of her trance. "No," she said softly, going around to the front of the chair. "I have not forgotten." She gave him one dark look, one containing a dare, and bent and rolled his stockings down. His knees were bruised but no skin was broken; he was not bleeding.

And it hurt her a little to look at his legs, because once they had been so strong and hard and full with muscle, and now there was a difference in their size and shape, slight, but there. Catherine stared at his shins. She had not realized a man's legs contained so much hair. Jon's was tawny, the color of a lion in fall.

Jon cleared his throat.

And Catherine realized that she had been standing there doing far more than stare; her hands had remained on his knees, touching him. She had never wanted to touch anyone more. The accident had not changed anything, not for her.

Slowly, she looked up.

His gaze was piercing.

The words wanted to explode out of her chest. *How I love you.* But she did not dare. With a small smile, she rolled his stockings back up. "A few bruises, but no real damage. Oh, Jon. Please, be careful."

He did not reply. He was spinning the wheels again with his hands, his brow furrowed with concentration—with determination. Catherine watched him pick up speed, moving across the room toward a different wall.

And suddenly it hit her. The fact that he could move—the fact of his liberation. A freedom both physical and mental. She cried out.

He was already slowing, but now his back was to her. "This thing needs brakes," he muttered, tossing the words over his shoulder as if tossing them at her.

And he *was* speaking to her. Filled with sudden joy, a happiness so intense she failed to breathe adequately, Catherine ran in front of him. She knelt before him, her face wreathed in smiles. "Jon! This is incredible! This chair—it allows you to move—it is as if you can walk again."

He stared at her with his too-blue eyes, and finally, slowly, reluctantly, the faintest smile curved his mouth. "Yes," he said, "this chair is incredible."

Blake waited impatiently in the entry of the prison, standing beside George Dodge, whom he had summoned immediately. His heart was in his throat and he was sweating. Dodge was telling the warden that Blake was Violette's fiancé and that he wished to see her. Fortunately, female prisoners were routinely allowed visits from their spouses—it was a fact Blake had only recently learned.

He needed to see her, desperately, to know that she was withstanding the rigor of her imprisonment. And although he was *not* her fiancé, it was easy enough to lie. He had contacted George Dodge the moment Inspectors Adams and Howard had taken Violette away. Dodge had immediately agreed to represent her. Blake had also sent word to Farrow. He was sure that Robert would agree that Dodge should handle Violette's case being as he was already intimately acquainted with it.

The warden told them to wait and sent two pockmarked male guards to get her. Blake paced impatiently. In the short carriage ride over, Dodge had grimly told him that they would most likely lose the trial if the real killer could not be found. Blake had sent a runner to Paris to locate Horn—if he could be located. He intended to interview Joanna Feldstone immediately. One of the two had to be the murderer, for there were no other possible suspects.

Footsteps sounded in the corridor leading to the entry from

the interior of the prison. Blake stiffened, staring, frozen with anticipation. The door, barred with iron, was opened. Violette appeared between the two guards and Blake jerked, aghast.

Only a single day had passed since her imprisonment. But she was filthy and disheveled, and her face was garishly pale and pinched and gaunt as if she had not eaten in days. But then, she had lost so much weight since having the baby. Looking at her now hurt Blake impossibly. And he was furious with everyone for what was being done to her. "Violette." He strode forward, leaving Dodge behind.

She stared at Blake, remaining motionless, her eyes huge. Very slowly, tears filled her gaze. She was trembling.

He could not stand it. The past fell away. Disappeared. He reached for her.

She fell against his chest, sobbing, shuddering, and he held her there, hard.

"You have five minutes, my lord," the warden said from behind him.

Blake wanted to kill the warden. Instead, he fought for self-control, and looking down, he met Violette's eyes and saw the fear and panic there. "Blake," Violette cried, her tone hoarse. "You have come to take me home?" Her tone rose sharply, bordering on hysteria.

"Have they hurt you?" he demanded, hugging her hard, incapable of answering the question, incapable of so thoroughly disappointing her.

"No." She shook her head, her mouth trembling. "Blake, I cannot go back down there. It's dark. Everyone is mad. They scream ugly things at me. One of the women says crude things to me, tries to touch me. There is dirt and sewage on the floors. They give us soup to eat, but it is gray, and filled with bugs. There are rats. They come out at night. I am so afraid."

"Everything will be all right, I promise you that," he said, shaking with anger and frustration and completely unsure of what he was saying and whether it was the truth. He stroked her back, her hair. He must do everything in his power to get her out of prison, yet he knew there was nothing he could do until the trial was over. "Everything will be all right," he repeated firmly.

"No." Her voice was husky. "I am going to die."

"You are not going to die," he cried, seizing her arms, almost shaking her.

"I am innocent, but I ran away, and they will find me guilty," she said, ashen.

"Why did you run away, Violette? Good God, why did you run away?" he cried, but it was an imploring question, with many layers, and what he was really asking was, *How could you have left me? How?*

She met his gaze. "I ran away because I loved you so much that I could not stand it," she said.

He did not move. In that moment, time stopped. The world was frozen.

She began to cry. "Living with you, as your wife, in a farce of a marriage, a true travesty of love, was a punishment too painful too bear. That is how much I loved you."

He could not speak. He was ready to cry himself. And then he realized that he was crying. Tears trickled down his face.

Dodge said from behind him, "I am sorry to intrude in such a private moment but we do not have much time. Lady Neville, I am afraid the Lords will not believe that you fled the country and your trial because you loved Lord Blake. And your trial is next week. What we must do is to find the real killer. And in the next week, before your trial, I shall advise you on how to answer all the questions the prosecutors shall throw at you. You must do everything I say, my dear," he said.

"I did not kill dear Sir Thomas," Violette told Dodge hoarsely, still clinging to Blake.

"Your time is up," the warden suddenly said, very loudly, and he spat on the floor, quite close to the tip of Blake's black shoe. "We don't make exceptions here. We don't care if you're the duke of Rutherford—my lord."

Blake clenched his fists, unwilling to release Violette. But the two guards were there, and he had no choice. As they were separated, he gripped her hand. "Trust me," he said. "Have faith, Violette. Please."

She nodded, her palm gripping his, tears spilling from her eyes. The two guards took her by her arms, tearing their hands apart.

Blake clenched his fists.

And suddenly Violette, who was being led away, dug in her heels like a recalcitrant—or frightened—child. "No! I can't! God, no!"

And Blake leapt forward as the guards dragged her toward the barred iron door against her will. Only George Dodge grabbed him from behind. "Stop," the solicitor said. "There is nothing you can do!"

"Blake," Violette screamed as she was pulled through the doorway, "Blake, don't let them do this, please!"

His heart shattered into a million pieces. He was immobilized. Powerless. For the very first time in his life.

She threw one desperate glance over her shoulder at him just before the warden slammed the huge door closed behind her. And she was gone.

Blake thought he could hear her sobs.

He whirled, facing the warden. "If anything happens to her," he said, "anything, if a single hair is missing from her head, I will personally see you torn from limb to limb and thrown to the wild dogs of London—do you understand?"

The warden paled.

Dodge reached into his jacket pocket, giving Blake a dark look, extracting his billfold. This was prearranged. Blake stared at the warden as Dodge peeled off bills and shoved them into the warden's hands. "Mr. Goody," he said. "Please make sure that nothing happens to Lady Neville—that she remains in good health."

The warden, his gaze glued to Blake, finally looked at the thousands of pounds stuffed into his palm, and his eyes bulged. He nodded. Sweat covered his bald pate.

The front door of the entry slammed. "Christ," the warden said, jamming the money into his shirt. "Another nob."

Blake turned to see an ashen and disheveled Robert Farrow striding into the room. Farrow saw him and faltered in surprise. And then he continued on. He was followed by a short, elderly man, one Blake recognized instantly as the family solicitor. "What the hell are you doing here?" Farrow said. And then, "Have you seen her? Is she all right?"

Blake hesitated. "She is unharmed and as well as can be expected." His insides were twisting up. He could not stand Violette's relationship to this man.

"Thank God," Farrow cried.

"Mr. Goody?" Farrow's solicitor was saying. "I am Lord Farrow's attorney. We have come to see Lady Neville."

"This ain't an afternoon tea," the warden said, his shrewd gaze shooting from Farrow to Blake.

Before the attorney could respond, Farrow confronted the warden impatiently. "We understand that. But I am Lady Neville's fiancé, and it is my right to visit her."

The warden stared. And then he began to chuckle. "Oh really?" he said. "Then who the hell is he?" And he pointed to Blake.

Farrow turned, and the two men's gazes met.

"I am not sure that this is advisable," Dodge said grimly.

Blake stood with the solicitor later that day on the front steps of the Feldstones' town house. "It is abominable that Violette, who is innocent, is suffering in such a state of incarceration."

"Accusing Lady Feldstone of murder could be considered an abomination as well," Dodge returned smoothly as Blake again rapped sharply on the door.

"I want her to break if she committed the deed," Blake shot back.

"My lords?" the servant queried.

"Lord Blake, here to see His Lordship and Ladyship," Blake said irritably. He still used the Neville title infrequently.

They followed the servant inside and were shown into a small but well-appointed parlor. Blake paced, fists clenched. Violette's anguished expression remained engraved upon his mind. He had never hurt so much before in his life—and now he was hurting for her, sharing her fear and her pain.

The baron appeared, his stout wife behind him. The baron's smile faded upon his seeing Blake's taut expression. However, Joanna appeared smug. "My lord?" Feldstone gripped Blake's hand and shook it. "Sir?"

"George Dodge, attorney-at-law, at your service." Dodge bowed smartly.

"I am not in need of a solicitor," Feldstone said with apparent bewilderment.

Joanna folded her arms beneath her massive bosom. "But Violette Goodwin is." She smirked.

Blake eyed her. "Lady Neville, my ex-wife, the fiancée of Lord Farrow, is in need of a solicitor, but only because she has been falsely accused of your father's murder and very wrongly imprisoned."

Joanna snorted. "We are back to that?! She is a murderess and the whole world shall soon know it! She is exactly where she belongs!"

Blake had never wanted to hit a woman before, but he wanted to do so now. Dodge placed a restraining arm upon him, as if he could read his mind. "Lady Feldstone, Lady Neville is innocent. She loved your father. Have you no pity, no compassion, for her?''

"None," Joanna said flatly. "None at all."

Blake interrupted. "Are you aware that your housekeeper in Tamrah was purchasing arsenic during this past year?"

Joanna gaped.

Feldstone stepped forward. "What is your meaning, young man?"

"My meaning is clear, is it not?" Blake said softly. But he regarded Joanna. "Did you kill your father, Lady Feldstone?"

The baron was gaping. Joanna's eyes were wide. She had turned white. "You think we are somehow responsible for Sir Thomas's death? Why—that is absurd!" the baron cried.

Blake knew that the man was not dissembling. "Lady Feldstone? Would you answer me directly?"

She inhaled, her entire bosom heaving. "I loved my father, Lord Neville," she said stiffly. "And if my housekeeper was purchasing arsenic, than I have no doubt that we had an attic full of rats." She stared.

Blake stared back. She remained pale, yet appeared affronted—or was he seeing what he wished to see? Was she guilty?

"Will you accuse me next?" Joanna cried. "I don't think so. Because in another few weeks your ex-wife will be swinging, my lord."

"Blake, we should go," Dodge said. "I think we have come up against a wall."

Blake nodded. He felt defeated. How bitter it was. He bowed stiffly. "I apologize for my accusations, my lord, my lady."

Feldstone was frozen. "Blake, if you were not an old family friend, regardless of your father, I would not accept your apology."

He, at least, appeared innocent. Blake turned away. He was grim. Nothing had been accomplished by his confronting Joanna, and Horn might never be found.

And time was running out.

Ralph squatted behind the thick shrubs outside of Blake's town house, sweating profusely, twisting his worn cap in his hands. He had, after all, come to London. He had not been able to sleep at nights thinking of the dangers Violette faced in returning to England—in spite of the fact that these days he no longer recognized her as the same person he had grown up and shared a lifetime with. He wished she hadn't changed.

But now he was frightened. More afraid than he had ever been in his life. He was clever and astute, how else would he have survived all these years? The moment Violette had left Paris, he had known her presence would be discovered and that she would be arrested. He had known he would have to go to her, and rescue her as he had done so many times when they were children.

And he had been right. Violette had left word with her staff that she would be staying at the St. James. It had taken him no time at all to learn that she had been arrested on her second day at the hotel and promptly imprisoned. But surely Blake would be able to get Violette released from prison. Ralph had little faith in the legal system, yet he knew how the high and mighty operated. Their wealth could buy anything. Surely it could buy Violette's escape. But once free, Violette would have to flee the country again.

In a way, Ralph was excited. Because this time he would tell her that it was too dangerous to return to Paris, and they would have to go somewhere else. Perhaps Rome. And it would just be the two of them, the way it had once been, the way it should have been ever since Sir Thomas had died.

Ralph crouched lower, recognizing Blake's phaeton as it halted by the curb. Blake stepped out. Ralph's pulse was pounding, and his instinct was to turn and run away. But he thought of Violette in a jail cell and he did not move. Too well, he recalled the moment she had rushed into his arms after escaping the poorhouse when they were children. She had been skinny and frightened, but she had wept with joy. He had been so glad to see her, hold her again.

Ralph stood. "Me lord," he called.

Blake, halfway up the block, froze. His eyes widened as Ralph strolled forward. Ralph managed what he hoped was a cocky grin. "Got to talk to yew."

For another moment Blake did not move. And then he gripped Ralph's lapels, snarling, "She is in prison. Suffering. You bastard—I want the truth."

Ralph gripped his wrists. "Let me go. I'm 'ere, ain't I? I'm 'ere to 'elp."

Blake flung him off.

Ralph recovered his balance and glared at Blake, then recalled what he had just said. "Did them bastards 'urt 'er?"

"No. But she is not well. She is far too thin, exhausted, terrified," Blake said harshly.

Ralph stared, thinking about all the stories Violette had told him about the poorhouse, remembering how scared she'd confessed to being—a fear that had lingered even after she had returned to him in St. Giles, for he had seen it there, haunting her eyes. "Can yew get her out?" he asked.

"I am not the Queen," Blake said.

"Wot do yew mean?" Ralph demanded, his heart sinking. "Yew got loads of money. Yew could pay off the warden, get 'im to look the other way. We can plan 'er escape."

"She is going to remain in prison until the trial, which is scheduled for next week. And then she shall hang—if the real killer is not found," Blake said coldly.

"Whoever killed Sir Thomas is probably long since gone. Wot's wrong with yew? Bribe them bastards. We'll set up an escape."

"And then what?" Blake stared. His tone dripped ice. "Violette must run away again, forever a fugitive, never able to return to this country—never able to see her own daughter again?"

Ralph's pulse was racing now. "Yew got to try."

"Did you kill Sir Thomas, Horn?"

" 'Course not!" Ralph glared. "We'll go to Italy—me an' 'er."

Blake's gaze was both razor-sharp and searching. "She is engaged, Horn. To Farrow. I doubt she will run off with you."

Ralph felt his heart stop, and then it began to beat again. "I don't believe yew," he said.

"She was wearing his ring."

Ralph began to shake. " 'Is Lordship ain't fer 'er!" he heard himself shout.

"And who is? You?" Blake asked grimly.

Ralph's fists were clenched. "Yeah. Me. It should always been 'er an' me. No one loves 'er more. I took care of 'er since she could 'ardly walk. 'Er father didn't care. 'E was always in them dens, smokin' opium. Everything was fine until yew came along an' taught 'er to be some fine, fancy lady!" Ralph shouted. He felt wetness on his cheeks. "I don't even know 'er anymore!"

Blake did not speak for a moment. Ralph was ashamed. He realized that he was crying. "I don't want 'er to die."

"She is going to hang," Blake said.

"No." Ralph shook his head. " 'Er and me, we're goin' to Italy." He wiped his eyes with his dirty shirtsleeve.

"No," Blake said softly. "She will hang—unless the real killer is found."

Ralph turned away blindly, almost staggering down the walk. At the curb he sank down, sitting, hands on his knees. He did not see the carriages and hansoms rolling by. He heard Blake walk up behind him. "I can't let 'er die," he said, low.

"Then tell the truth."

Ralph hugged himself, thinking about death. Death, and Violette. But not Violette Goodwin Blake, viscountess of Neville. Violet Cooper, a waif with hair chopped off at the nape.

"I did it," he said.

Blake remained silent.

Ralph laid his cheek on his knees. " 'E was goin' to die anyway, even a blind man could see that. 'E was sick. Old an' sick. I did it fer 'er, fer us."

"I understand," Blake said softly.

Ralph began to cry. "I don't want 'er to die. I begged 'er not to come 'ere," he said. "I thought we'd get the 'ouse an' money an' we could live there forever, 'appy as can be." He choked. "Better than the old times."

And when Blake did not speak, remaining motionless, Ralph said thickly, "But she fell in love with yew."

And he sat there on the stoop for a long time, crying, until the sun began to set and Blake finally reached down and helped him to his feet. His arm around the tall, gawky man, Blake guided him silently into the house.

⸫ *Thirty-nine* ⸫

BLAKE stepped out of his phaeton, his body taut with tension, staring at the grim stone facade of Fleet Street Prison. Violette's release had been ordered a short while ago, directly after Ralph's arrest. It was the same evening, quite late now, a dark cloudy night with a few snowflakes just beginning to fall.

His heart was heavy in spite of his relief that Horn had confessed to the police and Violette was being freed. It was very hard to believe, but he had first laid eyes upon Violette exactly one year ago. It seemed like a lifetime; it also seemed like mere moments.

George Dodge stepped out of the phaeton as well. He laid his hand on Blake's shoulder. "Smile, Blake. We have won."

How could he smile? Violette was being released from prison, but soon she would leave London, and marry Farrow.

They crossed the street and stepped onto the curb. Wide steps led to the large, square building which housed the prison. Blake shoved open the heavy front door. Guards barred the entryway, but then he saw the warden at the other end of the cavernous hall, who was clearly expecting him, and just behind Goody he saw Violette. He became motionless.

Violette's gaze held his. She lifted up her skirts, taking a single step forward, as if about to run to him. Blake started to smile, his gaze glued to her pale, strained face. Thank God she was unharmed, thank God her ordeal was now over—while his was about to begin.

Violette broke free of the guards escorting her and rushed to him. Blake almost held out his arms. When he did not, her steps faltered and she paused in front of him. "Oh, Blake," she said tremulously.

He stared at the woman he loved, wondering if he would ever be able to get over her, to let her go, to forget her. He did not think so. "Violette, are you all right?"

She nodded. Her eyes were suspiciously moist and bright. "Blake, I . . . ," she faltered. "I do not know what to say," she whispered.

He finally reached out and took her hand, squeezing it. "Perhaps prayers are in order, for the both of us." He forced a smile.

She searched his gaze. Her mouth opened, but no words came forth.

He wanted to embrace her, hold her hard and tight. He said, "I'll take you to your hotel."

She jerked her head slightly, an affirmation. "Blake? What has happened? The warden said I am free. Really free. I don't understand."

He took her elbow firmly. "There is no easy way to tell you this." His gaze held hers. How he wished to spare her the truth. "Horn confessed."

She blanched.

"He loves you, Violette, and not as a brother or a friend. He expected you to inherit something substantial from Sir Thomas, and for the two of you to live happily together at Goodwin Manor." Blake paused. "We did not have to go to Paris to find him. He came to me, and when he realized you were really going to hang, he confessed.''

"No," Violette whispered, tears filling her eyes. "Oh, God.''

He could not resist her anguish. Blake pulled her into his arms, holding her tightly, while she cried on his chest. "I'm sorry. So sorry,'' he whispered.

She finally looked up at him. "He will hang?"

Blake hesitated. "Yes.''

She cried again, like a small child.

And then Farrow was standing beside them.

Blake had known that the authorities would contact him, but not this quickly. The two men's gazes met. Something inside of Blake's soul seemed to vanish. He released Violette.

"What is going on?" Farrow asked stiffly.

"I told her about Horn," Blake replied.

Farrow started. "Why? Why did you have to tell her? She has gone through enough.''

At least Farrow loved her. Blake hoped his grief was not mirrored on his face. "I did what I thought best," he said quietly.

Robert slid his arm around Violette's waist. "I am sorry," he said to Blake. "God, I am sorry. For I owe you thanks, from the both of us. I cannot possibly express the depth of my appreciation. I owe you, Blake. We owe you.''

And Robert reached out to shake his hand. Reluctantly, Blake accepted the gesture. Yet he found it almost impossible to tear his gaze away from Violette. And she, too, continued to stare at him. Her blue eyes were huge and to him, it seemed, infinitely sad.

"You owe me nothing. I wish you both . . . much happiness.'' He was sick, in his heart, his body, everywhere. No other ending had ever felt like this. "Good-bye," he said.

She flinched, garishly pale now. Their gazes remained locked.

"Let us go," Farrow said. And Violette allowed Farrow to guide her past Blake, to the front doors of the prison. They were immediately swung open for them. She craned her neck to look at Blake; he wondered if she was crying. "Good-bye," she whispered.

They disappeared through the front doors, which remained ajar. Like a somnambulist, Blake followed in their wake. On the prison's theshold, he watched Farrow hand Violette up into his gleaming, dark brown coach. Farrow climbed in after her, settled down beside her, again putting his arm around her. Violette, Blake thought, collapsed into his embrace.

Oh, God. It was the only coherent thought he had. Any other would be far too unbearable.

And from behind him, very softly, George Dodge, attorney-at-law, whispered, "I am so very sorry."

Jon pushed his chair across the frost-covered gardens, unaware of the cold. As he approached the house, he saw two figures standing on the terrace, wrapped in cloaks. One was his mother, the other, Catherine. His gaze settled on the younger woman immediately. He wondered how long they had been watching him wheel himself around the gardens like a madman. Yet he was neither annoyed nor embarrassed.

"Jon, this is a miracle," the countess cried, tears sparkling in her eyes.

Jon smiled at his mother, but found himself looking at Catherine again. "I do not believe in miracles," he said, but without bitterness or self-pity. "Actually, a chair with wheels made supreme sense. And my chair is not the first. It was actually invented by a doctor in New York for one of his patients, a man with a similar condition to mine."

Before the countess could reply, Catherine said, very softly, "I believe in miracles."

Jon stared at her.

The countess stepped off of the terrace and bent to kiss her son's cheek. "In any case, this is wonderful." Her gaze returned to the steps she had just descended. There were only three, but clearly Jon would have to be carried up over them, chair and all.

"Mother," Jon said. "Would you mind if we took out one section of the terrace wall so I could build a kind of dock there?"

"A dock?" the countess asked, bewildered.

"Yes, a sloping dock, of the same stone. That way I could traverse from the lawns to the terrace and into the house without aid."

Her eyes widened. "Absolutely. Why, that is brilliant."

Behind her, Catherine wore a small, genuine smile. Jon found himself smiling back at her.

The countess looked from the one to the other and excused herself. But on the terrrace she paused. "Will you be joining us for supper tonight, my dear?"

Jon smiled at his mother. "Absolutely."

Her eyes brightened and she left them, hurrying back into the warmth of the house. It had begun to snow.

Catherine came down the three flagstone steps. "Your chair is wonderful. I am so happy for you."

He studied her exquisite face. "I can see that," he finally said, slowly.

She tensed, her smile fading. Their gazes were locked. Now her gloved hands worried the folds of her large, fur-lined mantle. "Your mother has invited me to supper tonight," she said uncertainly.

"Good," Jon said flatly.

She started.

"Than it shall be like old times." The words had slipped out. He was shocked when he realized what he had said. "Damn it," he muttered, reversing the wheels and moving backwards, away from her. He had had a different mechanism put on the wheels so he could reverse when necessary. A mechanic was also making him a brake, the kind used on the best coaches and carriages.

"No! Don't go!" She flew down the steps after him.

His hands stilled on the wheels. She paused in front of him. "Why can't it be like old times?" she asked.

He stared at her, unable to answer. An intense yearning swept him. But he had never lost it. He had merely pushed it as far down and as far inside of himself as possible.

Catherine swallowed. "Violette was released from prison today. The charges against her were removed. She is a free woman."

"I am very glad for her," Jon said.

"Your brother is deeply, miserably in love with her," Catherine said abruptly. Her cheeks turned brightly red.

Jon hesitated. He recognized dangerous territory when he saw it. "I know."

"You know? But you wanted me to marry him!" Catherine cried accusingly.

He gripped the chair's wheels, an instant away from fleeing. "She abandoned him. I did not realize how strongly he cared. I thought the two of you would suit perfectly."

Catherine stared at him, tears shimmering in her eyes. "You fool."

He knew he should leave. Leave the gardens, leave her. A small voice, one logical and proud, told him that. But he could not command his hands to perform the necessary act.

"I do not know how it happened," Catherine said. "I have always loved Blake, as a friend and as a brother. But to marry him? What a travesty of love that would be."

He opened his mouth to tell her to stop. No words came out.

"I am going to go to my grave loving you, Jon," she said simply. "And I would not have it any other way."

He was frozen. His heart warred with his mind, his pride. So many images, so many memories, swept through him then. Catherine in pigtails, racing him across the Yorkshire moors on horseback. Catherine in his arms, sharing too many dances at too many balls to count. Her smile, her regard, coming from across a crowded room, a shared instant, an immediate connection, in which he knew, without question, that she was thinking and feeling exactly as he was.

Catherine sitting on his bed, by his useless legs, just after the accident. The tears in her eyes, the fear—and the pity.

He finally spoke, groping for words, feeling how heated his face had become. So much was at stake. Yet he did not dare seize a shining star. "If I were still myself, Catherine, I would return the love you have offered me so courageously and unselfishly."

"You are still yourself!" she cried, cutting him off.

He stared. "No. I am half of a man. I . . ."

"Wait!" Her hands were fisted on her hips. Her eyes blazed. "You are right, you have changed. Once you were intelligent, now you have become an idiot."

He grimaced. "I am paralyzed. I have no legs."

"So you cannot use your legs!" she shouted. The wind carried autumn leaves in a swirling formation past them. "So what? Have you lost your mind? Your heart? Your soul?"

He could not say yes, because it would be a stupid, foolish, unbelievable lie. So he remained silent.

"Have you lost your dreams?" she whispered, tears sparkling on the tips of her pale lashes.

That he could answer, and honestly. "Yes, I have given up my dreams."

"Fool!" she shouted. And she did the most amazing thing.

She swung her fist hard, catching him right in the jaw. The blow only stung, because Catherine had not a clue as to how to hit anyone, much less a man, and Jon caught her wrist reflexively. The next thing he knew, she was in his lap. Her eyes widened, equally as surprised as he was.

His heart raced. But then, he had known that he was not immune to her. Losing the use of his legs had not caused him to lose his desire to touch her or kiss her, or even to make love to her—although the last he could not do. He wanted to push her to her feet. Instead, of their own volition, his hands closed on her shoulders.

"Don't turn away from me," she whispered. "Oh, Jon. I have loved you from the moment we met, and the fact that you cannot walk means nothing to me. Yes, I share your pain, and every moment of hurt and anguish, but if you let me, I know I can help take away that pain. I know it."

And he knew it, too. "But you deserve a whole man," he whispered harshly, just steps away from surrender. "A man who can give you children, Catherine."

"We can adopt," she said.

Adoption. Blake had also mentioned it, and it was almost unheard of—but not quite. His hands slid down her slim back. They were shaking. "I cannot make love to you. At least, not the way I wish to."

"And for you, being a man, that is the real reason to deny us a lifetime of joy?" She shook her head.

He stared at her.

She leaned forward and pressed her mouth to his.

Jon hesitated, using every ounce of willpower and iron control he had. He too had loved this woman from the moment they had first met. She deserved more, didn't she?

"If you reject my suit," Catherine said firmly, "then I shall remain a spinster until I die."

"Your suit?" His eyes widened.

"My suit. I wish to marry you. Be your wife. Be the mother of our adopted children. Be your partner in all deeds, great and small. Be your mate. In every way." Her cheeks had turned pink. "Even to your soul."

"You are asking me to marry you?" he whispered, in disbelief. His pulse was roaring in his ears, slamming against the bone of his breast. Genteel Catherine, tendering a proposal?

She nodded, cheeks aflame. "And you cannot say no," she said.

He started to laugh. And he hugged her, hard, his cheek pressed to hers, his eyes wet. And the laughter would not stop. And God, how good it felt to laugh again—to laugh with her. How good she felt, dear, sweet, genteel Catherine who had just proposed marriage to him.

"Is that a yes?" she whispered against his jaw.

"Yes," he said, looking down at her. His heart stopped. "Yes, it is a yes, and Catherine, I may never allow you to forget how bold you have been this day."

She laughed up at him. "You gave me no choice."

His laughter died. His smile faded. His gaze went from her almond-shaped green eyes to her small nose and bow-shaped mouth. There was no mistaking his racing pulse now. And as sorry as he was that he could not feel the desire rising in his loins, the desire was there, in his heart and in his mind. He leaned forward, touched her lips with his. And then he had her in an iron grasp, crushed against his chest, his mouth hot on hers. He could not get enough of her, how clear it was—not now, not ever.

And Catherine whispered, in the midst of the endless kiss, "Maybe now you can believe in miracles."

"I do," he whispered back. And he did.

"We have to speak," Violette said.

Robert faced her in the sitting room of her hotel suite. His expression was twisted. "I do not want to hear what you are going to say."

She looked at his handsome face, his anguished eyes, and it struck her for the first time how much this man truly loved her. But she did not love him back in the same way. And she would never be able to. "I am so sorry," Violette said, walking slowly toward him. She pulled off her magnificent engagement ring while he watched her. "Robert, you have become a great friend. I love you. But not the way I should. Not if we were to be man and wife."

He did not accept the ring. "It is Blake, isn't it? You are still mad for him."

Violette did not hesitate. "If I could change my feelings, I would. This is not a pleasant situation, to miss a man so desperately, one who does not care in return. But I cannot change my feelings. I am so sorry, Robert." She moved forward and embraced him.

He regarded her, appearing devastated. "Violette, you have

been through a terrible ordeal. Perhaps you need some time, time in which to recover. Perhaps you will feel differently in a few days, or even a few weeks."

She regarded him sadly, shaking her head.

His chest heaved. "I have never felt this way before. I love you. I do not want to lose you."

"I'm sorry. It would not be fair to either of us, Robert," Violette said softly.

"Why do you not let me be the judge of that?" He was suddenly angry.

"Because it is my life, my destiny," she said, lifting her chin.

He stared. A silence reigned. His eyes glistened. "Very well." He took the ring from her hand. "But my own feelings will not change. I think, though, that I knew this was coming. How I envy Blake." He wet his lips. "If you ever need me, I will be there for you. For anything."

She clasped her hands to her breasts. "Thank you," she said. "You are a dear friend."

He grimaced. Violette watched him quickly cross the room. He did not pause at the door. And a moment later he was gone.

She stared at the threshold, feeling drained and empty, feeling so very numb. Slowly she walked over to a window and stared down at the gaslit street. From the high floor where she was a guest, she could see beyond the square to Hyde Park. The trees formed a mass of darker shadows amidst the swirling snow.

Why should she not be exhausted, drained, numb? She had given up her daughter, been imprisoned in horrific conditions, had discovered that her lifelong friend had murdered a kind old man, and she had lost the single love of her life—all in a very short span of time. How could she survive? Violette gripped the windowsill, closing her eyes.

So much had happened. Too much. She was still stunned about Ralph. Yet perhaps she had begun to suspect the truth a few days ago in Paris. How sad she was. She would visit him when she was a little bit stronger; she would hold him and cry when she had more tears to shed. But she was also angry. He had changed so much, becoming bitter and ugly. He was not the boy she had grown up with. How could he have killed dear old Sir Thomas? How? She still loved him, but the action was unforgivable.

Violette sank down into a chair. She would miss Ralph. How

could she not? He had been like a brother to her since she was a very small child. And one day, she might stop missing Blake, how she prayed that was so, but she would never stop missing Susan. Violette covered her face with her hands. She intended to go back to Paris immediately, but she desperately wanted to see her daughter one final time.

Survival was going to be so very difficult, but she had no choice. She had come too far in this life. She would return to Paris, open up her ladies' shop. She would put all of her desire, her energy, her hopes and dreams, into that one maison. And maybe, one day, she would feel strong enough to be able to return to London to visit her daughter. Maybe, by then, she would be able to look at Blake without loving him so deeply, so impossibly.

"Violette?" Blake said.

She whirled. He stood a few paces behind her. She hadn't heard him enter the room. And in his arms was Susan.

She met his gaze, saw the anguish in his eyes, and that he held her daughter in outstretched arms. Violette rushed across the room to take her, cuddling Susan to her bosom, crying all over her. Susan laughed and cooed; Violette laughed through her hot tears back at her. It was the single most wondrous moment of her life—holding her infant daughter again. And then she looked up at Blake.

"I love you too much," he said solemnly, "to take your child from you."

She was frozen, in disbelief. Had she really heard him correctly?

"Besides," he said thickly, "a child needs a mother, and I shall never remarry. After you, and because of my feelings for you, I cannot wed another woman."

Violette clutched Susan tightly. Her heart was skipping numerous beats. "I . . . what are you saying?"

He raised one hand. "I know you are marrying Farrow. I did not come here to beg, or to create an awkward moment for you. I will support Susan, of course. But you and Robert can raise her together, giving her the home—and love—she needs."

Violette was incapable of speech.

Blake stared at her. She realized that his blue eyes were filled with tears. And then he turned abruptly away, about to leave.

"Blake!" She set Susan down on the couch carefully and flew after him, reaching him at the door. She ran around him, barred the door with her body, arms outstretched as well. "You cannot leave! What have you just said to me? Did I hear correctly?''

"Please, this is difficult enough as it is. Please, let me pass, Violette," he said, his shining gaze holding hers.

"I am not marrying Robert," she said.

He stiffened. "What?"

"I love you. How can I marry Robert, when it is you I think of every moment of every day?"

He stared at her.

Violette trembled.

"But you left me," he finally said.

"Because I loved you—and you did not love me."

"But I did love you," he whispered, reaching up to touch her face. And then he was cradling her face in his rough palms, the gesture impossibly tender, and Violette had never seen such a look in anyone's eyes before, such a look of devotion and love. "I fell in love with you the moment you knocked the lamp off of the table in the salon at Harding Hall," he said.

"You did?" she whispered incredulously.

"Yes," he whispered. "But being a very stupid man, it was a long time before I allowed myself to understand and even accept my own feelings."

Violette smiled at him through her tears. "But how could you really love me, Blake? I am not Lady Neville. I am Violet Cooper."

He laughed a little; he was crying too. "I love you because you were Violet Cooper, and now you are Lady Neville, and I would not have it any other way." He caught a tear on the pad of his thumb. "I would not change a single thing about you, not one single thing, not even how we met. My God, Violette, you are an extraordinary woman."

She could not reply because he was finally kissing her, his mouth feathering across her lips, a kiss at once tender but hungry, a kiss filled with pent-up yearning, with so much love. The kiss deepened.

Violette broke it. With her fingers, she touched his mouth. "Blake, it is you who is extraordinary, not I. It is you who is amazing. I admire you so."

"Then we are both vastly admiring of one another," he said gravely, and he laughed, kissed her again, then crushed her in his powerful embrace. Violette crushed him back. She had almost forgotten what this felt like—to be held like this.

And never had she understood what it felt like to be loved

and cherished like this. Warmth and trust flowed along with the love and desire and joy right down to her very toes.

Blake caught her chin. He was incredibly grave. "Violette, I did not think I could ever love again. But I have never loved this way before. Never."

And she smiled at him, a smile that came from her heart. "And I, Blake, have also never loved this way before—and will never love this way again."

Their gazes locked. Recognition and understanding flared between them. "Yes," he said, his hand on her cheek. "Yes." His gaze was brilliant. "Dear God, Violette, we have an entire lifetime to spend together."

Violette suddenly realized that too, and, filled with joy and excitement, she laughed.

His gaze darkened, holding hers, and he bent to claim her mouth.

And Violette thought that it was true. In love and dreams there were no impossibilities.

Don't miss Brenda Joyce's
extraordinary new novel

Splendor

. . . a novel of passion, divided loyalties
and scandalous secrets in the glittering
world of Regency society.

A December 1997 Bestseller
From St. Martin's Paperbacks